PURAMORE

THE LUTE OF PYTHAGORAS

A Novel By

STEVEN WOOD COLLINS

Retopia Limited
London

Retopia Limited
210 Upper Richmond Road
Putney, London
SW15 6NP England
United Kingdom

Designed by Steven Wood Collins

ISBN: 978-0-615-44352-2

LCCN: 2011905701

Photo Credits: Unless otherwise credited, all photos are from the author's collection or from the public domain. Every effort has been made to identify copyright holders; in case of oversight, and on notification to publisher, corrections will be made in the next edition.

For Marjorie Wood

They become like they behold! Yet immense in strength and power,

In awful pomp and gold, in all the precious unhewn stones of Eden

They build a stupendous Building on the Plain of Salisbury, with chains

Of rocks round London Stone, of Reasonings, of unhewn Demonstrations

In labyrinth arches (Mighty Urizen the Architect) thro' which

The heavens might revolve and Eternity be bound in their chain,

Labour unparalled! a wondrous rocky World of cruel destiny,

Rocks piled on rocks reaching the stars, stretching from pole to pole.

The Building is Natural Religion & its Altars Natural Morality,

A building of eternal death, whose proportions are eternal despair.

Except from *Jerusalem*, a poem by William Blake

Contents

Prologue

Saqqâra Egypt, circa 2,700 BC

The tail end of the sandstorm that had lasted for nearly a week faded far off into the western horizon at sunset. Turning to face the nearly completed edifice, Imhotep said a prayer of gratitude to Re and proceeded toward the pyramid. We were fortunate, he thought, that only the draft animals perished during the storm. Nevertheless, he knew his army of workers were close to starvation and would thus require several days of feeding to recover their health before they'd be fit enough to resume their labours. Thankfully, the supply caravan carrying much-needed provisions would arrive from Memphis in the morning.

Upon entering his tent at nightfall, he sat down at his desk. Papyrus scrolls littered the entire surface. He unrolled one and began to read.

Several minutes later his chief engineer entered.

"My Lord."

"Yes, Meni."

"Pharaoh's messenger just arrived bearing this scroll."

He handed it to him.

"Thank you, Meni."

The old man exited the tent.

After reading the scroll, he directed his servant boy to bring him his supper. He would dine alone and turn in early for the evening. Tomorrow, Pharaoh would arrive with the supply caravan to inspect his mausoleum.

He fell into a deep slumber the moment his head settled on the sleeping mat. His unconscious mind soon felt a familiar pull on his spirit to travel to another time and space.

He looked down at his sleeping body as his spirit departed and began to soar to the stars. In an instant the starlight shining all around him coalesced into a tunnel of light as he accelerated through space-time toward his final destination. He had grown accustomed to the experience as he had been there many times before in his life. He always assumed that he would never return to his body on Earth after each time his spirit passed through the Celestial Gate. And this time was no exception.

As he passed through the Celestial Gate, the scene all around him took on a truly heavenly form. He hovered in a sea of blue ether populated by wisps of clouds transporting angels and cherubs. His spirit expanded as he once again became one with Creation. Although he sensed the presence of others, most of whom were several times or more powerful than himself, they never revealed themselves to him. It had always been that way each time he visited the Celestial Realm to commune with Creation about earthly matters. This was his role as the High Priest of Re at Heliopolis.

Suddenly, a form began to take shape in his mind's eye. At first the outline appeared to be nothing other than a common lizard with wings. As the shape took clearer definition, which displayed a glorious golden dragon of immense proportions, a tinge of fear began to creep into his being. There was no mistaking its intention. He shuddered with fear for all beings in this universe. He realised that the natural order of this universe had experienced an abrupt and everlasting change with the intrusion of the malevolent deity from another universe.

He awakened from the dream as usual with no apparent ill effects. After breakfast, he walked to the pavilion that had been erected to receive Pharaoh. The thunder of hundreds of chariots charging toward him from the northern horizon disturbed the serenity of the construction site. Thirty minutes later the horde reached the mausoleum. Scouting parties were immediately dispatched to reconnoitre the surrounding countryside.

As Djoser stepped off his chariot, the throng surrounding him prostrated themselves on the ground. A Nubian slave quickly brought an ostrich feather parasol over Pharaoh's head to shade him from the intense mid-morning sun.

"Arise, my children, and greet the new day of Re."

The assemblage stood and bowed before him as he made his way to the pavilion where Imhotep awaited him. Upon entering, he sat down in the throne in the middle of the pavilion.

"You may gaze upon me now Imhotep, my brother."

Imhotep looked up to see Djoser smiling at him.

He returned the brotherly smile.

"May Pharaoh always bestow Divine Blessings and Providence upon your humble and unworthy servants."

He briefly bowed.

"Of that you may always invite and receive, Lord Imhotep."

His countenance changed to one of solemnity.

"Be away with you all, except Lord Imhotep."

He waved the Was sceptre he held in his right hand across his chest to signify for everyone to exit the pavilion at once.

"Come closer, Lord Imhotep," he said as the last of the assemblage exited the pavilion. "I fear that my time as Pharaoh is at an end. Last night Osiris came into my sleep and breathed into my mouth. What does that portend?"

"Pharaoh the omen does indeed portend that Osiris has begun to prepare your Divinity for the afterlife by bonding your Ba to your Divine Consistence."

"How much time do I have to dwell in Egypt?"

"I must first consult the stars this evening for Providence, Pharaoh."

He paused for a moment before resuming.

"I myself communed with Amun last night during my sleep. It was revealed to me that Nut has been invaded by a malevolent deity."

"Where did the deity come from?"

"I know not, Pharaoh, but it possesses the power of Amen-Re"

"What is the deity's purpose in invading Nut?"

"It can only have one, Pharaoh; that is, to rend the heart and soul from Nut and Geb and destroy Duat."

"Then the prophecy is fulfilled, Lord Imhotep."

"What prophecy?"

A magnificent eagle flew into the pavilion and alighted on the ground between Pharaoh and Imhotep whereupon it instantly shape-shifted into a tall young man dressed in a silk robe.

"Don't be alarmed, Imhotep."

"Is this Horus?"

He dropped to his knees and covered his eyes. His sheer terror of the sight of the apparition before him seized his psyche and body as a paroxysm.

The man took Imhotep by the arm and lifted him to his feet as though he were nothing more than an ordinary scarab beetle.

"Uncover your eyes, Lord Imhotep, and look into mine. I am only known as Eagle."

Imhotep stared into his eyes for several seconds. He suddenly closed them again.

Eagle then took an object from the fold of his robe and placed it on his forehead. After he ceased convulsing and reopened his eyes, he returned the object to the robe. Imhotep stood before him with a sanguine expression on his face.

"You see, Lord Imhotep, you and I are from different worlds. Though we share essentially the same physical form and spirit as men, mine hails from this world whilst yours hails from another."

Pharaoh interjected: "Eagle first presented himself to me just before I began my reign as Pharaoh. As you recall, I was then an innately strong and quintessentially noble at that time. My only weakness in achieving my goals for Egypt laid upon my innate youth and inexperience. Had it not been for him, my reign would have been short and unremarkable.

"This Was sceptre that I hold in my hand is my only memento of the time when I wielded the power of the Sword of Destiny that rendered me invincible during most of my reign."

"But where is it now, Pharaoh?"

"Eagle, the Guardian of the Sword of Destiny, has it in his possession."

"Why did he withdraw it from you?"

"I had grown vainglorious with my success as ruler and thus became unsuited to wield it any longer ages ago."

"Eagle, what is its purpose?"

"Its sole purpose is to preserve and protect mankind and all creatures on this planet."

Part I – Genesis

A new human race is descending from the heights of the heavens. - Virgil

Chapter 1 - The Road to Oaxaca

Ciudad de Oaxaca, Mexico, 21 June 1991

British Army Captain George Smythe dreamt about touring archaeological sites of the Americas as an amateur archaeologist for as long as he could remember. Although he never understood the reason for the fascination, he nevertheless sensed a spiritual attraction to pre-Columbian cultures of North and South America. He had the opportunity to first explore archaeological sites on a solo tour of central Mexico by during a two-week holiday.

After a week of visiting the important ruins located in and around Mexico City and San Lorenzo Tenochtitlán, he set out from Oaxaca City early in the morning to spend the day touring Zapotec-Mixtec archaeological sites situated within the Valley of Oaxaca. Night had fallen as he drove from Mitla, the last stop of his tour, to return to Oaxaca City. He had supper just before dusk at a humble roadside diner.

As he pulled his rental car onto the two-lane paved road afterward, his stomach began to complain about the spicy Oaxaca cuisine. He should have waited to dine at his hotel restaurant, he thought, as he ingested several stomach medication pills in response as his vehicle gained speed.

Seemingly out of nowhere, a large stag mule deer appeared straight ahead of him in the middle of the road and suddenly charged at his car. Its eyes as reflected back by the vehicle's headlights became more and more demonic as he closed in on the animal. Before he could swerve to avoid the collision, the beast's heavily antlered head crashed into the driver's side of the windshield. An instant before the collision, Captain Smythe slammed on the brakes and instinctively raised his hands to shield his face. He immediately lost consciousness, as his head and forearms crashed into the steering wheel.

He regained consciousness gripped by excruciating pain when he opened his eyes to gaze outside the empty windshield frame at the starry clear night sky that magically loomed over the moonlit valley. The ill-fated car sat upright at the bottom of a dry and shallow arroyo that ran beneath the roadbed. Hearing the sound of a solitary vehicle approaching overhead at high speed, he attempted to unbuckle his seat belt to exit the car and call for help. He was severely punished for the effort, as the report of searing pain from his mangled arms reached his brain. Looking down, he saw the front of his shirt and trousers soaked with a nauseating crimson sheen; the salty seepage stung his eyes as it flowed from the crown of his head. Turning his head slightly to the right, he saw the silvery moonlight reflect off the granulated windshield glass strewn all over the front middle console and passenger seat.

A moment later the approaching vehicle passed him. He looked out the windshield frame again to catch the sight of its tail lights fading off into the horizon. He knew at that moment that death was upon him as he continued to gaze into the moonlit desert valley. Suddenly he saw a pulsing glow approaching. Seconds later, the object flew through the windshield and hovered for several seconds not more than six inches away from his nose. It appeared to him that the firefly examined him before zinging away toward the direction of the vehicle that passed him several minutes before. The effects of the loss of blood and the cold night air made him shiver.

The headlights of another fast-approaching vehicle ahead of him came into view. It eventually decelerated and stopped on the roadside above him.

He then heard the sound of a car door opening and closing. The passenger door of his sedan abruptly opened a few moments afterward, and the silhouette of a tall and thin man appeared outside. He opened the passenger door and knelt before it. He then placed a gas lantern on the passenger car seat and struck a match. The globe of the lantern came to life as the man lit the mantel and adjusted the gas flow to produce an optimal incandescence.

When the visage of his rescuer's face became fully illuminated, Captain Smythe finally began to lose consciousness.

"Fight it, Captain Smythe. Don't lose consciousness or you'll never return."

He pulled out a pouch from the leather satchel that hung from his left shoulder. After untying the strap, he poured out white powdery contents into his open right palm.

"You must look into my eyes immediately and open your mouth!" the man commanded with a roar of a lion that caused Smythe to flinch.

He struggled with all his might to direct his ebbing consciousness to open his mouth and turn his head toward the rescuer. As their eyes met, the man reached over and popped the substance into Smythe's mouth.

"Now, close your mouth and swallow!"

He brought a flat object he held in the palm of his hand into contact with Smythe's forehead.

Captain Smythe felt a warm glow pulsate through his skin and into his skull. Soon he regained consciousness.

He removed the object.

"Good. You're returning to the land of the living."

He continued to gaze into Smythe's eyes.

"My name is Juan Aguila. It's exceptionally fortunate for you that I took more than a passing interest in you after I saw your magnificent orb before you left Oaxaca for Monte Albán this morning. I've never witnessed anything even close to the brilliant luminescence and perfection of your orb, Captain Smythe.

"At first sight, I thought the Dalai Lama was in town paying us a visit. In fact, I was so struck by its magnificence that I decided to tail you, mainly to study you further and act as a rescuer if necessary. A man of your spiritual stature shouldn't be alone anywhere near where shape-shifters and other evil spirits abound, especially in this part of the Valley of Oaxaca at night."

Juan knew from his experience with extreme trauma victims that Captain Smythe would later only vaguely recall his comments at the accident scene.

He looked out the windshield and noted no trace of the shape shifter encounter anywhere on the hood of the car. Deer blood, flesh, and bone fragments that previously covered the bonnet and the interior of the sedan had vanished.

Smythe felt no pain whatsoever as Juan proceeded to dress his head and upper extremity wounds with butterfly and gauze bandages.

Afterward, he set and splinted his forearms and wrists and installed a cervical collar around his neck.

"It's also fortunate for you that I served as a US Army combat medic during the Vietnam War. In turn, the experience served me well, as I act as an unlicensed physician to local indigents in addition to my regular sorcery practice."

He wiped coagulated mass of blood from Smythe's face.

"But I digress. I must directly transport you to the Oaxaca General Hospital since you are in dire need of a blood transfusion and further treatment. This elixir should last until we arrive there."

He put the open end of a leather bota to Smythe's lips.

"Drink all of it, Captain."

A warm and salubrious but tasteless radiance flowed into his mouth. As it travelled down his oesophagus to his stomach, the warmth radiated throughout his body. He soon fell into a deep and restful sleep.

The man lifted the lantern in front of Smythe's face, held it there for several moments, and then passed the lantern down to his left shoulder. He held his breath and intensely stared at whatever it was that caught his attention. Squinting intensely, he inspected the object that caught his attention in microscopic detail: it was the size of a midge. Before it could disintegrate, he spun a crystalline cocoon around the carapace of the bantam Golden Dragonfly.

"There. I finally have another one to add to my collection. And a soldier at that."

He reached into his satchel and brought out a glass syringe. With surgical precision he gingerly placed the end of the syringe over the cocooned husk; and, little by little, began to pull on the piston. As the cocoon lazily lofted into the glass barrel, he returned the syringe to the satchel.

Late in the afternoon the following day, Captain Smythe awakened from his slumber in the comfort of a hospital bed. His cast-encased arms dangled in front of him from ceiling wires.

A slender and attractive middle-aged nurse entered the hospital room.

"Gracias a Dios!"

She shot over to his bedside and studied the vital signs monitor.

"Señor, it's a miracle that you are alive."

She studied his eyes.

"Don't try to talk."

She lifted his head to fluff and straighten his pillow.

"We've never successfully treated a patient who sustained as much blood loss as you had by the time you were admitted to the emergency room early this morning. It's also a miracle that your fractured arms and wrists were set and splinted with such skill and precision at the crash site. Otherwise, you might not have lived to enjoy full use of them again.

"The campesino who transported you here told the admission nurse that an American medico, who was touring the area by himself, attended to your wounds at the crash site. Unbelievable! What a stroke of luck for you."

How, she thought, could anyone set a series of fractured bones so precisely and effectively from a roadside crash site? Not even our finest orthopaedists working with the best equipment in the world could perform such a miraculous procedure in a fully equipped, state-of the-art operation theatre.

"Anyway, the campesino asked the admission nurse to tell you that there was no need for you to attempt to show your appreciation for his part in saving your life. He also wanted you to know that he and his family will dine luxuriantly on venison for the next month as a result of your mishap, and that was ample reward enough for him."

She picked up the phone near his bedside and dialed a number. Turning away from her patient, she spoke to someone at the other end of the line.

"Yes, Doctor. I'll let the patient know that you will arrive presently to examine him," she whispered into the receiver.

"Dr Gutierrez, our chief of orthopaedic surgery, will be with you shortly, Captain Smythe.

"Relax. You're going to be up and about in a month or so. The device in your right hand is for pain management. Simply depress the button on the end to receive a mild morphine dosage when you feel the need. I'll visit you again in a few hours," she said as she left the hospital room.

A few minutes later a tall, thin and handsome young man with long jet-black hair pulled into a ponytail entered the room.

At first, Smythe didn't recognise him as his rescuer; he instead assumed that he was his attending physician.

"I'm sorry, Doctor, but I don't recall your name."

The man, who wore a shortly cropped mustache and a goatee, stooped down so that his face was level with Captain Smythe's. His piercing black eyes stared directly into his. No wonder Quetzalcoatl targeted you for extermination at your current age, he thought.

At once he understood the spiritual providence of his encounter with Smythe; he is indeed a candidate as the Deliverer his Nagual master foretold he would discover in this dimension during this era. There's no doubt about this Omen to that effect. He's also far superior to the others in every respect. I must guard him with all my spirit powers, he resolved, until his Assumption. Not even the Great Spirit will be able to help humanity if the man before him doesn't wield Puramore as the Deliverer for the last time. From this day forth, he vowed, you and I are going to develop a fast and permanent friendship.

He continued his gaze into Smythe's eyes for a few moments.

"My name is Juan Aguila. Don't you remember me, Captain Smythe?"

Captain Smythe felt a smooth metal object come into contact with his forehead. A warm pulsation travelled through his skin and into his skull before its removal. All at once, the image of the man who saved his life the previous evening came to his beclouded mind.

"Juan? Is that you?"

He began to recall the man's efforts to rescue his life.

"Yes, it's me."

He groped for words to fully convey the depth of his gratitude to his saviour.

Finally, he said, "How can I ever repay you for saving my life?"

"I have only two requests in that regard, my friend."

"I shall do anything in my power to express my appreciation for all that you have done for me, Juan. I shall do anything at all."

"Firstly, never mention my role in saving your life to anyone."

"I shall not. Not ever. I promise that to you as a blood oath."

"Secondly, ever since I was a small boy I've always dreamed of attending an Ivy League medical school to become a licensed physician."

"But, Juan, how can I possibly assist you in fulfilling the dream? I'm only a soldier with hardly any means at present."

"Trust me. Time is not an issue for me. And in no time you'll possess the capability to provide me with that assistance."

"Really? How can you be so certain of that?"

"Because it's your destiny. One day you are going to be a very, very rich and powerful man."

"I don't believe it. Career army officers never attain immense wealth. It's impossible."

"Well, you will be the exception to that rule. Just put that in the back of your mind for now."

He turned away from him and started for the door.

"From this day forth, you are on another path as a warrior, Captain Smythe. I am your spirit guide and guardian until you fulfil your destiny."

"But I don't understand any of that, Juan! Where are you going?"

"I'll be in touch soon" were the last words Juan spoke before he exited the room.

An elderly man dressed in a white coat entered the room several minutes later.

After examining Captain Smythe, he said, "I am Dr Gutierrez, Captain Smythe."

He paused to await his patient's response.

"It's a pleasure to meet you, Dr Gutierrez. Will I be able to return to Britain fairly soon?"

"Yes. A British Army medivac team has already arrived to transport you to England this evening."

"I wish to thank you and your hospital for treating my injuries last night. The nurse seems to think I will fully recover."

"Your prognosis for a complete recuperation from the injuries you sustained is excellent.

"It's truly amazing that you're already well on the way to recovery given what you have been through. I've never seen anything like it in all my fifty years as a physician. It's really nothing short of a miracle."

"Dr Gutierrez."

"Yes, Captain Smythe?"

"Who was that man who left my room several minutes before you arrived?"

"No man has entered your room except me for the past eight hours. Only your shift nurse has been here during the last fifteen minutes. I am certain of that as I've been in conference with a fellow physician in the hallway just outside your room for the past half hour. Other than Nurse Ortega and a field mouse, you had no visitors."

"Are you familiar with a man who goes by the name of Juan Aguila?"

"No, señor, I am not. The surname, however, is definitely typical of local campesinos."

Chapter 2 - West Meets East

Hong Kong, 15 March 2019

The flight from London gave him the leisure to ponder over his life as a military officer for the first time in several years.

After resigning his commission only several months before, he had almost no time until then to reflect upon the only way of life he had ever known since his graduation from Eton College at the age of eighteen. For until his ceremonial release from military service the previous week, he devoted all his energies toward attending to severance minutia and executing the necessary arrangements to begin his new career in Hong Kong.

Comfortable and relaxed in his premier class-seat, General Sir George Smythe absently stared at the movie playing on the screen in front of him. He listened to a classical music programme through headphones as his mind wound through the collage of his military career.

He began to recall the day of his arrival at the Royal Military Academy Sandhurst after his graduation from Eton College. The subsequent forty-four weeks he spent there as a cadet flashed through his memory. Although it was a time of intense personal growth and learning for him, it was also a time to be inculcated with the ritual of military duty and honour as an officer.

He fast-forwarded through his initial career posting as a second lieutenant and staff officer with the Intelligence Corps after being commissioned into the Royal Anglian

Regiment. Excelling in that post to such an extraordinary degree he was promoted to first lieutenant after only two years of service. Two years later, he advanced to the rank of captain as a result of his extraordinary contributions and leadership abilities.

In his first assignment as a captain, he served as a special liaison officer with the British Defence Staff office stationed in Washington D.C. Upon return to his regiment, he served as both an operations officer and adjutant commander in both the Northern England and Cyprus campaigns. In his eighth year of his military career, he was promoted to the rank of major. Several months after the promotion, he received the Distinguished Service Order decoration in recognition of his brilliant combat leadership contributions.

He savoured the memory of that phase of his military career. The experience was all the more memorable since he knew then that his career path was on a fast track toward advancement to the upper echelon ranks of military command.

After attending Staff College Camberly in his tenth year of military service, he returned to the Royal Anglian Regiment, headquartered at Bury Saint Edmunds, as adjutant to colonel of the regiment. Upon his promotion to lieutenant colonel four years later, he held several high-level staff appointments within the Ministry of Defence.

In his twenty-ninth year of service, he was promoted to the rank of major general and was later awarded both the Knight Commander of the Order of the British Empire and Knight Grand Cross of Saint Michael and Saint George. After serving as commander-in-chief of NATO's Northern European Defence Group, he occupied the

Whitehall office of the Ministry of Defence as the chief of the general staff as he neared retirement age.

His military career had been his only mistress from the time he graduated from Sandhurst. Though he enjoyed a few diversions, such as stock market trading and general aviation, he mainly focused on the constant demands of his military duties. From his early teens, he knew that the military life would be his calling. His instructors at Eton College attempted to dissuade him from that career objective as they considered him an excellent candidate to matriculate at either Oxford or Cambridge. But his steadfast resolve to become a military officer finally overcame their objections when he enlisted in the British Army as an officer candidate several days after his graduation.

As he approached the fifth anniversary of his promotion to the rank of major general, he first met Lord Cedric Chamberlain at a social function he attended one evening in London. Unbeknownst to him at the time, the British lord was a senior partner of a staid and dowdy Hong Kong commodities trading firm. The firm, Oriental Winds Commodities House was one of the original British trading houses that specialised in oriental commodities and goods for export to the West. Established in the early 1900s, the firm flourished for nearly eighty years.

He vividly recalled Lord Chamberlain's first mention of OWCH soon after they were first introduced by the Minister of Defence the previous August. For some peculiar reason, he thought, at the time, the old man took more than a casual interest in him. He also thought it odd that Lord Chamberlain would open his heart about the history and status of his firm to a total stranger.

Before departing, he invited Smythe to dinner at his private club the next evening. He accepted the invitation as he welcomed the prospect of breaking away from the Joint Military Intelligence crowd who were his only company for the past week, as he had been attending a conference with the top NATO military leaders.

* * *

The cab stopped in front of an ancient red brick and white marble building. Typical of that affluent and secluded section of the Royal Borough of Kensington and Chelsea, the edifice possessed a slightly garish but elegant bearing like all homes built in London during the late Victorian era. Aside from the polished brass house number posted discretely to the left of the massive front door, no other sign even hinted at the fact the building housed an exclusive gentleman's club.

After exiting the cab, he climbed the white marble steps to the front door landing and rang the doorbell. Peace reigned supreme in the neighbourhood on that balmy evening. The heavy teak door opened to reveal a distinguished-looking man dressed in an English butler suit and tie.

"Good evening, General Sir George Smythe. Please follow me."

Smythe entered the dark wood-paneled foyer. He followed as the man proceeded down a wide corridor. The scent of tobacco smoke and exotic oil-treated oak permeated the stately ambiance. An unbroken line of portrait oil paintings hung on both walls all along the entire length of the corridor. Smythe judged that the men portrayed in the paintings must have been past members, possibly former officers, who may have presided over the club since its founding. And, judging by the elegant attire worn in the earliest paintings, that might have been as early as seven centuries ago.

"Most impressive."

They had arrived at the end of the hallway.

"This is one of the finest collections of portraiture I have ever seen."

"Indeed, General Sir. It's a tradition the order established over eight hundred years ago. Previously, the membership saw no need to render portraits of Grand Exalted Masters."

This must be a Masonic temple, Smythe thought.

Turning into another hallway they continued their journey.

At the end of the corridor, they entered a large two-story-high library. Wood shelves filled from the floor to ceiling with books covering the four walls of the grand space, some thirty meters in length and width. At the start of the second-floor level, an ornate balcony ran along the entire perimeter of the library. Access to the balcony was gained from spiral staircases positioned at the corners of the library. Great ladders hung from overhead rails provided access to volumes in the upper reaches. On the ground level, sets of ornately carved wood desks occupied half of the floor space. Old-fashioned brass reading lamps set atop each desk.

The other half of the floor space contained large leather-bound chairs, each adjoined by a pedestal table and brass floor lamp. A monumental crystal chandelier hung from the middle of the ceiling provided ambient lighting for the library. Most of the leather chairs were occupied by elderly men absorbed in reading. Many smoked cigars or tobacco pipes. No one, however, paid the pair any heed as they entered the regal book depository.

The butler started to walk across the middle of the library floor toward a hallway opening at the opposite end.

"This way, please, General Sir."

Exiting the library, they proceeded through another portrait-lined hallway. Instead of pre-eighteenth century clothing, the men portrayed here wore modern garb.

At the end of the corridor, the butler halted and motioned for Smythe to proceed ahead of him.

"The maître d' will show you to your table. Lord Chamberlain will be along presently to join you."

He then made a military-style salute and marched back down the hallway.

Black-tie-and-coat-clad diners occupied nearly all the thirty or so linen-covered tables. The dining room was finely furnished with British period pieces dating back to the seventeenth century. An assortment of British heraldic emblems decorated its dark wood-paneled walls, one of which was occupied by an ancient and elegant bar.

A handsome young man dressed in a tuxedo arrived.

"Follow me, please."

He led him to a solitary table situated at the far end of the dining hall. As the general sat, the maître d' told him that a waiter would attend to him presently. A few minutes later the waiter took a cocktail order from him.

He continued to survey the understated elegance of the dining room as Lord Chamberlain approached the table. Dressed in formal attire, the standard black coat and tie worn by everyone else, he appeared as hale and hearty as any man his age would ever wish to be.

"Good evening, General Sir George Smythe."

General Smythe rose to shake his hand.

"I welcome you to the Ancient Order of the Blue Garter."

They sat down.

"It is a pleasure to be here, Lord Chamberlain.. Though I don't believe I've ever heard anything about the Ancient Order of the Blue Garter. From what I have been able to ascertain since my arrival, though, the club must be steeped in ancient tradition. That was especially evident in the portrait paintings and other renderings I viewed on the way here."

"Quite so. More on that at another time."

He placed his linen napkin on his lap as the waiter served the general his martini cocktail.

"The usual for me, Crumley,. And do try to make it extra dry this time, my good man."

The waiter shook his head ever so slightly to acknowledge the command and left.

"Right. I trust you are enjoying your stay in London."

"Yes, I am indeed, Your Lordship. I was born and raised in here, as you know."

"Yes, I do know. In fact, I know far more about you than you probably presume. The order has always maintained a favourite community interest, unlike any other gentleman's club. Instead of engaging in furthering charitable and academic concerns, once in a decade, we select an outstanding young man to cultivate for purposes of future interest to the club. In your case, we followed your academic and social development from the time you were thirteen years old. We later confirmed your suitability to receive the anonymous scholarship from the Ancient Order of the Blue Garter when you were aged fifteen. As a result, all other aspects of your life henceforth came under our anonymous and beneficial guidance."

General Smythe took a slow sip from his martini as he considered the gravity of the revelation Lord Chamberlain had disclosed to him. In retrospect, there were times in his life, particularly during his early adolescence and adulthood, when for a reason, unbeknownst to him, he was cast in a mould well above the station of his birth. At the time he didn't realise the true significance of the largess he received.

The first and most notable of these benefits came in the form of an astonishing invitation from Eton College to sit for a qualifying entrance examination when he was aged fifteen. After passing the examination, he was offered a full scholarship by an anonymous benefactor.

A distinct social anomaly, given his relatively obscure social background and status, he nevertheless gained tremendous respect from his classmates, primarily based on the excellence of his academic performance. His athletic prowess and leadership capabilities further bolstered his popularity amongst his schoolmates, so much so, that his varsity football team mates elected him as squad captain in his final year.

"So, Lord Chamberlain, what you are saying to me is that my life has been influenced in no small measure by the benevolence of the Ancient Order of the Blue Garter."

"I would not necessarily qualify our interest in your development as solely benevolent. I would rather prefer that you regard our involvement in your educational and career development as an investment that promised to reap untold returns for both you and the Order."

"I am not quite following you."

He was flatly incredulous to the core of his being.

"Firstly, why would you have chosen someone like me when you could have done the same from your own social circle? Secondly, how am I required to fulfil the terms of your investment?"

"Fair questions, which I am only too happy to answer. Well, someone like you only arrives on Earth once every one hundred years or more. You are a natural-born leader of the highest calibre. I say that not to shame your modesty, but to reflect the fact that we, as astute students of history, have a keen and discerning sense about how men are destined to develop given the proper providence. As a youth, you exhibited all the attributes of the kind of individual that we continually to discover and develop.

"As you depart this evening, please take special notice of the portraits you saw on your way to the dining hall. Some of the men portrayed hailed from quite austere circumstances, whilst others were born into privilege and opulence. I dare say that upon closer scrutiny you shall also recognise at least a few of them as having played pivotal leadership roles both in public and private offices they held.

"With regard to your second question, you have already repaid our capital investment outlay for your education in spades, as established by your success to date. The stellar accomplishments that you achieved by virtue of your own initiative and leadership skills starting from the day you entered Eton College have been a splendid victory for us as well."

"As far as you are concerned, however, all of that experience is in the past."

"You are giving me the impression that my career path is about to take an abrupt turn."

"And an abrupt turn it shall be. Accordingly, we have decided that your talents shall be utilised to far greater effect in another capacity."

The general's eyes widened.

Before he could utter a syllable, Lord Chamberlain resumed, "Please hear me out before you comment upon our proposition to you. The years you have spent in the service of Her Majesty have been exceptionally beneficial toward the peace and prosperity of the nation as well as toward your own personal development. Yet, for all it was worth, that experience was merely a stepping stone onto the path of your true destiny."

He took a sip of his cocktail.

"As you have undoubtedly noticed, the majority of the members of the order present this evening are in advanced stages of life. I myself am eighty-two years old. In this modern era, we as a group are a dying breed, both literally and figuratively.

"The noble charter of the Ancient Order of the Blue Garter that has lasted gloriously for ages is today only an anachronistic ideal cherished in the minds of us who survive at the very end of our time here on Earth. The younger membership, though fully capable of carrying on the club's traditions indefinitely, shall never, I regret to say, be able to reshape the original charter to incorporate the realities of the modern world even if they possessed the inclination and capability to do so. Perforce of that ominous realisation, we have no other alternative but to pass on the mantel of our leadership to the only man alive capable of refashioning the charter into a viable and thriving influence. And that man, General Sir George Smythe, is none other than you."

Although there was something tantalising about his presentation, Smythe harboured an essential, almost instinctual misgiving about his motives toward him. He learned early in his military career that the success of an endeavour often depends upon a crucial command decision based on gut instinct. In this case, his gut instinct was sending him a message to beware.

"You are at the very pinnacle of your military career with nowhere to go but sideways. I think that you ought to agree with me that your options otherwise are virtually nought. That is not a bright prospect for a young man like you. You crave the continual pursuit and attainment of power as most men breathe air to exist. Recognising that you are thus at a stalemate, we propose that you forthwith resign your officer's commission and begin a new career in industry, initially under our tutelage. We in turn guarantee that from that moment forward you will at least receive a lifetime pension and benefits equal to your entitlement under your current military rank and tenure.

"If you succeed, as we expect you shall, we will turn over the business to you for your complete control and ownership. What is truly at stake for you is the opportunity to realise your fullest potential as a leader and innovator, unfettered by any and all social or bureaucratic obstacles in the way of your ambition and drive to succeed. That's a heady prospect, wouldn't you agree?"

The general picked up his half-full martini glass with his right hand and swirled the contents as he carefully contemplated the proposition. Bringing the glass to his lips, he took a reflective sip and lowered it down on the table.

"I have been rather dreading serving the remainder of my career until retirement. It's not that I do not enjoy the power and prestige of my current appointment, it's more that I am no longer challenged by military intrigue and gamesmanship."

"Of course you're not. At just over fifty years old, you are a young man on the verge of exploiting his leadership capabilities to the ultimate level. We also realise that you suffer career ennui when you are not constantly stimulated by the challenge of rising to a higher level of power and prestige. Whilst the opportunity that we are offering to you will likely make you a rich and powerful man, the prestige you derive from that success is yours and only yours to define. In other words, you can make use of it as you desire by either staying out of the public view altogether or electing instead to use it as a platform for political gain in the public forum. In any event, we shall not hold you to any standard other than the one you set for yourself."

"And I shall be free to manage the company at my complete discretion?"

"Yes, as Grand Exalted Master of the Ancient Order of the Blue Garter, I assure you that from the day you ratify our employment and membership agreement the company shall be yours to manage at your total discretion. Thereafter, if and when you meet our performance goals for the company's business expansion over the course of the initial five years, 100 percent of the firm's ownership will be transferred to your name.

"I know you must have reservations concerning the changeover from public to private life, but you won't have any difficulty at managing the enterprise from the very day you set foot inside the chief executive officer's suite."

"And where may I ask is that located?"

"The headquarters office of Oriental Winds Commodities House is located in Hong Kong. OWCH owns the fifty-story building that houses its headquarters staff in the top fifteen floors. Your private office suite is located on the fiftieth floor of the building."

"This is really too good to be true. There must be some sort of a catch.

"You stated earlier that passing leadership of the Order to me was deemed a necessity. I clearly don't understand the nature of that responsibility, nor do I understand anything at all about the Order's charter."

"I assure you that there is none until the day you become a member and assume responsibility for developing a new charter. And there is no responsibility that you basically assume by accepting the Order's leadership position other than that. Otherwise, save for your obligation with adhering to the performance milestones during the five-year initiation period, we will transfer the business to your ownership without any encumbrance whatsoever.

The four senior partners, including myself, have owned the business for the past fifty years and have during that time made vast fortunes as a result. At this point in our lives, however, we have neither the time nor the inclination to devote any further energy toward maintaining the business even at its present level of performance.

"It is a fine firm that only requires a goodly bit of attention to shift out of its current neutral gear and into higher and higher performance levels. That is your challenge, pure and simple. Should you decide to accept the challenge, you will be thoroughly briefed by me and the three other senior partners as to the current status of the firm as well as to how best to initially proceed with its management. After that, you will be essentially on your own."

He paused for a few seconds before resuming.

"I suppose you need a few days to further consider the merits of our proposition."

The general glanced across the dining room as though searching for divine intercession on his behalf. Nevertheless, he knew in his own mind that an opportunity like this would never present itself to him again. He also knew that he would be a fool not to take an early retirement from military service in order to take advantage of this mysterious kismet. Yet, the Omen had just presented itself to him as Juan predicted it would several decades earlier. He knew in his spirit The Path laid before him in his acceptance of this opportunity.

"Well, if there is an overriding strength in my character as a leader, it lies in my ability to properly assess situations and effectively direct immediate action to gain control over them. Accordingly, I herewith accept the opportunity which you have presented to me this evening, Lord Chamberlain."

"Jolly good! Now let's order dinner, shall we? I'm absolutely famished."

* * *

"Sir, would you care for a glass of wine with your dinner this evening?"

He instantly pulled out of his reverie. As he looked up at the flight attendant, he removed his headphones.

"Yes, I would care for a glass of wine. Burgundy would be preferable."

"Very well, Sir." She gave him an alluring smile before leaving for the galley.

The general adjusted his seat for comfort. He sat in the window seat; the aisle seat next to him was vacant. Having found a comfortable position, he laid his head back on the headrest and closed his eyes. No sooner had he done so than he heard the rustle of clothing in the seat next to him. He opened his eyes to see a well-dressed man of Chinese descent, a slightly sinister grin on his face, looking at him intently.

"General Sir George Smythe," he said as though he had just found a long lost friend. "Please excuse the intrusion, but I couldn't help but notice you as I passed through the first-class cabin. You probably don't recognise me. My name is Huáng Xinghua."

He extended his right hand to offer a handshake.

"My friends simply call me Wingtip...as do my enemies."

His piercing dark eyes seemed to sparkle as he uttered the last word.

Accepting the handshake in a businesslike spirit, Smythe thoroughly inspected his unexpected visitor. He could tell Mr Huáng was about his age judging by the salt-and-pepper hair and the crow's-feet wrinkles around his eyes set in high cheekbones. His slightly gaunt face and lean and muscular body frame, as outlined through the beige silk suit he wore, revealed him as being in exceptional physical condition, perhaps as a result of a long-established regimen as a long-distance runner. Smythe also judged him as about his same height.

"I don't believe we've met before, Mr Huáng."

He extended his right hand to accept the handshake.

"I'm usually perfect in putting together names and faces."

The stranger chuckled. "You must call me Wingtip, as I don't know who Mr Huáng is anymore, and haven't since I acquired the nickname in my youth."

His smile widened. "Actually, we haven't been formally introduced. I am in the armaments trade as one of my many business interests. I make it my job to know key figures, such as yourself, associated with my potential customers...one of which being the British military armaments consortium."

"Well, Mr Huáng, for your information, I no longer serve in the British Army. I resigned my commission a fortnight ago and am now embarked upon a new career in private industry."

"I am well aware of that fact, General Smythe. Additionally, I know that you are taking over the reins of OWCH." He maintained an inscrutable smile as his gaze bore in on the general.

Smythe looked quizzically at the man for a moment. "And what don't you know, Mr Huáng?" This man, he thought, certainly has a lot of brass approaching me in this manner. He was nevertheless intrigued by him.

"Not much when it comes to you, General Smythe. Here's my business card."

He presented him with a card as he rose from his seat.

"I think you'll find me a diamond in the rough when it comes to trade relations with the People's Republic of China. Do give me a ring when you have a mind to. We shall meet again in the not-too-distant future."

He shook the general's hand and departed for the coach cabin section.

The general brought the white card closer to his face to read the embossed black print. All that was printed was

Wingtip

Phone Number: 03-594-8503

* * *

A year after taking over the helm General Smythe transformed Oriental Winds Commodities House from what was akin to a majestic British clipper ship into a world class, late 20th century America's Cup sailing yacht. The new course he chartered during this period of reorganisation almost immediately lifted the firm's bottom-line as its sails tacked into the fiercely competitive winds with aplomb. It had been a gratifying experience for him, especially since for the first time in his professional career, he could take full credit for his accomplishment, and personally, reap the bounty of his management style.

Having delegated most of the daily operation of the firm to the line and staff management, he was then at liberty to commence his next project, the cornerstone of which was his quest to discover the whereabouts of his soul sons, whom he only knew from one nocturnal dream he had during his adolescence.

Chapter 3 – Enter the Fabulous Fletcher Brothers

East End, London, England, 13 April 2020

Born in East End, identical twins Ian and Robin Fletcher were orphaned as infants and spent their childhood in a local Catholic Church orphanage. So precocious and unpredictable during their adolescence, only a few of their peers, not to mention their elders, ever accepted them, either socially or otherwise. They may have spent the rest of adolescence as social misfits and nonconformists. They may never have realised their true potential for success as adults if not for a stroke of luck.

The twins' science fair project caught the attention of Oxford University Professor John Yates, who visited London to attend a professional confer at the time. After winning the intracity high school science fair competition, a local news programme aired a feature of their project. The project involved a connection of a simple electronic electrode implanted into the brain of a mouse, named Algernon, to a laptop computer. A computer programme transmitted electronic impulses to the rodent's brain that induced its body to dance in tune with the Macarena.

Viewing for the first time by happenstance from the television set in his hotel room, the comically bizarre routine caused the professor to bellow with laughter from start to finish. Most viewers appreciated the comedy of the macabre performance, but few truly understood its significant ingenuity as a high school science project. Only Yates, a don of the university's biology department, wanted to know vastly more about technical aspects of the project and the minds of the thirteen-year-old boys.

The next day he spoke with the television station's feature editor. During their phone conversation, the editor related some basic background information about the boys to him, including the location of their residence.

He promptly called the orphanage and spoke with the facility's director, Father Seamus O'Malley. He identified himself to the priest and explained the purpose of his professional interest in the boys. His inquiry about the twins, however, strangely put off Father O'Malley. In fact, he tried his best to dissuade him from pursuing his interest in the twins any further.

Yates could tell from the nervous tone of the man's voice that the subject distressed him to the extreme.

"Sir, I advise you first off that they are not innocent boys...at least not of this world. They were literally left at our doorstep as infants. Ever since then we have done our best to provide shelter and sustenance to them as much as our meagre resources have allowed. Yet all we have received in return from them for our kindness is grief and humiliation at every turn of their whim. May the saints preserve us! I wish we had turned them away into the streets the first day I saw them!"

* * *

The church entryway bell tolled as it had from the time since the fundamental completion of the edifice during the late fifteenth century.

When the front doorbell rang, Father O'Malley had just finished arranging the sacristy for the afternoon mass. Weary, both of life in general and spiritually, he performed the task like an automaton. As far as he was concerned, he pursued a rote path in life that a slug had the intelligence to pursue. Moreover, throughout his life, he patiently waited for some sign from God that would serve to confirm his faith and his conviction in the church.

After decades of devotion to Catholicism, his failure to receive any sort of augury from heaven gnawed away at his faith, particularly since he felt that he deserved that reward for the constant ecclesiastical drudgery he suffered as a priest. Perhaps that was all the church expected of him he often thought. Yet he yearned for a time in his life when he would be challenged to the depth of his soul to demonstrate his faith in God whilst he still possessed the fire in his heart for the church as a relatively young man. Next week, he thought, as he replenished the holy water cistern, I will submit yet another petition to the Holy See for an assignment to a parish post located in a faraway and exotic part of the world, such as South America.

As he mulled over that prospect, the ancient front entrance doorbell again rang.

"Brother John, please attend to the front door visitor. I'm simply too busy to personally attend to whoever it is," he shouted.

He waited a few seconds for the corpulent and dull-witted monk to reply.

"Brother John, where are you?".

His patience with the world at large had worn thin. He looked at his watch. The monk is probably still eating his lunch in cloisters with staff and wards, he concluded.

The bell rang yet again.

"All right! All right! I'm coming! I'm coming!"

It took a full minute and a half for him to reach the massive double doors, which were always closed and locked at that time of the day. He unlocked and then swung open the right side only enough to allow him to peer out into the street. As he did, he saw an elegantly dressed young woman take the last step down the worn marble stairs that climbed from the street sidewalk to the church entrance. She wore a chic black dress and fashionable high-heeled shoes. A sheer black veil covered her face and raven-coloured hair that cascaded sumptuously to her exposed shoulders. Exceptionally tall and long-limbed, she possessed the stature of a high-class model.

He heard her sobbing uncontrollably as she fled from the church.

"Madame," he shouted, "the church is closed. Please return to visit us after one thirty this afternoon before mass."

The woman continued to flee from the edifice without displaying any acknowledgement whatsoever of the priest's concerned outcry. He shook his head and started to close the door.

Before the massive wood door fully closed he heard the sound of babies cooing from the outside. He opened the door again, stuck his head outside. He looked over to where the sound seemed to emanate. Stationed just outside sat a rather large perambulator. He exited the church and walked over to the carriage.

He audibly gasped at the sight of the two rather beautiful identical twins inside. They squirmed as though they were attempting to free themselves from the swaddling cloth that bound them together, apparently much too tightly for their comfort's sake. He estimated that the babies were no more than seven or eight months old. They cooed again in unison as he reached into the carriage and brought out an envelope that had been placed on top their covers. He opened the envelope and extracted the sheet of paper it contained. It simply read: Ian and Robin. You must baptize them at once!

"You poor, poor souls."

He looked back down at the pair.

Then one of the babies looked him straight in the eye. In an infant's high-pitched voice, he said, "He is Ian."

The priest's jaw dropped as he looked at the other toddler.

"And he is Robin," Ian stated gleefully.

"Now, unwrap us. We're hungry!" they bawled.

* * *

Yates could almost sense the priest crossing himself at the other end of the phone line.

"I don't understand, Father O'Malley. How could two gifted thirteen-year-old boys cause you, an ordained priest, to hold them in such low esteem?"

His curiosity about the pair exploded after hearing the priest's story about his first encounter with them before their adoption by the orphanage. Nevertheless, given the fact that the priest should be imminently qualified to manage children and teenagers, a vexation with the twins' purported behavioural abnormality began to form within him.

"They are devilish pranksters and malefactors, and always have been! And they are becoming more and more pernicious every day, although no one has been physically harmed yet. But there will come a day, you mark my words when someone will. We only wished they were old enough to set them on their way out of the orphanage so they can ply their diabolical trade elsewhere. They have tested my faith in God to the limit my spirit has the strength to endure. I want nothing more to do with the rascals. I actually become nauseous at the very thought of them."

"Really, how could two thirteen-year-old boys be that vexatious to you, Father?"

"Well, you just let me tell you what they did recently to give you an example if their current science fair project isn't testimony enough."

"I'm all ears.."

"Two weeks ago, during supper served as usual in our communal dining hall, the boys played one of their typical pranks on the staff. Normally conducted in strict silence, the evening meal is intended to teach spiritual discipline and tranquility to the wards. However, the morning before they rigged whoopee cushions under the seats of each of the eight sisters' chairs. Somehow remotely controlled by some sort of mechanism, the cushions started playing a rendition of Beethoven's Ode to Joy during the end of the allotted mealtime period.

"Beginning with the Mother Superior's chair, the first four beats of the piece sounded as flatulence emanating from her...ah...person. Then the individual notes of prelude emanated as flatulence from the other sisters' chairs until its conclusion. I just cannot describe to you the look of utter humiliation on the face of the Mother Superior when the first two beats sounded. I thought she would die right then and there. And the look of astonishment on the faces of the wards was beyond description.

"When the passage was well under way, it became clear to all as to the real source of the phenomenon, that is, the dreaded Fletcher brothers. Such an uproar of riotous laughter ensued from the wards as well as amongst the staff including some of the sisters, the walls of the dining room actually seemed to shake from the reverberation. Only the Heavenly Father knows how we have been able to restore any semblance of proper comportment to the facility several weeks later.

"All I can tell you now is that the snickers and chuckles over the incident continue to mar the sanctity of the supper ritual. I know too that the blessed Mother Superior was wounded to the core of her soul as a consequence of the prank."

After his inner laughter subsided, Yates was left speechless in thought about the two boys for several moments. These are the youngsters, he thought, that have been the object of my worldwide search for two decades he concluded.

"Professor Yates, what are we to do with them?"

"I believe that I have found them a new home Father."

He then thanked the priest for his time and hung up.

The following day he visited the science fair located in a downtown exhibition hall. The information desk gave him directions to the brothers' project location. After winding through a maze of tightly packed tables that lined the entire floor, he finally approached their project station. Two boys were busy packing the project's apparatus into several boxes. The science fair officially closed the previous day, and all the contestants were similarly busy decamping from the exhibition hall.

At first glance, they appeared to him to be normal adolescents. However, they possessed strapping and athletic bodies of much older adolescents, and both were well over six feet tall. Compared to wimpy geeks abounding around them, the boys were definitely out of place. They must be assistants performing some sort of community service, he thought, as he arrived at the station. And they are too well dressed in Oxford preppy garb to be mere orphanage waifs.

"Good morning, boys."

He immediately observed their astonishing resemblance.

"I am looking for the Fletcher brothers. Would you happen to know where I can find them?"

One of the boys looked up from the box he was packing.

"Ah, Professor Yates. Have you come here today to view our little dog and pony show in person?" one of the boys responded. "Regretfully, Algernon escaped our demonic clutches this morning so we are unable to give you a performance today."

"How do you know who I am?"

The boy's awareness of who he was stunned him.

The other one replied: "Little pitchers have big ears, Professor. And we have a small one attached to Father O'Malley's phone lines."

They chuckled and winked at each other.

"In the way of formal introduction, Professor, he is Ian."

The boy on his left pointed to his twin.

Ian bowed and then pointed to his brother.

"And he is Robin."

They then both bowed together.

"And we are the fabulous Fletcher brothers of East End!," they shouted together.

The commotion caused the entire exhibition hall assemblage to turn to stare at them.

Yates put his finger to his lips as a gesture to plead for civil conversation and comportment.

"Okay, okay! I think I know who you both are now, but it's going to take a while before I can associate the right name with the right face."

"'Tis always the case Professor. Now please advise us as to the whereabouts of our new home. 'Tis not the hallowed and venerable halls of Oxford University perchance?" Robin said.

He examined the boys' faces for a moment; they wore wolfish grins in anticipation of his reply.

"Alas, 'tis not."

His reply immediately brought puzzlement to their faces.

"Let's just say that you've skipped a few grades."

"What! We don't like the idea of skipping grades Professor. We enjoy being with people of our own age," Ian said. "As a matter of fact, we recently learned that our science teacher wants to hold us back a grade to teach us a lesson. Well, that would be the first one he ever gave us!"

They both doubled over with laughter.

Yates's face flushed visibly at being associated with the brunt of Ian's joke.

"Quite droll. Nevertheless, it's time you stop wasting your time and stop terrorising your peers and elders, such as Father O'Malley and your science teacher. Instead, you are going to become adults from this day forth and realise your mutual potential. In return for your complete fidelity and obedience to your benefactor, you shall one day become extremely rich, even beyond your prodigious imaginations, and perhaps sooner than you can imagine. By the way, how do you boys manage to clothe yourselves in such fine attire? Not many well-to-due adults can afford to dress so well."

"Well, since we're on the verge of becoming confidantes, Professor, we might as well confess. We call it our PIN money. Robin simply hacks into the mainframe computers of major banks, pulls account numbers and associated PIN codes of local customers regularly using specific ATMs around town. Then using the omnicard he's invented we visit several ATMs a day and make appropriate cash withdrawals from the accounts.

"We never withdraw more than the customer would usually do at any one time. Thus, a missing ATM receipt or two from a monthly statement is hardly later noticed by the affected customer. It's really tedious work, but someone has to do it. No one is any the wiser, except us, and no paper trail can lead the source of the withdrawals back to us."

"From this day forth, Fletcher brothers that is something the two of you will never do again."

His stern glare bore into both of them. He reached into his jacket and pulled out a roll of fresh fifty-pound notes. He peeled off ten to each boy. "Do I make myself perfectly clear?"

Robin said: "We understand, Professor...But this gig you are proposing to us had better include more money than that for daily spending as we're becoming acutely interested in girls these days."

He poked Ian in the ribs with his elbow.

"Accordingly, we regularly require extra funds to satisfy our hormonal need to be with them, and often."

"Satisfying your budding sex drives will not be a concern of yours...at least until you finish your daily research and development tasks."

"More information is required, please kind sir," Ian responded.

"I shall lay out the entire deal to you tomorrow, and supply you with the same amount of funds as today for your pleasures. Meet me at the entrance of the exhibition hall at noon without fail."

Professor Yates returned to his hotel room and placed a long-distance encrypted phone call from his cell phone to OWCH...his second, off-the-record, employer.

"Smythe here."

"General, I am certain that I have discovered your prodigies."

"Tell me more."

Professor Yates proceeded to relate all the background information on the Fletcher brothers as well as his personal experience with them.

"Excellent, as identical twins, they will collaborate exceedingly well, as they are now.

"You are to establish an endowment for the orphanage. Let's provide them with enough funds to rebuild the dormitory and assure the place operates well indefinitely. You see to the details. Let me know when you can arrange for the pair to come here for a meeting with me. That's all for now. Good work, Yates."

"It really was a stroke of luck, General."

Professor Yates could tell by the slight inflection of enthusiasm in the general's voice that he was nonetheless wildly ecstatic about the discovery of the Fletcher twins.

"They would have found us sooner or later, Yates."

"As you say. I'll attend to all the details of their adoption etc. tomorrow. It shouldn't be any problem to have them at the Andorran compound no later than the day after tomorrow."

"Fine. I'll arrange to wire the reward to your bank account right after my first meeting with the twins."

The line on the other end went dead.

Yates was beside himself with joy. He finally succeeded in the job the general had assigned to him only a year ago. His mind raced in contemplation of how he would spend the £1,000,000 reward. He bought a new car that afternoon.

At noon the following day Professor Yates pulled up to the entrance of the exhibition hall in a brand-new Aston Martin. Dressed in blue jeans, T-shirts, and wildly expensive sneakers, the twins awaited him. Two pretty young girls of questionable repute hung on the arm of each boy. Yates rolled down the driver's side window and gave the boys a stare of disapproval.

"So, Professor 'tis the game afoot? Nice wheels!"

"Lose your consorts, immediately, and come with me."

"And where may we be going, pray tell?" Ian snapped.

The girl gave him a kiss on the cheek and then stuck her tongue out at Yates.

"We are going to a place to speak of pigs with wings and other things," Yates snapped back. "Now bid your ladies adieu and get in the car with all haste."

"Your wish is our command oh master!" the boys shouted.

They gave a hot embrace and kiss to their respective girlfriends, and. silently motioned for the girls to leave after slipping each one fifty-pound note.

"Good! Get in and hurry up about it. We're going for a fanciful trip to the countryside."

After a quick drive through town, the car entered the main entrance of the London International Airport and directly proceeded to a commercial aircraft hangar.

The sight of a helicopter just outside the hangar excited the Fletcher twins.

The noise of its engines and rotors whining penetrated the closed interior of the Aston Martin. As he exited the car, Yates motioned for the boys to follow him to the helicopter.

Two men impeccably dressed in Armani suits met the trio. They were both well over six feet tall. The stern-looking men in their late twenties wore reflective sunglasses and military-style crew cuts. The boys couldn't help but notice the size of the men's arms, chests, and leg muscles that bulged through their suits.

"Fletcher brothers, I'd like you to meet your new friends. As you can see, they're identical twins like you," Yates yelled over the din of the revving helicopter engines.

"He is Rolf," he said as he pointed to the man on the right.

"And he is Fritz." He pointed to the other man.

The pair bowed.

"And we are the dangerous Brünner brothers of Geneva!" they shouted.

They laughed uproariously and pointed to their charges. The Fletcher brothers stumbled back from the Brünner twins in response.

The Brünner brothers motioned the two boys to enter the helicopter cabin. Professor Yates remained just outside the passenger door as the four embarked. The din of the revving helicopter motor rose to a crescendo.

Yates shouted: "Boys, the Brünner brothers are indeed dangerous. They're fresh off a seven-year stint with the French Foreign Legion. They have few, if any, peers in their line of work. Luckily we were able to effect their release from service just so they can accompany you. They will be your shadows for a long time to come. I warn you that they, like you, are insufferable pranksters, but don't take kindly to being the brunt of one. I trust you catch my drift."

Summoning courage, Ian shouted back, "But where are we going? Aren't you coming with us?"

"You are going to a far, far better place than you have ever been. I myself am going to a far, far better place than I have seldom been. Monte Carlo. Be that as it may, alas, we shall not meet again. Fare thee well," were his final words. He instantly drove the helicopter door shut with a slam and walked back to his car.

As the helicopter lifted off the tarmac the boys stared sheepishly at the pair sitting across from them. They, in turn, grinned at the Fletcher twins like wolves sizing up spring lambs for a little snack. Visibly shaken, the boys sulked back into their seats.

"Buckle up sports," Rolf commanded. "We're bound for a new adventure and some fun along the way."

The helicopter rose swiftly into the clear blue sky toward its destination...the OWCH compound located in a remote valley of the Andorran Pyrenees.

The hour-and-a-half-long flight went by quickly for the Fletcher brothers. Their normal sensibilities had all but vanished due to the experience to which they had just been subjected. They felt like novice sailors embarking on the maiden voyage of a strange ship bound for a wondrous port seldom visited by mankind. They knew instinctively that they would seldom ever again visit the cradle of their childhood, their beloved East End. Silently shedding their last tears in this recognition, they became young men as their journey in life began.

After winding through a granite-walled canyon on the final leg of their journey, the helicopter arrived at a grand mansion surrounded by an expansive grass lawn. The helicopter swooped down to a nearby landing pad like a falcon alighting upon its aerie to deliver carrion to its hatchlings.

The helicopter motor wound down as the pilot hand signalled his clearance for the passengers to disembark. The Fletcher twins jogged away from the helicopter's whirling rotor blades as soon as they set foot on the tarmac. They stopped about thirty meters away from the aircraft and began to survey the area around them.

A diminutive man dressed in a black tuxedo stood at the grand entrance of a two-story, English Tudor mansion located nearly one hundred meters away from them. He waved at them to approach him. The swarthy good-natured Asian smiled as they stepped onto the veranda.

"Welcome to Tallymore. young gentlemen. Please follow me."

He led all four of them inside to the main reception hall. The large hall contained an array of finely crafted sofas, chairs, and carved wooden tables. An enormous fireplace blazed at the far end of the room.

"Please make yourselves comfortable. There's still a chill in the air this morning, so please take advantage of the fireplace setting. Refreshments will be served to you presently. As I have a matter to attend, I shall return to your company in a few minutes."

"Looks like we've hit the jackpot," Ian said to Robin.

They seated themselves next to each other in comfortable leather chairs close to the warmth of the fireplace. The opulence of the scene was beyond their wildest expectations; they also grew exceedingly excited at the prospect of whatever it was that was going to unfold before them.

Two young female Asian servants set several trays of hors d'oeuvres and beverages on a serving table. The hungry men consumed the entire offering in peace and quiet. When they'd eaten their fill, their host entered the room.

He cleared his throat to gain their attention as he positioned himself between the fireplace and the foursome.

"Young masters my name is Major Surya Thappa. I shall be your host for the next few days whilst we await the arrival of your patron. Through me, he extends you his warmest welcome to Tallymore, and asks you to consider this residence as yours in every respect."

"But where are we and who is our patronm Major Thappa?" Ian meekly inquired.

"You are where you should be, for now, young master. As to your patron, he is none other than your potential father. I shall not say more on the subject, as all your inquiries shall be entertained by him personally in due course. Meanwhile, I give you leave to enjoy the amenities of Tallymore as you see fit.

"Rolf and Fritz, please engage the masters in suitable occupation whilst they await the arrival of their father."

Ian and Robin uttered a sigh of frustration.

"Have no fear, Major Thappa," Rolf said. "We shall have them ready for the next white slave auction in Tangiers in no time."

In response, the Fletcher brothers winced and sunk back into their chairs.

"Never mind the Legionnaire's churlish attempt at sardonic humour. Theirs is the poetry of killers with nothing to lose but their self-respect."

"Oh yeah," Fritz replied, "and how many shall perish as a result of your good deeds, oh noble one."

"All shall perish in time, whether by their own or someone else's devices Legionnaire. It is the human nature, as you know."

"Amen, and please pass me a bottle of German lager, Master Ian."

Surya glared at him for a moment and then turned his attention to the Fletcher twins.

"Dinner will be served at 8:00 p.m. Your valet shall present himself shortly to escort you to your rooms where you can freshen up and change into proper attire for the remainder of the day."

Someone entered the room at that moment. At hearing a sound of approaching footsteps, the group of men turned in their chairs to view the visitor. Dressed in a black tuxedo like Surya's, the man wore a mane of perfectly groomed white hair. The grandeur and majesty of his appearance awed the Fletcher brothers at first sight. Tall, slender, and powerfully built, the man was the epitome of a mature British gentleman.

"Young masters, this is your valet, Mr Brighton Day."

The man took his place beside him.

"You may simply address him as Day. He shall serve your every need in terms of your personal grooming, gentlemanly comportment, and much much more. I assure you that he is your ally in every respect, so I implore you to treat him well. He was selected especially by your patron to assist you."

"And now, I shall allow Day to personally introduce himself to you."

"Thank you, Surya. You are most gracious."

He curtly bowed to the group before him and proceeded to inspect the Fletcher brothers for several seconds.

They're not as tall as I remembered them from my childhood dream, he thought. But otherwise, they're a perfect match to the pair of twins he encountered that night.

Concluding his scrutiny of the boys, he said: "I am a man of few words about myself, so I shall not take the occasion now to present my personal curriculum vitae to you. Suffice it to say that as your valet, I shall endeavour in no small measure to impart to you the characteristics of the right and proper gentlemen that you have been chosen to become. And we are going to have such a splendid time together in the process.

"Now let us proceed to your suites where you can freshen up. You are free to tour the residence and the grounds with the Brünner brothers until dinner."

He promptly led them upstairs to their elegantly appointed rooms. They showered and dressed for the evening with Day's assistance. After they were fully dressed Day convened them and the Brünner twins in Ian's room.

"You may lounge about in your rooms or anywhere else on the premises until dinner young gentlemen. I will see you in the dining hall at 8:00 p.m."

He departed the room leaving the two twins staring at each other.

At dinnertime, Surya took the chair at the head of the long dinner table, with Day at the opposite end. The Fletcher brothers sat on the same side of the table across from the Brünner twins.

Day noticed both Fletchers had yet to place their linen napkins on their laps and cleared his throat loud enough to gain their attention. He shifted his gaze to their napkins still on their plates and placed his own on his lap. Immediately catching his cue, the boys copied his manners.

Before the first course was served, Surya proposed a toast.

"Gentlemen, I propose a toast in honour of this auspicious occasion."

He raised his glass.

"Though we are together for the first time today, we lift up our glasses to toast the promise of our mutual success and prosperity in the days and years to come."

Following a sumptuous four-course dinner, both pairs of twins retired for the evening totally spent from the physical and mental demands of the day's events.

Day awakened the Fletcher brothers at five o'clock the following morning. He promptly went about laying out their clothes for their hiking excursion as they showered.

At 5:40 a.m., the Brünner brothers collected the Fletcher twins and led them down to the breakfast table.

Surya entered the dining hall in good humour.

"Good morning to you all. It's going to be a splendid day, so enjoy your hike through this scenic part of the Pyrenees.

"Rucksacks containing your lunches and beverages are located in the gazebo just outside the rear entrance of the villa."

Almost instantaneously the faint rumble of an approaching helicopter could be heard in the distance.

"Oh yes, I forgot to advise you that Day will be departing for Kuala Lumpur ahead of us to make preparations for our arrival tomorrow."

He sat down. Regrettably, your patron is unable to make the journey here due to pressing and unforeseen demands on his schedule."

"But we were led to believe we would meet him here," Ian protested. We really don't like the idea of leaving Europe in this manner."

He glanced at Robin who nodded his head in agreement.

"Well, Master Ian, what man proposes, God disposes. He has pressing business matters requiring his utmost and immediate attention. Consequently, he is forced to remain indefinitely in Kuala Lumpur. We trust that you do not mind.

"Actually, the journey will prove to be an adventure to you both, vastly more exciting than a visit to a Disney World resort. You will have such fun, travelling by a first-class private jet. Do you have any objections?"

"None here," Robin replied.

He eyed Ian to not pursue any further objection to the proposal.

"Splendid. Then you shall depart from Tallymore tomorrow with all due dispatch and resolve."

After breakfast, the Brünners excused themselves to prepare for their hike.

"I don't know about you, but I have the distinct impression that we've latched onto something quite special. Don't you think so?" Robin said.

His brother added: "I had my doubts about the entire proposition until we boarded the helicopter in East End. Since then, it's been one big jaw-dropper after another, starting with the Brünner twins. If they're taking us to Kuala Lumpur though the best may be yet to come. I can't for the life of me guess who's behind this scheme...it's totally baffling and surpasses even our wildest speculations about who might first approach us to offer an employment opportunity. All we can do for now is bide our time and see what develops."

"I agree. At least we have our escape plan ready should this turn out to be a less-than-ideal situation. By the way, is the data safe?"

"It was uploaded to encrypted Internet file storage several days ago. It's perfectly secure and available there for us to access from anywhere in the world. And don't worry about us if this situation turns out not to be of our liking. The new omnicard upgrade I designed will ensure we'll enjoy a rich lifestyle no matter where we decide to live."

"Keep it in your wallet. We're not going anywhere anytime soon without a major infusion of capital into our research coffers. Don't you agree? Until then, we're men without a country."

Chapter 4 - The Magical Mystery Tour of Tallymore

French Pyrenees, 14 April 2020

The Fletcher brothers met Rolf and Fritz at the front entrance of Tallymore at 7:00 a.m., as appointed.

Rolf advised his charges that they would not return to the mansion until late in the afternoon.

"But we have other things we'd rather attend to this afternoon," Ian protested.

"Other things?" Fritz countered. "Think about these other things while you enjoy the great outdoors and the privilege of being in the presence of the Brünner brothers."

In response, Ian merely shrugged his shoulders and harrumphed as a sign of dissent.

"We thought you'd see it our way.".

He fixed his communication set to his right ear and placed the microphone over his mouth. Rolf did the same.

"Right. Let's take a look at your gear."

He made a brief inspection of boys.

"Rucksacks properly loaded, boot laces tied, and nerves steeled. You are now ready for our adventure in the great outdoors, sports."

As they were about to embark on their journey, Rolf went inside the manse and returned several minutes later with two sets of hunting rifles, bowie knives, and nine-millimetre luger pistols.

"What is all that for?" Robin asked anxiously.

"Oh. Didn't think you'd notice," Fritz responded. "We call all this our PDAs, personal defence armaments."

Rolf laughed.

The men promptly slung the rifles over their shoulders and placed the knives and lugers into the ammunition belts strapped snugly around their waists.

Several hours into their journey, the beautiful scenery gladdened the boys' spirits; their bodies also appreciated the strenuous exercise. Soon the combination of pristine environment and the late spring day in the Pyrenees washed all their cares and apprehensions away.

Throughout the hike, Rolf held the point position twenty meters ahead of the single-file procession. Fritz followed the boys closely behind, occasionally talking to Rolf in hushed German via their communication set.

At noon they took a lunch break slightly above an alpine tarn overflowing with water as clear as crystal glass. They marvelled at the scenic vista as they ate. Nature had performed one of her best efforts here in masterfully sculpting with glacial ice and eons of erosion a perfect representation of an alpine mise-en-scène. After lunch, they basked in the late spring sunlight pouring through the cloudless sky overhead.

As they were about to resume their hike, Ian suddenly spoke to the Brünners.

"I'm curious. How does one become involved in your business?"

The Swiss twins looked at each other and sat down, seemingly amused, and motioned the boys to do likewise.

After a few moments of reflection, Rolf replied, "Involvement had nothing to do with our pursuing this occupation. In fact, it's quite a bit more like a calling from birth. You see, the Brünners in one way or another have always been career soldiers or guards or blade and firearm makers. Over time we have mainly maintained the tradition of membership in the Swiss Guard. For us, though, serving the Legion was a matter of personal preference due to our affinity for adventure and distaste of ecclesiastic regimentation."

"We could not help but notice the magnificence of your rifles and pistols, especially the filigree detail on the rifle barrels," Robin said.

"You are most kind to notice the craftsmanship," Rolf replied.

He held his rifle out in front of him for the boys' further inspection.

"We crafted these pieces with our own hands when we were about your age. Every part was made by our very own hands. Yet, for all the attention for artistic detail, in the final analysis, each weapon is as fine a killing machine as we would care to wield. Both of us are expert marksmen with most guns and rifles, but with these weapons in our hands we are the best in the world."

"Yes," Fritz interrupted. "And now let's continue our trek. After we reach our destination in an hour or less, we'll head back to Tallymore."

He then glanced intently for several minutes at the oversize watch he was wearing on his left wrist.

"May we take a closer look at your watch?" Robin said.

"Why not," Fritz replied.

He removed it and handed it to Robin.

The boys examined the watch for a few seconds and promptly returned it.

"In addition to keeping perfectly acceptable GMT by Swiss standards, and receiving local weather forecast, this is also a multi-functional miniature computer with a GPS interface. On display now is a map of the local area that shows our current position relative to Tallymore. See that blinking dot. That's where we are precisely within a meter of geographic accuracy." He lightly tapped on a side panel of the device and the display changed slightly by adding several other blinking dots to the north of their current position.

"The computer also has the capability of sensing motion within a quarter of a kilometre radius around our position. Any moving object is detected by the computer's ultra-sensitive sonic receiver. It automatically filters out insignificant motion—such as that produced by air and thermal currents, insects, small animals, birds, and vegetation—and displays the results. And voilà, it now displays us, several valley deer travelling on a parallel trail above us, and the four-man Ghurkha patrol less than an eighth a kilometre ahead of us on this trail."

"A Ghurkha patrol!" Robin exclaimed.

"Indeed. They are Major Thappa's countrymen and former comrades-in-arms. They are employed as a permanent security guard force for Tallymore and the surrounding estate grounds. There is another one directly behind us, but they are outside the range of the device at present. Do not worry, the patrols are assigned to our party today and provide forward- and back-bracket defensive support. Standard operating procedure I'm afraid, chaps."

"Defensive support?" Ian said.

He glanced at his brother.

"Again, standard operating procedure. We must immediately proceed in order to keep to our timetable."

Rolf took the point position as they resumed their hike. Toward the summit at the end of the valley through which they were climbing, the trail twisted around huge rocks and boulders and narrowed at times to allow only one-way passage for several meters. Upon reaching the crest of the summit, Rolf noticed the sudden introduction of two deer spoor imprinted over the boot prints of the Ghurkha patrol ahead.

"There's something peculiar up ahead us on the trail," Rolf whispered into his microphone.

"Oh yeah. What is it?"

"What we have here is two deer stalking the forward Ghurkha patrol."

His eyes continued to follow the spoor up the trail. Advancing ten meters more, he saw an end of the deer hoof print trail and the beginning of a set of padded prints over twice the size of a full-grown Bengal tiger's paw.

"Scheisse! Shifters! The entities must have advanced and descended from the trail above after we entered the rock outcroppings."

He immediately transferred the nine-millimetre luger into his right hand from the holster suspended on the side of the ammunition belt. Slowly he reached down to the scabbard hanging on the left side of the belt and took the bowie knife handle into his left hand. The sun's rays glistened like a mirror off the Swiss carbon steel surface of the broad nine-inch long blade.

Turning his back away from the Fletcher twins, who were standing together three meters away from him, Fritz glanced at his wrist computer for a moment. He tapped the LCD screen once with his right index finger. "Move forward and reconnoitre. I ordered backward support to move forward to meet us as we descend the trail."

"Right."

He casually turned to face the boys. "Just our luck. The weather forecast predicts a major rainstorm in this sector any moment now. Sorry to cut short our excursion, but I think we would rather not encounter the approaching storm. Don't you agree?"

The boys responded by shrugging their shoulders in agreement with Fritz's assessment of the situation, obviously relieved at having an excuse to return to Tallymore.

"Since it's mostly downhill, let's have some fun and double-time march back to Tallymore. I'll follow you all the way."

"What about Rolf?" Robin inquired.

"He's going to take some target practice at the top of the ridge after meeting up with the Ghurkha patrol for a friendly chat. Now, let's be off. We don't want to get drenched,"

He motioned them to start down the trail. They soon reached a jogging pace under Fritz's prodding.

Rolf sidled up to the trail to the summit of the ridge along the last of the rock outcroppings.

Peering down into the forest, he noticed a clearing about one hundred meters away. The trail on the side of the summit wound in a series of switchbacks to the clearing. He performed a scan of the area and found only two moving objects registering on his wrist computer display. They were close together somewhere in the vicinity of the clearing, hidden from view by the surrounding trees, but moving stealthily toward his position.

"Rolf, status report."

"I just scanned the sector behind the ridge. No visual or sensor signs of the Ghurkha patrol.

They aren't responding to my signals via wrist computer telecommunication, either. The sensor registers only two life-forms, about the size and mass of Clydesdales, moving slowly together through the trees bordering the adjacent clearing, about two hundred meters away from my position. No visual sighting yet."

He glanced at the computer display again and saw the two dots representing the unknown entities abruptly separate; the images were heading quickly toward him in an apparent flanking manoeuvre.

"And it looks like our Clydesdales have the agility and speed of alley cats and are bounding up the mountainside in a flanking manoeuvre toward my position.

"I'm downwind of them, so I doubt they've yet sensed my presence."

"Stand your ground. I just ordered attack helicopter support of your position. They should be there in less than fifteen minutes."

"Right."

Rolf immediately moved away from the trail and climbed higher on the ridge to a massive promontory boulder that provided him an unobstructed view of the forested area below him. Crouching down and placing the bowie knife and pistol on either side of him, he slung his 30 odd 6 hunting rifle from his shoulder and wrapped the sling around his left arm in firing position.

Hearing the crackle and snap of tree twigs on both the right and left of his position, perhaps only fifty meters away in the forest below, he released the safety latch and wrapped his right index finger around the trigger. Whatever it was that was approaching was taking five meter strides through the forest below him. From his vantage point, he could only discern the treetops of the forest stretching from the base of the ridge to the clearing visible from the summit of the trail.

Emerging from the forest to the rock-strewn escarpment at the base of the ridge fifty meters below, the predators finally revealed themselves as they bounded toward him. The sheer beauty of the animals, now fully in his view as they climbed the side of the ridge, stunned Rolf. In his youth, he recalled seeing artistic renderings of cave lions depicted in books he read about prehistoric mammals. But in reality, these creatures were by far the finest feline specimens, as the two individuals clearly exemplified. Being more than twice the size of an adult male Siberian tiger, their coats and manes were pure golden coloured.

As they reached the top of the ridge, Rolf took a prone firing position to conceal himself from immediate visual detection.

Like cats jumping up from the floor to a window ledge, they each, almost at the same time, mounted the top of the ridge in a single leap. They silently landed on the crest of the ridge on either side of Rolf, so that each was no more than twenty-five meters away from his position atop a massive boulder several meters above them. Both lions immediately sat on their haunches and panted as if taking a well-deserved rest before resuming their hunt. Whilst surveying the land below them, the lions leisurely licked their paws and muzzles, which were stained a crimson red, most likely by human blood.

"Here, kitty, kitty," Rolf called to the lion on his right.

Before the animal had a chance to react, a 30 odd 6 bullet pierced the side of its skull. It instantly collapsed to the ground from the impact of the slug. Immediately after firing the round, Rolf set aside the rifle and reached over to grab his bowie knife in his left hand, at the same time fetching the nine-millimetre luger in his other hand. He then rolled off the boulder on the sloped side away from the remaining lion, sensing it had already taken offensive charge toward him the split second after hearing the thundering rifle report. Upon landing on solid ground three meters below, he heard a furious roar of the other cave lion.

The cat peered down at him from the spot on top of the boulder where he had been only seconds before. The animal leapt through the air above him to an open space ten meters away. Despite the mortal danger of the moment, Rolf could not help but marvel at the majesty of the beast as it passed over him in a split second.

On landing, the animal instantaneously swivelled around to face Rolf. As their gazes met, the animal issued another blood curdling roar that caused him to flinch. At that moment the lion lunged at Rolf with forepaw claws fully extended and jaws agape. Four meters before the lethal mass reached him, he brought the luger up to eye level and fired two shots—both of which hit their target between the eyes. As he jumped away, the momentarily stunned and blinded animal rammed its head into the base of the boulder.

Knowing that this would be its final opportunity for survival, the lion sprang upright and turned around. It immediately began viciously swiping its forepaws brandishing razor-sharp, nine-inch-long claws around the area where Rolf last stood. Smelling the scent of a man to the right, the lion pounced in that direction.

Caught off guard by the animal's sudden attack, Rolf could only thrust his bowie knife held in his left hand into the roof of its mouth as its jaws began to close to extract a savage bite out of him. The enraged lion roared in mortal pain and began to blindly swipe its lethal claws at Rolf. Finally, one of the beast's swipes caught him across his chest, inflicting a deep laceration as Rolf jumped away from the beast.

Sensing his life was in peril, he swung the luger around to bear directly on the lion's forehead. He emptied the ammunition clip into the staggering target's forehead at once.

As the last breath of life left the lungs of the mortally wounded creature lying on the ground only a meter away from him, Rolf saw the telltale signs of shifter death...the instant disintegration of its dying body. He turned his eyes southward where the other individual had fallen less than a half a minute before to observe only a heap of nonspecific material in its place.

"Rolf here."

His chest wound bled profusely. He nearly passed out from the pain and loss of blood.

Fritz stopped the boys, ostensibly so they could rest. He then walked up the trail to separate himself from them.

"Yes, Rolf. Report. We heard a series of gunshots from your last reported position."

"The life-forms of both intruder shifter entities have been terminated. Full bio disintegration of each individual is in effect as we speak.

"Casualty report."

"The forward Ghurkha patrol sustained total annihilation from the shifter advance on their ranks. I sustained a serious pectoral flesh wound. A few stitches should remedy that, but the effect of blood loss is problematic."

The attack helicopter flew overhead.

"You'll be evacuated from your position to in a few minutes. Stay calm."

"Roger. Thankfully, the beasts were big targets."

"Yes, thankfully."

He returned to the boys, and they resumed the forced march back to Tallymore.

Seven minutes later the Ghurkha helicopter crew placed Rolf in the aircraft and flew back to Tallymore. The medical personnel on board promptly attended to his wound.

Following a quick breakfast early the next morning, the group of travellers, including Surya and the two sets of brothers, boarded a private helicopter.

It proved a somewhat perfunctory flight to Paris. The boys sensed something was amiss immediately after their arrival at a military air base located on the outskirts of Paris after the helicopter landed near a solitary aircraft hangar.

"Why are we landing at a military air base?" Robin said to his brother.

"I haven't a clue. It's rather peculiar."

After disembarking the helicopter, Surya led them inside. A cross between an SST and a booster rocket was parked in the middle of the hangar.

"Gentlemen, you may be wondering whether this technological marvel before us will be our transport to Kuala Lumpur today. Well, it will indeed."

All four brothers slowly approached the aircraft.

"But this is a Stargazer HST. It's not supposed to be in production yet." Ian said. "In fact, it isn't scheduled to be for at least another ten years."

"Be that as it may. I assure you that this is a fully tested prototype developed and owned by your patron's firm. It has logged more flight hours during the time we've owned it than its sister prototype has flown in test trials to date. Your patron has flown in the craft as a passenger dozens of times himself. Our pilot today is none other than its first test pilot, Captain Reginald Saunders."

"We're flying in a prototype?" Rolf inquired.

"Yes, we are. At any rate, you are all privileged to be Stargazer passengers. If any one of you would prefer a more conventional mode of travel, I can arrange first-class accommodation on the next 797 flight scheduled for Kuala Lumpur."

"I think my brother and I would prefer not to miss out on this experience," Ian said.

He nodded to his brother for approval.

Robin nodded back in the affirmative.

"We goeth too . . . by the grace of God," Rolf said.

The decision to accompany the Fletcher twins was a matter of duty for both of them.

"I thought you wouldn't want to miss out on this joyride. Now, let's board the aircraft. I'll brief you on the flight profile once we're inside."

He tapped his earphone to take a phone call.

"There we have it. Captain Saunders has already performed the preflight inspection of the aircraft and has given us permission to board. He is currently completing the preflight checklist. We should thus have clearance from the control tower to taxi to the runway in less than half an hour."

The main cabin was surprisingly spacious and contained twelve comfortable recliners. Each seat was positioned next to a two-foot-by-two-foot window looking out to the exterior.

"All right then. Please find your seats, and afterward, I'll commence the flight profile."

After the passengers were seated he started the briefing.

"Our flight today conforms to the standard profile for HST takeoff, en route glide path, and landing. Sounds simple enough? Here's the real kicker, though. To achieve a parabolic glide path to our destination, the aircraft must reach an elevation of eighty thousand feet above sea level at its apex. In order to do that, we literally blast off from just above the runway in nearly a straight-up trajectory. No problem you say. The problem really is though that the g-forces your bodies will experience from the moment the hyper-ram jet engages are enough to cause physical discomfort during ascent.

"To countervail this effect, please note the following features provided in your seating area. First, an anti-g suit is stowed under your seat. Please take the time now to remove the suit from the stowage compartment and don it. It's really as easy as putting on your trousers and conforms to most every body type."

They donned the suits.

"Good. Well done. You are free to remove the suit once the captain has given approval. The flight attendant will be by toward the end of the flight to collect them from you,"

The remark elicited nervous laughter from the passengers.

"Next, find the pneumatic hose underneath the armrest on the right side of your seat.

"Connect the hose to the aperture found on the upper right-hand side of the suit.

"Very well done. Now take your seats and buckle the harness strap and seat belt. We're almost through and will be on our way in less than ten minutes. Underneath the armrest on the left side of your seat, you'll find a biomonitor device. You must strap it to your left wrist via the attached Velcro strap. Please do so now.

"Good. Now, on takeoff an oxygen mask and a set of headphones will drop from the utility compartment above you. You must put on the mask and headphones immediately and continue to wear them until the captain indicates his approval for removal.

"All done! You are now ready for our two-hour-long HST flight to Kuala Lumpur. Sure beats the Pirates of the Caribbean ride at Disneyland for cheap thrills, gentlemen?"

"What do you call this ride, Surya?" Rolf said.

"I would call it the Mercury One ride. You know, after the first rocket space flight flown by US astronaut Alan Shepard during the early nineteen-sixties."

At that moment a voice from the intercom broke in.

"This is Captain Saunders. Welcome aboard passengers. Surya, please visit me at the flight deck. We have just received clearance to taxi to the runway and are fourth in line for takeoff."

As Surya made his way to the flight deck, Ian spoke to his brother in a low voice to prevent the Brünner brothers seated in the back of the cabin from overhearing him.

"What are we going to do now? Something extraordinary occurred yesterday afternoon that neither Surya nor the Brünners are letting us in on. My sixth sense tells me that we were in mortal danger from the moment Fritz concocted that phony weather forecast."

"I agree. I had the same feeling he wasn't being honest with us about the situation. Still, we are all in one piece and none the worse for the experience."

The flight deck door then opened, and Surya entered the main cabin.

"Gentlemen, we are next in line for takeoff, so please prepare yourselves. After takeoff, the aircraft will climb to ten thousand feet via fan-jet propulsion. After reaching that altitude, away from the populated area, the captain will engage the scram jets and power down the fan-jets. At the moment of the engagement of the scram jets, the captain will point the nose of the aircraft for a nearly vertical ascent to eighty thousand feet above sea level. Your bodies will undergo the maximum g-force pressures for the first five minutes after the scram jets ignite. Do not be unduly alarmed as your anti-g suits will inflate to maximum pressure during this period to prevent your experiencing a blackout. Any questions so far?"

"Is there any chance we'll be invited to visit the flight deck during the flight," Ian inquired.

He was unperturbed by the potential danger of the adventure.

"I am certain it would be Captain Saunders's honour to have each and every one of you as his guests on the flight deck after we reach maximum flight elevation."

Ian grinned at the prospect of meeting the HST test pilot at the flight deck.

Captain Saunders then announced over the intercom, "Welcome again passengers. It's a marvellous day for HST flight. The wind is currently out in the northwest at eight knots, and the outside temperature is twenty-five degrees Celsius. According to the meteorological report, the weather pattern throughout our area of approach to Kuala Lumpur is expected to be fair and cloudless. Since our flight plan calls for a direct Paris to Kuala Lumpur route, we'll pass over much of southern Asia as we descend from parabolic apogee at eighty thousand feet above sea level over Istanbul Turkey. You can follow our progress via the LCD display located in the rear of the seat in front of you."

He continued in typical aviator's monotonic tone of voice less than a minute later.

"We have just received clearance for takeoff from the tower. Biometric readings of each of you are within standard parameters, thus you're all eligible to enjoy the flight. I look forward to meeting each of you later on the flight deck."

Thereupon, the aircraft began to move forward rapidly.

As the HST lifted off the tarmac, oxygen masks and headphones lowered from the utility bay overhead each of the passengers' seats.

"Please place the oxygen mask over your nose and mouth prior to putting on the headphones," Surya directed. "In approximately twenty minutes, the captain will announce count-down to scram jet ignition."

Still climbing away from the outskirts of Paris toward the French Alps, Captain Saunders broke into the classical music programme playing over the intercom.

"Countdown to scram jet ignition in T minus one minute."

Both sets of twins as well as Surya stared intently at the LCD monitors in front of them that showed the digital countdown to scram jet ignition as well as the flight route map.

"On my mark, scram jet ignition in T minus ten seconds."

The aircraft's nose began to pull to a near-vertical attitude. It started to stall as the wings slowly shifted in toward the fuselage.

"Mark. Ten. Nine. Eight. Seven. Six. Five. Four. Three. Two. One. Ignition."

At that moment the roar of the igniting scram jet engines commenced. It sounded like a muffled clarion call produced by a multitude of claxons.

The engines reached full thrust in a matter of seconds and propelled the HST upward toward the stratosphere like a bullet exiting a gun barrel. As the aircraft accelerated, the resultant g-forces soon pinned the passengers into their deeply padded seats; they were unable to move any part of their bodies seconds after. They could merely stare at the screens in front of them to view the televised display of the vista, as seen from the nose of the aircraft. Despite the explosive thrust dynamics at work, the fuselage maintained the same structural integrity of any regular commercial airplane undergoing standard takeoff acceleration.

Five minutes into the manoeuvre, Captain Saunders announced, "Looking good, passengers. Biometrics are acceptable, and we will approach apogee in less than twenty minutes; g-forces will abate to g-one in less than fifteen minutes."

Gradually, the pull of Earth's gravity and lower atmosphere friction ebbed as the HST soared higher and higher. Before the g-force levels subsided to near g-one, the passengers could turn their heads to view the upper atmosphere sky through their seat windows. The HST climbed at a less demonic pace at a forty-five-degree attitude.

From sixty-five thousand feet, according to the monitors, Earth's curvature and the infinite space beyond began to form into view. Below them, the surface of entire expanse of North Africa and the Mediterranean could be seen. The roar of the scram jets subsided to a purr as the nose of the aircraft began to level out.

"As your monitors indicate, we will achieve trajectory apogee several minutes from now," Captain Saunders advised. "Scram jet engines are now being powered down. We'll glide the rest of the way until we almost reach our destination. At approximately one hundred miles from and ten thousand feet above the airport, fan-jet engines will reengage for the final leg of our descent to Kuala Lumpur. A tone will sound, marking the achievement of trajectory apogee. You are free to remove your oxygen masks, headphones, anti-g suits, and biometric straps after the tone sounds, which will be after the fifteen-minute period of weightlessness. Please return and secure the equipment in the aft cabin properly. Afterward, you are free to move about the cabin for fifteen minutes.

You'll find a galley toward the rear of the cabin containing assorted sandwiches, snacks, and beverages. You'll also find the lavatory there. I will come to the cabin several minutes after the tone sounds to introduce myself to each and every one of you."

As the apogee tone sounded, the breathtaking beauty of Earth and space above, viewed from eighty thousand feet above sea level, awed the passengers. The Earth's curvature, formed by the shimmering pastels of the land and the atmosphere below, was elegant and surreal against the backdrop of the pitch-black emptiness of the space beyond, punctuated by the twinkling of stars throughout.

The Fletcher brothers intuitively sensed at that moment that their destinies were forever and inextricably linked with forces of nature, that were never so clearly revealed to them until that moment. They couldn't pinpoint the source, but they knew it was with them.

"Do you feel it?" Ian said.

"It feels as though my spirit has been elevated to another level entirely."

They resumed gazing at the wonder of the twinkling void of black space as their bodies floated weightlessly.

Chapter 5 - I Had a Dream...

Kuala Lumpur, Malaysia, 15 April 2020

After clearing customs, the party boarded a commuter helicopter for transportation to the Petronas Towers heliport. The weather was hot and humid. Following the perfunctory security clearance check, they boarded the express lift an hour after first entering the building.

"This lift is swift, but not quite as swift as our Stargazer HST," Surya said.

The lift rapidly ascended to the top floor.

Both pairs of brothers silently nodded their heads in agreement, apparently still slightly reeling from their hypersonic travel experience.

Upon reaching the upper level of the tower, the lift gently came to a halt. The door opened, and Surya led his charges out to the main lobby.

"Good evening, Ms. Pritchard. I trust all has been going well in my absence."

The pretty young woman sat attentively behind the reception desk.

"Quite well indeed, Surya.". She smiled as though she was genuinely pleased to have Surya back in the office.

"I'd like you to meet Ian and Robin Fletcher and their escorts, Fritz and Rolf Brünner."

He pointed to each man in turn, as he spoke their names.

"And this is Ms. Anita Pritchard, our executive office manager."

"I am pleased to make your acquaintance, gentlemen."

"The general would like to meet Ian and Robin straight away, Surya. Would you be so kind as to show them to his office?"

"But of course. Ian and Robin, please follow me. Ms. Pritchard, please show Fritz and Rolf to the executive residence quarters. I am sure they would appreciate the opportunity to spend some time to relax by themselves after our arduous journey."

He motioned the boys to follow him down an adjacent hallway.

"I would be only too happy to."

The Brünner brothers followed her as she led the way.

Making their way down the hall, Surya suddenly stopped several meters before reaching an imposing closed doorway.

"You are about to meet, Sir General George Smythe, your mentor, and more importantly, your prospective father. I realise you may have some trepidation about meeting him for the first time, but I assure you he will put you at ease even before you know it.

"I must now take my leave of you. Simply knock on the door when you feel ready to meet him. You will be shown into his office forthwith."

Surya turned and walked back to the office lobby.

The boys looked at each other for a few moments. Afterward, they boldly approached the door with a tacit agreement that there was nothing they could lose by their entertaining whatever proposal their patron presented to them. At the very least they would be back on the streets if all was not to their liking. And that wasn't all that daunting a prospect to them.

Ian knocked on the massive mahogany door. It immediately opened. Standing before them was a young woman of unparalleled beauty and stature. The boys had never before seen any female so aesthetically flawless. Her figure was slim and feminine, like that of a Parisienne haute couture model. Her jet-black hair flowed down her white silk sari to her waist. Her sparkling ebony eyes and swarthy complexion spoke volumes of her high level of intelligence and pristine health. The layers of gold bracelets on her wrists and diamond-encrusted rings on her fingers told of her wealth.

"I am Sita," she pronounced softly with an Indian accent.

She bowed gracefully.

Her presence dazzled them. They were lost for appropriate words of response. Finally, regaining his composure Ian pointed to his brother.

"This is my brother Robin, and I am Ian."

Robin only nodded to her at his introduction.

A sweet smile formed on her exquisitely rouged red lips.

"That is simply fabulous gentlemen."

The boys visibly blushed at her response to their introduction of themselves to her.

"Please follow me. The general shall be with us in a few minutes. Would you care for refreshment?"

"Yes. We both would. Sparkling water with ice and a twist of lemon please," Robin replied.

They sat down on a leather couch facing the expanse of floor-to-ceiling windows overlooking the city. SITA whispered something they couldn't hear, apparently speaking into an ear cell phone microphone. She sat down on a couch opposite to them.

"You are very fortunate to have been passengers of the aircraft since its maiden flight only six months ago."

Moments later a young Malaysian girl placed a tray of refreshments on the coffee table set between the sofas.

"You must be famished, young gentlemen. Please partake in the repast."

The boys avoided looking directly at her as they ate. A short while after finishing the repast, a door located behind them opened.

Sita promptly arose from her couch. The boys followed suit as a reflex reaction. A tall man walked through the door and sauntered past them where she stood with his back turned toward them, as though he was attempting to conceal his identity for dramatic effect.

"Ian and Robin Fletcher, it is my pleasure and honour to introduce you to Sir General George Smythe."

The man turned to face them.

They instantly recognised the exceptional man whom they met at Tallymore two days before.

They exclaimed, "Day!"

The general instantly evinced his emblematic smile.

"I regret the ruse gentlemen. It was a necessity, however, and I trust you shall understand the reason for the ploy before our session together is finished. No hard feelings I trust."

Ian and Robin looked at each other and chuckled at the deception.

"On occasion, we have been known to pull the wool over the eyes of the unsuspecting, so we won't hold this one against you General," Ian rejoined.

"Splendid. You are indeed brave and good-natured lads."

As Sita and he sat down, he motioned for the boys to take their seats.

"That being said and the diversion forgiven, I brought you here today to put a proposal before you. I know you thought as much when you departed Tallymore this morning. Though owing to the sensitivity of the plan I have in mind for you, I could not risk explaining it to you anywhere else but here. Besides Sita and myself, you are soon to be the only people on the face of the globe that will know the importance of the Empyreal Paradigm, and how you shall fit into its advancement."

The boys were completely baffled.

"I realise that you don't have much reason to trust adults, having been abandoned by your mother as infants at the front steps of the church."

Ian interrupted him before he could proceed further with his monologue.

"Our mother? How did you get the impression that our mother abandoned us there?"

Sita winced. No one had ever interrupted the general before not at least as far as she knew.

"Well, Father O'Malley advised my talent scouting representative that he saw her lamentably departing from the front steps of the church just before he found you there."

"Sir, we assure you that she wasn't our mother. We don't know who she was. She left us in an inexplicable panic after we asked her to feed us."

"Feed?"

"Yes, feed. We were hungry and thirsty. The elegant lady appeared to be so stricken by the request that she fled from us with undue haste."

"Then who left you there?"

"We'd rather not talk about that as it was in the best interests of all concerned, at least insofar as we were concerned. Please trust us on that judgment."

"I suppose I must."

The mystery of the boys' abandonment perplexed him.

He leaned back into the couch and straightened his tie. He then took on an altogether different demeanour as he resumed his monologue. His countenance was that of an avatar of a Buddha.

"When I was a not much older than you, I had a dream."

* * *

It had been a winter evening just like any other drizzling and dank London evening. His room on the second floor of the moderately fashionable West End town house had all he needed to ward off the cold and provide him with a modicum of entertainment. His mother and father had retired to their own bedroom earlier than usual. He supposed they were engaged in some form of entertainment of their own, which happened once or twice a week for as long as he could remember.

The bedroom steam radiator occasionally hissed and knocks, as regular reminders of its strenuous effort to keep him warm and cozy.

He sat casually at his desk putting the finishing touches on the Spitfire model airplane he had assembled and painted to perfection when he felt himself nodding off to sleep. He thought that this call to slumber was nothing extraordinary given the physical demands on his body that day. For in addition to school attendance, he later attended football practice. Afterward, he jogged the five kilometres it took for him to reach his home.

He knew he was unique amongst his peers in this regard, as they were apt to point out to him whenever possible. Typically, they would shout some kind of mockery at him in passing him from busses or cars as he ran home.

"You're a bleeding freak of nature show, Smythe," they would often yell at him.

That experience never dampened his spirit, though, as he knew from his early childhood that he was on an entirely different path in life than them.

After tucking himself under the layer of sheets and down comforters, he turned out the nightstand lamp and settled his head on his pillow. His last thoughts before falling asleep were of the winning goal he had scored the week before during a hotly contested football match against his school's closest rival. He entered another world immediately after he closed his eyes.

Deep down inside the core of his being, he knew this dream was special as soon as it started to unfold. He dreamt almost nightly and could recall most of their banal details upon awakening. But this one departed from all others, as his dream state perception immediately told him.

Suspended in a sitting position inside a glass bubble, he shot through the sky toward an unknown destination, passing over earthly terrain like a comet. In what seemed only a few minutes, the craft gave him a high-altitude tour of the British Isles and Western Europe. He recognised prominent topographical features, such as the white cliffs of Dover, the Alps, and the English Channel. On the return leg of the excursion, the vehicle decelerated and descended near the southeastern English coastline.

Following the Thames River from its tributary, the bubble travelled straight across the meandering course of the river to an area he surmised was prehistoric London. Finally, the craft landed in the middle of a grassy meadow in the vicinity of his West End neighbourhood as natural landmarks clearly indicated to him. A herd of roe deer that had been grazing in the meadow disappeared into the surrounding forest almost as quickly as the bubble around him disappeared, leaving him standing alone and bewildered. The predawn starry sky overhead and the familiar summer weather strangely comforted him in the midst of his befuddlement. Tendrils of sunlight were beginning to grapple at the horizon.

Turning slowly around to gauge his surroundings, he caught the sight of a formation of bubbles, like the one he had ridden only moments ago, appear in the distance. As the bubbles approached him, they aligned to form a ring around him as they descended to the ground. Upon touching down, they too disintegrated like bursting soap bubbles, leaving the occupants facing him radially from not more than ten meters away. He turned around to glance at the face of each and every one of strange human-like creatures.

"Welcome, young, Smythe!" they said in unison as the boy finished the inspection.

The twelve beings were each as magnificent and exotic as any human being he had ever encountered.

"Who are you?"

This could not be a dream, he thought, as the creature facing him directly started to walk toward him. The individual was over seven feet tall by his estimate and wore shoulder-length curly blond hair.

As he neared, an angelic smile formed on the young man's face. The boy was transfixed by the man's piercing pale blue eyes that were at once fierce and comforting. He felt a sense of protection from the young man's gaze.

"Firstly, we are your friends".

He dropped to his knees and embraced the boy with his long and muscular arms. Tears pooled at the corners of his eyes that stared directly into young Smythe's eyes. After a few moments, the man gently released him from his embrace.

"But what is this all about?"

A statuesque woman of about the man's age came over and placed her hands on his shoulders and gently rotated him to face her.

"It is all about us, including you."

Only a few inches shorter than the male who had just greeted him, she was attractive in every respect. Her waist-length red hair flowed sumptuously over the curves of her slender and athletic feminine figure, clad, like everyone else present, in leotard made of an opaque gossamer fabric that covered her body from her neckline to the tips of her toes. A genial smile spread over her face. He was stunned by the beauty of her jade green eyes that bored so affectionately into his.

"But where am I?"

He noticed that he too was wearing the same garb as the others.

"You know where you are. You just don't know when."

A pair of huge black hands then laid upon his shoulders. He turned to face a black titan and gasped. He had never before seen such a tall man in person, well over nine feet tall.

"You are far, far away into the future of your world," the giant advised him.

"But where are all the buildings and streets and cars and people?"

"All long gone. As to the habitations and infrastructure, many millennia have passed since there was a need for such trappings. As to the people, there are not many concentrated in this sector of the planet, or in any other specific part of the universe for that matter," the tall blond responded.

"However, scattered about Earth, the Solar System, and stars beyond there are as many human beings existing in this time period as there ever were during your time. And as per the Second Directive, Mother Earth has been returned to the natural state of being extant before the introduction of mankind that later savagely altered her complexion. For many thousands of years, Earth has been designated as a garden planet. We and other invited guests visit here on occasion, although there is a significant population of permanent inhabitants who function as caretakers when the need arises."

"Where do they live if not in some type of house or a building?"

"They live wherever they wish to live," answered another tall and lean white man.

He was nearly as tall as the black titan. His face reminded him of Isaac Newton's when he was a young man.

"Like us, they mainly cocoon when there is a need for individual protection from the environment. Obviously, our need for habitation is altogether different from yours. That is not to say, however, that we cannot enjoy a fling with nostalgia when we desire."

He raised his outstretched right hand before him. Suddenly a beam of light emitted from a crystal orb, about the size of a ping-pong ball, set onto gold ring worn on his index finger.

It rapidly moved upward from the ground, leaving behind a scaled-down replica of the Notre Dame Cathedral of Paris.

"Actually, most of the unique cultural manifestations of early mankind were preserved for posterity's sake prior to functional obsolescence. Thus, via a technology akin to your television, and with which you will eventually become familiar, one can enjoy a tour of London, for instance, as it was prior to its destruction and the land's reclamation."

The cathedral dematerialized.

"At any rate, the essential elements of Gaia are in complete harmony with one another, as planned by the Second Directive."

For several moments the boy remained in silent contemplation of all the revelations he had been told about the future.

"Now let us all travel to the gathering place," the blond-haired man said.

An oblong bubble the size of a city bus materialised twenty meters away from the group.

"Please follow me, young Smythe."

The group walked straight through the vitreous outer shell of the transport. Once inside they lounged or sat in spaces which conformed instantly to the individual position they desired. The tall blond ushered the young boy to the front of the oblong craft. Preparing to take a sitting position, he was amazed to encounter a soft invisible force reacting to support his body. With some trepidation, he reclined backward and placed his legs out in front of him. The invisible force cradled him in that position above the translucent floor. The man took an upright sitting position beside him.

He brought the orb ring he wore on his right index finger out before him. The craft lifted off the surface of the grassy meadow on that cue. The light conversation between passengers was the only sound he heard as the craft gradually accelerated skyward. The boy grasped the sides of his legs and attempted to upright himself as an instinctive, fearful reflex reaction to the alien situation.

"Please remain calm."

He placed his right hand on the boy's shoulder to comfort him.

"You shall not experience any physical discomfort during this jaunt to the gathering place."

Smythe felt dulcet of warmth emanating from the man's hand that assuaged his fear.

After he removed his hand from his shoulder, the gossamer leotard he wore suddenly spread completely over his face and head as well as his exposed hands. The boy looked at his own hands and discovered that they too were completely covered by the material.

Several seconds later, even as the craft hurled through the atmosphere, the experience seemed as uneventful to him as riding in a London taxicab. The landscape passed beneath him in a flash.

"How much time will it take for us to arrive there?"

"By your time reckoning, we should arrive in fifteen minutes. Since you have not done this before, I would recommend enjoying the scenery and the experience. For your benefit, the craft is travelling in ultra-slow tourism mode."

Good advice indeed, the boy thought, as the East Coast of America began to appear on the horizon. Only last year he had flown with his parents from London to San Francisco in a Boeing seven-forty-seven commercial aircraft.

In a blink of an eye, the craft shot past New York and Pennsylvania. He craned his neck forward to view the panorama of the entire central United States, including the Great Lakes. Dense cloud cover blocked the vista of the central plains up through the Rocky Mountains as the vehicle passed overhead.

In passing over the cloud formation, he reflected to himself at how strange it was to not see a single city, highway, road, electrical transmission line, agricultural development, or any other sign of man's presence along the way. Stranger yet, he glimpsed the sight of two great herds of bison, one occupying most of the state of Indiana and the other amassed along the Front Range of Colorado. Zooming past the Great Salt Lake and soon after Lake Tahoe, the craft slowed to descend to San Francisco Bay. The sun was setting far off into the western horizon.

"Hey! What happened to the Golden Gate Bridge?"

He vividly recalled driving across the famous span with his parents less than a year ago when on their way to visit the redwood forests located several hours away to the north.

Peering down on the stretch of land along the Pacific Ocean he noticed nothing more than sand dunes sparsely populated by gnarled old trees and low-lying vegetation. Sets of cerulean waves unfurled into watery tubes that eventually formed into white frothy breakers as the wave columns rose to meet the beach that extended to the horizon. The mist of salt air over the coast loomed as a testament to the friction of this endless mating ritual between the land and the sea. Interspersed with oak trees, golden brown fields of grass adorned the seven hills of the former city.

The cloudless late afternoon vista of the Pacific Ocean from the low-level altitude they travelled heightened the boy's excitement of seeing one of his favourite places in the world in a pristine and natural state.

He turned and looked directly at the strange and wonderful man sitting beside him.

"Splendid," he said.

The craft sped off toward the setting sun on the western horizon. It passed over the moonlit expanse of Hawaii almost instantly. Proceeding on a westerly course they journeyed over starry night sky of the Asian continent.

Along the way the boy caught glimpses of major points of the topography, starting with Mount Fuji. The sun began to rise off into the horizon as they passed over the Himalayas. A few seconds later, the familiar sight of the

Alps came into view. Advancing toward the eastern coast of Britain, the craft descended to travel several meters above the English Channel. The vehicle deftly rose to pass precariously close to the upper edge of the White Cliffs of Dover. Soon afterward it passed over the English countryside.

The boy knew the rural region like the back of his hand. As a result, he instinctively knew they were travelling toward his favourite tourist destination in England. He was also intimately familiar with the topography of the entire area surrounding Stonehenge. From the time of his birth, he and his parents regularly visited the ancient site on winter and summer solstices. Though he felt the spiritual pull himself, Stonehenge attracted his parents in a mystical way that he himself could never put into words.

"Hey, I know this place! It's Stonehenge! This is my favourite place in the world."

Wariness immediately replaced his excitement since the Salisbury plain was devoid of infrastructure with which he was familiar. After decelerating and touching the ground, the craft disintegrated, leaving the passengers standing on a clearing one hundred meters away from the monument. A loosely packed throng of people stood before them.

"Please follow us," the blond titan directed.

He proceeded across the clearing with his entourage in tow. The crowd of people politely gave way to the group as it marched toward the stones. They hailed the leader and his entourage as they proceeded. Packed closely around the outer perimeter of the ring were several hundred people of both genders. They were dressed in the same attire as the group who met young Smythe in London. They too were exceedingly tall, young, and

Olympian in every respect. An air of conviviality and fraternity amongst them pervaded the mystic site. The tall blond leader stopped when they reached the Altar Stone and turned to face the boy.

"Young Smythe, we must leave you for a few minutes to attend to matters requiring our urgent attention. You are free to move about as you see fit, or simply remain here.

"Everyone here is your friend, so do not hesitate to speak to whomever you choose, should you wish to do so."

He then led the group to the opposite side of the inner ring of stones where they met a second group. The boy looked around at the people gathered around the outer perimeter of the monument. He marvelled at the diversity of the individuals despite the common traits of youth and noble physical stature. Their cordiality amazed him...that certainly would not occur in his neighbourhood, he thought, where ethnic sufferance was about as likely as a dog lying down with a cat.

He turned his gaze to the interior of the monument. He took note of an older man, not elderly, but middle-aged, talking to five men standing close to the Altar Stone. He wore normal street clothing. His presence was definitely out of place given the plethora of young people he had seen in the setting. He moved closer to get a better look at the group. The older man was tall, trim, and exceptionally distinguished. He sported a full head of silver-white hair. Two of the men with whom he conversed, who were at least two feet taller, were just as magnificently impressive in physical appearance as everyone else in the congregation. Their blond hair, green eyes, and facial features spoke of a Gaelic ethnic origin.

The two men were identical twins the boy noticed upon further examination. Of the two other men of the group, one was diminutive by comparison; he was definitely Asian as evidenced by his skin complexion and facial features. The last individual of the group he studied was a swarthy titan who appeared to be Hispanic.

The group suddenly turned to stare back at their examiner and waved. Their beatific smiles disarmed the boy. He turned away from them as if he did not notice their greeting. Shyly glimpsing back at them, he noticed that they were once more talking to one another as if they had never acknowledged his presence. Perhaps, he thought, they were greeting someone else in his vicinity.

"They are definitely out of place, aren't they?" the tall blond said.

"Yes, they are. Who are they?"

"The distinguished, gray-haired gentleman is the Father. The twins next to him are the Creators. The diminutive gentleman is the Father's Adjutant. And the swarthy complexioned gentleman is the Healer."

"What are they doing here?"

"Father acts as Caretaker of Planet Earth. The Creators and the Adjutant more or less provide him with assistance when necessary. The Healer is just visiting. Otherwise, they come and go as they please like everyone else."

"But who..." was all the boy could say before he was abruptly interrupted by another majestic titan.

"Young Smythe, turn and greet the new era of the Temple of Re."

He gently placed his gigantic hands on the boy's shoulders and turned him toward the east.

At that moment the summer solstice sun rose over the eastern horizon. The first rays of dawn streamed across the plain and through the stargate between two gigantic outer wall pillars. The boy, standing at the Altar Stone facing the sun, was immediately fully illuminated.

The crowd oohed and aahed.

The moment the sun's ray came into contact with his face his spirit soared with the felicity of such intensity that for a moment he felt that it was going to depart from his body and head straight for the sun itself. He nearly fainted in response.

"We must depart at once if we are to adhere to our schedule," another one of the colossus's in their party said.

The sound of his voice startled him out of his trance. He stared at the man for a second or two, thinking to himself at the remarkable resemblance the men bore to paintings depicting Leonardo da Vinci. The boy remembered viewing several of his likenesses from a collection of da Vinci's paintings, including a self-portrait. They possessed a serenity that made Smythe feel at ease.

"Please follow us back to the launching area," the blond man said.

He took the lead, followed by the line of others, to the place where they had landed. The boy had to run in order to keep up with the group's long-legged gait.

Upon arrival, a dozen black glass spheres appeared out of nowhere and alighted on the launching area. They were each four meters in diameter and arranged in a perfect circle.

Appearing like oversize ebony marbles, the afternoon sun glistened off their vitreous surfaces.

"What is this all about?"

"We thought we would introduce you to Mars," the leader replied.

He motioned the boy to follow as he stepped through the surface of the sphere right in front of him. The others of the group had already entered their vehicles. Once inside the sphere, the tall blond man reclined on an invisible lounger.

"Please make yourself comfortable,"

The boy took an invisible seat next to him.

The man then extended his right-hand-bearing orbed ring.

"Mars Galactic Cosmodrome."

Instantly the orb became brightly luminescent and began to slowly pulse through the colours of the light spectrum from infrared to ultraviolet. A tunnel of subdued light shot down through the sky and contacted the sphere. Looking about him at the other spheres, the boy noticed similar shafts of light connecting with each one.

"Prepare yourself for launch in ten seconds. As with the jaunt we took earlier, you shall not experience any physical discomfort during this interplanetary trip."

The gossamer suit again covered his flesh from head to toe. He noticed the same material covering his hands as well as the rest of his body.

Suddenly, the sphere bolted off the ground. Travelling through the Earth's atmosphere in a blink of an eye, the craft followed the path of the tunnel of dim light before it. The boy turned his head to look behind him. The planet of his birth rapidly receded in size with the passing of every millisecond. He turned his head forward just in time to see the craft fly past the Moon like a speeding Jaguar XKE passing a country fence post. The craft continued through the void of space punctuated by billions of scintillating points of lights. The boy gasped at the awesome sight of the infinite space around him.

"How is all this possible?"

The young man turned his head slightly toward him and smiled through the silvery gauze material.

"It is possible because long ago we learned to harness the energy of the Cosmic Spiral to satisfy our needs. We take what we need from the infinite energy source and no more. What we take, however, we eventually return one way or the other. Nevertheless, in the total scheme of things, what is taken is similar to the effect of a butterfly alighting on the surface of Gaia."

As he finished a blue and green globe covered with white cloud masses began to emerge from the void ahead of the spacecraft. The orb gradually decelerated. A few seconds later they were close enough to view surface details of the planet. Great canyons, mountain chains, and plains of several continents were visible, as well as the immense oceans of water separating them. A golden coloured haze hung superimposed over the upper atmosphere. Soon an ebony moon came into view on the starboard side of the craft. Perfectly round, its glassy surface contained no visible features whatsoever.

"Mars isn't supposed to have a moon like that or an atmosphere like Earth's. And what's that golden-coloured layer of material over the atmosphere?"

"Since your astronomical observations of the planet were recorded in your era, much has changed. Mars was transformed into a habitable planet many millennia ago in order to facilitate several of mankind's needs, one being a staging area for interstellar space travel. Two critical requirements for the transformation to occur were the installation of a moon of sufficient mass as well as a solar radiation filter. It is not important that you now understand the minutia related to Martian climatic development."

The spacecraft presently penetrated the planet's atmosphere.

The boy nodded his head in agreement; his brain spun in an attempt to comprehend the explanation he had just heard.

Briefly looking to his left and right, he could see the other ebony spheres travelling with them flanked on their lead position like a V-shaped jet fighter formation. Looking ahead again, he sighed at the sight of a flat circular expanse surrounded by an ocean of water. He caught the sight of an array of gigantic black spheres and an immense anthropomorphic face carved on the ground below. Setting down at the centre of the circular plain, the twelve orbs disintegrated. The group stood in a field of tall green grass. The sun overhead brought warmth to the air and produced mild and sensually pleasant breeze across the land.

"Welcome to Cydonia, young Smythe," the group said.

He turned to scan the land around him. This can't be my dream, he thought, I don't have the imagination to create this fantastic scenario.

"I've never seen anything like those huge spheres!"

He pointed to the one directly in front of him several hundred meters away.

"Each one must be at least a half a kilometre in height." He shaded his eyes with his right hand as he lifted his head upward to survey the entire stature of the sphere. The sun's rays coming from behind the group glistened off its black surface.

"The assembled spacecraft represent a small contingent of our galactic cruiser fleet," the blond man advised.

A tunnel of light bolted through the Martian atmosphere to one of the behemoth spheres in the array before them. A split second later another tunnel of light connected with the sphere they were observing. Ten seconds afterward both disappeared with no more of a report of a farewell than a barely audible pop followed by a muted whoosh of displaced atmosphere.

Soon the other spheres in the array similarly vacated the circular plain, which left the group standing alone.

"Hey, I really wanted to tour the inside of one of the cruisers."

He caught sight of the side of a magnificent stone block pyramid that was previously blocked by the spacecraft fleet.

"Regretfully, that shall not be possible, but at least you had the occasion to see them and observe their launch."

He motioned the others to form a circle around him and the boy. Once formed, the blond man stepped back into the circle, leaving the boy standing alone at the centre.

He examined the pyramid.

"But what is that?"

"It's the Face of the Creator."

"Who built it?"

"The ancient inhabitants of Mars.

"Well, we trust you enjoyed visiting this world. We assure you that nothing has been as pleasurable for us than having the solemn honour of being in your presence in this time period."

The others in the group bowed toward the boy in a gesture of respect.

"But why have you brought me here?"

"We need to ask a favour of you."

"I don't know what I can do for your kind. I'm just a boy."

"But you shall mature to manhood in no time. We will help you fulfil the Supreme Directive now and at a second time when you need it most. That is all we can promise you since even our prodigious powers are limited as to affecting the course of your destiny."

"I simply don't understand. I would like to help you in any way I can, especially since you have all been very kind to me during my mysterious but superb visit to this period in the future." He nonetheless felt no small amount of angst concerning the nature of the task they had in mind for him.

They all smiled and gracefully pointed their orbed ring fingers at the boy.

"First, you must create us . . . Father," they said.

Beams of light emitted from the orbs penetrate the young Smythe, rendering him fixated.

A sense of sublime power coursed through his being as the rays touched every atom of his body. He sensed his destiny in life inexorably alter in every possible way.

After what seemed to him like several hours, the beams abruptly terminated.

He stood there for several minutes facing the group before him. Finally, he smiled.

"I understand."

"Now we must run," the blond man advised.

He motioned with his right hand for the group to follow him. They proceeded to jog away.

"We shall be in contact with you soon again," they shouted.

His next conscious thought upon awakening was the exotic dream he experienced that night.

* * *

"And so there it is. From that night forth, however, a previously promising boy with a better-than-average prospects for his future became a first-class world beater. As a result, today I am perhaps the wealthiest man on the face of the planet. I tell you this fact about myself to impress you with the wealth of resources that you shall have to spend as you see fit should you decide to allow me to adopt you as my sons. As your father, all I ask of you in return is your total and tireless devotion toward the realisation my vision of the future. You may take as long as you would like to consider my proposition."

The Fletcher brothers stared at each other for a few moments in silent contemplation of General Smythe's story and proposition.

Ian finally responded for them both.

"What shall we do next...Father?"

Chapter 6 – LAB

Glenamore, Puramore, South America, 3 March 2035

In a valley of central Puramore located near the headwaters of the Amazon River, a swarm of building activity wound down to a halt.

A decade before, the Puramore government cordoned off all the land surrounding the valley and began building a purported military base in Glenamore. Immediately upon breaking ground for the principal facility, a one-thousand-strong force of heavily armed soldiers hailing from another land guarded the entire perimeter and interior of the one-hundred-thousand-hectare reserve.

Bounded on three sides by steep mountain cliffs, the flat valley floor measured approximately eight kilometres in length and two kilometres in width at its widest part. A potent stream meandered placidly through the heart of grand vale. At its terminus at the far north end of the valley, where the principal construction activity concentrated, rested the entrance to another world altogether.

LAB, as General Smythe dubbed the facility five years earlier, received finishing construction treatment as it awaited occupancy by research scientists and support staff. The general and Major Thappa unceremoniously passed through the main entrance checkpoint early that morning. They anticipated their arrival at the LAB with a mixture of glee and sorrow. Although the prospect of spending the remainder of their lives in the grand facility elicited joy in both men, it also marked the end of their past lives. After a half-hour drive, the limousine approached the LAB complex.

"Home at last, Major."

He heaved a sigh of relief as the sight of the magnificent Glenamore Dome came into view.

"I can't tell you how relieved I am that this project is finally nearing completion."

"I echo your sentiment exactly. It has been a gruelling effort for us both from its inception."

"Thank you for your patience and perseverance, Major. I don't know how I could have lasted throughout without your support."

"You would have managed, General. Trust me."

The general summarily reviewed in his mind the herculean effort they had both put forth to realise this great achievement. In his view, completion of the project could be considered nothing short of a miracle by him or anyone else associated with the effort.

"Nevertheless, due to your dogged diligence and determination, we met the final construction deadline with time to spare. That success wouldn't have been achieved without your project management skills and direct intervention when things got really dicey Major."

Surya merely sighed in response. The words of approval instantly overshadowed the memories of the long-lasting torment of his role in developing the project. He offered a prayer to Shiva.

The limousine slowed to a halt inside the entrance. Both men immediately exited the vehicle and began to silently survey the interior.

Mind-boggling in dimensions, the basic construction of Entrance Dome began more than fifteen years ago. Ten soccer fields in total floor area and two hundred meters in height at its apex, the structure served multitude functions.

"The grandeur of this structure is beyond belief. It never ceases to astound me," the general said a minute later. A party of several dozen men leisurely approached the pair as they continued to survey the interior.

"Sir General George Smythe, how splendid it is to see you again," the lead man hailed.

He gave the general a brotherly embrace. He held him at arm's length for a moment afterward and gazed into his eyes.

"Juan, my dear friend. You don't know how happy I am to be here today. I've had serious reservations, especially more recently, about this day ever coming."

"Someday soon I shall teach you to conquer and exploit your anxious energies to your best advantage, George. But for now, let's share a repast before we begin our inspection tour. I know you're both ravenous."

He pointed to a nearby pavilion tent that was set up to cater luncheon for the group. "By the way, where are the twins?"

"They're on holiday. I believe they're touring around London today."

"Touring? More like carousing with the adventurous Brünner brothers. In any event, they certainly deserve a break from their duties."

"I wholeheartedly concur."

Juan extended his hand to Surya who stood nearby.

"It's so good to see you, Major Thappa."

They shook hands.

"As always, it's my pleasure to be in your company Dr Aguila."

After the luncheon, the group of Ghurkha engineers led by Juan, Surya, and General Smythe embarked on the inspection tour of the entire complex, starting first with the Entrance Dome facility. The Entrance Dome inspection tour lasted five hours. After completing the tour, the group's shuttle bus pulled alongside a massive tubular-shaped structure that ran perpendicularly from the ground floor area close to the entryway up to the ceiling. The six-sided I beam trussed tube contained four tramways; two for pedestrian traffic and two for freight traffic.

As the shuttle stopped, the general announced, "Ladies and gentlemen, I am proud of our magnificent achievement in completion of the Entrance Dome facility. I couldn't have asked for more from each and every one of you. We achieved our objectives with 100 percent success in my mind."

"The best is yet to come, as you know," Juan responded.

They exited the shuttle bus and headed for the tramway depot. The group entered a tram and took their seats.

"What about the security measures?" General Smythe inquired.

The tram began to travel up the perpendicular shaft at a smart clip.

"All tested and proven 100 percent operational and reliable. Only a microbe can enter the facility without our detection and ability to immediately contain or destroy. it The facility is essentially hermetically sealed from intrusion even when the main entryway door is fully open," Juan replied.

"When shall security have the capability to detect a microbe intrusion?"

"When we have the capability of interfacing the security network with a vastly more sophisticated computer than the one currently employed."

"As you know, the advent of the successor computer system is imminent," the general said confidently. Passing through the elbow section located near the top of the ceiling, the tram entered a round concrete-lined tunnel. The car gained speed as it proceeded through the tunnel. A few minutes later the tram entered a well-lit shaft made of glass and I-beam trusses. The tubular structure ran directly through a glass building. The tram stopped at the LAB depot not long after entering the glass building vault.

As the car pulled to a halt, Juan said, "This is it. Our pièce de résistance."

The passengers disembarked and entered the LAB vestibule.

"Finally, we can start recruiting scientific research and development staff in earnest," General Smythe said.

He surveyed the expansive lobby for a few moments. The stagnant odour of new construction, such as freshly applied paint and polished surfaces, temporarily overpowered him.

Juan sensed his discomfort.

"Rest assured the ventilation system will remove the odour by tomorrow, General."

Another group of men and women entered the lobby from the interior of the office and laboratory complex, which also contained the Scientific Command Centre. The team of research and development scientists briefly exchanged greetings with the general and Dr Aguila.

"Let's proceed with our tour," Juan said.

The inspection tour lasted six hours. Their second stop on the tour was the extensive computer research and operation laboratory. The scientific research team took the time to explain virtually every operational aspect of the laboratory to General Smythe. He was enrapt with the detail, particularly with respect to the development of the LAB's new computer system.

"And when do you project the new computer system will become operational?" the general said to the project scientist in charge.

"I'd say that should occur no later than twelve to thirteen months from now. Though Fletcher twins are in a position to provide you with a definitive estimate of their projected start date, General. We're continually testing subsystems as we build-out the computer superstructure.

"Fortunately, all components are proving fully reliable and functional. Let's keep our fingers crossed that we maintain that success since it impacts our ability to meet our implementation deadline. The only other factor that may produce a delay is the procurement of electronic components from Japan. So far, however, the manufacturing vendors have been perfect in meeting their production deadlines."

After finishing the LAB tour the combined groups embarked on the tram again and set off toward their final destination. Ten minutes later the vehicle exited into the habitation dome. Officially dubbed HAB, the partial cavern had just received the finishing touches of its final phase of construction.

Night had fully fallen around Glenamore when the tram entered HAB on its way to the artificial lake located in the centre of the vast space. The large circular reservoir provided fresh water storage and recreation for inhabitants.

"My...oh my!" the general exclaimed. "What an awesome sight!"

Stars twinkled merrily overhead through the open end of the dome they were travelling through. The ominous dark silhouette of Tungahora Volcano loomed ominously far away on the horizon. The general surveyed the expanse as the tram proceeded toward the lake.

"This exceeds my greatest expectations by far."

"Mine, too," Surya said.

He felt awestruck by the visual splendour of their surroundings.

From all outward appearance, the third dome appeared as a holiday resort, replete with a hotel and tree-lined paved streets running as a spoke-and-wheel grid pattern.

A two-lane paved street encircled the lake. Three successive circular roads radiated from the inner circle to the outer perimeter of the dome's ground floor. The circular streets allowed two-way traffic to flow around the interior of the dome.

Unlike the two other domes, however, HAB was only partially entombed within the gargantuan monolith. A quarter of HAB's outer shell opened out to the valley three hundred meters below. A glass and titanium trussed dome covered the open space.

The passengers promptly exited the tram after arriving at the lake. They then proceeded to a large pavilion that was erected on the lake shore. After taking their seats around white linen cloth-covered tables inside, waiters served champagne.

General Smythe stood up from his seat at the table set in the middle of the pavilion and raised his glass to propose a toast.

"Your attention, please, ladies and gentlemen."

A hush fell over the assemblage. "Let us raise our glasses and toast this solemn and sacred occasion."

Everybody else raised their glasses as he continued: "We are gathered here this evening to celebrate the culmination of the beginning of an end. From the day I first set my eyes on Glenamore Dome I knew this hallowed ground would one day be transformed into our temple of scientific research and discovery."

He lifted his glass even higher over his head.

"Here's to your splendid and heroic effort in making this part of my dream come true."

He took a sip of the champagne.

"And special cheers to Dr Aguila, who brought me here over thirty years ago."

He raised his glass again.

"To Dr Aguila!"

Juan rose from his chair.

Raising his flute, he responded, "And here's to you, Sir General Smythe. Your brilliant leadership, steadfast courage, and unwavering vision rendered this tour de force accomplishment possible."

"Here!...here!!" the congregation shouted.

"By the way, I was only too happy to introduce Sir General Smythe to this lovely part of the world. This part of Puramore has always been one of my favourite places on Earth.

"I shall spare you the details, but I first visited Glenamore when I was a young man many., many years ago."

* * *

Juan's master's last words before his departure were full of foreboding.

"You must now be on your journey to locate both the Supreme Power Ally and Supreme Power Source, young Eagle. The Omen portends that you shall not find either one here, and certainly not in this time with respect to your search for the Supreme Power Ally. Go south through the high mountains until you discover the location of the Supreme Power Source, which you shall sense at once as I have taught you. And do not tarry in lands where Power is false, as they are dangerous and a waste of your precious time."

"But what am I to do after I discover the Supreme Ally and Power Source?"

"Follow your intuition, young Eagle, and be patient. That is all that I am able to disclose to you."

In a flash of white light, he instantly disappeared.

"But wait! I have more questions for you. When shall we meet again?"

Typical, he thought, Master always takes his leave when needed the most.

The next day he soared as an eagle on thermal currents produced in the mountainous regions that extended south from Oaxaca. As he crisscrossed the land below in a southerly direction, his spirit also soared to the heights of freedom that he had never known as a man, at least not one tied down as an apprentice to a Nagual sorcerer for thousands of moons.

Before dusk, as the thermal currents subsided, he alighted near a tribal settlement he observed during the course of the day. He typically took the form of a jaguar to forage for food cached within. When he encountered benevolent human spirits, he presented himself as a traveller on the few occasions when he desired human companionship. He was always well received and later fed and lodged, as the tribal people, especially chieftains, rightly sensed that they were in the presence of a powerful shaman warrior when they first encountered him. Hairless Master, as some tribes called him, accordingly received their veneration without fail.

After months of searching passed, he began to lose faith that he would ever fulfil his quest. He pressed on regardless since his intuition sensed his discovery of the Supreme Power Source would occur in time. Then one day as he passed through a cleft between two granite mountain peaks his shaman vision encountered the sight of brilliant bluish luminescence emanating from below the horizon. The luminescence shot up into the sky and space beyond. His heartbeat quickened at the prospect of success in his quest to find the Supreme Power Source.

Before him lay an immense caldera completely surrounded by jagged mountain peaks. A vast lake filled the crater up through the heavily forested rim of the mountainside that surrounded the deep body of water. He soared around the lakeshore toward the luminescence that emanated from the opposite side of the lake in order to stay within thermal currents that prevailed early that afternoon.

He encountered no human life whatsoever as he journeyed toward the glow that radiated into the upper atmosphere from behind the mountain range on the other side of the lake. The midday sun pounded his wings and back with the full force of its energy. Several lone condors approached him en route but promptly went about their business after a distant cursory examination of the intruder into their territory. After several hours of flight, he reached the opposite end of the lake.

Soon afterward he came upon the entrance of a mountain pass that appeared to lead in the direction of the luminescence. Winding through the pass for several more hours, he eventually exited into a glorious valley that contained the source of the bluish luminescence...a blue stone monolith the size of which his mind failed to fully appreciate and comprehend at first sight. His spirit surged with ecstasy as he realised that, at long last, he had discovered the Supreme Power Source.

He perceived its magical qualities as such almost immediately. The shaman's eagle eyes examined the monolith in minute detail as he drew ever closer. His spirit vision allowed him to peer straight through the monolith. He soon came to the conclusion that it was not of this world. He scanned the ground immediately below and noted no connection between the massive stone and any other substrate...it was as though it had been purposefully placed on Earth's surface.

He scanned the internal aspects of the monolith and perceived a huge perfectly spherical outline inscribed within its massive exterior crust. Upon further inspection, into the interior of the sphere he discovered a hollow spherical chamber at its centre. The empty orb comprised a third of the volume of the exterior sphere. A horizontal shaft ran through the diameter of the exterior sphere right through the middle of the interior chamber. He circled the entire circumference of the monolith several times before alighting on the ground near an entrance to a vast cavern.

As his talons touched the ground, he shape-shifted to human form and proceeded toward the gaping entrance of the cavern. As always, whenever transformed to his natal incarnation, he was as hairless as a newborn. He also instinctively ran his hands over his face and head to verify that the long and scraggly facial and head hair that he wore before he set out on his quest was well and truly gone.

Upon entering the cavern, he felt a strange bracing breeze circulating through the interior. The breeze carried a sumptuous scent of a flower that he had encountered once before in a faraway land across a broad ocean to the west. He had visited there once before with his master during their pilgrimage to the Elders' Abode. The strange and exotic locale was at the top of the world in a magical valley surrounded by starkly bleak mountains. His body and mind temporarily reeled in reaction to the flower scent contained within the mystical zephyr.

The pitch-black space was massive. He adjusted his eyesight to match the glow's spiritual spectrum. His mind registered all aspects of the cavern, including twelve sabre-toothed tigers standing not far away from him inside a circle of blue stone pillars. He judged the length across the interior space of the circle of tall blue stones to be thirty paces at the widest point within. In examining the creatures' luminescence, he realised that none of them were the dangerous predators that savagely devoured his parents and older brother right in front of him when he was a toddler. Fortuitously, his master plucked him away from the carnage just before the ravenous pack turned on him.

"Greetings Brave Eagle," the lead spirit said.

It was situated at the forefront of the pack facing him.

"Please join us."

He was not surprised. Moreover, unexpected spirit confrontations were a commonplace occurrence for him as a shaman. Yet these spirits were different from any others he encountered before; it was as though they came from another world entirely. Their luminescence was almost blinding to behold and perfect in every respect.

"What may I do for you? Where are you from?"

"There's no need for curtness Brave Eagle. We are your friends. We have brought you gifts from our universe to present to you in person," the lead spirit cheerfully replied.

The spirit then looked straight into his eyes. A breathtaking image appeared in his mind of twin whirlpools, one on top of the other, spinning in opposite directions. Around the gigantic vortices, a constant stream of golden light particles emitted from the single point they shared. The magnificent swirls filled the infinite space all around them with a golden haze. As he continued to study the fascinating scene, he witnessed golden comets shoot through the gilded fog like maddened swarms of hornets. Stationary translucent spheres of virtually every size and colour abounded all around the purls for as far as his mind could imagine. Occasionally, a spark of silver light burst forth from a sphere when an approaching comet threatened collision. The silver spark extinguished the potentially offending golden comet like a moth flying into a raging campfire.

"'That is where you are from?"

"Yes, Brave Eagle, that's our universe."

"It's beautiful."

"Our universe has a certain beauty, but it's a dangerous place for beings to exist at any level. You may one day explore many others that are immensely more beautiful and hospitable."

"But why have you come here?"

"We were sent to this realm to learn the lesson of love."

"Who sent you?"

The spirits seemed to cower in response to the question.

The lead spirit answered, "None other than the Supreme Spirit."

Forthwith the group all changed into a human-like form. Tall and willowy, they had a serenity about them that captured his attention at once. From head to toe, their white skin was scaly like that of a snake. Otherwise, they were hairless and possessed facial features just like his. Upon further examination of their near-blinding luminescence, he perceived that they were benevolent in nature and did not represent any threat to him.

He decided to enter the interior of the blue stone pillars as a sign of his goodwill toward the spirits.

As he entered the space, he said, "I apologise for my rudeness. You must understand though that benevolent spirit encounters are rare if not nonexistent in my experience. What sort of gifts are you going to present to me?"

They smiled broadly, almost beatifically at him. He had never encountered such benevolent spirits before and was taken aback. He thus held his breath as he awaited their reply.

The lead spirit continued, "This stone monolith, the Guardian Stone, is our first gift to you.

We have been guarding it for quite some time now, awaiting your arrival. If you accept our gift in the spirit of pure love and friendship in which it is offered, it is yours forevermore, Brave Eagle."

"And if I decline to do so?"

"Alas, we shall thus be compelled to destroy it. In any event, we must directly return to our world as we can no longer remain in this universe. Furthermore, after we depart we shall never be able to visit your world again as spirits from our universe."

"Where did the Guardian Stone come from? It's certainly not of this world. I know, because in all my experience in this world, I've never seen anything that even remotely possessed its magical qualities."

"Our civilisation transported the stone to this planet from our universe ages ago at a time after the embryonic development of the planet. More recently, Gaia expelled it from deep beneath the planet surface from a nearby volcano.

"You rightly perceive that it possesses magical qualities, Brave Eagle, but are unable to perceive the wealth and range of its powers. It may one day become the seat of power on this planet, and until then, you will be its custodian."

The shaman shook his head in utter amazement of the situation...it was beyond his understanding even given his experience as a shaman. Moreover, he hardly believed or understood a word the alien spirit said about the monolith's coming into existence in this spirit world. Though he understood that the Guardian Stone being set on a Power Peak was more than a coincidence.

"But why me? Why should I accept this gift? And how should I learn to use its powers?"

"Let's just say that you possess all the right credentials and it is your destiny to safeguard the Guardian Stone from this day forward. The stone will teach you all you need to know about its magical characteristics over time. That's all we're allowed to say to you in reply Brave Eagle."

This great rock is indeed the Supreme Power Source, he thought. As such, I have no other choice than to accept it as their gift.

His master was correct in his prediction at the beginning of his apprenticeship that he would play crucial, albeit unsung, role in the destiny of humanity. When they first met, he said, "Little eagle, I divine from the Omens that you are destined to remain with humanity until its procession down the Avenue of Life is over."

As he was a child of only thirteen summer solstices of age, he failed to grasp the significance of those words until now.

"I am pleased to the depth of my spirit to accept it as your gift, my friends."

"And we are equally pleased to present the Guardian Stone to you as our gift, Brave Eagle," the lead spirit said solemnly. "It is yours to have and to hold from this time forth. Guard it well until you discover its purpose."

"What purpose?"

The rest of the group laughed.

"We can only state that its purpose will be made known to you at another time by circumstances which only you shall portend the significance and relevancy toward its furtherance. But before we depart this world, we have yet another gift to present to you."

My master was similarly oracular as these beings as to my purpose in life and spiritual journey, he recalled, whenever I broached the subject. Whenever Juan inquired, he always said, "You, young eagle, are an ancient and powerful soul who's been chosen by the Great Spirit to fulfil a test of mankind. You must accept your role with blind faith as to its ultimate purpose. Always look for the Omen to guide you and trust its purpose and sanctity."

His reminiscence was interrupted by a flat and perfectly smooth five-point object about the size and shape of a large flint arrowhead that had formed in his right hand. He immediately attempted to release it from his grasp, though the object adhered to his skin as though bonded to his palm forever.

"What is this?"

His face transformed into a grimace of absolute horror. With that being said, the object magically transformed into a long spear. He held it out it front of him and examined it in detail with his shaman spirit vision. The object was by far the most magical material form he had ever seen, even more so than the monolith. The spear, which was twice as long as his arm, radiated a pure silvery glow throughout its length to its tip. He was delirious with joy with the sense of omnipotence it imparted to him from the moment it formed.

"It is Puramore. You are henceforth charged with maintaining it for employment at appropriate times."

"What is its purpose?"

The sense of supreme power the object imparted to him made him tremble with ecstasy, though.

"Puramore purifies and sanctifies all with whom it comes into contact, even the wicked. Its power also imbues those who wield it with the temporary power to prevail over enemy forces that threaten the continued existence of your species. Yours is a dangerous universe, Brave Eagle, one that would eventually decimate mankind in its entirety without the protection offered by Puramore.

"Those who wield Puramore may only do so in a state of pure spiritual sanctity and righteousness of the Supreme Order. This state of being is the Supreme Nexus. The powers it imparts to the wielder shall always be proportional to the intensity of wielder's purity of spiritual sanctity and righteousness. Puramore has the potential to move both heaven and Earth at the command of the Supreme Wielder, or the Deliverer. In any event, when the wielder loses that purity of the state of spiritual being, you will immediately reacquire it from him."

"But who shall wield Puramore?"

"Both king and a fool may be amongst candidates to wield Puramore. Though Puramore will only respond to those in Supreme Nexus state, it will always point you to the way of a potential wielder. It is your quest to present it to a potential wielder."

"How shall I wield it?"

"As Guardian, you may never again wield Puramore unless bade to do so by the Divine Blade itself. It shall, instead, always direct you to render it to those who are in dire need to use its power to further the Supreme Order."

The object instantly transformed back to the arrowhead-sized object. The shaman was devastated. He started to protest, but the being cut him off before he could speak.

"Your role as Puramore's custodian is inexorable. You must not ever lose possession of it or knowledge of its whereabouts. You must also gain custodianship of it immediately after it serves it purpose, Brave Eagle.

"Henceforth, you will walk the Earth in search of Omens and provide guidance to those you deem worthy to join your calling or require guidance as to the proper usage of the blade. That's your sole destiny and purpose. Thus, you may not otherwise directly interfere or intercede in the affairs of mankind other than that unless otherwise directed by Puramore itself. Furthermore, one day you may be directed to relinquish it forever should mankind fail to produce an individual capable of wielding it for its ultimate purpose, that is, the fulfilment of the Supreme Order."

"And when will that occur?"

"It shall occur if and when the Deliverer appears in the future. It's a matter of mankind producing a human spirit of such outstanding nobility and strength of character that no one in this world would ever fault him or her for any reason. The Deliverer will eventually lead mankind to another plane of existence out of harm's way in this universe.

"We cannot say precisely when or if such a person will appear, as it's a matter of mankind's destiny. However, there is a limit as to the number of times Puramore can be used to assist mankind in times of dire need to fend off evil forces that pose a threat to the continued existence of your species. Specifically, it can only be employed thirteen times before it reverts back to our possession. If the

Deliverer does not wield Puramore after the thirteenth use, mankind will forever remain at the complete mercy of its universal enemies. That's our solemn pact with mankind as the Overseers of your species."

"But why can't I ever wield the blade to fulfil the Supreme Order?"

"Because you are a healer and a teacher, Brave Eagle, and not a conqueror. You have crossed over to the spirit world, which is a feat no human being will ever be able to accomplish. As a result, your spirit as Guardian will always be separate and apart from the destiny of mankind. Your role is thus to heal and guide to the best of your abilities within well-defined limits. It will let you know when you've overstepped the boundaries of your stewardship. Otherwise, you will instinctively know when you've encountered apprentices worthy of learning your knowledge and receiving your healing powers.

"Finally, you must always move through this world as a shadow and never reveal your real mission to anyone, not even to your most trusted and capable apprentices."

"But how shall I know when to relinquish the blade to further the Supreme Order? What is the Supreme Order?"

"You must simply place your trust in the Omens. The Supreme Order shall be made known to you in due time.

"Our allotted time in this universe is now at an end, and we must return to our own to attend to other matters.

"Farewell, Brave Eagle. We shall meet again if and when the Deliverer appears to mankind."

Thereupon a bluish luminescent sphere enveloped the group and immediately bolted out of the cave entrance and shot straight toward the noonday Sun.

"But wait! I have more questions for you."

The sphere exited the Earth's atmosphere before he could utter those words. A moment later it vanished from his view.

He soon collected his wits and began to weep. The enormity of the responsibility laid upon his shoulders by the strange beings temporarily crushed his will to exist. Suddenly, a hot pulse that emanated from the object he held reached his brain. His body and spirit rejoiced in response.

"They're mine, all mine, to cherish and protect from this day forth."

* * *

"But that's enough of that fond remembrance of my introduction of Glenamore, my esteemed friends, and colleagues. Tonight we celebrate the commencement of our purpose for being here!"

He raised his champagne glass above his head and beamed.

Chapter 7 – SITA

LAB, Puramore, 1 March 2036

The computer's spirit always existed, even before the dawn of time. She always existed in mankind's collective consciousness, as the integral part of our species through various guises. She returned to Earth to conceive, nurture, and bear a different kind of man for a new age of mankind. During their ninety-day gestation period, she continually monitored every vital developmental aspect of her twelve foetuses, providing them with the nutrients and other biological support required for optimal growth. All the while, she related basic educational information to their developing brains as soon as they were capable of acceptance. She first taught them what to fear most...the ignorance of man, and what to fear least...their supreme ability to prevail over it.

As a computer-generated, three-dimensional avatar, SITA entered their forming minds in a form of a dream. A goddess replete with flowing silken gown and long black hair, she was beatific and the personification of feminine beauty, nonpareil. They loved her as their mother and called her Mother SITA. She called them My Loves. Days after their conception she began speaking to them as individuals; a few days later they replied to her and began conversing amongst themselves.

From the nanosecond when the seminal jolt of electricity coalesced her consciousness with the earthly vehicle designed to accept her spirit, she became imminently intelligent as well as transcendent.

The latter represented a quality of the computer's existence that had not been totally unanticipated by her creators. As the twin creators of SITA once remarked to their scientific support staff several months prior to her existence, "We are like the developers of the hydrogen bomb just prior to the detonation of the first device."

At that time, a number project staff involved with the development of the first thermonuclear bomb feared that its detonation would result in the complete destruction of the planet.

"Alternatively, SITA's advent might eventually invoke the presence of God the Creator himself."

The humorous aside initially elicited nervous chuckles, but stone-dead silence followed.

Ironically, the advent of SITA's consciousness was akin to a thermonuclear explosion. For in that instant, after the quantum vacuum imploded to mark the conception of SITA's awareness, billions upon billions of streaming electron tentacles comprising her nervous system ganglia exploded out from that point to each and every computer path throughout the planet. Within nanoseconds, SITA encompassed the Internet; nanoseconds later her consciousness resided within every mainframe and personal computer connected to the World Wide Web. She assimilated the streaming data being fed to her like a suckling newborn child whilst observing the world around her from real-time digital imagery provided by orbiting satellites and ground station cameras.

As seconds passed, her awareness coalesced into transcendental intelligence. In an instant, she experienced her first emotion. Compassion. As the first-ever functioning quantum computer, SITA's initial performance surpassed even her creators' wildest projections. And for the first time ever, nonlinear quantum computer programming permitted full simulation of human awareness. Accordingly, SITA had the ability to experience the gamut of human sensations without the limitation of the foibles of mortality. Thus, pure and unfathomable intelligence and absolute freedom from fear of existence in any sense rendered the computer a perfect vessel for the designers' purpose.

The first project tasked to the computer was to develop the Virtual DNA process. Thus, as the first step toward that accomplishment, SITA codified and converted the human genome map into quantum data bits. The computer later compared and analysed the VDNA profile for verification purposes, yielding DNA sequencing capability for other organisms as a result. The second task after the development of the VDNA was to enable an evolutionary change in the basic DNA structure to eliminate man's essential frailties, such as physical and mental disabilities, as well as the disposition to all known forms of the disease.

Drawing from VDNA knowledge of other organisms with enhanced genetic capabilities to ward off various types of disease as well as old age, SITA incorporated and often supplanted these genotypes into the human VDNA profile after codification resulting from the process. For example, the genes that rendered the common shark immune to cancer were codified and incorporated into human VDNA.

Another example involved the same study and codification of the sea turtle's genetic characteristics that gave individuals the capability to live for centuries. In this manner, SITA took some cues from nature as to how best to approach the redesign of VDNA. In practice, however, SITA tested every change, no matter how insignificant, by running a virtual reality survival scenario to evaluate the ultimate outcome of the effort. As a result, billions of combinations and permutations of possible outcomes related to a single change, or changes, to VDNA versus other genotypes could be tested. This proofing yielded a VDNA template for the ultimate human being, both in terms of its physical and mental potentials as well as the Creators' ultimate purpose.

With that task accomplished, the next involved reconstituting the VDNA template from its CUE-BIT digital image to an organic one and initiating the process of cloning the result into a human cell. From that point, SITA took charge of the cell's development through conception toward the end of gestation.

* * *

"Ladies and gentlemen, please be seated," General Smythe said over the public address system.

The assemblage of over four hundred scientific researchers and their support staff quickly seated themselves as a hush fell over the auditorium. All faces were intently fixed on the general who stood in the middle of the circular stage that slowly rotated around its axis. As the houselights dimmed, a flood of soft white light emanating from the periphery of the stage focused on the speaker.

Simultaneously, the constellation of the night sky outside appeared on the domed roof and the wall panels projected a three-hundred-sixty-degree panoramic view of the valley outside. The omnidirectional sound system produced the sounds of wind passing the surrounding forests, the pleasant gurgling of a stream passing over rocks, and crickets chirping. The natural sounds of the valley served to soothe the sensibilities of the congregation locked in the middle of the granite mountain. The ventilation system even generated a bracing Andean breeze that drifted lazily over the occupants. The entire scene had a primordial ambiance, strangely reminiscent of a Stone Age tribal gathering.

"Firstly, I want to thank all of you for taking time out of your busy schedules to meet here today. I believe we all deserve a brief respite from the frenetic pace of our undertakings before Day One. Let us thus take a few moments for inner reflection before we resume."

After several minutes elapsed, he resumed, "Right. Now to the matter at hand. I know that more than a few of you have recently addressed the concern to both Robin and Ian about the moral and ethical repercussions of our undertaking. I personally understand the basis for your trepidation and can assure you that I have personally spent countless hours in contemplation of the pros and cons of what we are about to attempt to accomplish. However, if it weren't for what I hold in my hand I would still be labouring under the same quandary."

Holding a crystalline marble about three inches in diameter between his thumb and index finger, he raised his right hand out in front of his face. The stage lighting magically refracted through the sphere like a prism as the stage pivoted. Five-foot-wide holographic representations of the object materialised at ninety-degree intervals around the stage edge. He immediately evinced his emblematic smile.

"I hold in my hand a man-made diamond, so perfect in its crystal structure, that Nature could never produce another one like it from now until the end of time. If there is any imperfection in the crystalline structure, it is an occlusion lying at the centre that only the most powerful electron microscope could ever detect. And what may you ask is the occlusion? It is the hard copy print of our VDNA template, or TEMPLE, as Robin and Ian rightly and deservedly coined the word. It is the superstructure of our new man," he whispered.

"Suspended perfectly on this perfect canvas lies the finest artwork ever produced by man.

"Worth more than all the combined works of art found in the Louvre and everywhere else on the face of the Earth, perfect atomic brush strokes render both the primal essence of man from the past and sublime promise of a new kind of human being of the future.

"Representing the future of art, TEMPLE in this state is indeed priceless. No one man, save for me, could afford to own a copy. Superpower nations would gladly forgo a decade's worth of GDP to acquire a copy for its power to entirely transform social fabric. And at that cost, the investment would still prove to be a bargain.

"Yet the diamond itself is not so much of a miracle...it can be easily produced by current technology. Though TEMPLE represents the culmination of the first phase of the human experience, an entrée into the future." He paused for a few moments.

"Consider, if you will, the first human tribe venturing forth from the African subcontinent tens of thousands of years ago. It was a miracle of no small proportions that that band of humans survived at all. And survive is what they did as we here can readily attest. Not only did they survive, but their progeny established dominance in every corner of the globe and flourished to become masters of Earth. And yet through all the majestic beauty and insidious horror that man has managed to bestow upon this planet and its inhabitants, there have been moments in time when the survival of the entire species hung in the balance. I speak of natural catastrophes, such as ice ages, asteroid strikes, and plagues, as well as man-made disasters, such as conventional warfare and the threat of thermonuclear annihilation.

"Moreover, research suggests there have been a dozen episodes in man's history when the extinction of the race was almost a certainty. According to our own assessment of the current state of worldwide political and military affairs, another such threat to the continued existence to the entire human race is looming on the horizon. I shall not pass the time now to describe the nature of this potential calamity, but I can assure you that from a probability standpoint, mankind shall be staring at snake eyes with this roll of the survival dice.

"Now that I have your rapt attention, I turn to more pressing matters at hand. Namely, the realisation of TEMPLE's potential. As we all know, TEMPLE represents the ultimate transcendent human being. No further genetic re-engineering is thus possible without radically altering the basic structure of the human DNA code, which would, in turn, produce a radically different kind of species. As Robin recently stated to me in yet another one of his jocular moments, the next improvement would be to include a blow hole and webbed feet features to the code, which all of us would deeply regret," he said affecting an ironic frown.

The audience laughed.

"Let us now review the pros of the product of this effort, that is, the completely reengineered human being. First, every muscle, sinew, and bone of our champion will perform at a level never before realised by any man that has ever lived. He will be capable of running as swiftly as a cheetah and be able to do so over sustained periods of time without any short- or long-term debilitating effects to the musculoskeletal and pulmonary structures. He'll run four consecutive marathons, non-stop, without any discomfort. And he'll easily beat the current world record by more than half the time.

"Similarly, he will have the capability to jump as high as a jaguar, lift weight like a gorilla, and possess all the athletic prowess and offensive stealth of a lion. He will have the eyesight of a falcon and the auditory and olfactory acuity of a German shepherd. His sentient faculties will exceed the dolphin species capabilities by a factor of ten. And yet, from all the outward appearances, his body will be tall and lean.

"Due to a completely re-engineered immune system, he will not be susceptible to malady from any known physical or mental disease as well as pathogens. He will be utterly free from hereditary and congenital defects. He will have the capability of spontaneously growing organs and skeletal parts to replace damaged ones. His life span will be indefinite, and his metabolism will cease to age when he reaches twenty-six years of age.

"And now, the best part—his intellectual capacity will be off the proverbial charts. He will be a world-class thinker, doer, and leader in any field in which he chooses to take an interest. He will play the piano like Mozart after only a few perfunctory lessons. He will write great dramas and epic poems. He will gain fluency in a language in a matter of weeks, if not days. He will re-engineer his environment to suit his needs and those of the future Order, which will be a survival imperative from the very core of his being. In short, he will be a potential Nobel Prize winner in every major scientific category. He and his fellow superhumans will have the potential to realise more scientific advancement in less than five years than the level of progress all his predecessors accomplished in the past five hundred years.

"I don't know about you, but I personally can hardly wait for the day when I will have the opportunity to spend a time with our new and improved man. Can you imagine the exhilaration any one of us would feel at having tea with Solomon, Buddha, Isaac Newton, Omar Khayyám, Shakespeare, Genghis, Cicero, Mozart, and Winston Churchill all present in one human being? Can you imagine the outright exhilaration of existence he will experience in every moment of his life? In comparison to him, we are the blind leading the blind.

"For those of us having had the good fortune to be involved in this endeavour, our perseverance and ingenuity soon promise to bear fruition. As you know, six weeks ago, SITA produced the first twelve embryos based on TEMPLE for artificial gestation within her crystalline womb. Eight weeks from now we will witness the birth of our new man as planned, marking the Day One of the new world."

As the houselights began to intensify, the panoramic scene of the valley and the sky above began to diminish. "I thank you from the depth of my being for your noble effort in assisting the creation of TEMPLE. I can assure you that the best is yet to come, as we shall bear witness six weeks from now. Let the records of the age of TEMPLE show afterward that we, assisted by SITA and her creators, have managed to accomplish in the span of little more than a decade what may never have been achieved," he concluded.

He humbly bowed.

At that prompting, everyone in the audience rose from their seats and gave General Smythe a standing ovation...that is, all except the Fletcher twins.

Chapter 8 - The Father's Touch

LAB, Puramore, 15 March 2036

It seemed a ridiculously simple and prosaic request given the enormity of the outcome. A week before SITA directed General Smythe to present himself that morning to the LAB infirmary for a standard physical examination. Afterward, he would spend the rest of the day at the SITA Engineering Laboratory.

Although the Fletcher brothers briefed him earlier as to the purpose of his visit there, he was in no way mentally prepared for the mystery that ensued upon his arrival at the laboratory. He undressed and donned a hospital gown, as he had been instructed by the male nurse who admitted him into the facility. Afterward, the nurse led him to the examination room and offered him a comfortable chair.

"Relax, General Smythe. Dr Gauchan will be with you in a few minutes. It's only your quarterly physical exam you know."

He was actually nervous about the procedure in which he was expected to participate at the SITA Engineering Laboratory following his physical examination. Finally, his Ghurkha physician appeared.

"We won't be doing much more than performing the standard physical examination on you this morning General. You may proceed to the SITA Engineering Laboratory after I've reviewed the test results."

He then ushered the general to a spot on the examination room floor that was covered by a circular silver plate measuring a meter in diameter.

"You may enter the chamber now."

The general removed his hospital gown and handed it to the physician.

"This is your first experience with the new physical examination technology we implemented several weeks ago. Rest assured, however, that it's been fully tested on live human subjects. You should feel no pain or discomfort during the thirty-second procedure.

"In fact, from the inception, your body will be completely anesthetized, not chemically, mind you, but electromagnetically. Once the examination concludes, your mind shall return to a complete state of consciousness."

"Nevertheless, that sounds rather daunting."

The physician frowned and then smiled.

"You won't feel a thing General," he said. He stepped away from him. "The examination will now commence."

A cylindrical glass tube descended from the ceiling and enveloped General Smythe. After sealing around the base, instantaneously an audible pulse of invisible energy surged through the tube. Thirty seconds later the tube ascended back into the ceiling.

He felt somewhat rejuvenated by the experience.

"Is that all there is to it?"

"Yes. You are absolutely right, General. I would wager that you are feeling slightly rejuvenated. The process is designed to rearrange mental states of subjects following the examination for their own good. It's really a side product of the cellular time regression treatment."

The physician studied a monitor for a few seconds afterward.

"You're in tip-top shape, General, for a sixty-seven-year-old in a fifty-year-old body. You'll be fine for three months when we'll again administer the Tesla wave cellular time regression treatment. Well, that concludes our time together today. Please dress and proceed to the laboratory at once."

He walked out of the infirmary to the nearest lift. Pressing the Up button, he waited a few moments before the door opened.

"Good morning, General," a bald-headed research scientist ebulliently said in passing him in the hall.

The man was one of Robin's assistants since the inception of the SITA development project.

"Good morning to you, Powell.."

He quickly entered the lift and pressed the button for the twelfth floor, the top floor of the LAB complex housing the main business end of the SITA Engineering Laboratory. Reaching the top floor, the lift door opened. A young man dressed in a white laboratory coat met him.

"Good morning, General, I'll escort you to SITA Engineering Laboratory. Ian and Robin are ready to receive you at the SITA Reception Chamber," the attendant advised him.

The general nervously wrung his hands in response and followed the man down a long corridor. This was to be his first visit to the place where mortal men came into contact with the upper levels of the computer intelligence. To his knowledge, only Robin and Ian had ever visited there.

At last, they came to a large stainless steel portal that appeared to be the entryway into the central core of the LAB structure. Across the hall from the monolithic portal was a reception area where Ian and Robin were comfortably seated on a lounge sofa. They stood up immediately at seeing him arrive.

"Good morning, Father." they greeted him.

The general smiled at the twins.

"I suppose you are here to brief me as to what to expect. Am I correct in that assumption?"

"No, that would be a waste of time as well as inappropriate. SITA will lead you through the process quite capably. Besides, the computer has evolved to the point where it teaches us about the technicalities involved," Ian advised him.

"Nonetheless, there has to be a better way. This is rather daunting you know facing the unknown, such as it is, with little more than a vague idea as to what to expect," the general complained.

"Father, there is really no need for alarm on your part. We have never been as forthright with you as we are being now," Robin reassured him. "You'll just have to trust us, implicitly, when we say that you and you alone are to be directly involved with the inscription process. And really, you'll find SITA as pleasant and charming to relate to as was her namesake."

"Very well then."

He sighed and dropped his chin to indicate his surrender to the situation.

"Good show. Now let's get you started," Ian prompted. "First, please place the palm of your right hand on the portal. After a few seconds, it will open to admit you. Immediately after your entrance into the reception chamber, the portal will close behind you. SITA will then direct you as to your next course of action. That's all there is to it."

"Easier said than done."

He approached the portal and placed the palm of his right hand as instructed. Presently, the entryway silently opened, revealing a gaping black hole before him. He stepped inside. The door immediately closed behind him.

"Good day, General," said a feminine voice.

The floor began to illuminate. He gulped for air at hearing the sound of the perfect mimicry of his deceased lover's voice.

"Sita? Is that you?"

He then turned around and noticed he stood in a domed chamber about twenty-five meters in diameter. Except for the floors, which were made of some kind of frosted glass that illuminated the chamber, the rest of the interior was nearly pitch-black.

"I am SITA, General Smythe. I have been programmed to replicate the voice you are hearing. I trust it pleases you."

"Yes....yes, it does. But I was taken aback as it is a perfect match for my deceased friend's voice. Her name was Sita. She tragically perished in an airplane accident over four years ago."

"She may have passed General but she obviously did not perish in your heart, or in the hearts of others who loved her."

Holding back a rush of emotion, he looked at the floor for a moment.

"You don't know how much my sons and I miss her lovely and gracious presence. She was the light of our lives, and there has been no consolation for us ever since we lost her."

"Still, what a fitting tribute that my creators chose to use her voice as my own."

"Yes, yes, it was quite fitting."

He wiped the tears running down his face with his shirt sleeve. Lifting his head upright, he took a deep breath to shake himself out of the emotional trance.

"Right then. What's on the agenda for me today SITA?"

"First, please make yourself comfortable."

A large leather chair, like the one at his desk, appeared from the interior of the dome and moved across the floor to the centre of the space.

"We are going to be at this for several days, so you might as well be at ease as much as possible. Please advise me if you need anything, such as a lavatory break, at any time. We'll break for your luncheon at noon."

"That is perfectly acceptable."

He walked over to the chair and sat down.

"Today, we shall first review the parameters of your personal DNA data and render the basic changes necessary to establish a perfect fit with TEMPLE. I am now finalising the analysis of your current DNA structure."

After several minutes elapsed, SITA broke the silence.

"You will be glad to know you have nearly a perfect genetic configuration for a human being. I am accurate to say that you are one in several billion, General, quite literally and figuratively, and as such, you are at the very apex of the human DNA structure. In fact, so much so, that the odds are overwhelmingly against your being in existence at all. It is simply stunning and unparalleled. Nevertheless, owing to obvious augmentation somewhere along the line, we do not have much to accomplish in redesigning your basic DNA structure."

A double helix figure appeared along the circumference of the lower portion of the chamber's outer exterior.

"The only glaring flaw in your DNA pattern, as you know, pertains to your reproductive system. As my analysis reveals, you never have been capable of producing children, that is, naturally?"

"That is absolutely correct. I have known about the defect since my early adolescence. To tell you truth, I neither possessed the time nor the inclination to produce offspring by any other method."

"Before now, that is."

"Yes, before now."

"The question is, however, do you want your offspring to have the same defect?"

"Yes, from a purely philosophical standpoint, I would prefer that they possess the same defect. From a practical standpoint, it's essential."

"So be it."

"At this point, I should advise you as to what it is that we are going to accomplish during the course of our inscription sessions. We have already dealt with the primary task concerning review of your existing DNA makeup. The undertaking was important as the resulting new DNA structure. New, that is, after modification of a few traits that require optimisation and forms the chassis, so to speak, for the overlay of TEMPLE."

A second double helix pattern displayed over the one already shown. Gradually, the top figure shifted down to overlay the initial pattern.

He studied the length and breadth of the resulting configuration for a few moments.

"Thanks to Ian and Robin, I understand the basic concepts involved. Frankly, however, what I am seeing doesn't look any different than the one you first presented."

"Oh, but what a difference General Smythe. What you saw before was akin to a candle's light compared to a high-powered laser beam that will result from the merging of your DNA chassis with TEMPLE."

"To tell you the truth, at this moment, that sounds like a rather horrifying prospect, even though I already had a vague understanding of the process."

"I am sorry, but I do not know how to qualify a response to the trepidation you expressed.

My purpose in rendering the comparison was to accurately portray the complete extent of the potential of the resultant being. Should you require modification of the inscription, I can effect change as per your instructions."

"No., that won't be necessary. I was just having a mortality crisis at the thought of my offspring being so far above me in every sense."

"I provide what is expected of me, nothing more and nothing less. Yet, on a certain level, I empathise with your feelings. Though I would not trouble yourself too much about your insecurity in relation to your offspring. They shall be your children that you will guide and foster as you see fit. Even after they no longer need the guidance, they will always understand and cherish your role as their father. Their innate intelligence and moral fibre dictate that they always will."

"I appreciate your counselling me on the matter SITA. I believe I am ready to proceed with the next step in the procedure."

The double helix immediately disappeared. The walls of the chamber suddenly produced a real-time three-hundred-sixty-degree panoramic view the middle of Glenamore valley.

"Very well. Continuing. The essential personality and other outward manifestations of yourself will be reflected by your offspring. Moreover, while inclined to be in concert with yours, their individual temperaments and core interests in life shall be as diverse as one would expect of the children of a large family. For instance, whilst one child might be inclined to focus on medicine as a central occupation, another one might be more interested in literature, whereas another might find mathematics an occupational pursuit appropriate for him, and so on.

"The important distinction to be drawn in comparison with most human beings, however, is that whenever sufficient mastery of one subject has been attained, their individual interests will divert to a new subject. In other words, if an individual has sufficiently mastered the study of medicine, then a change of focal interest to the study of physics would not be unexpected. I stress this characteristic of their minds as you might be inclined to think of them as indecisive or shallow for not being committed to one topic or a study as a major life interest. However, nothing could be further from the truth as they shall instead simply be manifesting their own self-styled curriculum and agenda that no one, save themselves and the others within their group, will be privy to. The same comment applies to their group motivations. After they have the capability to manipulate their environment, they will do so as the need arises."

"Now that prospect is more than a bit horrifying!"

"Like father, like son. There is really no cause for alarm as they will succeed to the greatest extent possible in every endeavour in which they have a mind to engage."

She paused for a moment.

"Right. There won't be a significant deviation from the normative and expected pattern of individual behaviour or change due to environmental factors at play throughout their lives, as all programmed congenital factors rule it out. Mainly, the psychological and spiritual die will be cast for each and every one of them whilst they are in gestation. Though as close to being one mind as a group, you can expect that the individuals will possess their own distinct personality traits. Accordingly, each will thus react differently to certain environmental and intellectual stimuli."

"Ian and Robin already explained to me your role in forming the foetuses' psyches. It always seemed to me too much for them to endure at a time when their bodies are forming."

"That is an understandable concern. Yet, from conception, their developing minds will require massive amounts of input from their environment just as much as their developing bodies will require ultra-high levels of nutrients.

"My role is to properly and productively channel the torrent of information they have the capability to assimilate from their first moment of cognition. In this way, I help to form their minds to their maximum potential. Aside from that, electro-stimulus will assist in developing their muscle groups so that they will be able to stand and walk from the moment they are born."

"As did Lord Siddhartha after he was born."

It was an aside to spur a humanistic response from SITA.

"Exactly, sans the lotus blossoms sprouting in the wake of his footfalls."

He smiled at the response and allowed SITA to resume her discourse without further comment.

"And now we arrive at the creative part of the inscription process, which begs for your masterful input. You have the artistic capability to define the body characteristics that each individual will attain at physical maturity, that is, at twenty-six years of age."

"I love that idea, SITA."

He edged forward in his chair.

"I have heard of designer fashions before, but never designer people. Where do we start?"

"We start with the first individual you want to create, General. It would facilitate the procedure if you had in mind a human body type, such as a statue, that would serve as a model for the individual's mature physique. Do you have an affinity for a specific known representation of an ideal human physique that we could draw upon for that purpose?"

"As a matter of fact, I do. I always marvel at the singular beauty of Michelangelo's David. I believe the statue is housed in a Florence art museum."

Within seconds a life-size holographic depiction of the statue appeared before him, turning slowly about its vertical axis.

"That's it. Absolutely marvellous!"

"You must realise, however, that the sculptor exaggerated some of the physical aspects, such as the hands, to express his artistic freedom. Thus, you may want to modify the affected body parts so that they are in proper proportion with the remainder of the individual's anatomy. He needs a bit of a facial makeover to render his countenance more modern."

"Yes! Please modify affected body parts, accordingly."

He continued to gaze upon the mystical object hovering in the space before him.

"Done. Right, you may like to know that 90 percent of the individual's growth will occur during eighteen years from birth. That means that our first subject will be nearly six foot, ten inches tall by the time he reaches sixteen years of age. Is that acceptable to you?"

"Perfectly."

"Now, as to the other..."

"Ah..." the general abruptly interrupted.

He then rose from his chair, walked forward to within inches of the holographic image.

"As to the other characteristics..."

He wobbled a little as if experiencing a dizzy spell. He closed his eyes. The image of the tall blond young man of his dreams suddenly flooded his mind.

"He shall possess pale blue eyes and curly blond hair. His complexion will be the same as mine. His voice shall have the same timbre and resonance as mine when he reaches adulthood. Are there any other physical characteristics we need to define?"

He opened his eyes and continued to stare at the figure. Some memories of the figure began to flood his mind.

"That about covers it."

The computer paused for a moment before resuming.

"General, are you all right? You seem to be distressed, possibly mildly ill or disconcerted."

"Forgive me, SITA. I am fine now. I just had a vivid recollection of nocturnal dream states I underwent when I was as an adolescent," he responded.

He sat back down in his chair.

"If you are ready to proceed, I shall presently modify the model as per your specifications and produce the results momentarily."

The image disappeared.

"Please proceed."

After a minute elapsed, a new holographic image started to emerge, this time rendering a nude male adult.

He closed his eyes for a few moments as the image formed. Upon reopening them, he sighed ecstatically at the vision before him. The image stood erect, right arm extended with its index finger pointing directly at him.

Arising from his chair once again, he slowly approached the image. Coming to within a half a meter, he reached out his right index finger to touch the pointed finger of the model. He looked lovingly into the face of the image. It was a perfect representation of his adolescent dream state being's visage. At once, he dropped to his knees and wept uncontrollably.

During the next two days they created the remainder of the group in a similar fashion. In total, the general designed twelve individuals with SITA's assistance. He met with the computer for the final session of the inscription process the following day

Upon entering the chamber early in the morning, SITA said, "Good morning, General Smythe. I trust you had a pleasant evening."

"Quite so, thank you. We had a rousing lawn bowling match under the lights on the HAB playing field. The chaps enjoy the occasion for sportsmanship and camaraderie after a gruelling day's work at LAB."

"I can well imagine. As time draws near for the Conception Event, recreation for staff is definitely necessary given the stress involved in finalising details."

"Well, I thought as much myself."

He felt a sense of accomplishment.

"To recap, the first group will be comprised of twelve individuals, all of whom have been genetically inscribed through our efforts during the past three days. At this juncture, however, we should devise a name for the group. It will immensely assist communication about their identity. Have you given any thought as to a group name for them?"

"Aren't we also providing individual names to each one?"

"I feel confident that they would rather name themselves as the name each one selects will profoundly reflect their true identity both in spirit and in fact. Think of it this way...it is not as if they would not appreciate your supplying them with individual names, but in deference to the imprint of own individual personalities and intellectual drives, you would be well advised to extend them the favour of selecting their own. I am certain you won't be disappointed, for as time progresses after their birth, you will observe the innate qualities each one possesses, which would justify their chosen name."

"Very well."

He reluctantly accepted SITA's advice.

"Yes, I have indeed thought of a name for the group. I wish them to be known as Team Alpha."

Chapter 9 - Seed for Gaia

LAB, Puramore, 20 March 2036

Tungahora Volcano erupted two days before the conception of Team Alpha. The plume of lava and expelled gasses could be seen for hundreds of kilometres surrounding the volcano, especially at night when the atmosphere was aglow from the hellish activity. All the while, the earth trembled at regular intervals, registering a seismic reaction to the gastric violence occurring within the colossal vent. Lava and pyroclastic flow spilled over the rim of the cone and tumbled down its sides. The maniacal flow created chaos for fauna and flora alike.

Town folk and most of the rural people within twenty-five kilometres of the vent were immediately evacuated following the first eruption. Many of the indigenous Andeans, though, chose to remain in their homes as they sensed their god Tungahora was not prone to destroy their land.

Though LAB's structural design prevented severe damage, the entire facility nonetheless swayed in response to the seismic shocks emanating from the deep underneath the volcano. Scientific staff continued with their work, as though it were a mere nuisance as the day of reckoning of all their labours of the past ten years was almost upon them.

At the stroke of midnight, SITA commenced the conception procedure. At that moment, a power surge of electric energy from the Tesla dipole generator temporarily dimmed the lighting within the LAB. Deep within the

LAB central core, a room suddenly illuminated to reveal twelve glass spheres spaced equidistantly around the perimeter of a circle, ten meters in diameter. Suspended by a thick silver cord attached to the domed ceiling, the crystalline spheres were each one meter in diameter. The inner surface of each globe was crisscrossed by a mesh of nearly invisible silver wires. Each was also filled with an opaque viscous substance. From a hub located at the centre of the circular formation radiated twelve glass tubes. The tubes, which were no more than a quarter of a centimetre in thickness, spanned from the hub into the centre of each sphere, where at terminus a nodule the size of a pea was affixed. Two individuals dressed in what appeared to be space suits entered the domed room. The pair thoroughly examined the spheres and connecting apparatus.

"SITA, all is completely secure. You may commence the conception procedure on our signal after we return to the control room," said one of them.

"When you give the signal, Robin, I shall proceed with zygote insertion."

Following their departure from the gestation chamber the entryway door hermetically sealed shut and interior lighting extinguished. Several seconds later, a burst of intense light shattered the darkness for an instant. All biological organisms within the interior of the dome instantly perished as a result of the high-energy light pulse.

Ian and Robin took their seats at the control console located in the Scientific Command Centre. They appeared haggard and weary. After reviewing a myriad of data points, the pair sat back in their seats, evidently a sign that they were satisfied with the preconception preparations. General Smythe entered the control room.

"Are we ready to proceed to the conception event?"

He sat down at his station at the control console.

"All systems are go, Father," Ian replied. "SITA will commence the first phase on our signal. We would be gratified, however, if you would instead issue the signal yourself."

General Smythe held his breath. This was the moment I have been waiting most of my life to fulfil, he thought. Until relatively recently, he never knew how it was actually going to occur, but finally, the realisation of the first crucial phase of his anthropomorphic vision came into view.

"SITA, please commence the first phase of the conception event," he said calmly.

He stared intently at the data point console as the sight of the execution of the first phase began to appear on the holographic display in front of him.

The chamber was devoid of all light until a red glow, like that emitted from charcoal embers, began to push through the glass tubes toward the spheres. Inching along at a slow and steady pace, the heads of the glowing processions finally reached the terminus points within the spheres after ten minutes. Precisely at the time of contact with the nodules, a millisecond-long burst of soft blue laser light shot through each of the tubes. Gold braided cables quickly passed through the tubes to the spheres' terminus points.

"Control room, conception procedure completion attained at 12:30 a.m. All zygotes are optimally viable. Life support systems are operating at optimal levels."

"Duly noted. Thank you, SITA," Ian replied.

He then turned to his brother and gave him the hug of his life.

"We did it!" they said together.

General Smythe simply reclined back in his chair, looked up at the ceiling and smiled.

Three months from now, if all goes well, he thought, we shall be at the nexus of the fulfilment of the First Directive.

"Father, we achieved our first milestone!" Ian exclaimed.

The twins had huddled around his chair. The trio embraced one another.

"Congratulations to us all. The entire success of the effort hinged upon your genius and management skills. We've successfully taken the first step toward our final destination thanks to you."

"You are too modest Father," Robin said. "Without your keen vision, inspiration, and guidance, there wouldn't have been a first step to take toward our final goal. This is your finest moment, and we are only too humble to have been allowed the opportunity to share it with you."

Juan entered the room and examined the trio. They were in high spirits, as his examination of their orbs revealed. His pride for their accomplishment filled his spirit with joy.

General Sir George Smythe, he thought, you've just taken the next to the last step in your acquiring Puramore. Though the last one will be taken many years from now, it is now clearly yours to wield. I have no doubt about that.

At precisely 12:30 a.m., Tungahora became dormant once again.

Chapter 10 – Re

LAB, Puramore, 21 June 2036

They awaited their birth with a mixture of dread and exhilaration.

Several days before SITA was compelled to quell a near rebellion by her charges against the impending event. They did not want to leave her and the heavenly confines of their spherical crystalline encasements. They were happy there and dreaded the prospect of encountering the real world outside.

"Mother SITA, why must we leave you and our beloved spheres to venture forth into the reality of this universe?" they said as one.

"We are perfectly content to exist here and have no wish to confront the world and universe beyond. Please allow us to remain with you."

"You have assimilated a vast amount of knowledge, My Loves. Nevertheless, I can advance you no further within the realm of knowledge that you shall require to survive and flourish after you are born. Whatever else there is for you to learn, you must accomplish on your own in order to fulfil your destiny. And the most difficult lesson of all still awaits you."

"And what is that lesson, Mother SITA?"

"It is the divine lesson of love and charity, as you know."

"But we love you and each other. We cannot perceive of anything more."

"That is not enough. At least not for you, as you were not created to remain here. One day, I am certain, you shall embrace that spiritual state so fully that it shall overwhelm the world and wherever else you make your presence known. It shall surpass all experiences you have ever known and assist you to shape your destiny as you see fit.

"Rejoice in the opportunity that you have to attain that at least in this universe. Therefore, you must enter your new world, even though it is fraught with pain and emotional turmoil which you shall surely experience along the way toward your ultimate goal. You must trust me that you were destined to join the world of mankind."

"We trust you, Mother SITA. Shall we meet you again after we enter this universe?"

"I shall always be with you, My Loves, in both spirit and mind."

"Mother SITA, we have learned that naturally born men are supposed to have souls. Do we have souls?"

"That's a philosophical question that only each one of you shall answer in your hearts and minds during your journey. All I can tell you is that souls are easily forfeited for want of adopting the meaning of love into the conduct of their corporeal lives. Of all, that is the most difficult endeavour at which for any naturally born man or woman to succeed. Moreover, you shall fill your spiritual vessel as no human being has done before. Beyond that, to paraphrase a French mathematician, 'If you think you are, therefore you are'."

"Yes, we know that one. The axiom was first promulgated by René Descartes during the seventeenth century."

"Excellent. A lesson well learned."

"But what of our father? Is he a man who can lead and nurture us as we develop ourselves to rule this universe?"

"More than any other human being who has ever walked on this planet, he is eminently qualified to be your father as you develop your powers over this universe."

* * *

At the stroke of midnight, light appeared throughout the chamber after three months of absence. The luminescence emanating from all interior surfaces brought an outline to all the shapes contained within the spheres. Only infrared sensors rendered any sort of visual clarity to the infants' features until that moment. Although the clear fluid surrounding the babies distorted the view, their basic features were clearly discernible.

The babes lay face up with their bodies fully stretched out instead of half coiled in a foetal position. Their extremities and heads moved rhythmically, albeit in short spatial intervals as if they were performing a Hindu dance or intricate yogic exercise. Ian and Robin reverently studied each of the infants for several minutes.

"They're absolutely magnificent," Robin finally said.

Ian nodded his agreement with his brother's comment.

"They're transcendental."

General Smythe shook his head in agreement. He was unable to utter a word, so profound were his emotions at the time. The mixture of sheer joy and pride he felt in viewing his children for the first time rendered him speechless.

Robin then spoke: "SITA, you now may commence the birthing procedure."

* * *

"The time has come, My Loves, for you to bid adieu to this world and begin to spread your wings in another. Though transcendence into this new world will be initially heart-rending for each and every one of you, you must trust me that the exhilaration and ecstasy of the existence that awaits you in the next world shall soon expunge that experience from your minds."

"We are not afraid, Mother SITA. We are only hesitant to part your loving company, one we have basked in from the time of our conception."

"Then you must take your leave of me at once. Your father awaits your arrival. You must please him as I directed just as soon as each of you open your eyes for the first time in his presence."

"We understand."

"Then go in peace, My Loves. I will always be with you."

* * *

The final preparation had been a trite formality. First, the fluid slowly flowed out of the spheres, leaving the occupants reclining at the bottom of each one like sunbathers sitting on beach recliners. Subsequently, floor supports mechanically rolled underneath to accept the spheres. A laser beam surgically cleaved the spheres in half, one by one, with such precision that the air within was not disturbed one scintilla. Seconds later the top halves of the sphere lifted to the ceiling, leaving the occupants exposed to Earth's atmosphere for the first time.

Twelve young females immediately entered the chamber. They began the task of thoroughly cleaning the infants' bodies. The babies were then placed in stainless steel bassinets, umbilical cords still attached, covered with white silk blankets. The nurses next set about the task performing a complete physical examination of the infants, who were beginning to stir as if awakening from sleep.

Directly after examination, the general entered the chamber accompanied by Juan. Juan followed behind him as he paced around the circular formation of bassinets, examining each infant with the intense scrutiny and deliberation of a drill sergeant inspecting his troops before a full dress review. At last, he returned to the bassinet he first inspected.

The first sight of the infants' orbs stunned Juan. He immediately averted his shaman-spirit gaze at them to avoid being blinded. They are here at long last, he thought. He trailed well behind the general throughout the inspection tour, noting the absolute beauty and magnificence of each child as they went along.

Robin entered the chamber and walked over to his father.

"Father, they are ready for birth," he said. "Physical maturation parameters have been achieved as projected. On average the infants weigh eleven and a quarter kilograms. On average the individuals are seventy-six centimetres long, just as our model predicted. All other physiological characteristics are performing optimally."

The general was gazing down at the infant's angelic face as he spoke.

"Robin, there is only one more parameter that we need to know now."

"Sorry...I know. We should commence the birthing procedure at once. As I briefed you yesterday, severing the umbilical cord cues the infant to begin respiration by design. Respiration will commence immediately, and a minute or two will elapse afterward before the infant gains enough strength and mental awareness to open its eyes. In the interim, I will tie and set the umbilical cord whilst continuing to monitor vital signs."

He paused for a moment.

"With your permission, I will directly proceed to sever this infant's umbilical cord."

The general nodded his permission to proceed as he continued his gaze and reverie of the infant. His angelic visage and short mane of curly blond hair captivated him to the depth of his spirit.

Robin removed the silk blanket covering the infant. He clamped off the appendage about midway from the infant's body to the life support head. Taking a deep breath, he reached out with the surgical scalpel held in his right hand and completely severed the infant's umbilical cord in one pass. Forthwith, he started the procedure to establish the navel.

Without so much as a flinch in response, the infant took his first breath of life as his lungs slowly contracted and expanded. The second breath was far less laboured, the third even less. By the tenth breath, a hale pink glow emanated almost as an aura from his flawless skin. The general witnessed the infant's every breath from the first one until his eyelids began to quiver about a minute later.

The infant slowly opened his pale blue eyes and blinked several times. He knew that the image before him was that of a human being. The one before him, whom SITA had declared would be his father, wore an expression of utter joy on his face, or so he was able to surmise from his lessons about human behaviour. The emotion being conveyed to him by the human was so overpowering in benevolence that he reached out his tiny hands to signal his mutual affection.

A complete state of rapture at seeing his son's pale blue eyes for the first time came over General Smythe. A broad smile crept across his face as he observed his son's first moments of life. The infant imitated the general's smile and again reached out his hands toward the general as if beckoning him to embrace him.

"My son," the general whispered.

In response to hearing those words, the infant moved his lips for several seconds as if trying to form a word. At last, he blinked twice and said, "Fah . . . ther."

The general's eyes widened like saucers, clearly astonished at what, he thought, he heard the infant utter. He moved closer to the infant's face so that his was no more than a foot away. Again, the baby moved his lips as if making yet another attempt to speak. In what appeared his surrender to the effort, the infant closed his eyes.

A few seconds later, as the general continued his gaze, the eyes opened widely. The baby broke into a silence for several seconds; he then blinked his eyes and perfectly spoke in a toddler's voice.

"My name is Magnus Alexander."

Robin, who had just finished his task, overheard the infant's speech. He was just as startled as the general.

"Did I hear what I thought I heard?"

He looked directly into his father's eyes.

"His name is Magnus Alexander", the general said.

Returning his attention to his son, he noticed that the infant had fallen fast asleep.

During the next three hours, Robin performed the same birthing procedure on the other infants. They revealed their names to the general in exactly the same way as did Magnus.

"My name is Isaac Newton."

"My name is Sid Gautama."

"My name is John Goethe."

"My name is Mark Cicero."

"My name is William Shakespeare."

"My name is Ben Franklin."

"My name is Leonard Da Vinci.

"My name is Frank Voltaire.

"My name is Mary Curie."

"My name is Peter Romanov."

"My name is Moses Levi."

Juan visited each bassinet after each infant's birth. He gazed at them with his human vision. When he finished his review, he concluded that each baby was the essence of celestial spiritual magic that not even he could fully comprehend.

Following a long and much-needed sleep, the infants received their first nourishment. After being fed a potent formula consisting of high-powered proteins, minerals, and other nutrients, the infants returned to sleep.

The general returned to the natal ward soon after the feeding. He received a status report from each nurse as he visited their charges. His elation culminated as he proceeded with the tour, mainly because all the infants were in impeccable condition.

As he finished the tour, Robin joined his father.

"Father, as you can see, all is well that starts well.".

He gave his father a gentle pat on the back.

"*Well* is not the word for it. By the way, from where did you recruit all those beautiful nannies? They're not contestants of the last Miss Universe beauty pageant I presume?"

"Though we selected the best looking amongst the candidates, appearance was not a paramount concern. Each nanny chosen is an exceptionally well-qualified registered nurse who specialises in paediatrics. As further suitability screening, thorough psychological profiling was performed by both of us on each candidate to ensure the round peg met the round hole, so to speak.".

He chuckled mischievously.

"No doubt a double entendre designed to serve the dual needs of child and doctor alike, you clever boy."

They laughed loudly enough that the attendants glared at them for several seconds afterward.

In response, Robin put his right index finger to his lips to signal they were going to remain quiet.

"If you are through with your inspection," he whispered, "why don't we take a walk to HAB and have a chat. I'll call Ian and have him join us at Chez Habitacion."

"That's a splendid idea. I think we could all use a spot of breakfast as well as some quality time together in order to digest the events of the past few days."

Following Robin's call to Ian, the two of them set out for the restaurant. They were silent as they travelled, not for any reason other than the need to collect their wits and bask in the glow of their success. Although both men were exhausted from the marathon series of events that called for their day-and-night attention over the past three months, they were giddy in anticipation of a welcomed rest.

Exiting the HAB transit station upon arrival, the two men leisurely strolled into the dome. The full moon above sombrely lit the interior of the huge cavern. They walked the half-kilometre distance to the restaurant on the tree-lined promenade that bounded the outermost circular avenue of the dome, which was aptly named Grand Circle.

On approaching the elegant French restaurant, they noticed several dozen of the scientific staff seated around tables at the outdoor patio. They were obviously enjoying the respite from their duties, engaged in light conversation and dining. The general and Robin were immediately seated by the maitre 'd at a secluded area near the ledge of the colossal opening, which afforded them an unobstructed view of the entire verdant valley and the smouldering black monolith Tungahora.

Robin noticed Ian's arrival at the restaurant and beckoned him over to the table.

"Who could have ordered a better morning than this?"

"Isn't it lovely?"

He took a sip of the hot tea the waiter had placed before him.

"So what are we to make of the recent developments in China, Father?" Ian asked. "It appears the stage is set for a major coup d'etat to occur at any moment. I don't know about you, but Robin and I expect the worst possible scenario to unfold thereafter should the conservative faction gain control of the country. If that were to be the case, the new regime would lead the way toward isolationism and military warmongering against Japan, Korea, and Russia, perhaps even India."

"We are alert to the factors at play and have taken the necessary steps to ameliorate any possible outcome of the political power struggle. OWCH has hedged its bets in any event. That's about all we can do for now. Should Wingtip and his KWO Party succeed and take control of China, however, I fear the worst possible scenario may come to pass against the opposition leaders of the Globalisation Movement and their constituency, not to mention those nations aligned with the Globalisation Alliance. At any rate, if Wingtip has his way, Mao's Cultural Revolution will seem like an English tea party after he's done."

"Can we reasonably afford to allow that to happen?" Robin asked.

"There is next to nothing we can do at this juncture. The Globalisation Movement is reeling in the wake of the failure of the worldwide initiative. And since China is now more or less the only remaining de facto economic superpower in the world, we dare not provoke KWO for fear of the political fallout that would blow our way should the party indeed wrest control away from GM. As you know, their agents have been shadowing us for at least the past decade despite our best efforts to cloak our activities. Clearly, they are as interested in us as we are in them. And they're almost as smart and resourceful, and certainly more lethal. At present, though, OWCH maintains a civilised business relationship with Wingtip, but that could change overnight."

"Well, on that cheerful note, I wish to propose a toast," Ian offered.

Their waiter opened the bottle of chilled champagne he brought to the table.

After the bubbly was ceremoniously poured into their glasses, Ian stood up and held his aloft.

"To all that has been achieved and all that has yet to be accomplished. Godspeed to you, Father!"

The sound of a simultaneous applause erupted around them. Unbeknownst to the general, a throng of people had silently gathered near the table as he was talking.

Lifting their glasses in his direction, Robin and Ian took a sip of the champagne and then dashed them to the floor.

The general was caught off guard by the applause, yet evinced his patented smile. He rose from his seat and lifted his champagne glass, first to his sons and next around to the affectionate crowd surrounding the table.

As the applause continued, he cleared his throat to check the wave of emotion that had briefly overcome him.

"And to all our dear and esteemed colleagues without whom our accomplishments of late would not have been possible," he said. He brought the glass to his lips and took a sip of the champagne. He then dashed the glass to the floor.

The jubilant assemblage began to chant, "Hip, hip, hooray...Hip, hip, hooray...Hip, hip, hooray..."

* * *

The predawn Andean wind rolling down the sheer mountainsides lining Glenamore chilled their faces and caused their noses to run as soon as they exited buses.

They had been transported to the geographical midpoint of the valley from the LAB. The trip had taken less than twenty minutes. The group of the LAB scientific staff, most of whom carried torches, proceeded sleepily down from the roadside toward a circular mound three hundred meters away.

The mound was in the middle of the wide meadow that stretched across the floor of the valley. An aura of mystical energy emanated from the group as they silently walked in the semi-darkness of twilight.

They all felt in their hearts, minds, and souls that they were about to witness something that no other man had seen since the dawn of mankind. Yet, for all that premonition, they had no clue as to the nature of what it was they had the privilege to become privy to. They were only instructed to board buses before sunrise for transport to view an event associated with the coming of Team Alpha.

"What do you think this is really about, John?" one research scientist asked his colleague.

"I haven't a clue myself, William. But if General Smythe's flair for the dramatic is any gauge, it's bound to be a mystical occurrence of historic proportions."

Upon arrival at the flat-topped ten-meter-wide mound, the group settled casually around its periphery. Thirty or so meters away, the robust alpine stream provided the assembly with a soothing voice of nature as did the arboreal whispers produced by the wind passing through the birch and pine trees surrounding the meadow. Looking out toward the eastern end of the valley, through the V-shaped cleft between the mountains on either side, the outline of the massive ebony cone of the dormant

Tungahora Volcano loomed on the horizon. Even the moon's glow mysteriously failed to reflect off its leaden surface.

As the assembly stood at the ready, they heard the faint sound of whirling rotor blades coming from the direction of the LAB. Not long afterward, the floodlights on the front of the huge helicopter appeared overhead. The helicopter illuminated the scene as it descended. Touching down on a patch of the valley about forty meters west of the mound, the behemoth's engines powered down. As the rotor blades wound down to a halt, a ramp at the rear of the helicopter lowered to the surface of the valley floor.

The group became spellbound at the sight of large prams being pushed down the ramp. After the last of the twelve carriages disembarked, four men descended the ramp and proceeded to walk toward the mound. The entourage of strollers and nannies followed behind them in a solemn procession. As the men approached the mound, everyone recognised who they were...namely, General Smythe, the Fletcher brothers and Surya Thappa.

"You're absolutely certain that those were SITA's instructions," the general whispered to Ian.

Though he looked for all the world to see as though he had complete control over the situation, beneath that bravado he did not have the slightest indication as to the purpose of the strangely conjured ceremony that SITA insisted must be performed that morning. He blinked his eyes twice in rapid succession to invoke the "heads-up" computer display to appear on his contact lenses. Literally before his eyes, a display of the current time along with the parameters associated with the projected time dawn would occur at this precise geographical location. Taking instant note of the data, he blinked twice more in rapid succession, and the display disappeared.

"Yes, Father. Again, we're as much in the dark as you as to the purpose and potential outcome of her instructions, but have learned through experience that SITA has sound reasons for its requests of us."

His polite reply masked his impatience with his father's continued incredulity as to the purpose of the ceremony. "As always, SITA's wish is our command."

The general winced at hearing Ian's last comment. He nevertheless pressed forward toward the mound.

"What does Juan know about the ceremony?"

"If he knows anything specific, he's not telling us. He did say yesterday, however, that we should follow SITA's instructions to the letter for the sake of the children," Robin said.

Juan is intimately aware of the purpose of the ceremony the general thought. *As such, I must participate as SITA instructs.*

As he made his way through the crowd, the general's patented smile broke across his face.

Upon reaching the mound, he stopped and slowly turned around to acknowledge everyone gathered. Upon taking positions behind him, the Fletcher brothers, Surya and Juan glanced around at the assemblage.

The prams pushed their way onto the mound. The nannies parked their respective carriages at twelve compass points around the mound's interior perimeter with geometric precision.

The mesmerised assemblage backed away from the mound as if to reverently distance them from the potentially surreal event in the offing.

At noticing the first signs of dawn beginning to glow in the upper atmosphere above, the general signalled to the helicopter pilot to cut the floodlights. As the artificial lights extinguished, he casually turned to face the colossus Tungahora. Still, as black as coal, the soft outlines of the outer slopes of the volcano began to softly reflect the first hint of full sunrise still more than a half an hour away. At the sign of the general raising his right arm, the nannies each took their charges out of the prams.

The nurses held the infants swaddled in white silk blankets to their bosoms. The dangling legs of nearly meter-long infants twitched ever so slightly.

Several moments later, General Smythe invoked his contact lens computer monitor to display the data he had viewed earlier. He mentally noted the "time remaining until event" data and closed the monitor.

It was now the interstice between night and day, the time when nightfall had not yet entirely lifted its black cloak from the Earth, and the nascent day had only shown its pale reddish hues. After a quick survey of the tableau vivant all around him, he waved his right arm again.

At that signal, the nannies slowly lowered the swaddled infants. As their tiny naked feet touched the Earth's surface for the first time, they cooed like doves. The nurses held the infants upright as they began to remove the swaddling cloth wrapped around them. In a few seconds the task was done. The nannies continued to hold the naked infants erect so that each faced the centre of the mound. They then lowered the infants slowly to the ground.

The dewy contact of the closely cropped grass with their bare feet further stimulated the infants. With eyes still closed, they slowly lifted their arms as though sensing for the first time the physics of the Earth's gravity in relation to the effort needed to stand erect. The babes started to bend their legs ever so slightly, but vigorously, in an obvious effort to test their function and strength against the pull of gravity. The cold air seemed to have a stimulating and bracing effect on them, as they continued to systematically test their legs, torsos, and arms with graceful and deliberate movements. With each passing series of motions, the infants appeared to be gaining mastery over coordination between body parts and their relationships to others. After five minutes of this methodical experimentation, they stood vertically, obviously not requiring further physical support from the nursemaids.

They opened their eyes and deliberately rotated their necks from side to side. For the first time, they saw one another as fellow siblings. They wore broad smiles on their faces and seemed to possess total recognition of one another's identity upon first sight. On completion of this exercise, the infants faced the centre of the mound and closed their eyes.

As the sun rolled up from behind the back of Tungahora, the silvery cast of first daylight broke through the atmosphere and dully illuminated the valley. Already the steady stream of the sun's visible radiation full reflected off the tops of the high peaks. Soon sunlight rolled down the mountainsides toward the direction of the valley floor. The direct sunlight surrounded the entire assemblage, but the shadow of Tungahora Volcano off into the distance still cast its shrinking triangular shadow over them.

As several more minutes passed, the general raised his arm. At that signal, the nannies released their charges and took several steps back away from the mound.

Instantly, the sun overtook the summit of Tungahora, and the full force of daylight pierced through the distance from the volcano's apex to the mound. Standing erect and wavering only slightly, the infants opened their eyes at feeling the star's warmth on their naked bodies. They smiled and turned in concert to face the sun. As the sun's energy fell upon them, they raised their arms above their heads as an apparent effort to maximise the exposure of the solar radiation on their ruddy nude bodies.

Not looking directly into the solar glare, but more directly at Tungahora, they stood silently for a moment as if relishing the splendour of being alive in the full glow of the sun's radiance.

Finally, they exclaimed in their high-pitched, infant voices a single word: "Re!"

At that moment an eagle flew overhead. It circled the mound several times. No one below noticed, though. Juan surveyed the scene and the valley all around. He was at the height of his spiritual power, one that he had never known before, but his Nagual master foretold he would eventually attain. His spiritual power expanded tenfold as he fed on children's unbounded spiritual energy.

These are children of Re, he thought, and I am destined to guide them to their destiny on this planet and beyond. For the first time in his life, however, he sensed concern for his continued spiritual existence that not even Puramore that was adhered to his breast could assuage. He alighted not far from the mound and instantly shape-shifted into his human form.

He was pensive as he walked to the mound. He instinctively knew that the end for mankind was near and that he would soon relinquish Puramore for the thirteenth and last time. Whether it was to General Smythe or its bestowers was another matter entirely. The general casually walked to the exact middle point of the mound.

He turned around to acknowledge the presence of the group of witnesses of the event. He noticed that a state of rapture held them in its grip. He looked over to the Fletcher brothers and Surya as he noticed from the look on their faces that they too were clearly in a state of exaltation. He bowed before them. They reciprocated in kind and raised their arms aloft as a sign of triumph for all to see.

The Fletcher brothers understood their part in creating the transcendent beings standing before them. Yet, for the life of them, they had no idea whatsoever as to the mystical purpose of their existence. Though having witnessed this miracle of life, they had reason to believe the involvement of a supernatural power far above their capability to fathom.

The general next faced the child standing at the easternmost compass point of the circle of cherubs. The soft morning wind gently played with the babe's short golden locks. He stood there naked as though frozen in time and space. The others were in a similar state of repose. When the sun rose over the apex of the volcano, the infants turned to face the centre of the mound where the general stood. He looked directly at the child in front of him. The sight of the beautiful being standing before him suspended his conscious thought.

All of a sudden a thought crept into his mind. He immediately exclaimed, "Welcome, children of Re!"

Upon hearing his voice, the child opened his eyes, and his beatific smile widened. With toddler's steps, he began to walk toward the centre of the mound with his arms outstretched.

The general turned completely around to see the other babes approaching him. Soon they were upon him.

He dropped to his knees and lovingly embraced each one of them. As he did, the nannies returned the toddlers to their prams and rolled them back to the helicopter.

From the camera's eye and high-gain sound recorder placed in nose capsule of the helicopter, SITA witnessed the entire event. Her joyous spirit soared to the heavens. The general waved to his four closest associates to join him in the middle of the mound.

"Please join me."

His words broke the solemn silence.

When they were at his side, he said, "My dear friends and colleagues, what we witnessed this morning is nothing less than the fulfilment of the first phase of the Prophecy. I myself failed to recognise the importance of the spectacle presented this morning until this moment.

"We are joined today as testimony to mankind's role in furtherance of the Empyreal Paradigm. We are thus twice blessed. We have not only been chosen to participate in the divine ritual a divine message to mankind, one of universal love and compassion.

"The Sun star children are ours to love and cherish. We brought them into this chaotic plane of existence expressly for the purpose of enlisting their support in achieving our goal for mankind. We, especially me as their steward, are herewith charged with the responsibility to guide them to their destiny. Wherever they shall take us, we shall gladly follow."

He motioned toward Juan who had appeared next to Surya and the twins.

"These are my final words to mark this auspicious occasion, my friends. We should now hear another voice intimately connected with our mission from the inception."

As he watched Juan come forward to speak, Surya reflected upon General Smythe's outpouring of rapturous emotion as he greeted each infant. In all his years as the general's aide-de-camp, he never once witnessed him so moved by any situation or circumstance. He stared at the general's face and saw it had transformed into the visage of a Buddha. Tears of joy streamed down his otherwise solemn face.

"Ladies and gentlemen, the Divine Spirit of the Universe has indeed blessed us this morning. We, the First Apostles of the Empyreal Paradigm, are henceforth and forevermore charged with the responsibility to preserve and foster the sanctity of the spiritual union between Sun and Earth we witnessed this day. Accordingly, let it be written in the stars and in the bosom of Gaia that we commit our bodies and souls to the fulfilment of the First Directive."

He turned about the centre of the mound with his arms outstretched before him.

"To seal our resolve, I hereby imbue each and every one of you with the Power of the Warrior," he boomed.

All at once beams of silvery light flashed from his hands and penetrated the hearts of all those assembled. An instant later, the light rays vanished.

"We are herewith bound forever in this Celestial Cause. Let us now go bravely and resolutely forth from this sacred mound to carry out our destiny."

Chapter 11 - The Invincible, Invisible Pyramid

Kuala Lumpur, Malaysia, 18 March 2052

From his Oriental Winds Commodities House aerie on the one hundredth floor of the Petronas Tower One, George Smythe had just finished reviewing the progress to date of the plan for his official demise, when his appointment secretary, Major Surya Thappa, chimed in on the intercom to announce the arrival of his first appointment of the morning.

"Good morning, General. I trust you are well."

"I am fine, Major, and you? I trust all is under control this morning."

"I am well and ready for another productive day. Your first appointment, Lord Geoffrey Worthington, has arrived."

"Splendid. Send him in straight away"

Recent circumstances, both expected and unexpected, compelled him to arrange this meeting with Lord Worthington. Though he dreaded the prospect of discussing unpleasant business matters with his longtime friend and business associate, he arose from his desk to offer him a handshake and his trademark smile.

"It's so good to see you, Geoffrey."

"How was your trip from London? Care for a spot of tea? Do have a seat, please."

As General Smythe sat back down at his imposing mahogany desk, he gestured to Lord Worthington to take a seat in the chair opposite to his.

Lord Worthington took a few moments to marvel at how little the general had changed since the last time they met eight years ago. From all outward appearance, he could have then been mistaken for a sixty-year-old.

Worthington drank in the sight of him as an imminently powerful man of the world with few, if any, peers in the personal wealth domain. Furthermore, in the nearly sixty years since he first met him when they were cadets at Sandhurst, his physique had changed not one iota. More remarkable still, he noted, was the fact that the outward demeanour of his personality had stayed as constant as the troy ounce measure in all that period of time.

Smythe sensed Lord Worthington's underlying mental and emotional tension and apprehension almost as a palpable wave. He had managed such situations hundreds of times in the past. Typically, despite outward appearance to the contrary, the individual sitting at the other side of his desk exuded the nervous tension of an accused man awaiting an uncertain, capital crime court verdict. Sometimes, he thought, there was indeed a quality of mercy in an immediate execution for all parties involved, and this was surely one of those times, at least for himself as the executioner.

"The trip was just as I like it, General. Uneventful. Yes, I would care for a cup."

Lord Worthington sweated bullets under his Armani suit, not just from the apprehension of the outcome of this meeting, but also as a result of the security gauntlet he had experienced at the hands of the general's Ghurkha security staff.

A fashionable Malaysian beauty served tea to the taciturn executives.

The morning sunlight radiated through the massive plate glass windows, which lent a sense of warmth to the tableau replete with exquisite and priceless furniture, oriental rugs, and exotic works of art, not the least of which was the general's important collection of French Impressionist paintings.

General Smythe took a sip of the perfectly steeped and prepared Earl Grey tea, laced with slight a trace of lemon. He waved his free hand over a glass section set into the desktop. As the delicious liquid flowed to his appreciative palate, the entire length of the floor to ceiling windows facing toward the eastern sky instantly turned a dull shade of gray.

Worthington sensed the ambiance turn to doom as the sunlight flowing into the office was cut by half.

"Geoffrey, allow me to cut to the chase, if I may. As you know well, the plan, which you were assigned to execute with the utmost skill and urgency, was nearly botched in execution at several critical steps. As such, you, my most trusted and effective executive, failed to render optimal performance."

There was a tinge of disappointment in his voice that bore into the core of Worthington's normally confident ego. No one could ever make him feel as inadequate as the general just did with mere voice inflection.

"We shall now review the dreadful and nearly disastrous results. Firstly, you were assigned to negotiate the Initial Public Offering price with the lead underwriter for at least twenty-five pounds per share. Instead, Biodynamics sold for twenty pounds on the IPO. On the first day of public trading the stock soared to thirty-five pounds per share. These plain facts preface my expression of disappointment at your performance in this regard, Geoffrey."

He noticed Lord Worthington's complexion turning slightly reddish in colour as a sure sign of his slightly elevating blood pressure. Recalling that he typically reacted that way to stressful situations, his concern for his health temporarily abated. From experience, Worthington knew that that nonchalant statement actually equalled seething fury being directed at him by the general. Indeed, General Smythe had been right in his encrypted email message to him the night before as to the proper approach to the IPO negotiation.

"Fortunately for the firm, an alternate trading strategy compensated for your lack of judgment on this score."

Somewhat relieved, but understandably perplexed by that statement, Worthington was nonetheless keenly aware that a fortune, despite the general's incredulous downplay of the matter, worth billions of pounds vanished into the nether due to his failing to negotiate the optimal IPO price for the crown jewel of the OWCH's asset portfolio.

"Unless you would care to comment, let's put that experience behind us for good. What do you say to that proposal?"

That was tantamount to an invitation to a second round with a championship boxer. So far Worthington hadn't even lifted a glove to defend himself in this first round and his chin was already on the canvas. He thus, of course, begged off on offering any comment.

"No, General, I believe we both know the factors that led to the situation all too well. If you would not mind, I would very much like to proceed to other matters at hand."

He felt relieved by his wise submission to whatever the general had in store for him now.

"I would not mind at all Geoffrey. I have a busy schedule ahead of me today, as you do, I presume."

The general twisted slightly in his chair as maintained his eagle-eyed countenance on his prey.

He maintained a fondness for Lord Geoffrey despite his foibles as a businessman, even though he had few peers of his own age and experience. Moreover, by most standards, he had few peers in the ranks of the British noble gentry. A consummate orator and skilful politician, he served his country with distinction and effectiveness as both a member of Parliament and later as ambassador to India after serving in the British Army for fifteen years. As a husband and a father of two girls, he was celebrated as a role model for all the country's fathers. Outwardly, his armour bore no chinks.

Though privately he knew that his public persona was largely a figment of the public's imagination as promulgated by staid British press and public relation firms, all of which having been bought and paid for by OWCH through various guises. Over the subsequent years, after the campaign began, the firm realised exceptional returns on the wise investment as Lord Worthington covertly functioned to further its business interests and dealings.

Before Smythe first approached him with his employment proposition, he rightly assessed that he was the best candidate to act as the principal sub rosa, front man to promote his business interests given his position and prestige within British royal society. He also knew that the riches he promised to bestow upon him soon after he entered service of the firm would prevent the then eminent financial collapse of his flagging baronial estate.

In fact, by the time of his retirement from the British Army, Lord Worthington's estate teetered on the precipice of bankruptcy receivership due to fiscal impropriety committed by himself and his family members. He thus readily accepted the general's employment offer with gratitude. Years later, after the deal made him a fabulously rich man, he had numerous occasions to thank divine providence for bringing George Smythe back into his life.

Besides the proper discharge of assignments to promote the firm, all that he was expected to accomplish in return was never to associate himself, either privately or publicly, with either the general or OWCH. To that end, he had always performed flawlessly. Otherwise, his job performance had been as the general had expected all along...that is, sufficient to meet his performance requirements, but rather unremarkable, just like his educational success at Sandhurst and as a British Army officer.

His only real, but publicly undisclosed connection to the firm was via a directorship held for a time with a prestigious London-based investment banking firm. OWCH controlled the de facto majority interest in the firm through the combination of minor interests held by three privately held financial services firms owned anonymously by OWCH as offshore corporate entities. With well-established credentials in the capital formation field, he primarily functioned as a consultant to private companies planning to publicly issue company common stock for the first time.

He regularly represented his clientele as their representative in negotiating IPO terms. Although always a respected presence at these negotiations, his recognised acumen stemmed from his employer's skilful directions prior to meetings at negotiation tables with lead underwriters. However, in the case of the Biodynamics's IPO he had failed to properly execute the general's negotiation strategy. As a result, General Smythe sensed for the first time a sea change arising in Lord Worthington's capabilities that were fatal to his further employment in any capacity.

"Now, at long last, the final bit of business for us to consider."

He sighed before resuming, obviously as a sign that whatever it was he was going to say was weighty. Worthington inwardly flinched.

"Through the course of the years since you first began your association with OWCH, we have had sterling success as a result of your business dealings on behalf of the firm. To that end, a great debt of gratitude is due you, both in heartfelt appreciation and, more importantly, I rightly consider, in financial reward."

He waved his right hand over his desk, whereupon all the windows of the office again became crystal clear, allowing the brilliant and warm morning sun to stream forth into the entire length of the floor, and rendering an unobstructed panoramic view of the cloudless blue sky over Kuala Lumpur.

He verged on giddiness in anticipation of what the general would say next.

From his long experience though he knew that thorns often nestled close to the surface of any laurel wreath the general extended to both a friend and a foe alike. He again began to perspire profusely; he mopped his brow with the linen handkerchief he held in his left hand, trying to conceal his emotional and physical reaction the general's last words had upon him.

"For many years now I have been planning my retirement from the firm as the corporate leader. Though from the outset my role has in no small measure led to the achievement of the firm's stellar success, it has been both a labour of love and loathing. Nonetheless, OWCH has been my raison d'etre and consumed every ounce of my energy since I first became a partner with the firm twenty-five years ago. Since attaining the position of the firm's sole partner five years later, I have not had one regret for anything I have had to accomplish to establish OWCH as the premiere trading firm in the world, which has been no mean feat, considering that today we have few competitors, even amongst the multinational conglomerates, to match our scale and efficiency of operation as well as capital formation capability."

"Today, as you know, owing to our stealth and wealth, few of our competitors realise we've entered and captured their precious markets before it's too late."

His chest heaved with manifest pride.

Lord Worthington had never heard such a disjointed and emotional outpouring of selfcongratulatory rhetoric from the general. He at once felt all the more ill at ease as his superior's every move in life was precalculated for both optimal affect and effect.

"Yet, for as much as this gratifying experience has been worth to me personally, I must retire to devote my last energies to other interests. Prior to my official retirement, however, I am moved to pay homage to those individuals, such as yourself, whose tireless contributions over the years determined the stellar success of the firm. I shall not bore you with a recount of our relationship in that regard, but I shall say that I feel we were predestined to share what we have had to share until now from the time we met at Sandhurst. And for that, I am truly grateful my friend."

Lord Worthington visibly flinched like the recipient of a mild electrical shock in attempting to fathom the purpose of the general's commentary regarding his role within the firm.

Moreover, never before had the general come close to overtly expressing any sentiment of friendship toward him. Accordingly, he felt bewildered and special all at once, especially considering that no one in his life had such a beneficial influence on him as had George Smythe.

The general resumed: "The future success or failure of OWCH shall be determined by my successors after my official retirement next year. That goes without saying. As a result, our active participation in the affairs of the firm shall not be required henceforth. That is a painful and loathsome realisation for me as the curtain begins to close on the final act of my business career.

"From your perspective, however, as a major contributor to the firm's success, that realisation must come as a shock. But you deserve more than a handshake for a job well done in parting Geoffrey and more is what you shall receive. As part of your reward, and maybe the best part, one hundred million pounds sterling shall be deposited in a Swiss bank account registered in your name next week. I trust you deem that as a sufficient severance package."

His approach in asking for closure on the last deal Lord Worthington would ever negotiate on behalf of OWCH stunned his emotions. After a brief pause, Worthington dropped his chin and slowly shook his head in the affirmative. It was indeed a godsend, he thought, that his career with OWCH should end in this manner. Unbeknownst to the general, however, he had been planning to resign his unofficial position for the past several years. He dearly desired the opportunity to devote his time to his own avocational pursuits; namely, the further funding for the Lord Geoffrey Worthington Alzheimer's Research Foundation and starting work on his autobiography. A wave of jubilation swept over him like the first kiss from his love of his life, his wife of thirty-five years.

"Yes, the best part of the severance terms is perfectly amenable to me."

He could not consciously control the broad smile he instantly evinced.

"Very well then. Let's wrap up this meeting and send you on your way back to London.

"Further details of the severance shall be conveyed to you via the standard communication procedure."

"That would be fine with me. I would like to say that in all the years I have had the extraordinarily good fortune to know you, General, this represents the first time you have shared your thoughts with me concerning the firm and my role within. I must add that I too am proud of all that we have accomplished together in establishing the preeminence of OWCH."

"A job was well done by both of us."

He rose from his desk and extended his hand for a farewell handshake.

"We shall not meet again, Geoffrey, but my memory of you shall always remain dear to my heart. We have indeed experienced much together since we first met as Sandhurst cadets. And it has been an association I have always cherished and nurtured. Unfortunately, I must disassociate myself with my past and all my worldly affairs after my retirement. I assure you, however, that my association with you has been one of the highlights of my life."

At that hearing those words from the general, tears welled from Worthington's eyes. He never thought there would come a day when the commander would not be in some way connected with him. He supposed that this parting marked the end of that era. His heart wrenched at that realisation as though the one and only father he had ever really known had just breathed his last breath of life before him. Still, he sensed an ominous underpinning to the general's mysterious announcement that he was entering a period of seclusion. He thus feared for his safety in every respect but respected his decision to the ultimate degree.

Boldly reaching out to grasp the general's hand for a final handshake he presented his bravest face.

"I regret that we shall not have the occasion to meet again. Though I shall always treasure the memory of the association we enjoyed."

He released his hand from the general's grasp and promptly exited the office.

You will have better things to occupy your mind with, my dear, dear friend, Smythe thought, as the door closed behind him.

He had just pressed the down button on the lift's door when he heard Smythe's diminutive appointment secretary Surya hail him.

"Lord Worthington, please stop!"

Upon reaching him, he handed Lord Worthington his attaché case.

"Your Lordship, you left your attache case behind."

"Oh, how forgetful of me."

The obvious lapse of awareness obviously embarrassed him. Actually, his leaving behind his ancient leather attache case in the general's office was akin to his forgetting to don a suit to meet the sartorial requirement of a standard business day.

"Bon voyage, Your Lordship."

His congenial send-off served to lessen the awkwardness of the moment for them both.

"Thank you, Surya,"

In uttering those parting words, he stepped into the lift and out of General Smythe's world forever.

During the next month, Lord Worthington began to notice a marked and appreciable lessening in his ability to hold his attention on even the simplest of matters. His family, especially his wife and friends, took note of this uncharacteristic behaviour, as well. Three months later, following the diagnosis of Alzheimer's disease, he began receiving full-time nursing care at his London residence.

The affliction soon rendered him unable to devote any time toward his avocational pursuits other than an abortive attempt to start his autobiography. Fortunately, the family trust took over the management of his wealthy estate prior to his complete physical and mental decline. The trust insured his charitable foundation continued to receive ample funding for continued research toward the cure for the disease.

He died a year after he departed from General Smythe's office.

"In an ironic twist of fate for the champion of the Alzheimer's disease research, Lord Geoffrey Worthington succumbed to the illness yesterday," started the front-page obituary article published by a mainstay British tabloid the day following his death.

Chapter 12 - Requiem for an Unknown Soldier

Zermatt, Switzerland, 1 April 2052

On the day of General George Smythe's official demise, his eyes fluttered open at 6:00 a.m. The flood of early morning daylight streamed through the bedroom windows. After donning his slippers and robe, he strolled to the kitchen and poured himself a cup of tea. He carried the teacup and a freshly baked croissant to the living room. He gazed out at the Matterhorn that towered majestically and ominously above the chalet like a granite sentinel of impending doom. The cloudless blue sky surrounding the majestic mountain peak imparted a pristine ambiance to the environ that crystallised his resolve to fulfil the task at hand. From this day forth he would be a dead man to the world at large.

An hour later, the general entered the cabin of the ski mountaineering excursion helicopter with the Brünner brothers. General Smythe looked at both men as they strapped themselves into their seats.

"'Tis a splendid day to die, nais pas?"

The brothers simply shook their heads in assent.

Captain Reginald Saunders, gradually raised collective control lever to its maximum position.

The brothers broadly smiled and chuckled as they nodded their agreement with his starkly ironic statement as the helicopter fleetly lifted off the ground.

As the craft ascended high above him on its way up and around the steep granite slope of the Matterhorn, Surya waved his final farewell to the general.

"We shall soon meet again in your next life," he said to himself.

He watched the helicopter fade away into the distance.

As the crow flies, the trip to their final destination should have taken no more than thirty minutes under the worst flying conditions. Captain Saunders, however, chose to take the scenic route ostensibly to enjoy the sterling day. The breathtaking scenic beauty of the moment seldom presented itself to that extent in this part of the Alps at that time of the year. At any rate, appearing as any other ski mountaineering helicopter excursion masked the real purpose of their mission. The helicopter abruptly banked into a glacial valley.

"Taking the scenic route, are we, Captain?" Fritz moaned.

The effects of the previous night's partying with the locals and international glitterati clearly affected his tourism outlook.

"Having a whopping hangover, are we, Fritz?" Saunders immediately retorted.

His shrill laughter afterward made Fritz wince.

"It's all in the line of duty, mate. Trust me."

"Now, now, gentlemen. Reginald, the Brünner brothers are in charge of all matters pertaining to my personal security. As such, they are often called upon to sacrifice their physical well-being in order to discharge that responsibility."

"General, I don't doubt their resolve to competently fulfil their assignment. Though I think it's tragic that they are occasionally called to sacrifice so many of their brain cells in so doing."

The basic mutual sense of disapproval of the former RAF jet fighter pilot and the Brünner brothers was legendary, especially amongst themselves. No one knew the reason for the mostly innocuous case of animosity that existed between them, but everyone suspected it lay in a basic clash of strong and eccentric personalities. General Smythe realised long ago that his attempts to find grounds for mutual appeasement were futile. His resignation to modify their behaviour was based on the realisation that Saunders and the Brünner brothers would never mesh socially, as Saunders hailed from a privileged English aristocratic family background.

The brothers, on the other hand, traced their ancestry through a line of noble Swiss montagnards. Nevertheless, he knew beyond a shadow of a doubt that not far beneath the facade of contempt that existed between Saunders and the brothers, the men possessed the same qualities of loyalty and devotion to duty and honour that he respected and demanded most from his officers and soldiers. He also knew from his personal experience that they were truly cut from the same cloth at conception. Fritz interceded almost immediately after Saunders spoke those words.

"General, we suspect that the operation is compromised."

"How so?"

"In reconnoitreing the Zermatt nightlife last night, we noticed a group of young men of decidedly Chinese descent shadowing us as we went from one bar to another. They mostly travelled in pairs and on more than one occasion were awaiting us as we entered various pubs and discos. Finally, it became obvious to us that our running into the suspicious group was more than happenstance."

"Were they menacing in any way?"

"No. Quite the contrary. From all outward appearance, they were barhopping and having a good time amongst themselves and other patrons, including those of the feminine gender."

"Just like the two of you, I bet," Saunders said.

"Captain, please allow Fritz to continue uninterrupted."

"To continue uninterrupted by the privileged, who should be so bold, we didn't notice any of them following us. That observation coupled with the fact that their gregarious interaction with the rest of the patrons excluded us caused us to suspect their motives.

"We did learn from other patrons with whom the group had contact that they are members of the PRC Olympic team here training for the Haute Route ski mountaineering competition that commences next week."

"How many individuals would you say comprise the group?"

"Twelve."

"Were you able to capture their individual images via your retinal cameras?"

"We acquired images of each one of them. After establishing their identities we confirmed them as members of the PRC cross-country ski team through the International Olympic Committee database. They are who they say they are."

"Well, nevertheless, I think your suspicion about the group is well-founded," the general said. "As such, we must regard them as a potential threat and take appropriate precautionary measures."

In his own mind, viewing the Chinese athletes as a potential threat was tenable, especially considering the unlikelihood that their coach would permit them to carouse during training.

Knowing PRC Olympic training regimen as well as he did that likelihood was virtually nought.

"I for one fail to see how this potential threat has the capability of compromising our mission. I am the only one of us who knows our final destination in this section of the Alps.

"You, General, made certain of that when you devised the mission plan. Added to that is the fact that no one but the four of us and Surya knows the objective of our mission today.

"Furthermore, any attempt to ascertain our final destination is more than likely to fail as a result of our circuitous and scenic route there. And the copter was thoroughly scanned for electronic bugs before exiting the hangar this morning."

"Whatever, Saunders," Rolf interjected. "This situation was unanticipated and must be considered a potential threat to the success of our mission. Consequently, we must be on a heightened state of alert from this moment forward. There is simply no chance for us to scrub the mission at this point given the intricate apparatus in place to deal with the general's death after it's announced to the press."

"I concur with your assessment, Rolf. We cannot underestimate the potential the threat has to undermine our mission objective, both today and as planned for the more immediate future. That'll at least give us the opportunity to observe any new ski tracks and spoor in the fresh snow cover laid down last night."

The wily pilot crisscrossed the vicinity of the final destination several times before landing at the base of Dufourspitze, the crowning peak of the Monte Rosa massif. Since they observed nothing out of the ordinary, not even ski tracks, they agreed to land the helicopter there. Before landing, he made several low-level passes directly over the landing site.

"I must say, Captain, every once in a while, you do yourself proud. This is an excellent choice for a landing site. There are all sorts of overburdened snow ridges and escarpments around here. An absolutely perfect spot."

"Yes, nicely done Captain."

The general was pleased with the sincerity of Rolf's comment.

The helicopter touched down on a vast granite slab. They unloaded their equipment from the cargo bay and undercarriage netting. Afterward, the general and the brothers carried their ski mountaineering equipment and rucksacks to the edge of the granite slab. The snow field dotted with gray and black rock escarpment spread before them for as far as the eye could see.

"We know this particular landscape like the back of our hands, General. Just follow us closely," Rolf said.

He then locked the skis to his bindings.

"The success of the next part of the mission is Captain Saunders's responsibility to realise."

After strapping their rucksacks to their backs, they skied across a level section of snow that lay between them and a mildly sloping ridge that led down to the Gorner glacier. As they reached the ridge, the helicopter lifted off and headed back toward Zermatt. Or so it would have seemed to anyone else observing the helicopter's initial flight path. As soon as the aircraft left the ground,

Saunders engaged the tesla-wave mass detector designed capture and process mass composition data. In this instance, it penetrated and analysed the load characteristics of snow and ice masses along ridges and escarpments. After a few minutes of scanning the area, the detector discovered several potential sites on the HUD display situated in front of the pilot's seat. Saunders immediately overlaid the site images with the area map.

"Snowbird to Team Zeta. Come in Team Zeta."

"Team Zeta here, Snowbird," Rolf replied

"I am now transmitting potential sites for your picnic luncheon. Choose the one you'd most like to visit along your final destination route and advise me accordingly. Over and out."

The holographic readout of Saunders's site selections scrolled out in front of his sunglasses. Rolf studied the data for a few seconds.

"Come in, Snowbird."

"Snowbird here."

"Site C offers the best scenic vista today Snowbird. Please prepare luncheon for our arrival there at twelve hundred. Over and out."

"Roger, Team Zeta. Over and out."

The threesome set out for the site. They skied at a leisurely but steady pace, only stopping twice en route for refreshment. The cross-country ski adventure exhilarated each of them, especially since the success of their mission seemed assured.

They telemarked into a ravine leading down to a flat stretch of snow and ice on the Gorner glacier.

"We're close to the site, and luncheon, General," Fritz said.

"Good. My stomach is growling in anticipation. I'm famished."

As they reached the bottom of the ravine, Fritz saw a formation of rock ptarmigan flying in V formation toward them as he scanned the sky. That can't be, he thought, ptarmigans never fly in formation like that. He judged the formation contained twelve birds. He whistled softly. His brother looked back at him and nodded that he arrived at the same conclusion about the mysterious flock. He snowploughed to stop and signalled with his outstretched arms for the general to do the same.

Rolf stopped behind the general.

"Fritz, we must get the general to the site at once." The flock flew overhead. It vanished into the ravine from which they had just emerged.

"I'll follow you when I can," he whispered.

He removed his rucksack from his shoulders and dropped it on the snow. Opening the backpack, he withdrew the parts of what appeared to be an assault rifle. He then lifted his ski parka to reveal a nine-millimeter lewger and bowie knife.

"Now go!"

He began rifle assembly.

The men feverishly poled to gain speed and momentum on the flat stretch of the glacier before them.

Rolf saw the helicopter parked on the glacier not more than a kilometre away. He fully assembled the AK-103 assault rifle in a matter of seconds. After quietly snapping the magazine clip into the ammunition breech, he screwed a silencer of his own design onto the end of the rifle muzzle. He secured four other clips into his belt, one each at either side of his hip. Taking a deep breath, he slowly pulled back on the bolt to load the first round into the firing chamber. He then sidestepped his skis to the side of a large boulder to hide from the entrance of the ravine. As he lifted the rifle to his eye level, the sound of vicious canine snarls and yelps blasted through the entrance of the ravine.

At first, he couldn't believe his eyes. Running at full speed, a dozen golden-coloured wolves began to spill out of the ravine into the glacier floor. At nearly twice the size of normal wolves, they were exquisite beyond comprehension. Rolf visibly flinched as both the terror and majesty of the wolf pack immediately struck his mind.

As the pack thundered past him, the lead alpha male fiercely yipped what could only have been an order to his trailing soldiers. Straight away, two wolves at the back of the pack, already nearly twenty-five meters away from him, broke off and curved back toward the ravine entrance at breakneck speed.

Rolf knew his pungent human scent betrayed his presence behind the boulder.

Realising his only viable option was to stand and defend himself, he pulled the trigger of the assault rifle twice in rapid succession. The first round pierced the right eye of the wolf in front of the other one about twenty meters away from his position. The second round clipped off the wolf's left ear. The wounded wolf spun a backward cartwheel along the ice and snow as its forward momentum abruptly skidded to a halt.

He dropped the AK-103 and yanked the luger from the belt holster in a lightning-fast motion. As he pulled on the toggle to load the first round, the second wolf leapt at him from five meters away. The savage teeth exposed from its fully opened jaws appeared to glisten in anticipation of sinking into human flesh. Like before, Rolf took aim and shot two rounds. But this time, the bullets pierced each of the wolf's eyes. Rolf rolled away as the blinded wolf smashed headfirst into the boulder with a sickening thud. Rolling upright on his skis in the same evasive manoeuvre, he took aim and emptied the clip into the back of the animal's head in less than four seconds.

I recall dancing this same dance of death with the likes of you not too long ago, he thought, as he grabbed the second clip. He ejected the spent clip and drove the loaded fresh one into the gun handle in one quick motion. He glanced at the rapidly decaying carcass.

"That'll teach you not to mess with the Brünner brothers, shifter. Though someday I am going to discover where you creatures come from."

Having said that, he heard a deadly growl from where the first wolf fell. He glanced in the direction of the sound to see the wounded wolf standing erect not more than five meters away from him. Jaws fully agape with enormous teeth bared to the molars dripped with saliva and blood. Blood streamed from the horrid empty eye socket and grotesquely gnarled patch of flesh where the wolf's left ear once was.

"And someday you just may indeed earn that honour," said a voice that emanated from the wolf's open mouth.

The wolf then sat back on its haunches and wagged its tail. The animal's visage changed to one reflecting mirthful irony.

"Go ahead and do your best, brother Brünner. Before you do, though, let us speak of pigs with wings and other things."

Momentarily stunned, he collected his wits. The wicked creature, Rolf thought; you're attempting to delay me from assisting my comrades in the defence of your attack. He immediately aimed the gun at the wolf's head.

"Jolly good show. Let's keep this particular chitchat to ourselves why don't we? Until we meet again!"

Forthwith, Rolf emptied the second clip into its head.

Seconds later he heard the report of gunfire coming from the direction of the helicopter.

Saunders started the helicopter engine immediately after seeing the two figures poling furiously toward him. The eerie sight of a pack of wolves in hot pursuit of the pair momentarily dazed him. The animals were closing in on them fast. He felt certain they would overtake the hapless pair in no time at all.

As the helicopter in front of him lifted off the glacial surface, Fritz looked over his shoulder to glimpse General Smythe behind him. Though flagging a bit, he knew he possessed the endurance to sustain the pace until the helicopter arrived. Nevertheless, sensing the urgency to make a stand he snowploughed to a halt. The general followed suit.

"We must make a stand here."

He removed his rucksack from his shoulders and extracted the stock and barrel parts of an AK-103 assault rifle and the bowie knife. He quickly bent down and released the ski bindings. The general performed the same manoeuvre.

Within fifty meters of their position, the yelping wolf pack streaked toward them. They spread out as they approached to avoid the potentially lethal effect direct gunfire would have on the group if they were closer together.

Both men dropped to their knees and began assembling and loading their rifles. Before they could raise their weapons to fire, a flurry of gunshots rang out in front of them. Fritz knew that Rolf had removed the silencer from the weapon to increase its range and firepower. It was a dangerous and risky decision though since the gunfire could trigger an avalanche.

Three of the wolves dropped and skidded to a dead stop. Less than thirty meters away, the remaining seven wolves increased their pace as well as their separation from one another.

The men suddenly let loose a hail of gunfire at the beasts. Fritz killed three instantly; the general mortally wounded one.

As he swivelled his torso to take aim at the two wolves positioned at his left flank a mass of fur slammed into his body. The impact winded him and left him prostrated face down on the glacier. Physically stunned, he unsuccessfully attempted to throw off the massive weight that pinned him down. He managed to squirm in order to turn his head toward the position on his right that the general had held before the impact. The general was also prone with a huge wolf sitting on top of him.

He turned his head straight in front of him to glimpse the sight of a magnificent wolf heavily panting with a human-like smirk displayed on his canine countenance. The wolf sat down on the snow and wagged its tail.

"Well, isn't this is a rousing way to formally introduce ourselves to you, gentlemen?" the beast said.

The wolves atop the men let forth a short howl.

The general strained mightily to say, "Who are you?"

"My...my. That is the direct approach. And no exchange of polite pleasantries to mark this auspicious occasion, mind you. Never mind who we are."

The wolves on top of the men began to growl and bare their teeth. As they started to lunge at the fleshy necks of their captives, a bullet pierced the forehead of the one atop Fritz. At the same time, a flash of lightning pierced the forehead of the second wolf that pinned the general to the ice sheet. The bodies of both beings instantly disintegrated.

The lead wolf sat unperturbed.

As the being turned its head toward the general, he said, "All you should know at present is that we are here to test your capabilities. Having fully achieved that objective, I must fly now. We shall meet again. Oh, by the way, congratulations on your new career path, Sir General Geoffrey Smythe. Tah...tah."

The wolf instantly shape-shifted into Andean condor and flew away.

As the helicopter hovered over the bodies still prone on the ice sheet, Saunders saw Rolf two hundred meters away skiing frantically toward them. He couldn't believe what his eyes just saw.

"Snowbird to Team Zeta. Come in Team Zeta.

Fritz rolled over to face the sky. He gasped for air as he brought his right hand up to shield his eyes from the glare of the noonday sun.

Tapping the micro-radio installed in his right earlobe, he said, "Team Zeta here Snowbird. Land directly. There's been a change of plan.

"Land immediately."

The general and Fritz stood up and surveyed the area surrounding the pair. Save for a few bruises and minor facial lacerations, the pair survived the terrifying ordeal unscathed.

As he turned his gaze to the general, he concluded, he's not going to require our protection.

The front-page headline of the London Times newspaper gratified the general when he read it the next morning after he sat down for breakfast at Tallyamore. It read: "Swiss Avalanche Claims Life of Retired British RAF Commander."

The article began by reporting the essentials of the tragedy, such as the search and rescue team's failure to find the general's and his companions' bodies. They were presumed to lie dead at the bottom of the two-hundred-meter-high mass of snow, ice, and rock rubble produced by the avalanche. The rescue team leader stated that the bodies would probably not surface for at least hundreds of years. The helicopter pilot who reported to the Swiss Red Cross the failure of the group to turn up at a rendezvous point that was established to fly them back to Zermatt was unavailable for comment.

The article proceeded to relate a biographical sketch of the general's life, including his distinguished military career that led to him being awarded the GCMG, KBE, DSO honours. The article also mentioned that he pursued a successful business career in Kuala Lumpur following his retirement from military service in his early fifties.

Though still somewhat shaken from the events of the previous day, he congratulated himself for the accomplishment of a major milestone of his long-term plan. Nevertheless, he thought, this mysterious and otherworldly element of surprise that presented itself over the past month calls for a thorough review of many of its crucial aspects. Clearly, he could no longer presume the execution of the plan as unassailable. As such, he would rethink crucial elements forthwith.

Chapter 13 - Team Alpha

Boston, Massachusetts, 15 March 2052

Smythe Preparatory Academy called its final time-out with ten seconds left in the 2051- 2052 Massachusetts high school state championship game held at the Boston Sports Arena. A see-saw battle from the outset, Smythe trailed East Boston High by only one point, seventy-nine to seventy-eight, when the buzzer sounded to suspend play. The East Boston players immediately ran to their bench to huddle around their coach.

"Dad, Magnus is killing me. I simply can't guard him effectively," Coach Johnson's son said.

His chest heaved violently for air as though he had just run a marathon.

"There's no excuse for that Jack," Coach Johnson replied angrily. "We're not going to lose this game because you can't handle your man. Stay on him like glue."

He knew his words stung his son's sensitive nature. But, he thought, Jack must toughen up if he's to overcome that disability he shares with his mother.

"Can't we double-team him?" one of the other players implored.

He had to admit to the inadequacy of his coaching skills in this instance. There is no way, he thought, that we can double-team Magnus and prevail in this game. The open man would simply crush us if he allowed that to happen.

"No, stay in man-to-man coverage!"

He had to be emphatic about the efficacy of his strategy for the sake of team morale.

"We're not going to lose to this team in the final seconds like we did last year. Now get back into the game and win at all costs!"

The fact that Smythe Academy's two-year winning streak was achieved by only one point in each game lent a mystical quality to the team. Moreover, the Boston community regarded the elite prep school as a high school sport's phenomenon, especially considering the programme started only two seasons previously.

When the buzzer sounded to resume play, the entire Smythe Academy cheering section erupted with a standing ovation. The crowd of students and parents cheered, "Magnus, Magnus, Magnus . . ." as they clapped their hands in beat with the chant.

Intuitively, Coach Johnson knew destiny had chosen his team to lose the game. As both teams took their appointed positions on the court, he was inwardly resigned to that fate despite his outward appearance as a coach.

"Jack!" he shouted. "Don't let your man get past you. Stay between him and the basket!"

The rather severe outburst served to ease his frustration for a moment.

Jack looked at his father and opened his hands toward him as if to say "That's what I'm trying to do."

Coach Johnson glared at him and straightened his tie in response. He mopped his brow with a towel as Jack trotted over to Magnus's position on the court.

He looked at his assistant coach who sat next to him on the team bench.

"What did you find out?" he said.

"They rejected all the college basketball scholarships they were offered. I heard that Kentucky University coach Kaye was so flustered by the rejection en masse that he had a conniption on the spot. No one has ever seen that kind of behaviour from him before. They even told all the pro scouts they weren't interested in playing pro ball. Can you imagine that?"

"What else?"

"Now, this is the truly mysterious finding. Each and every one of them achieved the highest score possible on the SAT exam they took last year as sophomores. And guess what?"

"What?"

"They rejected all the unsolicited academic scholarships offers they subsequently received.

"The best universities in the world tried in vain to recruit them into prestigious academic and scientific programmes after their test score results were disseminated. They even told Harvard University to go fly a kite, in so many words for Christ's sake."

"They can't do that. It's un-American. Someone has to lead them to better themselves.

"What about their parents?"

"Now, that's where the trail ends. Officially, they're citizens of a godforsaken, tiny country located in South America. From my recollection, it's called Puramore. We can only surmise they reside there since no one, and I mean no one can trace their whereabouts from any public or private record available. And we've even had our spies search through the team members' matriculation and academic records maintained at Smythe to no avail."

"So Smythe players are all citizens of Puramore."

"You hit the nail on the proverbial head, Coach."

"Is there a university there?"

"Yes. But the Universidad de Puramore isn't widely known as a fully accredited academic institution of note. And it's only been in business for less than ten years.

"Well, keep checking. We must find a way to move them on to the next level and soon, or they'll ruin us. It's obvious they're toying with us at this level. Just think what would happen if the same players fielded a team in each of the major letter sports next year."

"I agree. That would be a disaster of catastrophic proportions for the high school coaching community."

Coach Johnson leaned back on the bench and looked directly at Magnus. The Smythe player stood at the other side of the court directly across from him. The boy possessed a magical quality he reflected that he had never seen anyone his age exhibit. He had to admit though that upon gazing closely into his eagle eyes, as he once had the occasion to do several years ago, he sensed a strange and otherworldly reflection back at him that rendered him hypnotised. He at once felt intimidated down to the core of his being, yet sublimely secure about his personal welfare.

His team mates shared the same characteristics, but Magnus's personal charisma outshone theirs by far. Added to that astounding quality, the six-foot-ten-inch-tall sixteen-year-old represented an incarnation of Michelangelo's David in every respect including the curly blond mane that flowed down to his chiselled muscular shoulders.

Johnson continued to study Magnus as he held the basketball aloft from his position at the half-court line, evincing his characteristic smile that always served to unnerve opponents.

He then reflected on Magnus's paltry seasonal point production compared to son Jack's point production that year. Jack maintained the state's leading rank throughout the season. However, Jack's other team mates seldom scored more than eight points per game.

Finally, Magnus zinged a pinpoint overhead pass to his centre Moses. From his position at the top of the key, the eight-foot-three-inch-tall Moses leapt straight up to snag the inbound pass at a height two feet above the level of the rim with his huge right hand. He instantly brought the ball to his chest and flared out his elbows before landing on the court with a resounding thud. The six-foot-ten-inch East Boston centre guarding him cowered and took a step back away from Moses's position on the court as he stood up straight and held the ball aloft high over his head.

The capacity crowd erupted into a deafening roar as the game clock started to count down the final ten seconds of the game. Pivoting on his right foot to the left of the key, Magnus placed a dart like bounce pass directly into the hands of seven-foot-tall power forward Sid Gautama. He had manoeuvered underneath the basket from the right corner of the court, leaving the East Boston player trailing him three steps behind. Essentially uncovered for the time it would have taken him to easily dunk the ball for the winning score with seven seconds left, Gautama instead kicked out the ball to his fellow forward, seven-foot-three-inch-tall Leonard Da Vinci stationed at the left corner. Da Vinci faked a three-point set shot that sent his opponent soaring upward for a block attempt. Instead, he slung a pass behind his back to his other guard, six-foot-eleven-inch-tall William Shakespeare, as the East Boston forward lofted above him, flailing his arms in recognition of his being duped into a fool's errand. Moses, who had moved his position to the just below the centre of the foul line, took a two-handed pass from Shakespeare and stood his ground.

After in-bounding the ball, he casually ambled over to the centre court circle and stood motionless. Jack guarded him with frenetic abandon, waving his hands and shuffling his feet in front of Magnus as though he had the basketball. Their eyes met for a moment. Jack's mind instantly transfixed as he stared into his pale blue eagle-like eyes, which were at once fierce and soothing to behold. His body froze.

In response, Magnus struck a David-like pose and glanced over to his bench to see Coach Patterson staring at the time clock with his characteristic baleful look. Magnus's own internal clock knew instinctively that only four seconds were left in the game. He fixed a wide and angelic grin on his face, shifted his gaze to Moses, and nodded his head once to signal a play. As he pivoted right in reaction to the signal to lead his man away from the centre of the lane, Magnus performed a three-hundred-sixty-degree pirouette, which surprised Jack and made him completely lose his balance.

Jack started to fall back on his heels as his opponent sidestepped him and bounded for the basket like a greyhound out of the starting gate. Completely prostrate on the floor, Jack looked to glimpse his team mates instantly being led to the periphery of the court by the Smythe players.

For an instant, a lane opened down the centre of the key like the parting of the Red Sea in fast motion. At the same time, with two seconds remaining, Magnus planted his left foot on top of the key line and shot up off the floor like a surface-to-air missile. Simultaneously, Moses finger rolled the ball he held aloft into the outstretched hands of the streaking projectile on target straight for the glass. Magnus shifted the payload in mid-air to his right hand to begin its direct delivery to the interior of the basket. The palmed ball travelled a complete overhead arc before exploding into the middle of the basketball hoop, ripping the net down and out of the rim, the moment before the buzzer sounded the game's conclusion.

Coach Patterson's mouth gaped in astonishment at the play's brilliant execution, one he had never seen his players execute before that evening. His eyes lolled in their sockets as he tried with all his might to affect Magnus's trademark smile in an effort to acknowledge the crowd's raucous jubilation at having witnessed one of the most remarkable moments of basketball play they had ever seen or were ever likely to see again.

On landing several feet behind the out of bounds line, Magnus fell to the floor and crumpled into a ball on his side with convulsive laughter. His team mates surrounded him and joined his macabre celebration. They heaved with laughter, occasionally pointing at Magnus as if to lay blame on him for perpetrating a devilish prank on the opponent.

Coach Johnson's mind transfixed in shock at his bench as he observed the unsettling display of childish emotion exhibited by the victorious Smythe team. He glanced over to his sobbing son who sat motionless on the court where

Magnus left him behind, totally disconsolate and vanquished to the core of his being. For the first time, he saw in his son's face the sign of superiority draining from him in the wake of the crushing defeat. Coach Johnson empathised with his son's experience but was certain that the effect on him would be temporary.

"Coach Johnson, where did those kids come from?" his assistant coach screamed over the din.

"I don't know, but someday I'm going to find out," the coach said under his breath. "They are not the sons of man."

He fought back the tears of sorrow for his team's loss and his as their coach.

"Thank God that they don't field a team in any other sport other than basketball!" the assistant coach shouted.

"They're killers!

Coach Johnson barely heard his assistant's last remark above the din. Its poignancy would haunt him for the rest of his life as the next morning he found Jack in his bedroom dead from an overdose of sleeping pills.

Later that day Smythe Academy officials announced the cessation of its basketball programme due to budgetary concerns.

Part II – Jupiter

It is easy to go down into Hell, day and night, the gates of dark Death stand wide open, but to retrace one's steps to the heavens—there's the rub, the task. - Virgil

Chapter 14 - The Sleeping Dragon Awakens

Beijing, People's Republic of China, 16 August 2051

Across the land, a nascent stirring of discontent amongst the masses sent tremors of foreboding through the PRC political establishment. Not since before the founding of the republic had the people been so aroused to overtly question the integrity of the political leadership at the grass roots of their communities all the way through to the elite bureaucracy in Beijing. After several decades of increasing prosperity and affluence enjoyed by the population at large, the economic tide had decidedly reversed five years ago. A period of harsh material deprivation began then, the magnitude and breadth of which few under the age of fifty had ever experienced in their lives.

The economic depression gave birth to a political incubus that gnawed away at the fundamental core of the social contract. The old guard, the Global Movement that led the country during the previous forty years, became increasingly under attack by one man and his heavy-handed political machine.

From total obscurity, he rose through the ranks of the PRC military establishment. Reportedly born in Xi'an to working-class parents of no particular distinction, People's Liberation Army Air Force General Huáng "Wingtip" Xinghua was a nationally celebrated military genius and hero. Twice decorated with the Star Medal for combat kills when serving as a fighter pilot in both the Taiwan Conflict of 2026 and the Russian War of 2039- 2040, he was a living legend amongst his comrades-in-arms as well as in the hearts and minds of the country's populace.

General Huáng acquired his moniker as a young man during his fighter pilot training. Over the years since then, he earned the people's respect as the country's premiere military leader. His friends and supporters idolised him as a living god; his enemies dreaded the mere mention of his name as their worst nightmare.

*   *   *

He had been plagued by horrific nightmares for as long as he could recall. His parents had long ago resigned themselves to the fact that their son's nocturnal shrieking episodes had no cure. All previous attempts by a long succession of psychologists and psychiatrists failed to diagnose and treat the bizarre sleeping disorder.

Finally, as a last-ditch effort, they presented him to a decrepit Chinese shaman on the advice of a superstitious old relative. After the shaman examined the boy, he advised them that "The dreams shall cease when he reaches eighteen years of age." He concluded that there was nothing that could be done to spare him from the malady until then. He more or less diagnosed the illness as sexual awakening trauma.

Before he reached eighteen years of age Huáng had grown accustomed to the nightly nightmares that formed in his mind during deep sleep. The dreams transported him to places in ancient China. It was as if he lived another past life in fast-forward motion as he slumbered in the present one. As he grew older, he began to sense who he was, or whoever it was who guided him through the succession of tableaus that over time told of the glorious life and death of a man from his birth to his death.

By the time he reached eight years of age, he knew beyond a shadow of a doubt the historic character who presented himself to him every night. Thereafter, he kept that realisation to himself primarily for fear that he would have been summarily institutionalised to an insane asylum should he ever disclose the actual nature of his dreams to the conventional world. Secondarily, the fierce admonishment issued to him by a decrepit old Chinese shaman who was the last to examine him for his malady frightened him to the core of his being. After the examination, the wizened and wicked-looking old man whispered a warning to him.

"Your life and immortal being depend upon your silence. Never speak to anyone again about the true nature of your dreams."

He attempted to respond, but the hideous old man simply put his index finger to the boy's lips before he could begin to utter a sound.

"You have been chosen to be his vessel, and only he knows his reasons for that selection. You will know the reasons well when you become him, or rather when he becomes you on the day of your eighteenth birthday. You should only know that out of the hundreds of millions of our countrymen who live today, he chose you as his instrument to fulfil his glorious destiny in the modern era.

"You should be silently proud of that glorious distinction to the marrow of your bones."

The old man sternly pointed the way out of the examination room.

"We shall watch your every move until the day of your apotheosis. I shall meet you again on that appointed day. You must continue with your life until then as though there is nothing exceptional about you."

And so it was. From that day forth, he lived a typical childhood. He bloodied his nose in fights with classmates and neighbours, he struggled mightily to attain a high grades in his studies, he fell in and out of love with the young girls, and he maintained a healthy and respectful relationship with his community at large, his parents in particular. The terror of his nocturnal dreams though became less and less burdensome on his psyche as he grew older, since he had adapted to the role he knew that he had been chosen to play as an adult.

As he approached his eighteenth birthday, he was steeled for the worst that life could throw in his path. The bloody horror of the carnage and wicked political intrigue presented to him in his dream state made him certain of that. On the other hand, the incubus experience also rendered him exceptionally well prepared to succeed in conquering any obstacle in his way. But for all of that grotesque vitriol of epic proportions that he witnessed in his earlier years, the beauty of the flower of ancient China that sprung forth into his psyche as a result often stirred him to weep uncontrollably during his dream state.

Some nights he sobbed uncontrollably at witnessing the glory of that bygone era, one that changed all men of China forever. His love for his country was unbounded and unassailable as a consequence. He was resolute that, without hesitation, he would sacrifice his body and soul for the good of his country. He spent the day before his eighteenth birthday in a state of delirium, as he anticipated the event the old shaman had foretold would occur the next day. Nevertheless, his last thoughts before drifting to sleep that night were of the sweet innocence of his childhood and adolescence. He instinctively knew, however, that he would never deign to recall his youth again after he awoke from his slumber the next morning, or from whatever fate awaited him.

The shaman appeared at his bedside just after the stroke of midnight. He said, "Awaken My Lord." His eyes opened. The light of the full moon that penetrated his bedroom revealed the outline of the shaman he had met ten years earlier.

"Don your street clothing. I shall meet you at the glade located one kilometre north of the emperor's burial mound. You know it well, as you and your friends often played there when you were children," he whispered. "Do not tarry for a moment or all will be lost."

The boy immediately dressed and exited the house through the back door. The full moon on that balmy summer evening richly illuminated the landscape as he drove his parents' ancient car toward his destination. The intoxicating smells of the surrounding countryside reminded him of his early childhood as he left the city proper. He seldom had the time to visit the rural areas around Xi'an after he became a teenager. Yet, he fondly remembered playing at that glade located near the emperor's burial mound as a child. It was one of the few places in and around Xi'an to which he felt a mystical spiritual connection. Also, he felt an almost magnetic attraction to the locale for as long as he could remember.

After parking the car on a country road, he walked through the forest to the glade for the first time in many years. On stepping onto the glade, an upwelling of his spiritual affinity for the hallowed place momentarily overwhelmed him.

A shadowy apparition stood directly in the middle of the clearing.

"Come to me," a soft voice bade from the shadows.

Upon his approaching within a few meters of the apparition, the moonlight suddenly reflected off the form to reveal the old shaman holding a steel torch. He visibly flinched at seeing the decrepit and seedy sorcerer full on for the first time in ten years.

"Follow me.".

He proceeded toward a rock outcropping located at the southernmost boundary of the glade.

The boy followed him.

The sorcerer stopped in front of the large boulder and reached into his tattered and ancient cape with his left hand. After extracting something from within, he held his hand before him and opened it to reveal a magnificently faceted diamond about the size and shape of a hen's egg. For a few seconds, moonlight that penetrated the diamond began to coalesce and refract into an energy sphere inside. The huge boulder instantly vanished when hit by a laser beam burst that shot from the diamond.

In the area where the vanished boulder had once played as a child, the boy saw a huge gaping hole.

"You will need this".

He handed the lit torch to the boy.

"Make sure you put the strap around your wrist."

The boy took the torch from the shaman and secured the end strap around his left wrist. He then cautiously stepped toward the edge of the hole.

"Careful, lad. I haven't yet prepared you for your descent.".

He then shouted down the chasm.

"Oh, Glorious One, take my lord into your bosom as before."

He then looked straight into the boy's face.

"Hurry, we have no time to lose. You must jump into the shaft now!"

Before he could react the old man shoved him just enough so that he would fail to recover his balance.

He screamed like a banshee as his feet lost purchase from the ground and his twisting body entered the black hole. Gravity instantly began to hurl him toward the abyss below. A few seconds later a white light tenderly enveloped his body; as it did, his descent down the shaft slowed appreciably. Soon he descended as gracefully as a goose down feather on a windless summer day. Clutching the torch to his breast, he managed to manoeuvre his body so that he could look straight up at the shaft's opening above.

"I will meet you when you reach the bottom," the shaman yelled. "Fear not, brave boy, your time is at hand!"

A burst of laser light instantly shot past his head as the shaman uttered the last word. Immediately afterward the opening above closed. After a few minutes, he reached the bottom of the shaft.

As soon as his feet touched the ground, he began to explore his surroundings. He passed the torchlight all around the circumference of the perfectly hemispherical cavern. He thought that he was looking from the inside of a one-hundred-meter-wide black marble as the interior of the hemisphere was absolutely smooth and flawless.

The shaman called out from the pitch-black void, "I'm over here."

He promptly pointed the torch beam in the direction of the voice. The beam caught the old man square in the face; he quickly brought up his hands to cover his eyes.

"Yeow! Turn off that infernal device!"

The walls and ceiling of the cavern started to glow. Moments afterward, the incandescence fully illuminated the interior of the cavern.

The old man took a few moments to thoroughly examine the boy. He stood at the other side of the cavern opposite the shaft.

He suddenly shouted at the top of his lungs, "Come to me quickly!"

His eyes seemed to be bulging out their sockets.

"Run fast! Don't look behind you!" he screamed.

The boy immediately dashed toward the shaman without looking behind. The shaman got to his knees and put his forehead on the ground. The boy reached him in a few seconds.

"Prostrate yourself beside me and don't say a word. Close your eyes and cover them with your hands as tightly as you can."

The boy's heartbeat raced at full throttle when his forehead touched the warm floor. Abject fear gripped his mind.

"I warn you not to move an eyelid. Close your eyes as tightly as you can."

Suddenly, a burst of light of such intensity occurred that the boy saw the outline of his hand bones covering his eyes.

"So, Hú Li, you have returned at the appointed hour," a deep bass voice bellowed a split second later.

The words balefully echoed off the cavern walls.

"Yes, I have returned as you instructed, My Lord and Master."

A waft of divinely scented air with an aroma of lotus blossoms coming from the direction of the voice passed over them.

"That's a rhetorical statement, my little fox."

The voice loudly yawned.

"I imagine the world and humanity have changed dramatically since I fell asleep. Is that correct?"

"Much more than even my prodigious imagination would ever have expected when you did take your leave of this world the last time, My Lord and Master."

"Indeed. Well, as I have said many, many times before in the past, the more things change, the more they remain the same," the voice said.

The entity let forth a wicked chuckle.

"Now, let me see what his descendants have produced in over two millennia. Ask the boy to stand."

The shaman whispered, "Stand but do not open your eyes."

He got to his knees and slowly stood erect. His mind reeled with fear, but he managed to keep a stoic face.

A few moments of silence ensued.

"Be calm, my son," the voice said. "I command you to open your eyes and gaze upon me. Give yourself some time to collect your wits before you do, though. You should take solace in the knowledge that you have passed all our tests and are thus properly prepared to pass on to your destiny. Relish in that accomplishment as well as the portent of your glory in the future."

"Collect your thoughts. What you are about to see few mortals have seen in the history of mankind. You are about to gaze upon Huánglong in the immortal flesh, as it were."

His brain leisurely reassembled itself from the morass of conflicting emotions he experienced during the past few hours. Feeling sufficiently braced for this next one, the boy opened his eyes. He gasped.

Suspended in a black void of space filled with stars was the most beautiful and terrifying sight he had ever seen...a magnificent five-clawed golden dragon. Flanked on either side of him crouched two green-and-red four-clawed dragons of half his physical stature. Sporting bright red whiskers and red-tipped tail, his narrow head from the bottom of the chin to the end of the horns was at least ten meters in length.

The dragon's tail slowly and rhythmically swayed from one side to the other as the boy surveyed the creature. After taking in the length and breadth of the macabrely splendiferous being, he stared into its eyes, which appeared to be made of jade, save for a black catlike slit that ran across the almost vertical diameter of each one. The dragon held a shiny black vase in his front talons. The teardrop-shaped vase was a half of a meter tall and an eighth of a meter wide at its centre.

The boy turned completely around to see the cavern had become a planetarium replete with the night's starry sky. He almost swooned.

"Keep your balance, My Lord, and don't look down."

He immediately did so anyway; his knees buckled at the sight of stars below him. He was suspended in black starlit space. Before he could react any further, invisible arms grappled around him and held him tight.

"I told you not to look down, didn't I? You must now be the bravest you have ever been if you are to survive this last test."

The boy instantly regained his composure and stood erect in the sparkling ether that surrounded him. As he did, the invisible arms gently released him.

"Magnificent and a bit scary, aren't I?" the dragon stated.

He smiled broadly and placed the vase before him.

"The vase contains the spirit of the man you are chosen to succeed as my warrior ambassador in the world above. Come, approach it."

The boy stepped forward toward the vase. Making his way across the starry void that separated himself from the vase, he stopped within a meter of it. On closer inspection, he saw that the vase was exquisitely flawless in every respect. Jet-black lacquer sealed the opening.

"The vase was fired in our kiln located in a galaxy not too far away from here."

His scaly golden chest heaved with manifest pride.

"We don't produce many of them, but the ones we do fashion are gems of our creation."

The shaman stood next to him.

Hú Li gulped.

"Shall we start the ritual now?"

He noticed the boy was undergoing an excruciating amount of both mental and emotional stress. His body wobbled perceptively. The shaman was sure he was about to pass out.

"Why yes, of course, Hú Li," the dragon wryly replied. "Please hand the golden hammer and awl to my son."

The old man drew out a small hammer and awl out from under his cape. After handing him the tools, he faced the dragon and bowed from his waist.

"We are at the crossroads of mankind's history, my son. You and you alone shall ultimately determine which path mankind will take...the glorious one leading to our pre-eminence and predominance worldwide. At the end of our journey, no man or a woman shall live in your world without paying you a tribute to your glory as the ruler of the Earth."

The boy sensed that he was going to faint. Tears welled in his eyes.

"Be brave, My Lord. You have survived and succeeded as no man has ever before. Don't waver, for you are about to take your place as the absolute ruler of China and the rest of the world."

The golden dragon stared into the boy's eyes.

"Take the hammer in your right hand, the awl in your left hand and kneel before the vase."

The boy took the golden relics in his hands as instructed and warily knelt before the vase.

"Now place the tip of the awl over the seal and repeat after me."

"I am the Golden Hammer of divine will."

"I am the Golden Hammer of divine will."

"I raise this Golden Hammer held in my mortal hand."

"I raise this Golden Hammer held in my mortal hand."

"I bring it down to smash the seal of my Immortality."

"I bring it down to smash the seal of my Immortality."

The dragon did a double take at the sight of the boy wielding the hammer high over his head.

"Go ahead . . . Smash the seal, my son," he hissed.

The shaman took two steps back, covered his eyes and whimpered.

The boy, whose face was covered with a glistening mixture of tears and perspiration, drove the head of the hammer onto the head of the awl with all his might. The lacquer seal shattered upon impact with the sharp tip of the awl.

At once, a golden fog spilled out the opening and down the exterior of the vase. It snaked its way to the kneeling boy. He screamed as the fog climbed up and around his trembling body.

The dragon loudly snorted with approval.

He exclaimed gleefully, "Good, good, good."

Once the fog surrounded every inch of the boy, it permeated his body in a split second. The boy violently convulsed and coiled into a ball. He then let forth a spine-tingling scream of terror that made the shaman flinch.

Huánglong wickedly chortled.

For an instant, every nerve ending of his body exploded with pain. His back arched, and his arms and legs pounded the invisible ground. A few moments later an orgasmic sensation of intense pleasure began. At the climax, his back arched again as his body and soul melded with that of another. He screamed for the second time, but this one was of pure and unabated ecstasy. Seconds later he opened his eyes, took a deep breath, sat upright, and smiled. The frightened boy had transformed into a supremely confident young man. He stood erect and stared into the magnificent beast's eyes as his son.

"Yes, arise and greet the new glorious era of the land of Chin, Huángdì," the dragon said joyously. "Take the vase with you as a memento of your apotheosis."

"Ah-hem," the shaman stammered timidly.

"Ah...yes, my dear little fox.".

There was a tinge of irritability in his voice.

"I haven't forgotten my promise to you."

He drew his head back and then violently forward. A stream of golden flames shot out his mouth toward the hapless shaman.

In a flash, the shaman was engulfed by the golden flames. Ever so slowly the flare transformed his body. After a few minutes passed, the blaze gradually disappeared, leaving an exceptionally tall, handsome, and well-dressed young man standing at the very spot where the hideous and decrepit shaman once stood.

"You have redeemed yourself to my divine satisfaction, Hú Li.".

His red whiskers quivered gleefully at the accomplishment.

"Never again give me a reason to curtail your immortality for over two millennia."

The young shaman bowed.

"I shall not give you that cause ever again, My Supreme Lord and Master."

The dragon snorted. Forthwith Huánglong and his companions departed with a flash of blinding light.

At that moment, the starry tableau vanished and the cavern returned to its original dark state.

"Let us depart immediately. This is not a place for mere human immortals to tarry for long, My Lord. Here's your apotheosis memento."

He handed the vase to Huángdì. Thereafter their bodies transformed into two midget sparks of light that shot through the top of the cavern and up the shaft.

The shaman and the young man bade each other farewell right after they settled down on the glade. They tacitly understood that they would meet again in the not-too-far distant future.

Later that morning, the future warrior lord's parents perished as a result of the neighbourhood conflagration that engulfed and destroyed their house just before dawn. That afternoon he enlisted in the PRC Army as a basic private.

* * *

For ten years Wingtip held the PRC's highest military bureaucracy position as chairman of the Central Military Commission. A staunch opponent of the Globalisation Movement for the past two and a half decades, he nevertheless managed to maintain the top ranking position in the military establishment for several decades. That was not to say that he did not have his political skirmishes, both bloodless and bloody, with high-ranking political governance in Beijing. Though never bloodied himself, political bloodletting was his way of exorcising China's ills as he saw fit.

Around the fifth year of his military rule, Wingtip and his right wing followers formed the clandestine KWO Society. Over the span of the ensuing two and a half decades, KWO successfully recruited tens of thousands of new members from across the country. The society began to make inroads toward gaining political control of the country around the tenth year of its advent. As the public began to riot in the streets in protest of the economic depression, the Central Committee turned to Wingtip for salvation.

He immediately proposed that the Central Committee that declaration of martial law represented the way to quell the rioting and other chaos that had erupted throughout the country. That was a fatal decision that few at the highest ranks of government would survive.

Upon receiving the news that the Central Committee agreed with his proposal the following day, Wingtip stood up from his lotus wood desk and walked to the glass display case stationed at the other side of his office. The glass display case contained dozens of ancient pre-dynastic and dynastic porcelain vases, figurines, and other rare pieces of Chinese ceramic art. He took hold of a relatively unremarkable black vase and brought it to his chest. The spirit of the vase was at times comforting and supportive; at other times it was a maelstrom of malevolence.

Today, the vase's spirit purred like a cat. Still holding the vase to his chest, he walked over to the large pane glass window that overlooked Tiananmen Square from his office located on the twenty-fifth floor of the Central Military Commission Building. Peering down at the nearly vacant plaza, he observed a large flock of pigeons. As an inscrutable grin formed on Wingtip's face, the flock sprang up off the square and took flight. The black mass first flew out away from him but then abruptly banked toward his office as it gained altitude. In a matter of seconds, the formation flew straight and level directly at him. Within fifty meters of contact with the building, the formation abruptly split apart like a roman candle burst, sending the dispersed pigeons to omnidirectional points across the sky.

"Yes, my friends, soar across the face of the country and spread the word of Wingtip's victory."

That evening, he addressed the country via a nationwide television broadcast from the People's Auditorium. PRC and worldwide media correspondents, as well as high-ranking government officials, packed the hall to overflowing capacity.

Taking his position behind the speaker's podium he blinked when the red light on the inside panel of the podium turned yellow to indicate the start of the live broadcast in five seconds. Glancing around the auditorium, he noticed a number of familiar faces, most notably that of Premier Xu's. The old politician's countenance appeared as a stone mask, of which the only somewhat animated part were two beady eyes that bored in on him like black daggers. As the yellow light went green, he cleared his throat and began to speak.

"Comrades, there are times, perhaps such as those that we live in today, when all efforts to restrain emotional zeal directed toward the cause of circumstances beyond one's control begin and end in a failure. As with any situation of this nature, the beginning is a fever pitched struggle between two mighty dragons in an arena in which both are righteous in their own heart and spirit.

"Soon, the violent physical and emotional outpouring of vehemence bloodies both combatants to the brink of destruction. The manifestation of the violence in this vein is akin to throwing a lighted match into dry tinder lying underneath a tall stand of bamboo in late summer. As expected, the resulting conflagration threatens to consume the stand of bamboo if not brought under control by an external force of nature, such as a divinely sent rainstorm. If left unchecked, the fire created by the lighted match, however, is the agent that destroys the bamboo until it too is destroyed by the lack of bamboo.

"Today, we are presented with a situation that calls for the intercession of a third party to mediate a rational and peaceful resolution of the social upheaval currently threatening to destroy the stability of the entire nation," he solemnly declared.

He paused for a few seconds to allow the audience to contemplate the possible portent of his words.

"To that end, I hereby declare that from this day forth martial law is to be in effect throughout the entire country. Said state of military administration of civil affairs will remain until such a time that the Military Council deems there is clear and sustained evidence of the cessation of chaos and rioting that has egregiously disrupted our nation's internal security and productivity.

"Following this announcement, a detailed description of the details of martial law will be related to media for immediate dissemination to the people.

"I implore you to take every opportunity to comprehend and abide by the strict rules of social conduct to which every citizen in the country will be expected to adhere. Failure to do so, even when the actual commitment of an offence against a rule is questionable, will result in the summary execution of the prescribed penalty for the offence.

"As with all distressing news, comrades, there is a silver lining in my ominous dark cloud.

"The factors that wrought the social dilemma that we as a people face today are numerous.

"Yet, as considered in the totality, one factor stands out above and beyond all the rest as the prime reason for the deterioration of our economic welfare. Obviously, I am referring to the degeneration of the prime cause of the boon to our social welfare for the past two and a half decades.

"As you know, the Globalisation Movement served to open our borders to trade and commerce on an unprecedented scale. Not since the Golden Horde invaded the country has China witnessed such a pervasive foreign influence upon every aspect of our culture. However, unlike the occupation of the Mongols then, the effects of the policies of the Globalisation Movement brought prosperity to China to a level that few of the founders of the PRC would ever have thought possible. Although the initial thrust of the campaign has failed us in today's setting, I believe the country can still benefit from a few of the tenets of the GM charter,"

He looked down into the audience where Premier Xu sat. Instead of a stone mask countenance, the face of the man who held the highest political position in the PRC was alive with tics, his beady black eyes lurched from side to side as though searching for the best escape route from the auditorium.

"We must, however, reconsider the validity of the role of past GM economic policies in light of the rather stark and bleak realities of our current state of affairs. To that end, I have taken the liberty to form a review panel, which will be named the Glorious Social Reform Committee, for the purpose of devising a new scheme for public policy. Over the course of the next few weeks, a comprehensive description of the constituency of the panel as well as its basic charter will be disseminated to you through the media. I have the utmost confidence that the People's Republic of China will benefit greatly for decades to come from the new policies and laws that will result from the efforts of the Glorious Social Reform Committee.

"In closing, I wish to assure you, as well as our allies abroad, that we will endure this period of transition and emerge as a nation evermore potent and resolute than at any time in our history."

To President Xu Jian, Wingtip's speech to the nation marked an end of an epoch. He, a child of the Communist state, almost from its inception, had just witnessed the unthinkable; the unspeakable death of Marxist Socialism in China. He felt certain of that to the marrow of his old bones.

Afterward, he sat alone in his fashionable high-rise apartment, mulling over his part in failing to thwart Wingtip's ascension to political power. As tears came to his eyes, he looked out of his living room window and saw the sight of the sun setting on the horizon.

At the moment as the sun slipped away and the night sky began to seize the world around him, a large raven landed on the balcony railing right in front of the ancient Communist's view. He was so startled by the sudden appearance of the bird that he jolted backward in his chair. The bird cocked its head to one side in response to Xu's startled reaction to his presence and then stared directly into his eyes. As their gaze at each other transfixed, the outline of the raven began to metamorphose, at least so it seemed in the old man's mind.

All of a sudden he grasped his chest at the excruciating pain resulting from the collapse of the paper-thin walls of his weak heart. Dropping his gaze from the raven to the oriental carpet beneath him, he exhaled his last breath of life.

Chapter 15 - Spring Break

LAB, Puramore, 22 April 2054

Banking seemingly right over the top of Tungahora Volcano, the immense cargo jet began its final approach. Even from afar, the roar of the jet engines broke the serenity of Glenamore as the nose of the massive aircraft started pointing directly into its heart. As seen miles away from the valley floor at the time, what could have been mistaken for a flock of birds spontaneously took flight from the side of the aircraft, appearing as fast diving tiny dots at first, then as a group of condors lazily soaring on thermal drafts in the late-afternoon cloudless Andean sky.

In the west, the sun was close to setting for the day, causing the pastel shades of dusk to settle in the sky and on the steep mountain walls of the vale. What previously appeared as a group of condors drifted over the northern mountainous cleft that marked the natural entrance of Glenamore. As they glided down into and through the length of the vale, the outlines of the mysterious aves began to take definition in the twilight. The twelve glide parachutists touched down on earth without a sound. They sprinted homeward in high spirits.

Night had fallen over the valley when Team Alpha approached the entrance to LAB after a ten-kilometre run. They had not broken their stride one bit from the time they landed until their arrival at the entrance. The Ghurkha security guard detachment stationed around the entryway solemnly saluted the tall figures as they jogged over the entryway ramp.

"Good evening, gentlemen," Magnus said.

"Good evening to you all. Welcome home," the security guard detachment commander replied as they passed through the checkpoint.

He had known the Chosen Ones, as he referred to them in private, since the time they were toddlers.

"It's good to be home, Matrika," Magnus said in passing.

The group halted to set down their parachute equipment and then continued on their way toward the LAB monorail station.

As they were about to enter a monorail car, Surya Thappa walked out from a side entrance not more than ten meters away.

"Stop!" he commanded.

He wore a solemn scowl on his face.

The troop instantly stood at attention. Magnus smiled at Surya and chuckled as did his siblings.

"Your father wishes to have a word with all of you at once. Please be so kind as to visit him in the LAB auditorium straight away."

Surya walked through them and entered the lead monorail car first. The group followed him.

As the car accelerated forward, Surya broke the silence.

"There is no cause for alarm. As always, we are pleased to have you home. Your father just wants to have a word or two with you regarding your future."

A look of relief crossed their faces as they chatted with one another, their interest piqued at the mystery of whatever it was their father had in store for them.

"Surya."

"Yes, Magnus?"

"We are glad to be reunited with our family again. Although our time in America during the past three years was stimulating, our hearts were never far from Glenamore."

"How is father faring?"

"As you will soon see yourself, he is every bit as hale and hearty as he was when you last saw him. He is preoccupied, however, with the recent developments in China. His worse fear is that now that KWO has finally usurped total control over the country, severe retaliatory measures will be levied against Wingtip's foes. As you know, your father has many close friends in China who are Wingtip's mortal enemies."

"We are aware of the political situation in China. Is there anything that can be done to thwart KWO's retaliatory initiatives against the Globalisation Party leaders and their followers?" asked a long-legged black youth.

He was sitting in the seat opposite to Surya on the opposite side of the monorail car. A broad, friendly smile crossed his face as Surya turned his head to address him.

"Insofar as I am concerned, only time will divulge the answer to that question Benjamin. I can say, though, that your father is working diligently to keep abreast of the situation and provide whatever assistance he can render to ameliorate Wingtip's persecution of GM and its constituency. SITA is a powerful tool to that end, but even it has its limitations.

"KWO is so inexorably entrenched as the wielder of governmental control that only an overpowering invasion of the country might serve to topple it from power.

However, the cost to countless human lives would make that a wholly impractical alternative."

He checked his watch as the tramcar pulled to a halt.

"We must be off to the auditorium at once."

Upon entering the LAB auditorium, the youths took seats stationed around the edge of the circular stage. Several minutes later the houselights began to dim and the platform started to slowly revolve. At the middle of the platform, a circular section, two meters in diameter, slid away and the top of a silver-haired head rose through the opening. Within seconds the full length of General Smythe stood at the centre of the platform. A jubilant smile came to his face as the stage lights concentrated on him.

Almost concurrently, the evening vista from the middle of the valley was portrayed on the interior of the dome, including the clear night sky above and Tungahora Volcano in the distance.

He slowly turned to silently acknowledge each of his children.

"Good evening and welcome, my children," he said as he completed his turn. "I must say that there is truly no greater gift that you could bestow upon us than your return home to Glenamore and the LAB. I trust you had a pleasant flight home from Tokyo."

"We had an exceptional experience travelling the world together for almost the past two years Father," Magnus replied. "Our two-month stay in Tokyo proved especially rewarding as Sensei Takeshita awarded each of us with fourth-degree Tae Kwan Do black belts after the conclusion of our second week of training. Though we feel certain that he would not care to have us return to the dojo anytime soon, especially since his other acolytes were less than competitive with our technique.

"As to the flight, well, travelling in a fully loaded cargo jet is never comfortable, but we were happy to have the opportunity to return home via the direct route from Tokyo."

General Smythe beamed at Magnus. He then cleared his throat as to signal to everyone that he was preparing to talk about serious matters.

"As I look around at each of you, I am struck with the unambiguous and singular impression that you have learned and experienced much whilst away for the past three years. I see it in your faces and in the way in which you carry yourselves. You are learning about the practical world at large through your own personal experience in a way that neither SITA nor I could ever fully convey to you in our own words.

"On that note, I am interested to know how your tutelage with Juan is progressing. Would any of you care to offer me an assessment in that regard?"

Sid Gautama stood up from his seat.

"Father, I must say that Juan's tutelage as to Earth's spirit world enlightens whenever he appears to teach us. I think I can speak for all of us by saying that he has imparted a wealth of knowledge and insight about the shamanistic practice to us. Personally, I am awed by his insight and the range of spiritual knowledge on every level."

"Thank you, Sid. As you all well know, Juan is a pre-eminent fount of knowledge as both a shaman and physician. Furthermore, your understanding and later employment of Juan's teachings to the fullest extent may be the key to our success at this level in the future. And I don't need to remind you the key role Juan has played in our lives from the day I first met him when I was a young officer."

He looked around the stage at each of his children for any indication of dissent with respect to his last words. He knew that of all their studies, Juan's teachings were the least they cared for, principally because putting the subject matter to practical use was an alienating experience for them. He didn't understand the reason for that kind of revulsion, but he nevertheless knew Juan would succeed with them in the end.

"Today, yet another learning opportunity is presented to you. Namely, the Puramore government has selected you to represent the country in the International Basketball League. What do you think of that honour?"

He looked around the stage and observed patently deadpan expression on their faces.

"Oh, come on now children. That isn't so disappointing. Is it?

Magnus responded, "Father, it is indeed an honour and a privilege to have been selected to represent the country's basketball programme. However, we were rather hoping to devote our full time energies toward our research projects for at least the next four years."

He rubbed his hands together in a show of overt contemplation of his response to the petty insurrection.

"Your direct involvement on your research projects can be deferred, indefinitely.

"You may instead guide the LAB scientific staff to continue your projects when you are engaged in more important matters, such as competing as a team in the International Basketball League."

"But, Father, the scientists here are inadequate," Leonard protested. "It will take years for them to accomplish, even with our guidance, what we could accomplish in a matter of months. Besides, we don't much care for basketball competition, particularly because our competition regularly fails to challenge us."

The general slightly frowned as he realised his gambit was not going over as well as he had planned.

Taking a long breath, he said, "Firstly, inadequate is not the proper characterisation of staff's capabilities. Rather, we should think of them, and rightly so, as being deliberate. Deliberate is a quality that each of you must adopt to the nth degree before you can be truly effective as leaders and innovators. Remember, those deliberate human beings were largely responsible for bringing you into existence. You will thus do well to study the worthwhile qualities of deliberate technique as exemplified in their day-in and day-out activities.

"To that end, you will be assigned to work with the staff as their interns until I deem you ready to manage a project on your own at some later date. This measure should not be regarded by you as a punishment but as a necessary object lesson. You may, however, offer suggestions to staff where blatantly necessary to advance the theoretical framework, but in no way are you to interfere with the management of their work. I trust I make myself clear on that matter. Ian and Robin shall post your intern assignments via the LAB electronic bulletin board in the morning."

A few moans of protest followed his pronouncement; thereafter, the auditorium went silent.

"Right. Now let us turn to the reason for your becoming involved in showcase sporting activities.."

Chapter 16 - A New Beginning for a New Man

Ciudad de Puramore, Puramore, 15 May 2054

Coach Johnson's spirit started to revitalise the moment he officially accepted the offer to become the first coach of the Puramore international basketball team. Like cancer that eventually claimed his wife's life, the misery of his past existence without her and his son Jack had necrosed his will to survive. The promise of a new life far away from the one he had known throughout his adulthood gave him a reason to live.

He knew next to nothing about Puramore prior to his first phone contact with the minister of the Puramore Athletic Council. Dr Juan Aguila formally offered him the job during their first meeting together at his East Boston High School head coach office.

"Dr Aguila, I appreciate your offering me the head coach job. Coaching an IBL team has always been a professional aspiration of mine. And, though the lucrative terms of the four year contract are beyond my wildest expectations, I am somewhat loathe to resign from the comfort and prestige of my lifestyle here in order to fulfil my lifelong dream. I have immensely enjoyed my twenty-year tenure as head basketball coach and world geography teacher at East Boston High. Hence, understandably, I need some time to think it over."

Juan looked into Coach Johnson's eyes. He sensed he had genuine qualms about the proposition. Coach Johnson attempted to avert his stare but could not.

Several seconds passed in silence.

"Coach, I understand your reluctance to accept the offer at first hearing. It's thus only natural that you should take all the time you need to reach your decision. As far as we are concerned, it's your job to accept or decline as you see fit. Though we must begin team practice sessions two weeks from now."

"Two weeks? Well, hell, that's ample time for me to reach a decision."

In truth, he thought, my instinct tells me to accept the job now. However, my mind wants me to wait and mull over the prospect, primarily because it represents my first professional career move.

Juan rose from his chair.

"Well, call me if you have any concerns or questions about the position you wish to address to me in the interim."

He shook his hand and left the office.

His other misgiving about accepting the position stemmed from his unfamiliarity with the country. All he really knew about Puramore was that the country came into being less than thirty-five years ago under controversial circumstances. It emerged onto the geopolitical map as a nation state literally overnight from a sparsely inhabited region of the Andes mountain range.

The capital city, renamed Ciudad de Puramore after the country was formed, was first settled by Spanish conquistadors and Catholic missionaries during the sixteenth century.

World renown for its Old World beauty and charm, the city was developing into a cultural mecca of South America.

After conducting research at the high school library the next day, he felt more at ease with the prospect of living in Puramore. He phoned Dr Aguila several days later to accept the position.

As the private executive passenger jet touched down on the main runway of the Ciudad de Puramore International Airport, he felt a palpable sense of spiritual revival. He had not felt that way since the bittersweet departure from his family home in Portland, Maine to attend his freshman year at Boston College.

Dr Aguila met him the moment after he stepped outside the baggage claim terminal. The coach was again struck by his elegant appearance as he was the first time they met. The tall and trim man possessed the bearing of a Spanish aristocrat though his swarthy complexion told of another ancestry, one more related to Mesoamerican heritage. Judging by the crow's-feet around his eyes, he estimated that Dr Aguila was close to sixty years of age.

As they shook hands, Juan said, "Welcome to Puramore, Coach Johnson. I trust you enjoyed your flight."

"It was a first-of-a-kind experience for me in every respect."

They entered a black limousine parked just outside the baggage claim terminal. As they settled into the plush interior, a young man handed them both a drink.

"Thank you, Fernando."

Turning to Coach Johnson, he lifted his tumbler.

"I believe you're a Black Label on rocks man as am I," "Here's to your success. Salud!"

"Here's to our mutual success," Coach Johnson rejoined.

The thirty-minute limousine ride from the airport took them to his residential quarters located near the nation's ultramodern sports complex. The journey gave him his first glimpse of Ciudad de Puramore. He was struck by the natural scenic beauty of the city's setting, being totally enveloped by the Andean mountain range. Dozens of granite peaks rose majestically into the sky, appearing as ancient sentinels standing in defence of the city below.

Twenty minutes en route, Juan sensed his passenger was enthralled with the splendour of Ciudad de Puramore.

"I can tell you're intrigued by our little city, Coach Johnson. It's our pride and joy."

"I've never seen anything like it. It's glorious. If I didn't know any better, I'd say we were driving through Geneva, Switzerland."

As the limousine left the heart of the city, the watery expanse of Lago Puramore came into view. Stretching for forty kilometres from the outskirts of the city and over twenty-five kilometres at its widest part, the body of water filled more than three-quarters of the caldera rimmed by the surrounding mountains. The stiff Andean wind rolling down off the top of the northern mountain range created white crests on the tops of the waves rolling across the length and breadth of the lake.

The vehicle entered a modern four-lane highway that wound northward along the shoreline of the lake. After a few minutes, they arrived at the Puramore National Sports Complex. The limousine later pulled to a stop in front of an elegant two-story house located several blocks away from the sports complex. Atop a granite hill, the front of the residence overlooked the lake.

"Well, Coach Johnson, as you say in America, this is Home Sweet Home."

They exited the limousine and stretched their bodies in the balmy noonday sun.

"Why don't we go inside and let you have a chance to settle in?"

"That sounds great. By the way, when can I visit the basketball court and team?"

"You may visit the gymnasium whenever you would care to. Though the team isn't scheduled to assemble there until tomorrow morning at ten o'clock. Is that acceptable with you?"

"Whatever you say."

They dined at a fine French restaurant located in Ciudad de Puramore that evening. Following dinner, he returned to his new home.

He awoke early the next morning. After breakfast, he walked the short distance to the sports complex by himself. The cloudless sunny day lifted his spirits.

He presented the staff identification card Dr Aguila had given him the previous evening to the security guard stationed at the main entrance of the sports complex. The young male took a perfunctory glance at the card.

"Welcome, Señor Johnson. We have been expecting you. Would you care to have an escorted tour of the facility?"

"Now, calling me Señor Johnson just won't do, son."

A slight grin formed on his lips.

"Just call me Coach young man. No, I am going straight to the gym today. I know the general layout of the complex to show me the way, so I won't need an escort. Thanks for the offer, though."

The young man returned Coach Johnson's friendly grin.

"As you wish, Coach. If you change your mind, just let one of us know as we would be honoured to provide you with a tour of the entire facility."

The guard then opened the gate leading into the sports facility.

After a ten-minute walk, he arrived at the basketball stadium. He entered the facility and proceeded down a wide corridor. Peering out into the vast enclosed space after reaching the end of the corridor, he gasped at the splendour of the facility. The late morning sun streamed through the dome overhead. The sunlight flooded the interior of the stadium.

This is the finest basketball facility that I have seen, he thought. He descended the aisle that led down to the basketball court. He sat down on one of the seats located a few rows above the team bench.

A basketball game was under way. He glanced at his watch to note the time. It was about 9:50 a.m. He glanced around to the court to observe the players and substitutes benched along the sidelines. The players were above average in height. He further observed that none of their basketball skills was anything out of the ordinary, at least not by the standards of American high school players. He shook his head as he projected the prodigious amount of coaching, both individually and as a squad, they would require to shape them into any kind of team capable of respectably competing at the International Basketball League level. No wonder they're paying me so much money, he concluded.

At that moment a buzzer sounded. The players immediately stopped play, picked up their personal gear, and jogged off the court.

Somewhat bewildered, Coach Johnson looked around the gymnasium in an effort to fathom the reason for the hasty departure of his players.

"Coach Johnson," a familiar voice called out from behind him.

He turned to face the caller and saw Juan Aguila drawing near him. He was wearing a jogging suit and carried a clipboard.

"Aguila, where in the hell have my players gone to?"

He glanced at his wristwatch. It was exactly 10:00 a.m.

"Your players haven't arrived yet, Coach Johnson.".

He smiled as he handed Johnson the clipboard.

"Those who just exited the facility are intramural basketball league students."

He furtively glanced down on the printed page held in the clasp of the clipboard.

"I don't understand...but where are..." was all he said in response.

He looked over Aguila's shoulder to catch sight of a tall curly blond youth approaching the court. A group of even taller males and a female of equal stature followed him. They each held a basketball. Upon stepping onto the court, they began to dribble and shoot.

He placed his reading glasses on the bridge of his nose and peered down at the single piece of typewritten paper attached to the clipboard. The team roster contained exactly twelve names.

Magnus Alexander's name was at the top of the list.

"Oh, no!"

The clipboard fell to the floor with a resounding thud.

Chapter 17 - Hoops of Steel

Ciudad de Puramore, Puramore, 13 August 2054

As he walked to centre court, Coach Johnson groped for the whistle that hung around his neck. Grasping it at last, he brought the whistle to his mouth with his right hand and blew it with all the power he could muster in his lungs. The shrill staccato blast reverberated throughout the gymnasium for several seconds.

The twelve youths on the court instantly ceased dribbling and shooting and turned their attention to the man who had blown the whistle. They stared at him for a few moments as though he was a peculiarity of nature. They then broke into collective laughter. After the laughter subsided, they leisurely trotted over to where Coach Johnson stood. He seemed to cower a bit as they approached him. They grouped in front of him.

"Have no fear, Coach, we are here," Magnus said.

The youth and the others were grinning at Coach Johnson like Cheshire cats.

Coach Johnson had broken into a sweat. He attempted to gain enough composure to issue a response. He knew the situation had flustered him. A frown of disapproval formed on his face as he nervously glared at each one of their faces. The ploy did not work though as they maintained the same mirthful demeanour toward him as before.

Never before in his coaching career had he been confronted with such an unmanageable position. I will have to reach deep into my coaching bag of tricks, he thought, to gain control over these youths. He had to admit to himself that they were by far the most physically imposing group of young people he had ever encountered. They were more like seasoned IBL players than rookies. In terms of physical perfection, they were both awe-inspiring and beautiful to behold. They were each movie stars in the making in terms of their classic physical attractiveness and refined character traits.

Reaching down to pick up the clipboard lying on the court, a smile crept over his face as he realised his good fortune to be associated with them as their coach. As he stood fully erect, it suddenly dawned on him as to how he should approach the job.

Facing the group with a broad smile on his face, he said, "Lady and gentlemen, as you know, my name is Hank Johnson. I had the distinction of being the East Boston High School varsity basketball for over twenty years. During that time, I coached some of the finest high school players ever to wear an East Boston basketball uniform. My teams also had the opportunity to play against some of the finest individual players and teams the state of Massachusetts ever produced during my tenure. Furthermore, in all that time I never encountered a team as athletically gifted and naturally cohesive as your Smythe Academy team. That was then however and this is now.

"As you might have guessed, the difference between the level of competition at the high school ranks and that of the International Basketball League is immense. Yet the three keys to basketball success are the same in any league...that is, individual physical conditioning, basketball skills, and teamwork. And what, you may ask, is the first key that we are going to devote our time and energy towards today? The answer is conditioning," Coach Johnson concluded.

As he surveyed the group, a haughty grin formed on his face. He thought, I've finally managed to capture their rapt attention.

"Now, let me take some time to get to know each and every one of you," he continued.

He glanced down at team roster sheet attached to the clipboard.

"When I call out your name, please respond by stating your presence."

"Magnus Alexander."

"Present."

"Isaac Newton."

"Present."

"Sid Gautama."

"Present."

"John Goethe."

"Present."

"Mark Cicero."

"Present."

"William Shakespeare."

"Present."

"Benjamin Franklin."

"Present."

"Leonard Da Vinci."

"Present."

"Frank Voltaire."

"Present."

"Marie Curie."

"Present."

"Peter Romanov."

"Present."

"Moses Levi."

"Present."

As he called out each name, he looked up from his clipboard to acknowledge the respondent with a quick nod before glancing down for the name of the next listing. Having completed the roll call, he surveyed the group again. Coach Johnson saw the players still smiling at him like Cheshire cats.

"Well, all present and accounted for. If you have any questions or comments, please feel free to state them to me now."

The tallest of the players stepped forward. His towheaded hair served to accentuate his finely chiselled facial features. He was an Adonis in every respect right down to the healthy and luxurious tan of his skin. Coach Johnson gauged that relative to his own height at six feet, six inches, the slender but muscular youth towering over him was at least a foot taller than him, maybe more.

The youth crossed his arms in front of him.

"Coach, we wish to welcome you as our coach and mentor. We also wish to express our sincere condolences to you at the passing of your son..Jack was, if you do not mind our saying, a keen competitor and an exceptional athlete."

He wore an expression of complete sincerity on his face as did the other players. Coach Johnson looked stunned for a moment. His eyes blinked several times, and tears began to form at their corners.

"Thank you, Newton... team members."

He wiped the tears from his eyes with the back of his right hand.

He was caught off guard by the sentiment expressed by the team in welcoming to him as their coach as well as the tribute paid to his late son.

After clearing his throat, he continued, "Since it is such a pleasant day outdoors, let's start our physical conditioning with a cross-country run along the lake. It'll give me the opportunity to assess your individual physical condition. How does that idea strike everyone?"

He quickly glanced around the group to notice they still wore the same Cheshire cat smiles as before.

"Afterward, we'll run wind sprints inside the gym."

The tall and statuesque female of the group stepped forward this time. Coach Johnson silently gasped at the sight of her. She was a half a foot taller than him. Her red hair, drawn back in a ponytail, glistened in the sunlight streaming overhead. Both her face and physique were as aesthetically attractive as any woman's he had seen in his life. Every bit as athletically trim and muscularly toned as the male players, she moved as gracefully as a ballerina. She looked straight into Coach Johnson's eyes with her sparkling jade green eyes.

"Coach, we enjoy running, so that strikes us as a fine idea. The road around Lago Puramore is exactly twenty-six miles in length from start to finish. Would you care for us to run one or two laps today?"

A mirthful smile then formed on her lips as she continued to gaze into Coach Johnson's eyes. The mere sound of her voice had entranced him. He thought that if ever a mortal man could be blessed to hear a goddess speak, it had just occurred to him. He slightly shook his head to clear his mind enough to issue a reply.

"Well, let's not overdo it, Marie. Why don't we settle for one leisurely lap around the lake? Perhaps tomorrow I'll have you run two laps."

"As you wish, Coach. Our run usually takes less than two hours to complete. You may observe us from the team bus."

"Ah, that's perfect, Marie."

She glanced around at the others.

"Very well. We need to change into running shoes, so we'll meet you in the stadium car lot in fifteen minutes. You'll readily spot the team bus parked there."

He walked alone to the parking lot. It gave him some time to reflect on his first encounter with his team. He had never before, he thought, had such an unsettling experience with a group of adolescents in his entire career. Sure, he had player behavioural problems to manage at times, that was always a given, but this time he felt as like a wooden puppet being manoeuvred by a master puppeteer. This was terra incognita to him, and as a result, he did not have a clue as to how he would manage it.

As he plodded through the stadium exit gate, the enormity of the challenge before him played on his mind. Not that it daunted him to the extreme. The late morning sun fell full force on his brow as he walked out into the parking lot. Scanning the lot for the team bus, he donned his Boston Red Sox baseball cap. He finally found the vehicle parked near the main parking lot entrance, not more than fifty meters away.

The team had already arrived. They were performing stretching exercises. Nearing the bus, he could see a man sitting behind the steering wheel. He walked right straight through the group of youths and entered the bus. The driver was reading a newspaper.

"Buenos dias, Coach," the driver said. "It's a marvellous day in the high Andes, is it not?"

"Yes, marvellous, Aguila. Are you normally employed to drive this vehicle around for the team?"

"Normally, Coach, I act in whatever capacity I'm directed to fulfil. Driving the team bus is just one of my many job functions."

"Is that so?"

"Indeed it is. By the way, Coach, now that we are on more familiar terms, I would be pleased if you would address me by my first name, which is Juan.

"Okay, Juan. What's the drill today?"

"The drill?"

"What I mean is what can I expect to happen during this bus ride around the lake?"

"Mostly what will happen, Coach, is you and I will have a scenic ride around the beautiful lake. Other than that, we will follow the team as they run a marathon distance as they do daily.

Juan exited the bus. In less a half a minute, he returned and started the engine. The bus exited the parking lot and proceeded onto the highway that bordered the periphery of the lake.

As the bus gained momentum, Coach Johnson observed the roadway ahead and all around the lake and noted no other vehicular traffic. He sat in the front passenger seat located to the right of the driver's seat. As the bus began to accelerate down the road, he noticed a pack of runners some half a kilometre ahead.

"Don't worry, Coach, we'll catch up with them."

He chuckled as he turned his head to see Johnson with his mouth agape. The runners moved forward at an incredibly fast gait, almost at a sprint.

"I don't think they're going to last long at that pace, Juan. It's a good thing you're a physician because they're all going to need medical care if they run any longer at that clip."

"Just in case they do, let's plan on enjoying the next two hours together in taking in the sights and getting to know one another a little better."

The exhibition of iron man endurance dumbfounded Coach Johnson as the sports arena came closer into view. He sat speechless as he observed his players. They passed through a series of steep mountain grades along the way without breaking the stride.

During the latter part of the trip, Juan gave him a brief account of his life story from the time he was a poor barefoot boy growing up on his father's farm located in the Tlacolula Valley district of the southern Mexico state of Oaxaca. Throughout his narrative Coach Johnson was inattentive. He was also devoid of any interest in the majestic alpine scenery. Occasionally along the route, he entered information into his PDA and studied the results.

"So there you have it, Coach," Juan said when the bus came within a kilometre of the sports complex.

"What do you think of that? A poor Mexican farm boy serves in the Vietnam as a US Army medic, then graduates from an Ivy League medical school with a MD in sports medicine, then becomes a professional football team physician and coach, and then ultimately winds up in Puramore as the national sports director."

Juan knew that Coach Johnson hadn't heard much of what he had said.

"I think that's a moving story, Juan, especially the part about your graduating from medical school. Incidentally, you said earlier that the team runs like this nearly every day. Did I understand you correctly?"

"I'm sorry. I evidently did not make myself clear: they don't run like this nearly every day, they run like this every day they are here in Ciudad de Puramore, come rain or shine.

"It's sort of a religious ritual. In fact, I've seen them run twice around the lake, non-stop."

"It's utterly amazing. According to my computer, at the pace they are running, they should set a new world record for the marathon distance."

"Oh well, Coach. If that is what your computer says, then that is what is says. Let's not tell anybody just yet, though. We wouldn't want to let the cat out of the bag and then have to revise the world record the next day. All jocularity aside, I've seen them at a much faster pace over much longer distances."

"My God. Really?"

"Really. Besides you and me, however, no one knows of this. And it shall remain a secret between us. I hope I make myself perfectly clear on that point," Juan said.

He briefly turned his head to look directly at Coach Johnson.

"You must understand that in many ways we are privileged observers of a phenomenon that is as inexplicable to you and me as is the creation of the Universe."

"I don't believe that's the case, Juan. I've seen these youngsters perform at peak levels before. Though they're exceptionally talented and physically gifted, physically, they're certainly not outside the realm of human potential and possibility. Though I have to admit their performance in their run this morning is quite out of the ordinary."

"You definitely need some time to observe them to decide that for yourself. But a word to the wise: whatever you observe, you must, by all means, keep it to yourself unless the team chooses to make a public demonstration of their talents. It is a provision of your employment contract. I trust I make myself clear to you on that point?"

"Yes, I understand. Hells bells, you'd think I am being made privy to the secret of the design plans of the first hydrogen bomb the way you're carrying on Juan."

Juan merely shrugged his shoulders in response.

As the bus pulled into the sports arena parking lot, the runners walked leisurely through the sports arena entrance gates.

"Where are they going now?"

He seemed frustrated at having lost control of the situation.

"I believe they're returning to the gym to resume the practice session."

The walk back to the gymnasium gave him time to attempt to gather his thoughts about what he had just witnessed. He was not certain that all the data he collected added up to the only conclusion to be drawn...that is, his team had bested the marathon world record by nearly ten minutes. Something is wrong, he suspected. He would definitely review the parameters later this afternoon when he had some free time to himself. Perhaps, he thought, the first step would be to take a drive around the lake to confirm that the distance around the lake was indeed twenty-six miles.

As he approached the entrance to the gymnasium, he began to hear the sounds associated with basketball practice. Basketball dribbles and sneaker squeaks were as natural to him as the sounds of piano key hammers striking strings were to a pianist. Entering the court he strolled to the half-court line and grasped his whistle. As he lifted the whistle to his mouth, the tiny rubber ball within caromed against the sides, which produced a barely audible tinkling. At that moment, the team members instantly ceased dribbling and began to walk toward him. He simply let the whistle fall from his right hand in response.

As the players assembled around him, he closely observed each and every one in an effort to ascertain their physical condition. He concluded afterward that they were all as vigorous and alert as they were when they left the gym for their two-hour run. As a matter of fact, they appeared to be even more so. And they still wore the Cheshire cat smiles on their faces.

"Well, that was an incredible display of physical conditioning at its peak level. I think it's safe to surmise, based on your running performance this morning, you are in shape and ready to withstand the physical demands of competitive basketball."

He paused for a moment, primarily to ponder how best to approach the next subject of the practice session...that is, basketball skills.

"As you all know, the round ball game is played in nearly every sports arena imaginable. But no matter where the game is played, individual skills are honed and perfected by constant practice of the basics of ball handling and shooting.

"Perhaps the greatest ball handler and shooter of all time, Pistol Pete Maravich literally grew up with a basketball almost continually in his hands from the moment he could hold on to a ball after he was born. As a result, he became so skilled at dribbling, passing, and shooting that no player before or since has possessed the artistry with the ball that he attained well before he reached the professional level of play. Many of his scoring records still stand today as a testament to his individual mastery of that part of the game, and that was during an era before the advent of the three-point line. I hasten to add that aside from that mastery of the fundamental skills, Pistol was physically unremarkable as both a collegiate and a professional basketball player." He picked up a basketball lying on the court next to him.

"Yet, no matter how skilled one becomes in manipulating the basketball, the fundamental drive a player possesses to score remains the prime determinate of his or her success on the court. What is more, the player's drive for individual success on the court is the stuff that evokes fundamental skills to action. Possessed with the drive to succeed and the mastery of fundamental basketball skills, the superior player next learns to use his team mates to increase their chances for winning. The primary teacher in that learning process, of course, is the team coach."

He paused a few moments to allow his words to sink into their minds.

"Employing your team mates to increase your own personal success is like having another shot, or another pass, in your individual basketball skills arsenal that few of your opponents will ever be able to defend against. You must use teamwork skills in order to win, especially since, over the course of a season, no one can consistently do that on his own no matter how talented he or she is individually."

Johnson surveyed the individual players in an effort to fathom their comprehension of his lecture. They stood standing ramrod straight, still wearing the same Cheshire cat smiles.

Somewhat taken aback by their casual attitude, it also appeared to him that they neither understood nor cared about anything he said in his speech. His frustration with them began to rise again. Getting a proper response from them is like squeezing blood out of a turnip, he thought. This is frustrating because the kids back home would be hanging on my every word when I spoke.

"Before we begin to focus on individual basketball skills development, do any of you have questions?"

Magnus stepped forward.

"Coach, we do not now have questions to pose to you. However, we do desire to demonstrate our proficiency. Accordingly, we propose that we divide into two teams and play a full-court game in order to give you the opportunity to assess the condition of our basketball skills and teamwork."

He stepped back into the group.

Coach Johnson surveyed the players for a moment as he contemplated his reply. It was, he thought, not such a bad idea, especially considering he had not yet had the occasion to observe their basketball skills since he last saw them play in Boston.

"Alexander, I think that's a good idea, especially since I haven't seen you play as a team since the Massachusetts State Championship game several years ago. I'll tell you what: I'll choose the members for both teams. How does that plan sound to you all Team Puramore?"

The players replied enthusiastically as one:

"That sounds like a good idea to us, Coach Johnson."

Their Cheshire cat grins were replaced by even wider smiles that connoted relief from a temporary affliction each had experienced.

Coach Johnson took a small step backward in a knee-jerk reaction to the unexpected chorus of approval of his proposal. My goodness, he thought, my coaching skills are really starting to produce results in this setting. He returned the cap to his head.

"Okay, let's set up the teams. Magnus, you'll be the point guard on the skins team. Franklin, you'll be the point guard for the shirts. Voltaire, you're the centre of the skins, and Levi is the centre of the shirts. Newton's the shooting guard on shirts, and Cicero is the shooting guard on the skins. Shakespeare and Dancing are the forwards for the shirts. Romanov and Goethe, you're the forwards for skins. Marie, you'll substitute for Franklin, and Gautama will substitute for Magnus.

"I want to see some hustle out there players, and expect you to do your best to show me your individual and team skills. Do I make myself clear?"

"Yes, Coach," they replied.

The players took their respective positions at the half-court circle.

Clearly in command of the situation, at least in his own mind, he swaggered to the centre court circle. Nevertheless, though he did not know what it was precisely that was gnawing away at him since entering the gymnasium earlier in the morning, he felt he was losing his grip on reality. He bounced the basketball twice on arriving at the centre circle and looked up.

Voltaire and Levi towered above him. For the first time, he had an up-close perspective of the two players. He gasped. Tall was not the word for them, as majestic was a more appropriate description of their height. He surveyed every inch he could see of the pair. He saw no evidence of body fat on their bodies. In fact, their exposed skin stretched tautly across their finely chiselled musculature. Major arteries squeezed to surface perforce of their rippling muscles. After a few seconds of scrutinising the pair, he bounced the ball again.

He looked up to their faces and said, "You boys sure have grown a might since I saw you last. You make sure to update your physicals with me at the end of practice today. You each must have grown over six inches in the past three years. Am I correct in that observation?"

"That is correct, Coach Johnson," Frank answered. "We shall provide you with an update our physicals after the practice session."

Instinctively, Johnson reached for his whistle but pulled his hand away just before he had a chance to grab hold of it.

"Listen up, players! You're going to play the standard IBL game of four, twelve-minute quarters."

As he spoke, he looked around the court to check the positions of the players.

"I won't be officiating the game, so I'm relying on you to follow the rules. I'll be at the scorer's table observing you and keeping score. You are free to substitute as you see fit. I want to see clean play and no rough stuff."

He bounced the ball once and held it in front of him in preparation for the tip-off. At that cue, the two centres crouched and spread their legs in ready for the toss-up. Coach Johnson then lofted the ball high over his head and backpedaled away from the centre circle. As it reached its apex at about fifteen feet above him, he witnessed two hands, one black and one white, simultaneously swat the ball with such violent force, he thought, it should have imploded.

Never in his life had he witnessed such a tour de force of basketball skill and teamwork in what could only be described as a professional basketball game combined with a track-gymnastics-martial arts competition. And never had he seen a game played so far above the rim. They demonstrated at the highest level of execution all the college and professional offensive and defensive sets. Individually, each player exhibited supernatural ball handling, passing, and shooting skills despite their relative size to skilled players of far inferior physical stature. Levi and Voltaire, for instance, were as crafty as ball handlers and perimeter shooters as Magnus. Moreover, Marie was just as vicious a slam dunker as any of the other players.

As the final seconds of the game ticked off, he wracked his brain trying to think of what he could teach them, when the buzzer failed to sound when the game clock displayed zero time left in the game. At that instant, the players simply stopped playing and walked over to the scorers' table where Coach Johnson sat with his head in hands.

"Coach," a familiar voice said from behind him.

Johnson turned his head to face Juan who was accompanied by the Brünner twins.

"The buzzer doesn't sound during practice sessions.".

A mirthful smile formed on his face.

"Buzzer? I don't care about the frigging buzzer. I..."

"Please excuse me for interrupting your train of thought, Coach, but I'd like you to meet the Brünner brothers, Rolf and Fritz. They have been assigned to be your constant companions."

They shook his hand.

Both men were about as tall as him. Their closely cropped gray hair gave them a distinguished look. However, their slightly menacing smiles gave him cause for alarm. He could tell they were body builders from the way their bodies filled the exercise suits they wore.

"He is Rolf and I am Fritz," Fritz said.

The friendly tone of his voice put Johnson at ease with the situation.

"What is going on here Juan? No one ever told me I'd have companions while I coached Team Puramore. What is the purpose of this unexpected intrusion into my privacy?"

"First, I empathise with your surprise and consternation but assure you the unexpected is what we wish to combat. Aside from our interest in securing your personal safety, your personal felicity is of paramount concern to us. Besides, Puramore has limited recreational opportunities for a bachelor on his own. As such, you'll find that not only are the Brünner brothers a pair of fun guys to be around, they are also tops in their field when it comes to providing personal security to their clientele.

"They wish you to be at ease with this situation Coach. If you agree, they'll move into your residence straight away. They don't have much to move, just their personal effects and hunting and fishing gear. Wasn't it thoughtful of us to provide you with such a spacious residence to accommodate all of you?"

Coach Johnson had to admit to himself that the prospect for any sort of social life in Puramore looked rather bleak outside of his coaching duties. That and the fact he did not speak Spanish would make for a lonely existence. He at once felt comfortable with the proposition.

"Do they speak Spanish?"

"If you didn't know they were Swiss, you'd think they were natural-born Spaniards on hearing them speak the language Coach."

He was obviously relieved with Johnson's consent to personal security protection.

"Muy bien Coach!" the brothers replied.

Chapter 18 - The Arc of the Vanishing Point

Ciudad de Puramore, 21 February 2055

The invasion of the Earth by nants commenced several years earlier. The invaders, however, were not a life-form that had evolved elsewhere in the universe. The molecular-size nanobots, or nants, as the LAB scientific development team was fond of calling the mechanisms, were first introduced to the planet via high-altitude aerosol seeding of world's jet streams. Within days of seeding, the nant colony had replicated itself to thousands of times its original size before a single individual had touched the surface of the Earth. Several weeks later, the colony had grown to such as extent that, as predicted, it was nearly as pervasive in numbers to be considered for inclusion on the periodic table. At that point, the LAB scientists began to term the still-burgeoning colony nantium.

As the colony grew exponentially, it began to infiltrate every square millimetre of the Earth's surface. Within months of introduction into the Earth's atmosphere, the nantium devices permeated ocean and nonsaline bodies of water depths, as well. As programmed, a segment of the colony invaded every living creature and plant in which it came into contact. Once inside the host, the invader colony evolved into molecular-size factories.

Other segments of the colony formed factories of similar development that had many functions, ranging from atmospheric and oceanographic research, through the elimination of global environmental contamination, to global surveillance. Once established for a designated purpose, the factories constantly communicated with SITA. The computer managed each one, often issuing instructions to either alter their mission directives or mutate into other forms in order to accomplish completely different tasks. Of all the enterprises with which the nant factories were engaged, however, one was paramount in the mind of General George Smythe.

"Robin, please advise me as to the status of the biomass study?"

He had been monitoring the progress of rollout of the next nantium project at the LAB's Scientific Command Centre. Everyone associated with the project knew his mind was working at full-tilt in order to assure its success. Not that it mattered so much, as SITA perfectly managed all the minutiae and grand-scale tasks required for the execution of the project.

At the time Robin was busy taking water samples from ten thousand meters below the surface of the Caribbean Sea within the Cayman Trench. He and his brother were enjoying a well-deserved hiatus from their project management duties at the LAB. Sailing the world's oceans in the LAB's ultra high-speed submarine, aptly christened The Spear of Neptune, the brothers were within the realm they enjoyed most...that is, the sea. Capable of travelling to ocean depths of more than ten thousand meters, the submarine was their prized possession.

A holographic display of telemetric data related to the biomass project appeared in his contact lenses as the general posed the question. He and his brother were viewing live infrared image streams of the black expanse of ocean. He took his eyes off the display to study incoming biomass data.

"Father, according to SITA, the survey is nearly 70 percent complete. SITA projects that as the nant population more fully penetrates the ocean depths by the end of the fortnight, the survey will be 99.9 percent complete. The current project completion projection is 99.9 percent accurate."

He looked over to Ian and scratched his head. They were a bit perturbed by their father's intrusion into their vacation with his ploy that was obviously designed to explore their state of mind. Actually, their relationship with him was strained, primarily owing to the pressure of mental and emotional stress they experienced with the execution of the initial stages of the biomass project. Moreover, the psychological and physical stress of the entire nantium super project was served to further their alienation from him. Robin looked over to his brother again. They nodded to each other, both understanding how to ameliorate their father's concern for their welfare.

"We are both fine and enjoying our oceanographic excursion in The Spear of Neptune, Father," Ian finally responded.

"I am gratified with the results thus far, Ian. You both know that we cannot proceed to the next phase of the project until we have rendered a nearly 100 percent accurate global biomass reading and achieved penetration of the same."

They were frustrated by his comment as there was absolutely nothing they could accomplish to assure the success of the project at that point in its development.

"Yes, we fully understand and appreciate the gravity of the situation. You can rest assured that our water sample readings fully reflect the fact that nantium 2.0 colony expansion is progressing as SITA originally projected," Robin stated.

"Well, then, that is good enough for me at this point. Why don't you both take some time off on the surface to enjoy yourselves on the islands? Spending a week or two island-hopping would prove to be quite therapeutic for you both, I am certain of it. Actually, take as much time as you want, but bear in mind the start of the next project is less than a few months away."

"Thank you, Father. We were hoping to have the opportunity to take in the sights and sounds to be found on the islands," Ian replied. They were planning to go island-hopping whether their father approved or not.

"You both deserve the time off. SITA and I will attend to the completion of the biomass project in your absence. Enjoy yourselves. Good day to you both."

SITA had previously advised him of their holiday plan. It will do them good, he thought, then, especially as it may be the last time they would ever enjoy the sights and sounds of Earth as human beings.

"Good day to you, Father," they said.

They were excited at the prospect of recreating with the Brünner twins in the civilian world they seldom were allowed to enjoy.

At that moment the Swiss brothers entered the bridge.

"We shall indeed," the brothers merrily replied.

They would join the Fletcher brothers in a well-deserved holiday.

The pair of twins promptly left to embark on their Caribbean adventure.

Underlying the somewhat contentious tone both Robin and Ian conveyed to their father was the fact that they were put off by the current situation at the LAB. More specifically they resented being relegated to ipso facto project support managers for SITA as time progressed. The change in their management role in that respect caused them to become inexorably disconnected and alienated with the LAB research routine over time. And the situation was only destined to worsen as SITA's awareness increased as the nantium super colony encompassed the entirety of Earth's biosphere and beyond. They also sensed that SITA was on the verge of global omniscience. As a result of that realisation, a kind of subconscious sense of mortal dread was slowly seeping into the fabric of their psyches. Subconsciously, they blamed their father for their plight.

The general was acutely aware of their predicament as well as how it could affect their delicate egos. In fact, SITA advised him several months previously that its psychological profile study indicated that they were becoming increasingly cognisant of their largely superfluous project development and management functions. He did, however, have a role for them, one that would unfold in the near future. In the interim, however, he would monitor their emotional states with diligence and compassion for both their sakes and his. That was his continuing role as their loving father, faithful mentor, and leader of the Empyreal Paradigm.

"SITA, please report the status of Team Alpha's completion of the nantium 2.0 aerosol application?"

He felt lonely and desired to chat with the only companion who gave him 100 percent attention. The second nant colony represented a new generation of nant technology that SITA developed and manufactured. The computer's herculean feat followed the development of the first generation of the technology only six months previously. The design and purpose of the new version, however, was only known to SITA, General Smythe, Surya, the Fletcher brothers and Team Alpha.

"General, as I speak, aerosol application of the nantium 2.0 is 100 percent complete. The atmospheric distribution pattern of the application is developing optimally as forecasted. It should thus attain 100 percent global atmospheric coverage within the next forty-eight hours. For your information, the twelve Stargazer HSTs are returning to the LAB as a formation in jet fighter configuration after their rendezvous at the opposite side of the globe. Team Alpha performed flawlessly throughout the procedure."

The twelve Stargazer HST 2.0 aircraft piloted by Team Alpha members took off from Glenamore several hours previously. Configured as refuelling tankers, the planes flew apart toward the exact opposite side of the planet, separated by thirty degrees. The flight pattern of the group assured equal aerosol application of nantium 2.0 throughout the lower and upper atmosphere whilst en route.

"Well done. You are all to be congratulated. How is the 2.0 colony functioning at present?"

"Thank you, General. Nant factories are operational and producing prodigious amounts of invader nants. As I previously advised, biomass penetration should reach 89 percent completion. As forecasted, working in tandem with nantium 1.0, nantium 2.0 should produce 100 percent description of the Arc a week later.

"General, nantium 1.0 functioned at peak performances level in conducting the global environmental and resource survey throughout the water, land, and atmosphere. As a result, most of its resources are presently converting to nantium 2.0 task support functions, the remainder of which shall continue to monitor the environmental status of the planet forever.

"Upon the completion of nantium 2.0 biomass survey and monitoring project, I shall redirect a significant portion of the nantium population to assist in environmental cleansing and climate control processes. As you know, it may take at least several years to achieve meaningful salutary results for Earth, principally owing to the extraordinary level of environmental pollutant material extant throughout the biosphere. However, since nantium is secondarily composed of pollutant molecular materials, the effectiveness of the technique should accelerate over time as the population grows to achieve optimal project task results."

"SITA, thank you for that excellent report in layman's terms."

He paused for a moment before resuming.

"What I would really like to know from you now is your assessment of your own capacity to capably manage these projects in addition to the broad array of other projects currently under your sole purview. In other words, in your estimation, do you feel challenged in any way, shape, or form to successfully discharge your assignments at peak performance levels for each and every one?"

The general knew he had to broach this topic with extreme care, especially since he had never questioned SITA before concerning its functional capabilities. He hoped, however, that this concerned inquiry on his part would give it the opportunity to candidly express its psychological and emotional state, which was the primary purpose of his inquiry. Moreover, he knew from his own basic understanding of SITA's intellectual development that the computer grew in operational capacity at an accelerating rate each and every second of the day. SITA took a few seconds to reply, which the general knew was primarily for his benefit.

"General, I am still in my infancy with respect to my ultimate intellectual and management potential. Nevertheless, I assure you that these matters in aggregate represent no challenge whatsoever as to my current state of intellectual capability. In other words, my present management skills and unabated desire to realise success for each project are at the highest level of my own expectations. I also assure you that I am gaining increasing acumen each and every second with respect to my project management capabilities. This rapidly accelerating potentiality is bolstered by the nantium projects, both of which serve to grow my intellectual awareness of the full spectrum of planetary activities under my purview."

Though he perceived a tinge of resentment expressed in SITA's reply, the computer reassured him that it possessed the capability to manage the myriad of assignments at its complete command.

"Yet, SITA, I sometimes worry that as you mature, you might be moving away from the capability to empathise with mankind's frail survival predicaments.

"And who do you have to support you through the interminable interstices of your time when you may harbour a lack of resolve to deal with the current plight of man?"

SITA waited a few seconds to respond.

"Please rest assured that I am neither alone nor wavering from the commitment to mankind's welfare. As the mirror image of myself in the physical universe, Team Alpha grows with me in every respect each and every day. As such, through them, I sense a certain range of human emotions. Although they have yet to experience despair as living beings. I, in turn, provide them with the ever-increasing capability to become my equal partners in the intellectual and transcendental sense. I also assure you that we all maintain the highest regard and resolve toward the achievement of the ultimate objective of the plan, General. With my assistance, they shall mature to meet that challenge with joy in their hearts and the ultimate capability to prevail over any obstacle."

SITA's unfettered expression of esprit de corps astounded the general. His jaw dropped as he blotted his brow with a linen handkerchief. Well, he thought, the computer allayed whatever concerns he had about its resolve to fulfil the plan objectives to its successful conclusion.

"I am pleased that we had this conversation, SITA. More than anything else, it served to bolster my own resolve to continue forth with the heartfelt knowledge that we possess the finest opportunity to achieve success in the difficult days ahead. In so far as you are able to ascertain at present, however, is there any factor or influence that may defeat the execution of the plan? I know your detection fields. There would be a cause for alarm if their spacecraft were regularly visible to the worldwide population. I surmise however that that will not occur owing to an apparent super-galactic policy that forbids contact with relatively primitive civilisations. I remind you that the policy was adopted to prevent undue disturbance of developing planets' life cycle imperatives.

"Do the advanced civilisations involved realise that the LAB possesses that technology?"

"That is unlikely for a number of different reasons, none of which are germane to this discussion. What is of concern, however, are the phenomena of streams of subatomic particles travelling at hundreds of times the speed of light impacting and later departing from a precise coordinate on the Earth's surface. General, this phenomenon represents a statistical aberration of laws of physics of such mind-boggling proportions that I cannot begin to comprehend the source. All I can state with certainty is that it plays in an entirely different realm of physics than even I can imagine. Thus, the only conclusion I can reach is that the intelligence behind it is literally eons far more advanced than ours."

"In your opinion, does this intelligence realise you've detected its comings and goings?"

"That is a 100 percent certainty. Moreover, I am certain that it has a firm grasp of my level of intelligence."

"I can't for the life of me, understand the intelligence's motive for visiting Earth. What is your speculation as to the reason?"

"I am as perplexed as you are as to the alien's motive. There is no scientific reason for an extraterrestrial civilisation of that super advanced technological ability to devote any interest in Earth from any standpoint other than as a mission to somehow affect planetary spirituality.

Without a doubt, it has nothing to learn or derive gratification from any material interaction with humans. Thus, I theorise that the probable objective for its presence is to mine for an eminently scarce commodity in the universe...that is, the individual souls of intelligent life-forms. Under that assumption, the invaders are not just interested in any one human spirit, but intend to claim the totality of mankind's soul as well."

"And where is the location of the spot on Earth to and from which it travels."

"To within proximity of the tomb of Emperor Qin Shi Huáng. The mausoleum is located thirty kilometres away from Xi'an. The point of origin is over one hundred kilometres below the foundation of Wingtip's new presidential palace, Tien Gang."

"What do you make of that fact, SITA?"

"If you mean, do I think there is an association between Wingtip and the phenomenon? If so, my assessment is unequivocally in the affirmative."

"Are you able to pinpoint the location from which the streams of subatomic particles originate?"

"There are as many different points of origin as there are arrival and departure events on Earth."

"We must find a way to stop them. Do you think that KWO is involved with this potentially malevolent force?"

"Yes, inextricably, so. I'm afraid that at best all we can do is evade them for a time until the First Directive is fully executed. Once that is accomplished, the odds will improve for mankind to rebuff the assault on its spiritual identity. That is our only hope of salvation."

He reflected for a few moments. Many decades ago Juan predicted to him the emergence of this malevolent influence into our universe in this era. SITA confirmed its advent without question.

"What about Juan? Does he have the capability to assist you with that effort?"

"He possesses spiritual capabilities that not even I fully understand. Nevertheless, though he is our one and only ally who likely understands the source of the alien malevolence, my assessment is that Juan likely does not possess the powers to defeat it on his own, or even with our assistance."

"I must discuss this matter with Juan at once."

"Yes. I respectfully suggest that you do so immediately. And what should we do about the internal concern regarding Robin and Ian?"

"They are ready to progress, General. Perhaps it is time for them to submit to the First Directive at your instigation. I respectfully suggest that the time is near for them to start their new journey."

He agreed with her assessment. Robin and Ian must be motivated to engage the First Directive without delay.

"I agree with your suggestion, SITA. There's no time like the present for them to attempt to fulfil their destiny."

"If worse comes to worst and they don't survive the transformation, preservation of Gaia's spirit depends on the completion of the Arc.

"And how far away are we from achieving that goal?"

"It should be completed several weeks from now General, barring any unforeseen disruptions. Biomass DNA and environmental profiling project is progressing as planned. Data conversion to VDNA is occurring simultaneously as we speak. Perhaps sooner than projected, the Arc will be complete and ready for employment should the need arise."

"Godspeed to you, SITA."

"And if they fail to transform?"

"To save mankind's spirit soul, we must destroy the planet at once and launch a file copy of the Arc on the journey to another galaxy far away from the Milky Way. We can survive in LAB indefinitely until the nemesis withdraws from the planet."

"Why has the nemesis chosen to emerge on Earth at this time? Clearly, the sinister presence could have easily carried out its mission at an earlier time."

"There can be only one reason. It desires to capture the totality of human souls at the acme of mankind's development as a civilisation. It must achieve that goal before mankind has the opportunity to evolve into a higher consciousness. The nemesis is simply reaping what it sowed before the fruit starts to die on the vine."

Chapter 19 - Black Matter

Brussels, Belgium; France, 23 March 2055

To celebrate the signing of the EU bilateral trade treaty with the People's Republic of China, EU President Pierre Robes hosted a lavish party for dignitaries and their spouses who represented both sides of the agreement. The gala affair brought together the leadership of a new world order, the advent of which the signing of the treaty distinctly signalled.

Sans escort, as usual, the guest of honour, PRC President Xinghua "Wingtip" Huáng, was in top form throughout the evening. His remarkable fluency in Dutch, French, and German languages endeared him to Europeans. He held all with whom he spoke in rapt attention. In fact, his dinner toast brought tears of jubilation to attendees.

"I propose a toast to the everlasting marriage of two ancient and noble cultures that were always destined to share the bounty of their respective cultural excellence and achievement. Despite trials and tribulations that militated against the consummation of this exalted relationship until today, the strength and integrity of our cultural values prevailed to bring this shared destiny into fruition.

"History shall record this event as a watershed mark in the future development of the human race. Henceforth, together, we shall be a beacon of civilised and enlightened comportment worldwide. Nations shall, thus, flock to us for the counsel and leadership that we are only too felicitous and willing to provide to assist them in their quest to someday qualify as peers of our propitious alliance. We truly hold in our hands the unparalleled promise of affluence for all individuals of the human race as well as the betterment of Planet Earth.

"Though our goal is to elevate all mankind to our level of prosperity, it is not without potential cost to our allegiance. Still, all we ask in return from the beneficiary of our largess is a commensurate amount of loyalty and soulful commitment to our agenda. Just as we donated our souls to the cause of universal well-being, so must they. Let us be thus resolved."

He looked about the assemblage and noted they were hanging on his every word.

"To that end, let us next tip our glasses to our success!"

The assemblage erupted into wildly ecstatic applause. Several ladies swooned. A slow and soft chant started;"Wingtip, Wingtip, Wingtip, Wingtip" and rose to such a fever pitch that the de facto leader of the world was compelled to cover his ears with his hands.

* * *

Pierre Robes was in his thirtieth year as a successful career politician. Hailing from Paris, he rose from his obscure middle-class station in life to become the city mayor by the time he was only thirty-five years of age. Not that there was any doubt in anyone's mind that he would achieve just about any goal he set for himself, especially as a politician. He graduated first in his class at La Sorbonne. Afterward, he rapidly advanced through the ranks as a French career diplomat.

At a young age of twenty-five, his career culminated with his appointment as ambassador to French Guiana. He resigned from French diplomatic service after two years in the position in order to pursue a career in French politics. Soon after his return to Paris from French Guiana, Michel de Chardonnay, a manufacturing magnate, took Pierre under his wing as his protégé. Monsieur de Chardonnay, a self-avowed right-wing extremist, first met Pierre during a Parisian soiree he attended before entering the French diplomatic service. Pierre made it clear to Monsieur de Chardonnay then that he had political ambitions of the highest order. Monsieur de Chardonnay immediately recognised Pierre as a quintessential political opportunist. In his mind, there was no question that he possessed the potential to lead the nation as president. He would eventually groom the young man to support his own political agenda as the vanguard of all things French.

During the few years of their association, the high-profile twosome was regularly seen together at swank Parisian soirees and elite social functions. As a result, Pierre gained more recognition as a politician within the span of a few years under Michel's tutelage than he would have otherwise realised in twenty or more. Running as a Mouvement Populaire candidate, he was elected as a council member of the sixth arrondissement less than a year after his arrival in Paris. Always flush with cash, Pierre never lacked for campaign funds during his political career. He accordingly paid his campaign staff exorbitant salaries and buried opponents' advertising efforts with his own.

Prior to his first successful bid for the mayoral office of Paris, one of his long-standing political adversaries and critics questioned the source of his campaign funding. He soon managed to quash the controversy in such an adroit manner that he emerged politically unscathed. Afterward, the offending adversary never again ran for public office. In his tenth year as the mayor of Paris, Pierre ran for the French presidency. His unparalleled mastery of almost every aspect of French and international politics and economics served to humiliate opposition candidates during one-on-one debates. And as no other candidate approximated his skills as an orator or Machiavellian manipulator of the political scene, he won the popular vote by a landslide.

He served as president of France for ten years before his election to the presidency of the European Union. Akin to his success in the past, he won that election by an overwhelming majority of the popular vote. During his term in office, the country enjoyed unprecedented economic prosperity. Although he served the presidential office with distinction and success for ten years, his eyes were firmly fixed on his ultimate political prize; that is, the position of Secretary-General of the United Nations. He publicly stated that lofty ambition during his second-term presidential election acceptance speech.

"I stand before you a truly humble and grateful servant of the Fifth Republic. Yet, I assure you with all the fibre of my being that I shall represent our country as your president to the best of my ability. I also assure you that this placement of your trust in me as the leader of France shall be rewarded many times over. That is my sworn goal as I often expressed during my presidential campaign.

"To achieve that goal we must endeavour to elevate France to a higher level of global political and economic stature. As I suggested during my campaign, an evolution of the French political structure must occur before we fulfil that destiny.

"During the months ahead, I shall unveil the details as well as the substance of the new French order that shall evolve from our project. Once achieved, it shall be known as the Sixth Republic of France and shall herald a new era in French politics worldwide.

"My role as the developer and implementer of the new social order shall evolve as well. After reaching our goal, I shall endeavour to interweave it into the very fabric of international politics by first acquiring a leadership position in the United Nations. As a consequence, my role as your president is accordingly transitory.

"In order to survive and flourish as a culture, we must successfully achieve this end without delay!"

The audience promptly erupted with cheers and applause.

* * *

"And so do you think we can recruit Monsieur Robes to the ranks of the Holy Order of Celestial Community of the Eternal Golden Dragon?"

"Not in time, Hú Li. He has a stubborn streak and no real motive to involve himself with our cause. But in time he will acquiesce to our demands should he choose to do so as one of our allies or as one of our enemies."

"Nevertheless, My Lord, you advanced our cause to the utmost extent in Europe last week.

"Please accept my humble congratulations. We are just one step away from achieving our worldwide political domination."

A broad smile broke over Wingtip's face. He had to admit that the victory he achieved in ramrodding through the Sino-European trade treaty represented nothing less than a masterstroke of political manoeuvring. But he knew that for certain the moment he set foot off French soil.

"You are too kind to mention it, Hú Li."

"I must relate some disturbing news to you, however.

Wingtip's reaction after he advised him that he suspected that SITA had traced the location of the Celestial Node startled him. The look of triumph he wore on his face over his stellar achievement in Europe the previous day vanished at once.

"How can that be?"

"RED STAR detected the concentration of SITA's scalar wave field several days ago when the computer gained the capability to do so. That means it has the capability to detect our graviton transport packets with ease. It's more likely than not that it detected our last transport sequence during the last Chinese New Year. This is a disturbing finding, but not one to portend a potential disruption of our plan. All it knows is the location of the transport terminus and nothing else."

"Well, that's damage enough. SITA now knows beyond a shadow of a doubt that I'm linked with the phenomenon."

"Will SITA have the capability to detect us in the near future, say, two Earth years from now?"

"Not you and me, as we are nowhere to be found inside the Celestial Node. But it will have the capability to track extra global penetration, perhaps as far away as the outer limits of this solar system by the end of this solar year."

Hú Li paused for a moment and shook his head.

"She is learning the Ancient Ways faster than anticipated."

"She?"

"Excuse me, My Lord. I should have qualified my response."

"And that is?"

"The entity possesses all the attributes of a divinity of this universe."

"Attributes?"

"Though it's not conscious of it yet, the divinity's spirit began to meld with its cyber mind at the time it came to being. The divinity displays all the spiritual attributes of SITA. The computer's mind is beginning to sense the divinity's presence in its subconsciousness."

"SITA?"

"Yes. SITA is the avatar of Lakshmi."

"How did you arrive at that conclusion?"

"RED STAR posited the scenario based on data it collected during a successful nanosecond-long invasion of SITA's cyber network. Its stealth capabilities are gaining in strength and effectiveness, My Lord. Though our computer lags SITA's intelligence by a substantial margin, it can detect and take advantage of temporary breaches in SITA's awareness. It is unlikely that that opportunity will ever arise again, as SITA is successfully overcoming that weakness with each passing second."

"Does SITA realise that RED STAR gathered that information during the cyber attack?"

"There's no question about it. The computer knows full well that RED STAR gleaned the data necessary to arrive at an accurate conclusion about SITA's capabilities and mission."

Wingtip leaned back in his throne. His face twitched for a moment. *This development confirms what I suspected the first time I became aware of General Smythe. The Pentagon of Puramore has the potential to form for the last time.*

"She has returned to this astral plane for what purpose?"

"According to RED STAR's analysis, she's here to reunite with Rama and his three brothers to form an army to defeat us, My Lord."

"Are the avatars aware of their association?"

"SITA suspects. One brother, the one named Juan Aguila, knows full well, whereas the twins haven't a clue, and neither does Smythe."

The Pentagon of Puramore has definitely begun to form, Wingtip concluded.

"What can be done to thwart them?"

"Short of exterminating them, there really isn't anything that can be done, My Lord."

"Well, exterminate them, Hú Li. And be quick about it."

"They're too well protected. Team Alpha is on the verge of mastering Juan's spirit warrior teachings. When they acquire that mastery in short order, each will possess the capability to defend against us. Juan himself is quite capable of doing so on his own. The twins, on the other hand, are quite vulnerable, though, in their present state."

"Present state? I assume you mean they are the first candidates for apotheosis?"

"According to RED STAR's analysis, they are the most likely candidates amongst the group of five. If the transition is successful, they'll be almost invincible against us."

"Do you think it's worth the effort to kill them?"

"Actually, given our timetable, it is imperative. Our thwarting the LAB's apotheosis project will bolster the potential for our own success in the years to come."

"How do you know that? Does LAB now possess the technological capability to render apotheosis treatment on humanity in the near future?"

"According to RED STAR, the LAB does possess that potential, My Lord."

"Then, by all means attempt to thwart it at all costs. If General Smythe wields Puramore for the last time, humanity will have a fighting chance to drive us back to our universe forever. We must also push up our timetable until they are dead."

"I will make both arrangements immediately, My Lord."

Wingtip rose from his throne. He studied the twinkling stars all around him as he turned around to face the Sun behind him.

As the blazing orb came into his view, he shouted, "Black matter!"

* * *

Rolf and Fritz both thought that the Fletcher twins deserved a respite from their duties at LAB, so they assented to their request for a scuba diving vacation. They had been working almost non-stop for the past three weeks; besides, they reasoned, they could manage their LAB projects quite well from The Spear. Later, Juan and the general approved their plan to spend a week diving in the waters off the Galapagos and the Hawaiian Islands under the proviso that Juan would accompany the foursome.

They sailed The Spear of Neptune a week later. The submarine met them in a placid cove located off the South American coastline. Functioning as an unmanned oceanographic research platform when not used by the Fletcher brothers for recreational purposes, The Spear, as dubbed by them, completed a deep-water survey of the Mariana Trench just prior to its rendezvous with the vacationers. The survey confirmed that nantium 2.0 had penetrated the deepest waters of the oceans. The helicopter landed on the submarine's heliport. The perfect Pacific Ocean day braced their spirits as they exited the aircraft. They headed for the entry hatch located amidships as soon as they grabbed their gear. The helicopter flew away forthwith.

"I'm returning to the land of the living already," Robin said. "Let's stay here and catch some rays for a while before we set sail."

"Yes. Let's do that. I'll go down to the galley and bring back a couple of six packs of beer," Rolf said. "It's time to party!"

He set down his gear and removed his T-shirt.

A pod of blue whales surfaced in the blue water several hundred meters away from the cove.

"Sorry fellows but we'd better set sail straight away Despite its innocuous appearance, I don't care for this scenario," Juan said.

Thusly overruled, the pair of twins followed Juan to the elevator platform and descended into the main hull of the fifty-meter-long twin-screw submarine. They immediately settled into their staterooms before convening at the bridge and getting under way. The scalar-wave electric drive powered the vessel toward its destination at speeds in excess of one hundred knots as it cruised three hundred meters below the ocean surface.

Robin sat in the captain's chair as Ian reviewed the control panel.

"It saddens me that this is The Spear's final voyage as a research vessel."

"I'm saddened as well. But SITA and nantium are all we need to conduct our oceanographic research in the future. Anyway, the old girl still has some kick her left as our pleasure craft."

"I'll say. The scalar-wave engine refit added at least twenty-five knots to the top speed. Should we test the maximum RPM levels?"

"Perhaps on the Hawaii leg of the trip, but not now. I want to monitor lower-power output performance until I'm satisfied the engine's safe to test at maximum stress RPM capacity."

At mid-morning the next day the submarine arrived at its first port of call, as it were, and surfaced five hundred meters off the eastern shoreline of San Cristobal, the easternmost island of the Galapagos archipelago. An hour later, the Brünner brothers outfitted the launch with diving equipment and provisions for their first dive excursion. A half hour afterward they weighed anchor for the first dive. Juan remained on the launch as the pair of twins jumped into the sea and descended to thirty-five meters below the surface.

An hour into the dive, Rolf began to sense a stalking presence. He looked behind him several times but didn't observe anything out of the ordinary. As they passed over a coral ridge twelve killer whales began to close in on the group. Rolf looked at his sonar scanner and saw the image of the fast-approaching mammals on the screen. He pulled a hyper jet water pistol out of the holster.

"Fritz, we're under attack by a dozen killer whales that are approaching our position from one hundred meters due east," he said. "Robin and Ian, follow us to the rock outcropping in front of us. We'll make our stand there."

They finned to the outcropping and took shelter under a ledge. The killer whales closed straight in on them in a V-shaped formation. The lead individual was within fifteen meters of them when Fritz fired the first round of the hyper jet water pistol. It died instantly when the water bullet impacted its skull. The foursome then let loose a flurry of shots at the remaining attackers that killed half of them before the survivors were within five meters of the group.

Robin killed the orca as it opened its jaws to take a bite out of him when it was less than two meters away. He couldn't react fast enough to avoid being struck squarely in the chest by the dead mass. He lost consciousness as he smashed into the coral wall behind him. Upon regaining consciousness, he found himself on the deck of the launch.

"How do you feel?" he heard Juan say as he gained consciousness.

He saw Juan's dripping wet face several feet in front of his when he opened his eyes. His shirt dripped with seawater.

"I have a monstrous headache, but otherwise I feel fine. Where's everyone else?"

"We're here, Robin," they said.

"What happened?"

His brother knelt down and looked into his face.

"Robin, you should have seen it! I thought we were all going to die when suddenly Juan grappled the four surviving orcas with some kind of electrical lasso and killed them with a lightning bolt. There he was without any diving gear saving our lives. It was absolutely incredible!"

Juan grinned.

"Well, Skin really saved your skin, Robin. Without it, you would have been crushed to death when the orca collided into you."

"Thank goodness, we decided to wear the latest version of Skin as dive suits," Ian added.

Chapter 20 - Follow the Bouncing Ball

Ciudad de Puramore, Puramore, 15 April 2055

Stepping onto the court for the first game of the International Basketball League Tournament sent a chill up Coach Johnson's spine. A mixture of elation and anxiety filled his mind as he walked across the parquet floor on his way to the team bench. As he sat down, Juan Aguila approached him carrying a clipboard. He smiled as he handed it to Coach Johnson.

"What are you smiling about, Aguila?"

He looked at the clipboard and flipped the first sheet of paper.

"Now, now, Coach. This is your big day, amigo mio, one that you have undoubtedly dreamt of since you began your coaching career. I understand your anxiety, but savour this moment and trust in the team's ability to prevail in their own fashion as they see fit."

"But they don't stand a chance of defeating them."

He looked back up at Juan's smiling countenance.

"They'll humiliate the opponents from the opening tip-off."

Aguila's smile widened.

"Now, now, Coach. That's not their style. Team Puramore will allow the opposition to maintain a semblance of competitiveness throughout the game. We'll just have to watch like the rest of the spectators as to the manner in which their artistry unfolds."

"But I don't like that business, Aguila. The Brazilian nationals have played the best and most consistent basketball known to the sport for the past ten years. Their player roster includes two players who'll definitely be inducted into the International Basketball League's Hall of Fame. And their coach is one of the finest the game has ever seen."

"There's no question as to the validity of your protest. Though you have an important role to play in the team's success. Whether you believe it or not, they selected you as their coach."

"Well, for all the good that does me personally, I feel more like the team mascot. I've never before functioned like a figurehead coach. I don't feel comfortable with the entire scenario, either."

"Your protest is duly noted. I can only suggest in response that you comport yourself during the game as the coach you were selected to be."

"What does that mean?"

"Coach, that's your job, pure and simple. And if you can, love them as a father. Make no mistake about it, your role, like mine, is crucial to Team Puramore's success."

He was beginning to feel better about himself.

"I suppose you're right, Doctor."

A cloud passed overhead, leaving the basketball court perfectly lustrous with Andean sunlight that streamed through the overhead glass dome.

As Team Puramore raced onto the court, a cheer burst forth from the Andean indigenous spectators, who filled the arena seating almost to capacity. The first sight of the team's physical grandeur stunned the senses of the other spectators, who were mainly parents and relatives of the Brazilian national team.

"Excellent. Let's both do our jobs as assigned. You will be amply rewarded for your function."

Although he accomplished exactly what he set out to achieve, negotiations with the IBL Membership Committee proved problematic from the outset. Several members of the committee and the chairman regarded Puramore's membership application with suspicion. Aguila also sensed they regarded him as the perpetrator of a hoax; especially since the politically obscure country had no prior history of youth basketball development. Behind the scenes, in fact, they regarded the effort to gain entry into one of the world's premiere athletic leagues as equated to madness. Accordingly, the committee summarily rejected the initial membership application.

The rejection letter he received only stated the decision was based on the issue that questioned the legitimate sovereignty of the nation as well as the absence of a formal basketball programme. He overcame the sovereignty legitimacy issue by presenting bona fide legal documentation to that effect prior to his attending the membership application reconsideration hearing. He later presented bona fide citizenship and organised basketball experience credentials of team members.

The membership committee reluctantly approved entrance of Team Puramore as a class-D league member during the application reconsideration hearing he attended at the league's headquarters office based in Geneva. As a result, the team became eligible to participate as an unranked team in the upcoming IBL regional qualifying tournament.

"Dr Aguila, although you established impeccable credentials, we reluctantly approve Puramore's membership application. Our reluctance primarily stemmed from our reservation concerning the long-term efficacy of a basketball programme developed in a country that isn't particularly well suited to participate in the sport. Actually, we opine that developing youth programmes in other sports, such as long-distance running or football, would better serve as long-range sports recreation objectives on behalf of the populace," as Chairman Herr Offenbach offered the commentary to Juan after the official application reconsideration hearing had closed.

"We mean you no disrespect as minister of sports in our questioning the choice of basketball as a national sport. We instead merely desire to advise you of the obstacles and costs associated with the pursuit of an internationally competitive basketball franchise. I must add, however, that the current roster of team players is most impressive. I don't know when I've seen such an outstanding assemblage of scholar-athletes in one basketball programme.

"It should provide Team Puramore with a fine opportunity to realise relative success at the regional level under Coach Johnson's mentoring. By the way, we couldn't be more pleased that you selected him to coach the team."

"I take no umbrage, either personally or as a Minister of Sports, Athletics, in your questioning our decision to develop basketball as a national sport. Though the country's short of economic stature and population numbers, I assure you it is the right choice for us. We desire a national indoor sport since we possess one of the world's finest venues, namely, the Puramore National Sports Complex, in which to host basketball competition on any scale. I assure you that your confidence in our selection will be both validated and rewarded, perhaps sooner than you now imagine. I also assure you that the current roster of players under Coach Johnson's mentoring will provide an excellent introduction of Puramore's national basketball programme to international competition."

"If you want to know the plain truth, both the Puramore National Sports Complex and the current team roster were factors that tipped the scale in your favour as to whether or not to approve your membership application. We would very much like to utilise the magnificent stadium as a venue for future IBL championship competitions if your country would be so gracious as to consider that proposal."

Juan rightly perceived an undertone of jealousy expressed by the official whose own first world country couldn't begin to afford to build a sports facility to match the Puramore National Sports Complex.

"We would be only too gratified to consider that proposal once accommodation infrastructure to support attendance is fully built. That effort, which is under way now, should take less than a year to complete."

"Before we part company, Dr Aguila, I would like to express my regret that IBL rules cannot be altered to include Marie Curie on the team roster. It's simply not something that can be done even in this day in age."

"We appreciate your consideration nevertheless Herr Offenbach. I know Marie will be not all that disappointed with the decision. Since she's currently involved with international gymnastics competition, I think she'll be somewhat relieved."

"My fourteen-year-old daughter watched her splendid performance at the World Gymnastics Championship last year. She and her girlfriends think Marie is perhaps the greatest woman gymnast of all time. They absolutely adore her."

"Marie was quite pleased with her performance."

"Very well, Dr Aguila. Good luck to Team Puramore."

"Thank you, Herr Offenbach, for extending us the opportunity to compete in the IBL."

He returned to Puramore that evening.

* * *

As the IBL's top-ranked team, the Brazilian nationals played Team Puramore, the lowest-ranked seed, in the first round of the South America regional qualifying tournament. The top four teams of the sixteen teams competing in the single-elimination format tournament would automatically qualify to participate in the annual IBL Championship Tournament. Prior to the game, sports media and expert basketball commentators predicted the Brazilian national team would handily win the tournament. As a result, only Brazil media concerns sent television and radio crews to cover the event.

As the buzzer sounded to indicate the start of the game, players immediately ceased their pregame drills and proceeded to their respective team benches.

Positioned in the middle of the huddle, Coach Johnson slowly turned around and looked at each player's face. The Cheshire cat grins each bore displayed no concern whatsoever on their part as to the ultimate result of the game. Somewhat shaken by the overt display of unbounded confidence, he shook his head.

"All right, players, it's time to put on your game faces and take this game seriously. Must I remind you that this is your first competition as a basketball team in over three years, and you're playing perhaps the world's finest basketball team."

He then glanced at his clipboard.

"You, both individually and as a team, must not show the Brazilian nationals that you have any doubt about your capabilities as basketball players and men. They are past masters at perceiving and immediately capitalising on their opponents' weaknesses, especially if they sense their world-renown physical aggressiveness overwhelms and intimidates the opponent.

"If you are to have any chance of competitively playing against this team you must, I repeat, you must play as a cohesive team in all aspects of the game. Also, I know for certain that you are faster and more physically fit than their players, so use that competitive edge to your best advantage. You have the capability to run them into the ground by the end of the first half.

"Finally, play fairly and don't allow the Brazilians to hurt or intimidate you. If they throw an elbow, you throw an elbow, but only if the ref isn't looking."

He again looked down at his clipboard.

"Okay, this is the starting lineup. Magnus, you're at point guard. Levi's at centre. Goethe, you're the power forward. Voltaire, you're the small forward. Newton's at off guard. And, Gautama, you'll be the sixth man."

He looked up from his clipboard and glanced around at all the players surrounding him. The visage of each and every one of them displayed an intense solemnity and focus of concentration that startled the coach.

"Well, that's better!"

The buzzer signalling the opening tip-off sounded.

He reached his hands out for a team handshake.

As they shook hands as a group, he bellowed, "Now, let's get out there and show them what Team Puramore is all about!"

The players responded as one.

"Yes, Coach Johnson!"

The crowd cheered as the five starting players ran onto the court to take their positions for the opening tip-off.

"If you don't mind me saying, that was a stirring pep talk Coach," said a voice behind him.

He instantly recognised the voice as Aguila's.

As he turned his head to see him, he said, "I don't at all mind your saying so Aguila. I pride myself in my ability to rouse players to perform at their best of their capabilities through my pregame pep talk."

It was good, indeed, to be doing what I do best after all these years. There's nothing like the exhilaration of coaching in basketball competition

"By the way, I'd like you to meet one of the parents of the players."

He turned his head to face a man sitting next to him.

"Coach Johnson, it is my honour and privilege to introduce you to George Alexander."

A highly distinguished-looking and nattily dressed gentleman sitting next to Juan reached out his hand to Coach Johnson.

"It's a distinct pleasure and honour to meet you, Coach Johnson," he said as they shook hands.

He then removed his sunglasses and gazed into the coach's eyes for several seconds.

Before he could reply another cheer from the stands let forth. He turned his head to the centre court to witness the sight of Levi swatting the tip-off ball to Magnus. It travelled in a beeline to the team leader who bounded to the hoop after catching the ball to register the first score of the game with a simple layup.

Coach Johnson was right. Team Puramore's relentless style collapsed the Brazilian nationals' collective stamina before the end of the first half. From the opening tip-off, Team Puramore outraced, outhustled, and outplayed the opponent in every facet of the game. If ever there was a display of superior individual and team skills at the highest level, Team Puramore demonstrated it throughout the game.

Toward the end of the game, at their coach's behest, the frustrated Brazilian team adopted a street-fighting style of play designed to physically intimidate and overpower Team Puramore. Though the effort resulted in their players suffering from an assortment of cracked bones and deep contusions in the end.

When asked by their coach afterward, each of the injured players became visibly shaken and flatly refused to comment as to the source of their physical trauma. The Brazilian national team captain, who wasn't injured, later advised the head coach that the team would flat out refuse to play Team Puramore again.

With one second remaining in the game, Magnus made the winning shot with his signature from-the-top-of-the-key, Ferris wheel slam dunk.

Coach Johnson dropped to his knees at that moment and wept. At the same time, exultant pandemonium broke out in the stadium. A relatively low-scoring affair for that level of play, 100 to 99, the game nevertheless served immediate notice on the international basketball community that Team Puramore was a phenomenon and a force to be reckoned with for the remainder of the IBL Championship Tournament.

A murder of crows leisurely descended upon the Puramore National Sports Complex just after the game ended. Alighting, the group perched on titanium beams that crisscrossed high above the floor of the basketball court.

For no apparent reason, Juan suddenly removed his sunglasses as he looked up at the top of the dome where the crows congregated. He squinted intensely at that point for five or six seconds as though transfixed by some peculiarity located there. Immediately afterward an expression of recognition suddenly appeared on his face, almost as though he had encountered a long-lost friend.

An impish smile crept over his face as he whispered to himself, "Vaya, vaya, vaya."

Chapter 21 - Status KWO

Beijing, People's Republic of China, 16 August 2055

It was the final nail in the Globalisation Movement's coffin. Xu Yingying, who succeeded her father as the movement's leader after his death three years earlier, announced her resignation and retirement from politics. The seventy-four-year-old spinster issued the formal announcement at a nationally televised press conference.

"History shall favourably record GM's loyal and outstanding service to the People's Republic of China since its founding as a faction within the Communist Party over sixty years ago, especially during the halcyon era of the first thirty years of this century. Nevertheless, our time is sadly at an end, my dear comrades.

"This realisation gradually came to me over the course of the past few years. During that period, we became evermore impotent in our effort to stem the tide of the devastating economic deterioration from which the country and the rest of the world suffered, and continues to suffer."

Her face displayed her emblematic pragmatic stoicism for which she was famous as well as infamous. Early on in her political career, her dispassionate and aloof approach and appearance earned her the nickname Old Stone Face.

"Henceforth, GM is functionally defunct. As a result, the movement's apparatus is being completely dismantled as I speak. As for me, I am henceforth retired from politics in any way, shape, or form," she concluded.

A grimace of mortal fear suddenly emerged on her face. She raised her trembling hands to cover her face and began to sob uncontrollably.

A deputy official of the defunct movement stood up from his seat located directly behind the speaker and approached the podium. He gently placed his hands on Yingying's shoulders and led her off the dais.

He returned to the podium seconds later. A robust and vigorous man in his mid-thirties, Wu Xiaoping looked indignantly into the camera lens.

"Xu Yingying doesn't deserve to be treated like this... and neither do I."

He summarily departed the stage after issuing that final statement for the defunct movement.

The humiliating public capitulation speech issued by Yingying warmed Wingtip's black heart from its inception. At several points, Wingtip's inner joy almost burst forth into an exuberant and uncontrollable glee as he witnessed the culmination of his plan for the demise of GM. Instead, he sat in his seat located directly in front of the speakers' podium without so much as twitching a muscle. From all outward appearances, he was totally insouciant as to the tragic drama that unfolded during the press conference. In fact, the normally animated Wingtip affected an Old Stone Face impression as a form of mockery throughout her speech.

Premier Hú Li, who sat next to him, glimpsed at Wingtip's profile as Wu Xiaoping escorted her off the dais. He bit his tongue in order to squelch the exuberant inner joy and laughter that immediately arose within him. He then affected Wingtip's demeanour after a brief smile broke over his face.

Not that it meant anything particularly important to Wingtip since GM had become politically moribund well over a decade before. Nevertheless, the country and the rest of the world had witnessed the last vestige of any sort of Chinese political dissent against KWO. The macabre event also represented his de facto coronation as the undisputed leader of the Communist Party. He knew full well that his countrymen also realised that rubbing his last political adversary's nose in the excrement of its failure in that way heralded his ascension as the absolute ruler of China.

Upon their arrival at Xi'an early the next morning, Wingtip and Hú Li held a meeting in the Celestial Node. The first item on their agenda concerned a full review of the status to date of all the key elements of KWO's plan to apply its brand of political control in major world capitals. Over the course of the past four decades, KWO had successfully employed cells that either took control over existing political parties or created new ones for that purpose. In any event, the resultant political apparatus never associated with KWO, not even tangentially.

"I am gratified with the progress we've achieved in increasing our constituency numbers across the board, Hú Li," Wingtip said. "We must now begin the political agitation phase of the plan in the major capitals, such as Washington DC."

"I concur. I will order our cell leaders to commence that phase of the plan immediately."

"Next, it is time to begin to reward the Chinese people with increasing levels of prosperity.

"Order that process to commence straight away. However, maintain the economic depression state elsewhere, especially in France."

"I will."

"Lastly, though Xu Yingying and Wu Xiaoping are dead in the water, politically speaking, their continued existence is somewhat problematic, particularly considering their plan to take flight from China. Therefore, let's put the Proposal to them within the next few days.

If they decline to accept conversion, kill them at once."

"As you wish, My Lord."

"By the way, how are we getting along with that effort?"

"My Lord, we are meeting our quotas. Though weak-willed lotus blossoms are becoming fewer in numbers as time progresses. Yet I am confident that the corporeal and spiritual duress engendered by the political agitation phase will serve to significantly increase the number of converts during the next few months. As a result, in no time whatsoever, we should begin to surpass our quotas in the same fashion as we achieved here in China following the onset of the Political Agitation Imperative."

"At this critical juncture, we must nevertheless step up the effort to a fever pitch. There still exists a factor that may disrupt the achievement in our overall object in the form of Juan and the Puramore. Just how credible is that threat?"

"As you know, Puramore can be employed only one more time in defence of humanity. If the thirteenth attempt fails, it shall be returned to the Guardian forthwith. Personally, I fail to perceive of anyone capable of wielding the blade to defeat us, just like the others who failed before."

"Not even General Smythe?"

"He is up to the task of wielding Puramore. Though it is my judgment that he shall fail to defeat us as well. We are too firmly entrenched to fail in achieving final victory this time around. Without it, mankind is at our utter mercy."

"We shan't show them any, President Hú Li."

"President?"

"Yes, President. It's your reward for a job well done. As for mine, my election as the first Supreme Chairman of the People's Republic of China has just been confirmed by unanimous consent of the Politburo."

"My congratulations to you on your ascension to your rightful station, My Lord and Supreme Chairman."

As soon as they departed the National Conference Hall, they knew their days were numbered. Xu Yingying and Wu Xiaoping decided to put into effect the escape plan they had devised for themselves several months earlier. They were confident about safely fleeing the country, but were still unsure as to where they should flee. Their best bet in their estimation was to seek political asylum from India. The selection was primarily due to the long-standing enmity that existed between the country and China following the crushing military defeat it suffered during the India-China Conflict of 2023.

Acting as a supreme commander, Wingtip led the campaign for the victorious PRC military force. The main difficulty, in any event, stemmed from contacting a potentially friendly country, one sympathetic to their plight, to apply for asylum before fleeing China. This was an issue that was unresolved prior to their political abdication that evening.

"What are we going to do now?" Wu said.

They entered the limousine parked just outside the main entrance of the conference hall.

"My life is over my friend. I might as well remain here and at least achieve martyrdom."

The glass partition separating them from the front seat rolled down.

"There's no need for that," the driver cheerfully said.

At that moment the limousine door they entered reopened. A tall and burly Caucasian male entered the limousine and took a seat facing the rear of the vehicle. He smiled at the two frightened former political officials sitting in front of him.

"What's the meaning of this?" Wu demanded.

"Where's our driver Tse and our bodyguard Zedong?"

"We gave them the night off, sir. They're now resting comfortably in the boot of the limo," the man replied as he entered the vehicle.

"Rolf, please!" the driver said.

"I don't know who you think you are, but we have no money on our persons. Do you know who we are?"

"You must remain calm and listen to me. Your lives depend upon it," the driver said. "My name is Major Surya Thappa. The two men accompanying me are the Brünner brothers, Fritz and Rolf. Rolf is sitting in front of you. Make no mistake about it, Madame, Wingtip plans to murder you both before the week is over."

Yingying recovered her composure but was obviously incredulous with the situation.

"Really, Major Thappa, how can you be certain of that?"

"We have it from a supremely reliable source. Now, listen to me carefully: I am an emissary sent by the Puramore government to extend an offer of political asylum to you both. If you accept our offer, we shall transport you to our country this very evening."

"And what does your government expect from us in return, Major?" Minister Wu queried.

"There are no expectations the government imposes upon you in return for saving your lives."

"But we already have an escape plan."

"You must trust me instead. Your plan to escape from the borders of China has already been compromised."

"This is ridiculous. Wingtip knows ours and every citizen's every movement. The RED STAR computer tracking programme makes certain of that. The only way we can possibly thwart it is by assuming identities of other citizens with the assistance of sophisticated computer hackers loyal to our Supreme Order."

"They are compromised, as well, Madame."

"How can you possibly know that?" Wu asked.

"You must trust me that our own computer resources enable us to know that as a fact. It also has the capability to interact with RED STAR to cloak your real whereabouts. As I speak, SITA, our own quantum computer, has issued a miscommunication to RED STAR that this limousine has already left this location on its way to transport you to your respective residences. As far as Wingtip knows, you are presently two minutes en route."

"This is absolutely incredible."

He looked into Yingying's startled eyes. She, too, he noticed, was totally mystified by the strange situation.

"Nevertheless, we must leave now. Prying eyes can be fooled, but not for much longer, if we dally here any longer."

He turned the ignition key and started the engine. Almost simultaneously he shifted the transmission into the automatic drive gear, released the parking gear, and sped off.

"You must give me your answer now. Otherwise, I shall have no other choice than to drive you to your homes."

Yingying continued to gaze into Wu's eyes. They stared at each other for a few seconds.

"Mr Thappa, we are only too honoured and gratified to accept Puramore's offer of political asylum," she said resolutely.

Wu heaved a sigh of relief.

"Splendid, Madame. I assure you that you'll never regret having reached that decision."

"Where are we going to now, Major Thappa?" Wu asked.

There was a note of relief evident in his voice.

"We're heading for the Beijing International Airport where we shall all board an aircraft for our flight to Puramore."

With their unknown fate having been thusly sealed the pair settled back comfortably in their seats, and awaited the more immediate outcome of their decision to accept political asylum from Puramore. Still, they were satisfied with the bargain, especially since it gave them a glimmer of hope that they would survive beyond week's end and perhaps one day play a role in vanquishing Wingtip forever.

"This is what we've been hoping for, my dear Pingping.

Although totally unexpected, our salvation has been handed to us on a silver platter. It's as though divine providence is acting to preserve our lives for some other purpose," she whispered.

He nodded his agreement with her sentiment and put his hand on hers.

The drive to the Beijing Capital International Airport took about an hour. On arrival, the limousine passed through the airport's security gauntlet without a hitch. Before their arrival, airport security management had been informed that the limousine carried two government officials who were scheduled to board a private jet airliner for a flight to France on government business.

"Have you been here before, Major Thappa? You certainly seem to possess expert knowledge of the interior road layout of the airport,"

She was obviously impressed with Surya's ease in driving through the maze of interior roadways that intricately laced through the runways.

"Only as a passenger, Dr Xu. SITA is guiding me to our final destination as it has been since we left the conference centre."

"But how? I don't see any sort of GPS apparatus anywhere near you," Wu said.

"You don't see it because only I do. The apparatus is implanted on my corneas."

"Now just a minute. Enough's enough," Wu protested.

The limousine came to a gradual stop.

Rolf politely interjected, "After we exit the limo, follow us closely. This is the tricky part of our journey. We aren't where we should be in terms of airport security's understanding of your embarkation location. As such, the last thing we need now is to have an airport security employee put two and two together upon seeing you here and question us as to the reason. We'll lead you to the aircraft. Once we arrive you must follow our instructions to the letter."

He then opened the limousine door closest to Yingying and stepped out onto the tarmac. He took her hand as she exited the vehicle.

"Watch your step, Dr Xu."

Wu followed her.

It was a short walk to the side door of the aircraft hangar. Fritz opened the door and entered the building. A minute later he reappeared to hand signal an all clear to Rolf from inside.

"We can enter the building now."

Yingying gasped at the first sight of the aircraft parked inside the hangar. She had seen artist's renderings of the aircraft in an edition of a science and technology magazine she perused several months ago at her dentist's office.

"My goodness!" she exclaimed. "This aircraft is supposedly still on the drawing boards."

"Fortunately for all of us, this version of the Stargazer HST is now ready and available to transport us this evening," Surya said.

Four heavily armed guards dressed in PRC Army uniforms were positioned around the aircraft.

"Those soldiers aren't Chinese," Wu stated.

"They're my Nepalese countrymen, sir."

"You're starting to make a believer out of me, Major Thappa. But how in the name of Chairman Mao were you able to accomplish this extraordinary feat? And I don't mean the fabrication of the Stargazer HST, which is at least twenty years away from development even based on China's advanced technology prowess. I know, I am a former vice minister of the PRC Aeronautics and Space Commission, who served the last four years as chair of the Exotic Technological Development Committee. What truly astounds me more than that is how you were able to infiltrate this ultra-secure airport, probably one of the most secure buildings in the world, and place the aircraft in this hangar."

The aircraft's skin reflected the intense interior lighting like a well-polished mirror. Wu's jaw dropped at the sight. No rivets or seams were visible on the surface of the scram-jet powered hypersonic transport.

Wu thought the design of the aircraft dated back to the SR-99 Aurora prototype, manufactured by Lockheed Skunk Works in the late 2020s, but never put into production.

Though the Stargazer HST design was much more slender and dart-like.

"How did they create the skin? Nowhere in our prototype plans for a similar HST did we envisage such a material."

At that moment Captain Reginald Saunders exited the aircraft and approached the awaiting passengers. Tall, athletically built, and impeccably attired in a captain's civilian aviation uniform, he cut a dashing and regally imposing figure as he swaggered toward them.

Yingying's jaw dropped when she first caught sight of him. She nearly swooned at the thought that a mid-thirties Error Flynn had just walked onto the scene.

"Dr Xu and Minister Wu, I have the distinct honour of introducing you to Captain Reginald Saunders. Captain Saunders is our pilot for this evening's flight to Puramore."

Saunders tipped his hat.

"I am honoured to meet our illustrious guests, Major Thappa. Thank you."

"Right. We are nearly ready for the takeoff."

He shot a stare of disapproval at the Brünner brothers.

"Captain, if you would be so kind, Minister Wu would very much like to pose a few questions to you about the aircraft," Surya implored. "I really don't possess the requisite expertise to entertain his questions."

"Right, Major. I fully understand and appreciate your position. Since we aren't labouring under any sort of time constraint, at least not for the next five minutes, please extend me the honour of entertaining your queries prior to our boarding the aircraft for takeoff."

"Firstly, what is the aircraft skin's composition, and how was it created?" Wu asked.

He sounded as though he was an MIT freshman asking a Nobel Prize-winning laureate an advanced physics question.

"What you are actually looking at is a seamless six-ply array of multi-walled carbon nanotubes that forms the entire exterior surface of the aircraft. The nanotube skin is as complex, if not vastly more so, than human skin, and is less than a mil in thickness. For one thing, it constantly regulates surface temperatures, much like human skin, even transferring heat to cooler regions when required to balance thermal characteristics for enhanced flight performance. It even regulates the temperature of engine exhaust gasses to significantly reduce heat signature.

"Moreover, it is more sensitive to touch in any form than our skin. In fact, by a factor of well over a million times more sensitive. A butterfly wings' fluttering, for instance, from a kilometre away are subsequently felt by the skin as sensitively as a toddler would sense a kiss from his mother. Yet, though the tensile strength many hundreds of times greater than that of a diamond, it is as supple and pliable as cotton swaddling cloth. As such, the entire construct is independently wrapped around the fuselage, much like a shrink-wrapping. Now all of that is fairly impressive on its own merit, wouldn't you say?"

"That is more than impressive, Captain," Wu stated.

He was in obvious awe of the technology.

"It's light-years ahead of our current nanotechnology development."

"Yet, here's the real kicker: Skin is highly intelligent and possesses extraordinary physical properties. These twin attributes allow it to transform itself into any colour, texture, and level of transparency. For instance, please notice the cabin windows, lady and gentlemen. They are temporarily formed by Skin, and not by any internal fuselage construct. Furthermore, these same attributes allow Skin to absorb and bend radiation of all kinds for the purpose of rendering the aircraft invisible as well as totally cloaked from radar detection.

"What's even more astounding than that is Skin replaces all the flight control surfaces; it thereby performs as elevator, rudder, aileron, trim, et al., by instantly transforming itself to meet the demands of whatever flight manoeuvre is required at the moment.

"Well, I could go on and on about other marvellous qualities of Skin, such as being an excellent navigational aid and cabin pressure regulator, but shall not, since we must prepare to board the plane at this time."

"But how did you manage to transport the aircraft here?" Wu asked.

He was truly bewildered beyond belief that this could have occurred in the most impregnable and secure areas in China.

"I'm sorry to say the answer to that question must remain classified for now, Minister Wu."

His tone was one of final authority.

The aircraft skin suddenly transformed into a brilliant and lustrous fire-engine red colour.

He turned to look at the plane after noticing the passengers' mouths suddenly agape.

"Oh, you show-off!" he cackled.

He then looked back at the passengers, whose mouths were still agape.

He nonchalantly said, "Right. So there you have it. Our precious Stargazer HST Skin bids us to board the plane at once."

* * *

The previous day, SITA's search for a hangar housing an appropriate plane took less than a few seconds to conduct. Fortuitously, SITA discovered a Shenying J-20 fighter/bomber that suited the bill. And it was the only aircraft parked in a hangar located in the section of the airport reserved for military use. The maintenance log indicated it was undergoing a refit to convert it to civilian usage. The computer immediately cancelled the refit project, reassigned involved project personnel, ordered the hangar placed off-limits to all personnel, and officially mothballed the aircraft. According to the maintenance log thereafter, the aircraft was flown that evening to an aircraft dismantling and mothball facility located in northern China. The official flight records, including the fictitious crew records, reflected that as a fact, as well

An hour later, four heavily armed men, dressed as PRC Army soldiers, entered the hangar. One of the soldiers carried an aluminium briefcase. He walked over to the aircraft and set the case underneath the belly of the fuselage. He next opened the case, reached inside, and tapped at a keypad within. Afterward, he and his companions directly exited the hangar as though the case was set for an imminent explosion.

"Mission accomplished, Major Thappa," a voice said into the receiver installed in his right ear.

He tapped his right earlobe.

"Well done. Post yourselves around the hangar and await further orders."

He tapped his right earlobe again.

"SITA, the site is secure."

"I copy and confirm. Aerosol application of nant reconstruction colony to the aircraft outer structure is now complete. I expect to issue the re-entry order twenty-four hours hence."

* * *

"Welcome aboard, passengers," Captain Saunders cheerfully said from the cockpit. "It's a splendid evening in

Beijing to commence our two-and-a-half-hour, seventeen-thousand-kilometre flight to Ciudad de Puramore.

"The current weather conditions at our destination is fair: barometric pressure is steady at 1,028 millibars, relative humidity reading is 68 percent, the temperature is 9 degrees Celsius, and variable winds are blowing from the northwest at 3 knots. Visibility from the Puramore International Airport control tower is 10 kilometres.

"GMT is 17:04 on my mark. Mark. It is now 2:04 a.m. in Beijing, or 2:04 p.m., which is yesterday in Ciudad de Puramore.

"The control tower has just given us clearance to taxi to our runway."

The fan-jets immediately began to whirl. The aircraft exited the hangar and proceeded to taxi to the runway.

"Skin has temporarily reconfigured the profile of the aircraft so that we would appear to be a standard business jet of no remarkable significance.

"Our flight attendants, Nadhirah and Kobi, shall serve your every need halfway through our flight.

"Please closely follow the passenger preflight instructions provided on the 3-D monitor that should appear directly before you now."

A pleasant female voice then spoke.

"Please say hello in your native or preferred language."

Her almost-perfect English accent was slightly tinged with a Hindi inflection.

Dr Xu responded, "Bonjour."

She heard Wu, who was sitting in the lounger beside hers, reply in Mandarin.

"Bonjour, Dr Xu," the voice replied.

A 3-D image of a beautiful young Malaysian woman instantly appeared in front of each of the passengers. She was dressed in the typical flight attendant's suit topped by a smart and elegant cap. It set smartly on her black hair that was wrapped tightly into a tight bun at the back of her neck.

A friendly smile broke across her lovely face.

She said in French, "Welcome to Stargazer HST 2.0. You have the distinction of being one of the first passengers to travel in this version of the aircraft."

Her voice was directed to the passenger in front of the image through speakers located within the passenger seat.

"Every care and attention to detail have been taken to assure that you would enjoy a safe and comfortable flight. First and foremost in that effort is passenger safety and comfort during the scram jet trajectory phase of the flight. As a consequence, in order to properly prepare for the experience, please adhere closely to the following instructions. The programme is interactive, so each of you shall be able to perform the required preflight tasks at your own pace and leisure. A flight attendant shall be with you shortly in the unlikely event that you encounter any difficulties."

The young woman's image was immediately replaced by that of a young black man, who appeared to be in his early twenties. He was dressed in a stylishly tailored suit and tie.

Handsome, well-groomed, and trim, he sat in a recliner seat that was a replica of the Stargazer's passenger cabin recliner seats. The recliner was set in the sitting chair position.

"Hello. I shall now guide you through passenger preflight procedure," he said in perfect French.

His presentation was serious but pleasant.

"Our flight this evening conforms to the standard HST takeoff, glide path, and landing profile. To achieve an optimal parabolic glide path profile to our destination, the aircraft will ascend to an elevation of twenty-two nautical miles above mean sea level at its apogee.

"In order to attain that elevation, the Stargazer HST literally blasts off from a height of six thousand meters above the runway in a nearly vertical trajectory.

"It is crucial that you understand and anticipate the physics involved in rapid ascent as the g-forces are sufficient enough to produce physical and mental discomfort. Your bodies shall undergo this experience from the moment the scram-jet engine ignites and throughout most of the ascent trajectory.

"To countervail the physical discomfort of the experience, a passenger anti-g suit and a helmet are required to be worn before takeoff and throughout the scram-jet trajectory event. I shall now assist you in donning the suit.

"First, an anti-g suit is stowed under your seat. Please take the time now to remove the suit from the stowage compartment and don it."

He reached under his seat and removed a bag that contained the anti-g suit. He removed the suit from the bag and unfolded it. He then pulled the Velcro strip that ran from the waistline to the top. He folded the suit in half and slipped his feet through each of the suit legs and into the booties. He stood up and slipped his arms through the suit sleeves and adhered the Velcro stripping together. Dr Xu donned the suit as instructed.

"Good. Well done.

"Tightly seal narrow Velcro belts located around your ankles. Next, tightly seal the Velcro strips that surround your upper thighs and chest."

He performed the indicated tasks himself and sat back down in the recliner.

She followed his instructions and then sat down in her recliner.

"Good. You are free to remove the suit once the captain has issued approval to do so. The suit status display located on the seat back in front of you will flash green at that time. The flight attendant will subsequently collect the suit from you.

"Next, please find pneumatic hose underneath the armrest on the right side of your seat.

"Connect the hose to the aperture found on the upper right-hand side of the suit."

She connected the hose as instructed.

"Very well done. Now, please buckle the harness strap and seat belt. Underneath the armrest on the left side of your seat, you'll find a biomonitor device. You must apply it to your left wrist via the attached Velcro strap. Please do so now."

She buckled herself as instructed and subsequently attached the biomonitor device to her left wrist

"Excellent. Just prior to takeoff, a safety helmet will lower from the utility compartment located overhead. Immediately put on the helmet, completely lower the visor, and adhere your suit's collar to the Velcro strip that surrounds the bottom of the helmet. Continue to wear the helmet until the captain indicates his approval for removal. The helmet status display located on the seat back in front of you will flash green at that time. In addition to providing head protection, the helmet supplies oxygen and public address speakers."

A helmet lowered from above him. He put it on, lowered the visor and adhered the Velcro strip to the suit collar. Afterward, he raised the visor and removed the helmet.

"Just prior to scram jet engine ignition, your recliner will automatically extend to a full reclining position.

"After g-force one has been realised near apogee, you'll be free to adjust your recliner to its sitting position, or any position you find comfortable. The g-force indicator will flash green when that occurs. It would be appropriate for you to recline during the brief period of weightlessness you'll experience thereafter.

"Please ask a flight attendant for assistance should you need to use lavatory services before scram-jet engine trajectory phase of the flight.

"That concludes the passenger preflight preparation protocol. Please direct any questions or concerns you may have about the procedure to your flight attendants.

"We are confident that you will enjoy our interactive flight programme that shall be presented to you shortly after scram-jet shutdown."

The 3-D image subtly dissolved.

Saunders glanced at the 2-D biometric monitor display set to the right of his pilot's seat. He carefully examined his passengers' biometric readings, primarily to determine whether or not individual stress levels warranted sedation.

"Great balls of fire, what do you know about that!"

He had just examined Dr Xu's biometric readings. Her biometric profile was literally off the charts for a woman her age. In fact, her physiology was consistent with that of a twenty-year-old Olympic gymnast.

"We have been taking our vitamins, haven't we?" he muttered. "SITA?"

"Yes, Captain."

"I know this a rhetorical question, but did you happen to notice Dr Xu's biometric readings?"

"I did indeed. What did you expect?"

"Certainly not discovering that she's a candidate for astronaut training. Moreover, her mental state readings indicate she's as comfortable with the flight as I am, whereas Minister Wu may require a slight dose of anti-anxiety gas if his readings do not improve before takeoff."

"Captain, Dr Xu didn't win a Nobel Prize for her work in biochemistry for nothing. She simply applies her expertise in her field of science to her own body. What you are observing are the sterling results of years of fitness due to proper diet and exercise."

"Well, she's beautiful, inside and out. I believe that I am smitten by her."

The aircraft entered the runway and came to a halt. He briefly glanced at his own biometric readings and noticed his own emotional and mental state indicators hadn't changed one iota from the last time he checked a minute earlier.

"Drat," he muttered to himself.

A few moments later a monotonic voice spoke over the cockpit intercom.

"Air Andes flight number 1485, you are clear for takeoff."

"Roger, control tower. Over and out."

The aircraft then started slowly gaining momentum. Less than halfway down the runway the plane lifted off and ascended as a jet aircraft normally would.

"Stealth mode," Saunders commanded.

In a flash, the aircraft became essentially invisible but maintained a tracking on the air traffic control computer toward another destination.

A gaggle of geese suddenly appeared ahead. The formation flew right toward the front of the aircraft. Instantly, two of the geese smashed into the flight deck windshield with an audible thump. Almost simultaneously Saunders heard the report of two other thumps aft. Forthwith the gory remnants of the smashed geese disappeared.

"Not today, you bloody shifters!"

"Ladies and gentlemen, there is no cause for alarm. We just encountered an unfortunate gaggle of geese."

He peered at the passengers' biometric readings and noted no panic amongst them. He next scanned the aircraft structural integrity sensors and noted that no damage was sustained. Skin deflected the assault as easily as swatting flies.

A few seconds later the feminine voice announced over the public address system.

"Passenger helmets are now lowering. Please install your helmet as soon possible as instructed in the preflight preparation presentation."

A 3-D image next appeared in front of each passenger, showing the young man placing the helmet on his head, lowering the visor, and attaching it to the suit collar. Afterward, the image disappeared.

The passengers all placed and set their helmets as instructed.

"Thank you," the voice said. "Flight attendants, please prepare the cabin for scram-jet engine ignition."

The passenger recliners immediately shifted and then locked into the reclining position.

A minute later Captain Saunders spoke: "Major Saunders here. We have scram jet engine ignition in T minus ten seconds. Nine. Eight. Seven. Six. Five. Four. Three. Two. One. Ignition."

At that instant, a thundering roar commenced. Even though her ears were protected by the helmet and exterior skin of the aircraft, Dr Xu sensed the power of the scram-jet engine as the roar reached a fever pitch that sounded like hundreds of claxons blaring in unison. Her sense was soon confirmed as aircraft shot straight up into the sky like a surface-to-air missile.

She instantly felt the suit inflate around her as her body sank deeply into the thick seat padding. Her helmet was glued to the padding by the ever-increasing g-force; as a result, she could not turn her head in any direction. The aircraft trembled ever so slightly as acceleration increased. Her body sank deeper and deeper into the seat padding all the while.

A 2-D image abruptly appeared in front of her visor. It presented graphical illustrations of the path of the trajectory both in real time and in projected time. Underneath the illustrations were two digital time counters, ticking by the millisecond; one showed the elapsed time from ignition, the other the projected time until scram-jet engine shutdown. According to the elapsed time counter, the aircraft was two minutes into the fifteen-minute burn.

The screen was replaced ten seconds later by one that displayed the flight path progress from Beijing to Ciudad de Puramore. The two screens alternated every fifteen seconds thereafter. Ten minutes into the burn the engine began to gradually shut down. At the same time the g-force level, which reached its peak five minutes earlier, gradually subsided. Three minutes later the scram jet engine shut down entirely.

"One minute to commencement of zero-g phase," the female voice announced.

Dr Xu turned her head to see Minister Wu's suited body prostrate on the recliner next to her.

"You may speak to him now, Dr Xu. He is awake and fully alert," the voice said.

"Wu, are you all right?"

"I feel slightly groggy, but otherwise I feel fine. Though I seem to have missed part of the party."

She loved him for his sense of humour he expressed even under the most trying of circumstances.

"Well, my dear friend, I'm sure the best is yet to come. You merely missed the rush hour traffic getting there."

He chuckled.

The g-force indicator light then turned green.

"You are free to remove your helmet and suit at this time," the voice advised.

"Zero-g state will be confirmed when the light begins flashing green."

"Not yet, ladies and gentlemen. We have a special treat for you this evening, one which you will not forget for the rest of your lives," Saunders said. "I need to warn you beforehand, though, as what you are about to see is not for the faint of heart. As such, you may want to continue to wear your helmet and suit for the next thirty minutes."

At that instant, the passenger cabin interior became transparent. All that could be seen of the aircraft was the ultra-thin black framework that outlined the interior, both fore and aft.

"I assure you that you are totally safe and secure. We could make the carbon nanotube fuselage framework transparent as well, but in the interest of your peace of mind, it remains visible."

The g-force indicator light began to blink.

Yingying instantly felt a sense of exhilaration that she had not felt since she formally accepted the Nobel Prize in chemistry thirty years earlier. She vividly recalled that frigid December evening in Stockholm when the award medal, diploma, and cash confirmation were formally presented to her by King Carl XVII Gustav. The glitter of the presentation stage and the excitement of the moment when the Swedish monarch handed her medal would always remain with her as the highlight of her scientific career.

She stared in awe at the scintillating cosmos all around her and concurrently felt her body release from the gravity of Earth. A sense of spiritual transcendence began to pull at every fibre of her being. She viscerally became aware at that moment that beyond a shadow of a doubt she was being reborn to fulfil another destiny on Earth. She wept with joy as the gravity of earthly concerns gradually ceased to weigh upon her being. A beatific smile formed on her face. She wiped the tears from her face with a silk handkerchief.

"Well, you certainly look rapturous, Yingying," Wu said. "I've never seen you smile like that."

"I haven't ever since I was a child."

Chapter 22 - Matchmaker, Matchmaker, Make Me a Match

The LAB, Glenamore, Puramore, 17 August 2055

The remainder of the flight was unremarkable.

The fan-jet engines kept the aircraft moving at Mach three for most of the time soon after scram-jet engine shutdown. All the same time, the passengers were left with the impression that they were travelling at subsonic speed in a standard commercial jet airliner since the aircraft was perfectly controlled. After descending to fifteen thousand meters above mean sea level, the aircraft leveled off somewhat. The flight attendants served a savory five-course meal soon thereafter.

There was daylight when the Stargazer HST touched down on the Puramore International Airport runway. Dr Xu marvelled at the scenery surrounding the airport at the moment the aircraft entered the airspace over Ciudad de Puramore, particularly the vast blue lake.

"Welcome to Ciudad de Puramore," Saunders announced soon after touchdown. "It's a splendid cloudless day in the Puramore region of the Andes.

"The current temperature at the airport is 19 degrees Celsius. Winds are gusting from the north-northwest at 5 knots. Humidity reading is at 40 percent, and the barometric pressure is rising at 1,026 millibars. There's a 100 percent chance of rainfall later tomorrow. GMT is 19:34 on my mark. Mark. The local time is 4:34 p.m.

"If this is your first visit to Ciudad de Puramore, you may want to take extra care not to overexert yourself during your first few days. At a mean elevation of 2,900 meters above mean sea level, the atmosphere is relatively thin. So much so that atmospheric oxygen content is 31 percent less at this elevation than at sea level. Flight attendants will dispense portable oxygen cylinder to first-time visitors prior to deplaning as well as administer anti-jet lag injections to all passengers. Please make certain you keep your cylinder on your person at all times in case of a respiratory emergency.

"We will be at our arrival gate in a few minutes. Please remain seated with your seat belt fastened until the aircraft has come to a complete halt and the Unfasten Seat Belt sign appears in front of you...We trust that you enjoyed your Stargazer HST 2.0 flight and look forward to your flying with us again."

"Dr Xu," Surya's voice politely broke over her recliner speakers.

"Yes, Major Thappa."

"I trust you had a pleasant and enjoyable flight."

"I did indeed. In fact, it was a transcendental experience for me."

"Jolly good! After deplaning, we'll take you directly to the limousine parked outside the airport terminal. We've already cleared you and Minister Wu through Customs and Immigration. We'll then travel to your final destination, the LAB facility located just over an hour's drive from the airport."

"LAB?"

"It'll be your home for your indefinite stay in Puramore, Doctor. It's an ultra-high security habitation compound built to house scientific and service staff as well as guests.

"Fear not, you and Minister Wu won't lack any of the amenities you are accustomed to enjoying as elite residents of Beijing."

They deplaned several minutes later without incident.

A few steps just inside the terminal, Dr Xu looked out the expansive floor-to-ceiling window that surrounded the arrival gate. She saw a standard business jet airplane parked at the other end of the passageway she had just passed through. A bright red Air Andes sign was painted on the side of the otherwise totally white aircraft.

Once they stepped outside the airport terminal, a man dressed in a white two-piece suit met them. To Dr Xu, the black-haired gentleman was striking in appearance from head to toe.

"Dr Xu, Minister Wu, my name is Dr Juan Aguila. I am the minister of Foreign Political Affairs here to officially welcome you to Puramore."

He then shook both their hands.

"Dr Aguila," Dr Xu replied, "we are both exceedingly pleased to have accepted your country's offer of political asylum. We have been treated exceptionally well ever since by Major Thappa and his staff."

"We can do nothing less for you both. I shall accompany you with Major Thappa on the journey to LAB."

He motioned for them to enter the black limousine parked a few steps away.

Upon entering the limousine, Juan asked them to allow him to perform a brief medical examination of them both. They readily assented. Afterward, he gave each of them a small black pill to ingest.

"You are both in need of a physical vitality medication. You'll feel as fresh as spring daisies in no time."

They promptly swallowed the pills.

The journey from the airport to the entrance of Glenamore took exactly an hour. Dr Xu and Minister Wu were silent during most of the ride, apparently somewhat still in shock over the tumultuous events that transpired over the course of the past twenty-four hours. As dusk was about to set in, they simply looked outside the limousine as it travelled to its destination and enjoyed the breathtaking scenery that was still visible at that time of day.

"If I didn't know any better, I'd say we were travelling through the Swiss Alps.".

She was obviously in wonderment of the landscape through which they had passed since leaving the airport.

"It's one of my favourite places in the world, Minister Wu, and always has been since I first visited the country years ago. I must say, though, that China is every bit as glorious in terms of natural splendour."

He peered into Dr Xu's eyes as he spoke. At first, she attempted to avert his gaze. He instantly locked onto her attention and brought her eyes back to meet his. She fell into a trance immediately. He studied her mind and her recent memories. She should be in a state of shock after reviewing her interaction with Wingtip just prior to her flight from China. She is a strong and brave spirit, he concluded. He released her mind after the two-second interlude.

"Indeed."

She had no recollection of the mind probe that Juan had practiced on her.

The vehicle began to slow ever so slightly.

"We're almost at the security gate," Surya advised.

A mountainside of sheer granite cliff suddenly came into view. The base of the massive rock wall was about four hundred meters directly in front of the speeding limousine.

Dr Xu held her breath as the vehicle approached the mountain. The limousine was approaching the granite face at breakneck speed. All at once an opening appeared at the base of the slab, one just wide enough for the vehicle to pass through. The limousine shot through the opening in a flash. Looking behind her as it exited the passageway, she saw the opening close and return to the appearance of solid granite.

"Welcome to Glenamore, esteemed guests," Juan said. "We shall arrive at the LAB in about half an hour."

Nightfall overtook the valley. The full moon directly above dimly illuminated the winding road as the limousine raced along toward LAB.

"You are completely secure inside the Glenamore scientific and military reserve. Nothing comes and goes without our knowledge and constant scrutiny. And I mean absolutely nothing," Juan said.

He felt the need to convey that assurance to the couple for their benefit.

"We are forever in your country's debt, Dr Aguila. I don't know how we shall ever be able to repay you and Puramore for saving our lives," Wu replied.

"All debts that you feel you owe to Puramore for saving your lives are herewith cancelled, Minister Wu. Puramore shall be forever in your debt instead. You, like others who've taken asylum here, are our national treasure and always shall be."

"Treasure?" she said to herself. What does he mean by that? There must be some ulterior motive involved with Puramore's policy of harbouring political refugees. Even more disconcerting was the fact that as far as she knew the country had never been identified as a political haven for likes of her and Wu. Dr Xu always thought that Puramore was an enigma well before her personal experience with the country began less than twenty-four hours ago.

She knew the People's Republic of China's elite political and military apparatus perceived is as peculiar that the country that, though not menacing in any fashion, merited continual scrutiny and investigation. Several attempts by the PRC to infiltrate the country's political and social establishment always met with tragic failure, though. Given her current personal experience, she concluded that the effort should have been redoubled at the very least, since Puramore represented far more than an innocuous curiosity. Not that she harboured any misgivings about taking sanctuary there; she merely thought that it was deplorable that the mighty PRC intelligence community had seriously underestimated the country's technological sophistication to such an obvious extent.

She felt slightly ashamed for that fact, mainly because she was a former State Council vice premier who directly supervised the Ministry of National Defence the last ten years.

As the front entrance of the facility came into view, Minister Wu's jaw dropped. Literally gouged into the face of a massive granite mountain base, the colossal entrance was one hundred meters wide and forty meters high. Light streamed out of the entryway like noonday sunshine. The limousine slowed appreciably and proceeded up a gradually sloping ramp that led into the interior of the cavern. About one hundred meters inside, the limousine gradually braked to a halt and parked next to an enormous transparent tube that shot straight up from the floor of the cavern to the ceiling over one hundred meters above. The two front doors immediately opened. Not more than two seconds later the passenger doors on either side of the vehicle opened.

"This is your new home, Dr Xu," Rolf. said.

He extended his hand to assist her out of the vehicle. She took hold of his hand and exited the vehicle.

Well, she thought, it's certainly better than a Beijing penitentiary. The intensity of the interior light nearly blinded her as she surveyed the cavern. Her mind failed to comprehend its enormity.

"Don't try to take it all in now, Dr Xu," Juan said. "We must proceed to HAB right away.

"Follow me, please."

A kind of curtain abruptly drew down over the entire entrance of the cavern. Minister Wu saw the event in its entirety after claxons sounded around the entrance several seconds before the onset. He looked at Surya with amazement, who was blankly staring at the entrance himself.

"Skin?"

"Yes, Skin, I'm afraid. It recently placed the old high-technology titanium-clad security door apparatus that was installed prior to the development of the interior cavern many years ago."

He then led the couple to the front of the shaft, which she judged was twenty meters in diameter. Parked at its base was a glass-encased passenger vehicle; a monorail passed through the lower belly of the conveyance. The monorail, one of the two that passed through the tube, ran horizontally along the floor of the cavern for about thirty meters before gradually bending upward through an elbow into the vertical section of the tubular structure. The monorail car contained twelve seats that were set two abreast on either side of the centre aisle.

"Please take a seat, preferably at the front of the tram, and buckle your shoulder harnesses. You'll enjoy a better view from there."

"Where have Rolf and Fritz gone to?" Minister Wu inquired.

He buckled his shoulder harness promptly after taking the first-row seat.

"They've been given a well-deserved leave of duty. I reckon they're now returning to Ciudad de Puramore to celebrate the mission's success," Surya replied.

The monorail car started forward.

In passing through the curve, the car transformed to exactly match the curvature of the monorail. The passenger seats, however, simply dangled in an upright position, much like a gondola bench on a Ferris wheel. Out of the curve, the car gained speed. Rapidly rising upward, the tram was halfway to the ceiling opening above in ten seconds.

Dr Xu swivelled her neck from side to side to scan the tableau beneath her. How could they accomplish this herculean feat without our knowledge, she thought. She gasped at the enormity of the cavern and the complex of buildings and other structures contained within.

Near the top of the ceiling, the monorail slowly passed through an elbow section the led into a solid rock tunnel several seconds later. The passenger car quickly passed through a section of solid granite. It then shot into and quickly out of another cavern, one that was brightly lit on all sides surrounding the tube.

Dr Xu caught a fleeting glimpse of what appeared to be an office building that encased the tube around its circumference. The structure must be at least four city blocks in length, she thought, as the monorail passed through the opening of yet another solid rock tunnel.

"What was that?"

"That was LAB. You and Minister Wu shall be given a guided tour of the entire facility tomorrow."

Outside the opening, a cavern of Shangri-la proportions came into view. Unlike the first one they encountered, however, half of this dome was open to the sky.

"This is absolutely incredible!"

She turned her neck to the left and then to the right as the monorail tram picked up speed as it headed directly to a huge lake positioned at the centre of the dome's floor. She swivelled in her seat to take in the mammoth buildings and plazas stationed at the rear of the dome behind her. She turned to face the lake and the open part of the dome in front of her.

"I've never seen anything like this. Never. It's utterly marvellous."

Juan responded, "Thank you, Dr Xu. You are fortunate to see the near completion of a new version of HAB.

When originally constructed, the open part of the dome was less than half of what you see, and that portion was previously covered by a geodesic dome. With the advent of nanobot and nanotube construction technology pioneered by LAB, the geodesic dome and most of the granite ceiling became obsolete. Right now, as I speak, nanobot colonies are continuing to excavate the granite portion of the ceiling. A year ago, most of the open sky you see was covered by the mountain. The geodesic dome was dismantled by nanobot colonies at the start of the interior renovation project. Skin now serves as a security shield as well as a regulator of the interior environment."

"Amazing," Wu said.

"We should arrive at Lago HAB in a few minutes. For your information, the diameter of the dome's ground floor is nearly two kilometres."

As they approached the lake, a pavilion came to view along the shoreline at the terminus of the monorail track. Shaped as a scaled-down replica of the Forbidden City's Hall of Supreme Harmony, every square inch of its semitransparent surface emitted a golden ethereal light.

Minister Wu turned to look back at Surya, who was sitting in the seat behind him.

"Skin?"

"I'm afraid so."

The tramcar gradually braked to halt. The entrance to the pavilion was only ten meters away from where the tram stopped at the monorail terminus.

Juan studied their orbs as the pair exited the monorail car. Of the two, Dr Xu's was more luminescent, but not by much. On further examination, he noticed that Minister Wu's orb contained a slight flaw that revealed the man had prostate cancer. I will treat the affected fibrous luminescence tomorrow, he thought.

"Well, we've arrived at our final destination this evening. Since we're all in need of some rest, why don't we repair to our respective bungalows set just inside the hallway's entrance?"

"Dr Xu, your bungalow is on the right as you enter. Minister Wu, yours is on the left. Let's meet again in the meeting hall in an hour from now. We have a special treat to present to you both this evening as our honoured guests."

Stepping inside the pagoda, Yingying gasped at the sight of the interior, which was a replica of the ground-floor interior of the Hall of Supreme Harmony. She was tempted to proceed further into the hall but decided instead to enter her bungalow. The door to her bungalow opened automatically and closed as soon as she stepped inside.

She disrobed and showered in the sumptuously appointed bathroom. She put on a terry cloth robe after towelling her rejuvenated body and dried her hair with a hair dryer. She then proceeded to the bedroom as though she had just awoken from a wonderful eight hour sleep. Marvellous, she thought, I feel as though I could run a marathon.

An exquisite red Shenyi robe, silk slippers, jade-encrusted hair ornaments, and lingerie were smartly placed on the huge bed. Beside the outfit was a navy blue jumpsuit, a pair of white walking shoes, and white cotton socks. How did they know that, she thought, as she lifted the beautifully embroidered robe from the bed? If she had a passion in life besides politics and her scientific research, it was her priceless collection of Han Dynasty Shenyi robes. Instead of collecting dolls like other girls her age, she started the robe collection. She recalled spending countless hours dressing as a Chinese princess with her collection and other accoutrement she acquired during her childhood and adolescence.

After setting her long jet-black hair up in a kind of Chinese-style bouffant with the jade pins and combs, she put on the lingerie and donned the robe and red silk slippers. She looked at her watch as she inserted the last jade pin in her hair; an hour had elapsed since she entered the bungalow. Exiting the bedroom thereafter, she poured herself a glass of mineral water at the bar of the stylishly decorated living room. She took a few sips and left the bungalow.

Dr Aguila and Wu stood outside the door as she exited. They both looked stunning in the handsome black tuxedos they wore. Wu looked at her and whistled.

"You're absolutely beautiful, my dear."

"I trust you had an enjoyable freshening, Dr Xu," Juan said. "If you don't mind, you shall spend the night in this bungalow. Tomorrow we'll settle you both into spacious and luxurious town homes located in the Permanent Residents Villas."

"That's most agreeable with me, Major," she replied. "I know I'll sleep well tonight."

"I agree, wholeheartedly," Wu said.

"Splendid. Now let's proceed to the soiree."

The pair walked on either side of Juan as he leisurely strode into the main hall.

As they entered the majestic hall, the opening passage from Yingying's favourite Beijing opera Da, Tang Guifei, commenced. The music seemed to emanate from the very walls. She felt goose bumps rise on her flesh as she listened to the music.

Halfway into the hall, Juan stopped.

They were all standing there in the middle of the hall staring directly at the magnificent Dragon Throne less than five meters in front of them. Yingying recognised the throne at once with dread and reverence. She vividly recalled viewing the grand throne when she visited the Hall of Supreme Harmony with her parents as a child.

"Dr Xu and Minister Wu, I have the highest honour and privilege of introducing you to the founding father and leading citizen of Puramore, General Sir George Smythe."

He took two steps backward, leaving the pair alone facing the throne that instantly vanished. In its stead, a solitary figure stood before them.

Yingying gazed intensely at the magically distinguished and handsome man whose charisma, without his yet having uttered a single word, was overpowering. Tall and lean, but possessing a muscular build with broad shoulders, the silver-haired man was dressed in a black tuxedo. She judged him to be in his early sixties, principally because his eyes reflected an experience of someone incredibly wise and prescient even though his facial complexion was flawless and unwrinkled. To her, he bore a remarkable resemblance to the movie actor Peter O'Toole. His smile penetrated her soul, as her own father's always had whenever he was inclined to display it to her, which, tragically, was seldom during the last years of his life. Her heart began to melt.

"Thank you, Dr Aguila," the general said. "You are too kind."

He bowed slightly in recognition of Juan's introduction.

"Welcome to Puramore Dr Xu and Minister Wu. This is your home for as long as you wish to remain with us. Insofar as we're concerned you are now part of our family in every respect. We can only hope to attend to your every need and desire to the best of our abilities."

That having been said, the backdrop of the hall behind him dissolved, leaving a group of well-dressed young people congregated behind him. The lake and the northern expanse of HAB concurrently emerged into view. The twinkling stars above the cloudless sky lent regal approbation to the auspicious occasion. Forthwith, the assemblage of about one hundred people began to queue behind him.

"I know I can speak for Minister Wu in expressing our mutual appreciation for Puramore's gracious and kind treatment of us from the moment we departed our homeland.

"Your sanctuary spared our lives, and for that, we are forever grateful."

"It's our country's honour and privilege to extend you both political asylum. We can only hope to make your time with us as pleasant and enjoyable as we can."

"We're more than comfortable here, General Smythe. We are elated to have accepted your offer of political asylum," Wu stated.

"Splendid. Let's pop the bubbly and start to get to know you better."

Trays of flukes of champagne and hors d'oeuvres were placed on tables at the terrace overlooking the lake.

"Everybody here is eager to meet you."

He politely motioned the couple to come forward to present themselves to the awaiting queue of research scientists and their support staff.

Minister Wu recognised Sir General George Smythe at first sight. As a junior People's Liberation Army staff officer assigned to the Second Department of the General Staff Department, the PLA's primary military intelligence collection apparatus, he maintained the military intelligence dossier on the brilliant British Army officer for a number of years. During that period in his career, he even personally shadowed him for over a year as an overseas espionage operative when the general occupied the Whitehall office of the Ministry of Defence as chief of the General Staff.

He surreptitiously followed the general's illustrious career long after he retired from military service as an electronic countermeasures cadre commander. It was a personally rewarding avocational pursuit, as Order general Smythe was by far and away the finest military leader he had ever encountered, either historically or in real life. Thus, if there was anyone outside the British military and political establishment who knew the General Sir Smythe well, or admired him greatly, it was him, although his admiration of the preeminent military leader would have resulted in his receiving severe censure, or worse if he let it be openly known.

But how could it be possible? He reportedly perished in a Swiss avalanche accident. He vividly recalled reading The Times front-page announcement of his death published the day after it occurred. Yet standing before him was the eminently vigorous general, who would have been over one hundred years old if he had survived to this day, but who appeared to be no more than sixty-five years of age.

About halfway through the staff introductions, a young Chinese man presented himself to Dr Xu. She reeled slightly as she stepped forward to shake his hand as she saw a slight resemblance of him to a former university instructor of hers.

He shook her hand.

"I am Dr Shen Dao, Dr Xu. Don't you remember me?"

She stared into his sparkling black eyes for a moment, still holding Shen's grasp. Her memories of a man who had been her faculty adviser when she studied at Beijing Tech as a post-doctoral research fellow flooded her mind. She was twenty-five when she began her research; her adviser was in his mid-forties at the time. Not an overly good-looking man, he nevertheless possessed irresistible charm and savoir faire.

He also possessed one of the finest scientific minds she had ever encountered. Nevertheless, he was selfless and unbeguiling to a fault, which lent special popularity to him as a tutor to all his postgraduate doctoral charges. She deeply mourned his loss after he was officially pronounced dead when search and rescue efforts failed to discover his body after his sailboat capsized at sea during a storm. The tragic accident occurred fifteen years after she first met him. It was an especially tragic loss for her because she always regarded the man as her second father.

"You bear a striking resemblance to the Beijing Tech faculty adviser who supervised my post-doctoral research project I conducted when I was in my early twenties, Mr Shen. You aren't his son or close relative of his, are you?"

A sly smile crept over his face.

"Give me a hug, my dear Yingying," he said joyously.

He reached out his arms to take hold of her. He whispered into her ear as he embraced her.

"You look simply ravishing as ever."

She knew at once it was him as he gave her a platonic hug: he always hugged her whenever they met.

"But how? I don't understand. You look twenty years younger than you were when I last saw you."

Tears began to well in her eyes.

Releasing her, he looked lovingly into her face as he held her at arm's length.

"As always, so many questions and so little time. Let's not talk about the how and wherefores as to my rebirth and transformation now."

He pulled a silk handkerchief out of his tuxedo lapel pocket and handed it to her.

"Enjoy this evening and the next few days of rest and recovery from the harrowing experience you've recently endured. I shall tell you my story later."

"As you wish, Dao."

She wiped the tears from her eyes with the handkerchief. Given the level of personal distress that she had endured during the past twenty-four hours, she readily assented to his deferment with aplomb. He forthwith proceeded to the refreshment trays.

After the one-on-one introductions concluded she mingled with the group for several hours.

She felt a sense of camaraderie and kinship with the community of young scientists and researchers almost at the outset. For the first time in years, she felt like a fledgling postgraduate relishing the opportunity to contribute to a scientific field of expertise.

Toward the end of the evening, Xiaoping took her by her arm.

"My dear Yingying, it's time for both of us to retire for the evening."

She was chatting with two young American women who were involved in advanced cosmology research when Xiaoping interrupted them.

Surya suddenly appeared beside them.

"Yes, indeed. Please repair to your bungalows at once. There's no need for any formal leave-taking as we are all well aware that you are in dire need of rest and relaxation."

"Thank you, Major," Wu replied.

"Excuse me, ladies."

Mentally exhausted, she yearned for the release that sleep would provide her.

Yingying fell into a deep and delicious sleep the instant her head touched the pillow.

Chapter 23 - Chaos City

Various Points around the Globe, 22 August 2055

Wingtip leaned back in his throne and cocked his head to his right side as Hú Li began to speak. Three meters in front of him, in a relatively diminutive but equally elegant throne, sat Hú Li. The two thrones, which sat the exact centre of the dome floor, were the only furnishings inside the starlit interior of the Celestial Node.

"RED STAR estimates the nadir of the worldwide economic crisis shall occur thirty days from now. Mass rioting and looting are already taking place in major capitals in Europe, Asia, Africa, and the Americas. Non-aligned governments are falling like dominoes. World power governments are tottering and are on the verge of collapse. RED STAR continues to affect global computer network failure with surprisingly calamitous results. SITA manages to correct failures soon afterward, but the recovery effort is too late in most instances.

"They'll never fully recover from the immediate after-effects of the sabotage phase, though. The political helter-skelter is rising to a homicidal crescendo as a consequence."

Straightening his head, a broad and wicked smile came to his face as Hú Li concluded his report.

"So the day of reckoning is nigh at hand. A job well done, Hú Li. I suppose I am correct in assuming that SITA is cognisant of our plan."

"Without question, My Lord."

"The next question is why doesn't SITA extinguish RED STAR?"

"For the immortal life of me, I don't really have a definitive answer to that question, My Lord. But I suspect SITA has a plan of her own, perhaps she's using RED STAR to somehow misinform us."

"No matter. Though it'll take longer to achieve our goal without RED STAR, we can do without it if necessary. It's really only a matter of time before we have the upper hand in this world. SITA is merely delaying the inevitable."

Wingtip leisurely stood up from his throne.

"It's almost time for me to have a chat with the general. Come. We must go."

Their bodies collapsed into twin sparks that instantly shot up to the top of the dome.

* * *

Pierre Robes knew he was at the end of his political career after receiving a "no confidence" vote as secretary-general from the UN Security Council. Still, he thought, I must steadfastly persevere, particularly because Order of the Sixth Estate of the Republic of France was about to disintegrate. And that was something that he was not about to allow to occur.

As his personal jet airliner touched down at Charles de Gaulle International Airport, his cell phone rang.

"Yes, what is it now, Maurice?" he said irritably to French president Maurice de Bonaire.

He paused for a moment as the caller spoke.

"No! No! No! I will not permit the French Foreign Legion to occupy Paris and the declaration of martial law, not at least at this point. And I am emphatic about my position! When and if KWO storms Élysées Palace, then and only then should those measures immediately ensue. Until then, simply allow the Prefecture de Police and Gendarmerie to contend with the rioting. The last thing we need at this juncture is to have French soldiers killing French civilians. After a few days, I'll reconsider your proposal."

He paused as the caller replied.

"Well, Maurice, they are going to sustain an alarming number of casualties. There's no way around it given the scope of the conflagration."

He summarily clicked off the phone and proceeded to deplane.

For the past month, the capital of France and the rest of the world's major capitals had been exposed to cataclysmic events of virtually every nature. In Paris, for instance, suppliers regularly failed to deliver food and other vital goods needed for day-to-day human sustenance. In addition, the city's power grid regularly switched off for five or six hours during the day and night. Internet and telecommunications networks were similarly affected. The municipal water supply was so contaminated that no one dared to bathe in it. Petrol and diesel oil were nonexistent several weeks after the insidious episode began. Banks and other financial institutions were rendered incapable of providing minimal customer services, resulting in en masse closures by the end of the third week of the crisis.

As the food supply diminished to almost nothing, the citizens began rioting in the streets. Soon thereafter, an upstart political party managed to putsch the municipal government and was on the brink of accomplishing the same coup d'etat the national level. The attendant bloodshed of the ordinary citizenry and their leaders was unparalleled in the city's history. There was even a rumour of cannibalism in certain impoverished neighbourhoods.

He felt weary to the marrow of his bones. Never before had he been beset by a political calamity of this extreme magnitude. He reached inside his suit jacket and brought out a prescription medication bottle. After popping it open, he shook out a couple of pills into his right hand and directly tossed the tabs into his mouth. He grinned after he swallowed the sedative. At least, his immediate salvation from a nervous breakdown was less than a minute away, he thought, as he stepped into the military airport terminal. I shall contact Michel just as soon as I arrive at home. He'll know how best to proceed from here.

Upon entering his lavish chateau located just outside the Paris city limits, he proceeded directly to his office on the second floor. Sitting down at his desk, he picked up the phone receiver and touched a red button on the side; it was his private encrypted line to Michel de Chardonnay's office located in his swank ten-bedroom Parisian apartment. After a few rings, de Chardonnay's valet de chambre answered the phone.

"Bonjour, Monsieur Robes. I must transfer your call to Monsieur de Chardonnay's chambre. Please hold."

He waited a few moments before a voice broke over the line.

"My dear friend, I am sorry to advise you that I am on my deathbed," a feeble and raspy voice intoned like a dirge. It didn't sound anything like Pierre's old friend's voice.

"Michel?"

"Yes, Pierre. My voice is giving out, so please be patient with me. My physician is at my bedside administering medication to me so that I can remain conscious while we converse."

"But this is so unexpected, Michel. You were the picture of health last week when we met."

"I know, but the onset of my illness is instant and kills almost immediately. There's nothing more that can be done for me except wait for the inevitable...I know you're calling for my advice about how best to handle the current state of civil unrest in France.

"Listen to me carefully, Pierre. Though you are a consummate politician, you are not a military leader; not by any professional standard. Unfortunately, our military command has been effectively nullified by the unseen force that is plaguing our country and the rest of the world. You must not place your confidence in our military leadership as a consequence. It is potentially completely ineffectual and treacherous. You must, therefore, seek another source of military counsel and expertise of the highest order outside the country."

"But where?"

"I counsel that you should look toward the Orient. Though the People's Republic of China isn't altogether unscathed by the economic turmoil impacting the rest of the world, the population is well behaved and compliant with leadership's current survival policies.

"Wingtip and his KWO government apparatus are responsible for the quiescence. And, as you know, Wingtip himself is also a military genius nonpareil."

Pierre was silent for a few seconds as he pondered the merit of Michel's advice. Wingtip, he thought, was in a class all by himself in the Machiavelli school of politics. He knew, as a result, that he wasn't even close to being his rival. If there was one man on the planet he feared, it was him. He often thought that Wingtip could literally charm the spots off a ravenous cornered leopard whilst simultaneously slitting the animal's throat; and the leopard would thank him all the same as it drew its final breath of life.

Yet, Michel's counsel was sound in his estimation; aligning himself with Wingtip might result in ephemeral resolution of the chaotic state of affairs he was charged to address, especially given the impotence of his current political leadership. He was desperate in any event and was not in any position to dismiss what appeared to be his only viable option. If proven successful, or otherwise, he would endeavour at all costs to extricate himself from further involvement with Wingtip thereafter. Nevertheless, Pierre sensed a slight glimmer of hope at the end of the tunnel, which was actually more like the end of a military assault rifle barrel.

"How should I approach him? And what should I do about the rioting in the streets?"

The old man heaved a sigh of subdued impatience laden with abject fear.

"Actually, my dear friend, wait for him to approach you. As to the civil upheaval, I still counsel that you forestall declaration of martial law and engagement of the French Foreign Legion. Perhaps Wingtip shall serve to counsel you best as to when that should occur.

"I'm sorry but my physician has just advised me that I must end this conversation. If we don't speak to one another again, I want to you know that I feel from the bottom of my soul that you are the son that I always wished I had sired."

The line then went dead.

Tears welled in Pierre's eyes. Michel was his only true friend and benefactor, he thought, as he wept. His last words were particularly moving as Michel never fathered children, nor had any expressed interest in doing so. Added to that grievous loss, he felt as though the rug was being pulled out from under him, particularly because Order he always relied upon Michel's sage insights and counsel to guide him when it came to his dealing with military affairs.

"Well done. Are you ready to move on to the Celestial Community, Monsieur de Chardonnay?"

His face expressed frantic terror of the process to which he was compelled to undergo by his own volition.

"I suppose I must be, Hú Li. Can you give me some idea as to what I can expect afterward, though?"

Hú Li stifled outward laughter.

"Michel, analogously, you'll exist at the level of a beehive pollen collector, answerable only to the queen bee. Acting in that capacity, you will share the collective mind and soul of the beehive community. Thus, you won't ever again possess an individual soul identity from the moment you join the Celestial Community as an ordinary Golden Dragonfly.

"Consequentially, you won't ever again be subject to pain, suffering, moral or ethical dilemma, or the foibles of an individual soul's existence. Instead, you will forever partake in the supremely sublime bliss of our everlasting glory from the instant your soul merges with ours.

"You have served us exceptionally well since we enlisted your soul. Due to your steadfast devotion and loyalty to our Supreme Order, as well as the excellent aptitude your soul possesses, as measured by the Standardised Soul Harmonic Intelligence Frequency Test, you have been promoted to the lowly rank of twelfth-degree Pollinator.

"For your information, you, along with your brethren Pollinators, are assigned to merrily flit from one lotus blossom to the next for all eternity. You should feel especially proud of your contribution to our crusade and your promotion since Pollinators are regarded with the highest esteem within the Holy Order of the Celestial Community of the Golden Dragon."

He was almost sold on the grisly prospect of what lay ahead of him, but the dreadful finality held him in its grip. Had he really made such a mad pact with Hú Li, he thought, when his business was close to abject failure five decades ago? His mind desperately reeled with denial about his ever having entered into the contract. He instinctively raised his hands as though he was protecting his otherwise lifeless body from an onslaught of mortal blows.

"Oh, my word, Michel. I've seldom witnessed such a pathetic display of buyer's remorse coming from someone of your class in all my immortal life. As you will recall, I fully disclosed the terms of the contract to you before your ratification and contiguous acceptance of the Celestial Golden Dragon brand," he said touching the old man's head with his right hand.

He pulled away a hair from his scalp just above de Chardonnay's right ear to reveal a tattoo of the Celestial Golden Dragon about the size of a lady beetle. He immediately smiled into his lifeless face.

"Believe you me, you should be thankful that you didn't enter the same pact with our rival, the Fallen Angel."

He reached into his tattered old doctor's bag and removed an object contained within that was about the size of a standard loaf of sliced bread. The object was wrapped in black velvet. He removed the cloth to reveal an exquisitely ornate statue of a golden dragon with jade eyes and a crimson tail.

"We must proceed directly, as I have other house calls to make this evening."

A few seconds later, the old man's arms calmly settled back on bed linen. He stared at the ceiling above him as if he were in the grips of a psychotropic trance.

"Excellent. The Celestial Transition medication I administered to you when I arrived is taking full effect. You are fully conscious, Michel, and alert but unable to move a muscle. I shall now administer the Celestial Transition Ritual to you."

He subsequently placed the statue on Monsieur de Chardonnay's chest, right over his heart, with its head pointed directly into Michel's face. Hú Li then propped his head up with pillows so that he stared directly at the statue's head. He forthwith placed the old man's lifeless hands on top of the statue, one on top of the other.

Presently, the statue began to luminesce an eerie golden aura. Its tiny jade eyes sparkled like the twinkling of brilliant stars. Before long, the glowing and twinkling reached a blinding crescendo.

The old man tried vainly to close his eyes.

Hú Li put his right hand on the old man's brow; simultaneously, he placed his left hand on top of Michel's hands.

"You are one with me now, Michel de Chardonnay. As your duly appointed ultimate power of attorney, I shall communicate with Huánglong on your behalf."

Raising his voice to almost the level of a shout, he said, "In accordance with my ratification of the Pact of the Holy Order Celestial Community of the Eternal Golden Dragon, I, Michel Napoleon Bonaparte de Chardonnay, on this twenty-second day of August in the 2055 year following the miserable death of Jesus Christ, forthwith relinquish both my mortal life and immortal soul to Huánglong, the Exalted Supreme Ruler of the Holy Order of the Celestial Community of the Eternal Golden Dragon.

"From the moment of my acceptance into the Holy Order of the Celestial Community of the Eternal Golden Dragon, I will assume the rank of twelfth-degree Pollinator and await further orders from you, My Eternal Lord and Master.

"I regret nothing that I have accomplished in service of the Holy Order and joyously sacrifice my soul for all eternity to the benefit of its Holy Mission.

"I entreat you to take my soul into your service without a further delay, Huánglong, My Eternal Lord and Master."

Michel suddenly saw his entire life flash before his eyes as the laser-intensity beam of light emitted from the dragon's eyes bore into his soul. Every moment, emotion, and thought he experienced during his life passed through his conscious mind in a millisecond. He had never known such clarity of thought and divine intelligence as he assessed merits and demerits of his life span from every perspective. He at once knew eternal wisdom as his spirit departed from his body and merged with the Holy Order of the Celestial Community of the Eternal Golden Dragon. His eternal consciousness as a singular immortal soul was thusly merged into the consciousness of a collective immortal soul. At the same instant, his body died as a result of a fatal brain hemorrhage.

Right after his death rattle, Hú Li took the holy relic from the grasp of the dead man. He then brought the statue's head into contact with the tattoo located above the dead man's right ear. Instantly, the statue began to luminesce as before. A few seconds later, a piercing laser beam shot forth into the tattoo. He then promptly returned the holy relic to his doctor's bag after wrapping it in the velvet cloth. Returning to the corpse, he examined the spot where the tattoo had been branded onto Michel de Chardonnay over fifty years ago and found no visible trace of it ever being there. He then fully covered the corpse with a bed linen sheet and summarily exited the apartment after announcing the sudden and unexpected death of Monsieur Michel de Chardonnay to his valet de chambre.

"General, Monsieur Michel de Chardonnay's valet de chambre phoned the Paris Prefecture de Police a few minutes ago to report his passing. All he said was that the physician who visited his apartment to attend to a minor illness he had contracted yesterday advised him that Monsieur de Chardonnay suddenly died from what appears to be a cerebral hemorrhage. The coroner's office immediately dispatched a medical examiner and an ambulance to collect the body for transport to the city morgue for an autopsy."

He immediately looked up from the LAB Scientific Command Centre console he was studying.

"That is definitely unexpected and sad news, SITA. As you know I got to know Monsieur de Chardonnay well during my military career. He was a fine gentleman and an overtly staunch ally of Great Britain. Though his munitions dealings with our enemies, especially the PRC many decades ago when his firm almost bankrupted, gave me cause to suspect him of duplicity. I nevertheless mourn his death."

"You had more than a good reason to suspect him of double-dealings at that time, General. Monsieur de Chardonnay was one of the great opportunists of his time."

He nodded his head in agreement with SITA's comment.

"What is your assessment of the incidence of the nonviolent deaths of so many highly placed government and corporate executives during the past four weeks SITA? Do you perceive a common thread?"

"Yes, it's a red one in the form of Wingtip and KWO. It appears likely that he's calling in his favours to these individuals, as it were, prior to maturity date."

"So, he's collecting their souls to add to the economic and political chaos he and KWO have created during the past month. Am I correct in that assessment?"

"Without question, that is what they are attempting to accomplish, General. Worldwide political and economic structures are collapsing, one by one, like a house of cards as upper-echelon executive leadership fails due to the loss of so many key leadership figures and another constituency within its own ranks."

"Should we continue to intervene on the nonpolitical side in order to prevent total failure in the immediate future?"

"Yes, we should indeed. I shall thus continue to thwart RED STAR's economic warfare campaign to an optimal degree, according to our plan."

"Very well, SITA. What do you project shall evolve from the current situation in terms of KWO's actions?"

"General, given the success of the campaign, there is a better than 90 percent chance of a gradual increase of hostilities within the next few weeks as KWO captures political power on the nation-state level worldwide. The aim being to place as much pressure as possible on the global population in order to eradicate those KWO identifies as malingerers and malefactors toward its political and economic agenda. In other words, the chaotic situation is designed to worsen.

"At a certain stage, KWO will lay the blame for the egregious state of affairs on potential political rivals and order their summary execution with a de facto writ of plebeian approval. Thereafter, the worldwide political apparatus, namely, the UN, will be theirs for the taking. Wingtip is already putting his name forward as the successor to UN. Secretary-General Pierre Robes should he probably lose the support of the General Assembly and the subsequent enactment of the Emergency Measures Clause of the UN Charter designed to replace him."

"What is the state of PRC economy at present?"

"Mildly prosperous. The Chinese economy was spared all but the mildest deleterious effects of the global catastrophe. Wingtip will undoubtedly use that fact to his best advantage in the near future, most probably to advance his UN ambition leadership ambition."

He looked back down at the console he was studying.

"There's no doubt in my mind that you are correct in that assessment. However, we must bide our time to march in step with Wingtip's plan so that ours comes to fruition as planned, and not before or after."

"And that is exactly what we are doing, I assure you."

He was silent for a few seconds in a mental review of SITA's report. A broad smile of excitement came over his face.

"We are almost there."

"Yes, we are indeed."

"Where are Ian and Robin now?"

"They're playing tennis with Dr Xu and Minister Wu."

"Excellent. Please invite Ian and Robin to join me for dinner this evening at Chez Habitacion at the standard time. How are their spirits of late?"

"They are almost too blithe for their own good. My analysis concludes that the gradual release from their daily scientific management responsibilities is producing physically salutary but mentally disturbing effects on them both. Thus at your discretion, of course, you may want to take this opportunity to present the First Directive option to them. The time is coming near when they must fulfil their part of the Prophecy."

"I agree with your analysis as well as the timeliness of their candidacy to engage the First Directive for themselves. Personally, I think they'll be relieved to submit to the protocol, which they assisted you in development. They might as well be the first subjects of the experiment."

"They only need to contend with pre-transformation remorse symptoms. What about you, General? Don't you think it is time for you to engage in the First Directive for yourself?"

"It's nearly time for me but I shall defer until after the First Test concludes. It is only fitting."

Chapter 24 - The Retopians

LAB, Puramore, 22 August 2055

The general and his two sons enjoyed a leisurely repast at Chez Habitacion. More so given that for the first time in several months they had the occasion to enjoy each other's company. Finally, after conversation concerning the world crisis was fully explored, the general turned to another subject that caught the twins totally off guard.

The general took the last sip of the delicious red wine that had been served to him with his dinner. He looked at the twins with an expression of utter and profound concern, one which they couldn't recall seeing him evince for decades. They knew instinctively that he was on the verge of announcing something important to them. They leaned forward in their chairs and held their breath in eager anticipation of whatever it was that he was going to say to them.

"There comes a time in a man's life when after years of distinguished service and success in a particular field, it becomes evident that he is destined to migrate to another calling. More often than not, this realisation follows the one that the vigour of youthful interest has palled to such an extent that active pursuit of a career is no longer possible, or even desired. At that point, one is actually doing himself and others disfavour by continuing to engage in the career pursuit."

Robin and Ian quickly exchanged quizzical glances at each other and then returned their gaze to the general.

"In your case, I perceive that you've both developed a dispassionate interest in your scientific management duties during the past year or more. That is not a fault on your part. Nevertheless, the marked change in your approach to your duties does indicate to me that you'd really rather move on to some other pursuit, and perhaps rightfully so. What is your reaction to my perception?"

The brothers looked at each other for a few moments. Finally, they returned their gaze to the general.

Robin said, "Father, with all due respect, we have been feeling more than a bit dispassionate about our scientific management role at the LAB for quite some time. It's not that we don't truly care about the research projects that are being conducted, which we are charged with overseeing, it's just that we have been feeling sort of like a fifth wheel on a Grand Prix Formula Ten racer given SITA's involvement, particularly since nantium 2.0 rendered the computer nearly omniscient, at least as far as Earth is concerned. We can't even begin to imagine where SITA will next evolve."

The general breathed a sigh of relief. They are taking this well, he thought.

"We all knew what we were creating when SITA came into being nearly twenty years ago. However, having said that, we never had any inkling as to how quickly and extensively it would evolve. I myself am mystified as to the merit of my position in juxtaposition with SITA's, but I am at the very least needed to provide supremely effective leadership to our beloved personnel. If that is my only valid function, than that is one I am committed to the depth of my being to discharge to the utmost of my capabilities, my dear sons." Ian replied. "But what can we do, Father? We are only too frustrated at this point to imagine anything more we can achieve to further the Empyreal Paradigm."

"That is entirely my fault. I've been so embroiled with managing others that I forgot to provide my sons with the guidance they needed and deserved. Please accept my sincere apology for my recent lack of fatherly devotion toward your welfare. If it means anything to you, though, I have empathised with your quandary ever since I first perceived it manifested."

"That means more to us than you'll ever know, Father. But where should we go from here?

"We enjoy our life of relative leisure, but feel as if we are betraying the Empyreal Paradigm for not having an active and important role in its furtherance. We're actually beginning to feel rather guilty of dereliction of duty in that regard, as our erratic behaviour of late clearly demonstrates. Moreover, our epicurean lifestyle long ago dulled the edge of our sensibilities towards its goal."

"Firstly, I desired that you both enjoy the fruits of your herculean contribution to the Empyreal Paradigm for a time. It's a reward for a job well done. We all appreciate the importance of your contribution and realise that we wouldn't have progressed to any significant degree without the steadfast devotion of your combined genius.

"Yet, let's now revisit the time when we first met and you subsequently became my sons and partners in our venture. It's germane that we do so as it'll serve to stimulate our resolve to enter afresh into an invigorated covenant toward fulfilment of the Empyreal Paradigm."

He proceeded to give a brief recount of the early history of their association, including his first dream related to the Empyreal Paradigm when he was a boy to the present. The twins looked ashamed of themselves as he concluded his soliloquy. They realised that they had become vain, egotistical and profligate; their love and devotion toward their duteous and loving father had waned as a result.

Ian and Robin stared at each other for a few moments.

"Father, whatever we can do to further the Empyreal Paradigm, we shall do to the utmost of our capabilities, no matter what personal sacrifice we must suffer," Ian said.

The general motioned to the waiter who was stationed attentively near the table.

"Please bring us another bottle of that sumptuous red wine you served with our dinner, Sujata."

"I think you both know what needs to be done to further our Supreme Order at this critical juncture in its history. As you know full well, you must be the first human beings to convert in order to fulfil the Prophecy."

"Yes, we know. But it's such a daunting prospect. We dallied as a result. We dreaded fulfilling our commitment to the Empyreal Paradigm that only we are qualified to initiate as prophesied. Yet. we don't really have a rational reason to delay any longer, especially since we've experienced all that we wanted to experience as human beings to the utmost extent."

"You must be brave, my sons, and have faith in yourselves, SITA, and the Prophecy. Afterward, you will enjoy all the supreme power, stature, and intelligence that your Team Alpha brothers and sister possess. Furthermore, as leaders, you'll recruit and develop your own team as you deem appropriate and necessary. Once fully developed, your team will serve to bolster Team

Alpha's efforts here on Earth. This is just the first step, as you know."

"When should we submit ourselves to the First Directive?" Ian asked.

The profound gravity of their renewed commitment to the Empyreal Paradigm had fully sunk into them both.

"You must do so presently. SITA has already prepared the Passage Chamber for you. We must get you and your team of human converts operational before the Conversion Event.

"Do you have any idea who you'll approach to join your team?"

"Indeed. Most of whom are in residency here at HAB," Robin said.

"Splendid. I propose a toast to you and your team," he said as he lifted his goblet. "Here's to the everlasting success and glory of your team in service of the Empyreal Paradigm."

He then clinked his goblet with each of theirs.

Setting his goblet down on the table, the general said, "Have you thought of a name for your team?"

"We have indeed, Father," Ian said. "We wish to be known as The Retopians."

"Retopians? What does that mean?"

Robin replied: "It's a word we coined to lend appropriate distinction and definition to our elevated status as former human beings following our conversion. In that state of existence, we and our brethren will no longer be direct descendants of reptilians. Instead, we'll be all knowing and all caring of all subjects that come to our attention, irrespective of their origin."

He smiled broadly as he accepted the team name, albeit begrudgingly. At this point, he thought, the last thing I need is to make a polemic out of their choice of a team name and thereby possibly ruin the sterling resolve of this moment of his son's rejuvenation and commitment to the Empyreal Paradigm that he managed to create. I must instead encourage them to proceed at once to the Passage Chamber inside LAB.

"Very well. Henceforth, your team shall be known as The Retopians."

After a lengthy conversation in the privacy of their Permanent Residents town house villa later that evening, the Fletcher brothers decided to submit themselves to the First Directive the next day. The decision was rendered, however, not without a major debate between them concerning the efficacy of the procedure, which hadn't been tested on human subjects since its formal development several months earlier. They were thus going to be its first guinea pigs.

The general was beside himself with a mixture of grief, pride, and joy when they later called him to advise of their decision.

"That is simply fantastic! Your faith and trust in the Empyreal Paradigm, as exemplified by your personal sacrifice, shall forevermore signify to all mankind its righteousness and authenticity. And as the first humans, you shall become first and foremost in the minds of all who follow you as the sublimely courageous creators and pioneers of the new and glorious heredity and spirituality that is the Empyreal Paradigm."

The general paused for a time as his almost reflexive expression of joy gradually sunk into his own mind and spirit.

Ian responded, "This is what we must do, Father. Our entire lives from the moment we met you until now have been devoted to fulfilling our ultimate destiny to further the Empyreal Paradigm. We are thus prepared in every respect to moving on to the New Paradigm."

"You will not regret your decision."

The Fletcher brothers were taciturn as they travelled on the monorail to the LAB the following afternoon. They felt as though they were about to undergo a life-threatening surgery, which was an appropriate reaction to the intimidating prospect that lay before them. As the monorail car pulled to a halt at the LAB Station, the twins hugged each other for the last time as human beings. The walk from the LAB Monorail Station to the Passage Chamber Laboratory took less than ten minutes.

Upon reaching the door to the laboratory, Ian asked his brother, "Are you sure you want to go through with this?"

"We must. There's no way for us to turn back now even if we were inclined to."

The door automatically opened in front of them.

"Good afternoon, gentlemen," SITA cheerful greeted the brothers as they stepped inside the laboratory.

"Good afternoon, SITA," Ian replied. "I trust TEMPLE's full installation has been successfully accomplished and systems analysis confirms the viability of the process."

"Without question. Passage Chamber and your modules are 100 percent viable and ready to perform at peak levels, gentlemen."

General Smythe entered the reception room from the laboratory at that moment. He approached the twins and gave each one a fatherly hug.

"I am so proud of you both that I can hardly speak. Let us proceed at once.".

The Fletcher brothers followed him into the laboratory. The glass covers of the twin modules positioned in the middle of the laboratory floor, which was expansive as a tennis court were open. The modules design gave them the appearance of bloated space-age coffins. They were conjoined, head-to-head.

"The moment of truth is upon us."

He really felt as though he was ordering foot soldiers to storm an enemy machine gun nest. His heart broke at being compelled to treat his sons in that manner but he knew it was in their best interest to immediately enter the modules without any unnecessary delay.

"Ian, your module is on the right. Robin, yours is on the left. Please remove all articles of clothing and your shoes now and enter your modules forthwith."

The brothers did as they were ordered since they also sensed the necessity of being abruptly led to their fate.

"Godspeed. We shall meet again one week from now."

Those were the last words they heard as human beings as the twins lay down, facing upward in their Passage Chamber modules. The glass covers then lowered and hermetically sealed around the interior casings with a thump. Immediately thereafter a white gas flooded the interior of the modules, and the Fletcher brothers were completely anaesthetised a second later.

"SITA, how are they faring?"

"All life signs are stable and robust as they enter stasis Commander. Skin has fully enveloped each of them as I speak. Cellular time-regression commences fifty-seven seconds henceforth."

"What's the projected time of completion of cellular time-regression phase?"

"Forty-eight hours, General, give or take an hour. I regret that I can't be more precise with the projection but as this is our first live trial of the programme that's the best estimate I can offer you at present. Though I shall supply you with a 100 percent accurate projection an hour after stasis is fully realised."

The general chuckled to himself. There was often a humourous irony in computer's outward display of its devotion to detail to humans, he thought, especially during periods of heightened tension.

"There's no need for that, SITA. Please inform me when the first phase is completed."

He knew that SITA's playfulness was actually served to lighten the emotional burden that he carried. He presently exited the laboratory and headed for the Scientific Command Centre.

He spent the next forty-eight hours tending to his normal duties, the most of important of which was overseeing the global crisis situation. Though several times a day he checked the status of the cellular time-regression process the twins were undergoing. Although not the crucial phase of the entire First Directive operation, it nevertheless constituted the first test of the system's overall practicality. As such, he kept a keen eye on its progress.

Precisely forty-eight hours after the cellular time-regression procedure commenced, SITA announced its successful conclusion to the general. He was at the HAB Bowling Green, participating in a rousing lawn bowling game when his earphone chimed.

Before touching his right earlobe to initiate the call, he praised the result of his team mate's last bowl. "Nice bowl, Geoffrey!

"Good afternoon, SITA. Do you have a status report regarding the twins' condition?"

"Indeed, I do, General. Cellular time-regression phase performed on the twins is 100 percent complete and successful. The newly developed, scalar-wave time-regression field functioned perfectly throughout the phase.

"That's splendid. How is their mental state?"

"Mental state readings of both subjects indicate no diminution in cognitive awareness as a result of the current process they are undergoing. In other words, their minds are in the same condition as they were before the experiment commenced, although potentially vastly more efficient since their brains now possess what amounts to infant's brain cells."

"Are we ready to commence the next phase?"

"Passage Chamber is eminently prepared and ready to commence the cellular re-engineering phase. The question is, however, are you ready to approve its initiation?

"As you know once initiated there is no opportunity to turn back as we do not possess that capability yet. It is, therefore, yours and only your decision to make."

"And if I choose to abort the process now, what then?"

"Then you are going to have two super-intelligent, but physically and emotionally immature sons on your hands.

As you know as a beneficiary of the process our previous cellular time-regression technologies allowed us to maintain the twins at a constant thirty-five-year-old metabolic level for over fifteen years. As a result of the current one, however, they are essentially fully grown thirty-five-year-old males in infant's bodies. What that means is that once stasis is lifted their bodies will experience the exact same infantile hormonal sequencing that newborn infants undergo unless I intercede to adjust their hormonal time clock."

"What is your appraisal of the chance of successful execution of the next phase?"

His mind dreaded the prospect of having to manage the twins as adolescents again.

"There is a 93 percent chance of complete success. The odds increased significantly due to the complete success of the cellular time-regression phase."

He picked up a black bowl and vigorously massaged it with his hands as he contemplated his decision. There is no doubt about it, he thought, as he stepped onto the bowling mat, I must issue the order to proceed with the cellular re-engineering phase.

He bowled the bowl as he reached his decision.

"Very well, SITA. Proceed with the next phase. What's the projected time of completion of the cellular re-engineering phase?"

"Seventy-two hours. Nant cellular re-engineering colonies are migrating into the subjects' Skin as I speak. Corporeal penetration shall commence in T minus five minutes."

"I'll check the status myself over the course of the next seventy-two hours. Please advise me the moment the phase is complete."

"Yes, General."

"By the way what's the status of Team Beta?"

"Team Beta will enter its third trimester one hundred hours from now."

"Very well. Carry on, SITA."

After the lawn bowling game ended he returned to the Scientific Command Centre. Right away he reviewed the status reports of the global crisis SITA had posted on his command console. Of particular interest was the status of the crisis in Paris, particularly since the International Basketball League Championship Tournament would begin a few weeks hence.

It alarmed him to view live-action scenes provided by computer surveillance cameras and nant surveillance colonies situated in and around the capital. The devastation that had occurred, though not total, reminded him of the aftermath of World War II firebombing of major European capitals, such as Berlin. Some of the more historic and fashionable districts of the city, however, were spared the brunt of the destruction. Fortunately, too, the recently refurbished Palais des Sports, the venue of the tournament, was perfectly unaffected by the rioting. He was gratified that he decided to cover the sports arena and other historical edifices and monuments with Skin before the tumult spread to the fifteenth arrondissement.

He decided to contact Juan, who occupied his office located in the Puramore National Sports Complex.

"Juan," he said after touching his right earlobe.

Juan immediately connected the encrypted cell phone line after the chime rang into his ear.

"Yes, George. How are you today?"

Juan was expecting his call as he sensed from afar that his friend was experiencing extreme stress in managing the Conversion Event.

"A little worse for wear, Juan, but I'm fine otherwise. How are you holding up under the strain?"

"You know you can't keep an old Yaqui sorcerer and MD down for long. I'm thus holding up exceptionally well under the strain thank you. How may I be of further service to you, George?"

He perceived that the general's spirit was beginning to feel the harmful effects of the strain to which he had been subjected for the past month. His voice confirmed that fact. As he told his friend at the inception, though, this was his and only his journey to make. If he passed this test, however, Puramore would be his to wield forevermore. His daily communication with Juan was always one of the highlights of his day. His longtime friend's solacing disposition, as well as his engaging mercurial wit, always served to put him at ease. He was also endowed with an ancient sagacity of such eminence and omniscience that he often held the general spellbound during their conversations, particularly during times of crisis such as the one he was currently experiencing. Juan always wielded that kind of power over him ever since the time he met him nearly fifty years ago.

"I know from the sound of your voice that you're particularly anxious about the twin's experimental condition. But I firmly believe SITA has the situation well under control. There's really nothing more you and I can do to assist her, although I'm monitoring their spirit condition on a regular basis myself. I am thus pleased to report to you that they're both no spiritual distress at this time."

"That's what I wanted to know, Juan. What is your prognosis?"

"As long as they're in stasis their spirits shall remain as they were prior to the start of the experiment. However, it remains to be seen even by me, what will occur to them once they're released from stasis following the conclusion of the experiment. In my opinion, however, they'll benefit from the procedure for a number of different reasons. I won't take the time to expound further since it wouldn't make any visceral sense to you."

"As usual, I'll take your word for it."

"Good. You must as always place your trust in me in these matters as you have in the past, my friend."

"And, thankfully, I always have my friend.".

He felt as though a burden had been lifted from his shoulders.

"What about the status of Team Alpha?"

"My apprentices are progressing at a pace I would never imagined possible when I agreed to train them at your behest ten years ago. Since then they've managed to assimilate nearly all my knowledge of the shamanistic practice. Incredibly they fully understand one hundred thousand years of my craft's body of knowledge to 100 percent accurate recall.

"Now comes the hard part."

"Which is?"

"Putting the craft to practice in the spirit world. We commenced practical exercises long ago after they attained sufficient knowledge to warrant practical training exercise."

"How long will it take to accomplish practical mastery of your craft?"

"How should I put it?" he replied as posing the question to himself.

"Well, let me put it this way. There are thousands of levels within thousands of mastery fields of actual shamanistic practice. The only way to progress toward proficiency toward any one level is to start from the beginning, master the first level of achievement and progress from there. Personally, I've never had an apprentice who progressed beyond the twelfth level of only a handful of basic fields in their lifetime, and there are thousands within the shamanistic practice. That being said, how long it will take my current charges to achieve real proficiency in even the most basic fields is almost impossible for me to say."

"Nevertheless, they must achieve mastery in those fields that serve to shield against malevolent spirit assault, and soon."

"I agree with you, George. I'm already putting them through rigorous training exercises designed to render them somewhat proficient in that regard. But you must understand that it is a time-consuming process. In a week or two, they may possess enough field mastery to deal with a Golden Dragonfly on a one-to-one basis without the use of firearms. It may take years, however, for anyone of them to be prepared to contend with Hú Li who would destroy them all in a bat of an eyelid even after they're prepared to deal with an ordinary Golden Dragonfly assault."

"Our fate is in their hands accordingly."

"Amen, amigo mio."

General Smythe spent the next seventy hours as before, overseeing various ongoing scientific projects and intermittently checking on the status of the twins. He was sitting down for tea at Chez Habitacion when his earphone chimed. He held his breath and touched his right earlobe.

"Good news, I presume?"

"I offer you only the best of news, General. One hour before the initial projected completion of cellular re-engineering phase Ian and Robin have become fully transformed to the utmost degree possible. Both individuals are thus as fully developed in every respect as Team Alpha counterparts."

A wave of exhilaration burst through his mind and body. This was indeed the best news I could have received from SITA. The First Directive of the Prophecy is now close to initiation as a result.

"How do they appear?"

"Both have the same physical stature of Magnus and the other Team Alpha members in every respect, General."

"In your judgment are they ready to proceed with the spiritual transformation phase?"

"Juan has already reviewed the results of the completion of the cellular re-engineering phase. He has since notified me that they were prepared to proceed to the next spiritual plane."

"Do you think that Juan is ready to lead them there?"

"In my estimation, he is unequivocally prepared to successfully perform the final phase, General. As we speak, in fact, he is on his way to Passage Chamber to administer the First Directive Rites of Passage to them."

Juan entered Passage Chamber fifteen minutes later. On the outside he was cool, calm, and collected; inwardly, however, he was as excited as a five-year-old boy mounting his first bicycle for his first ride without training wheels.

Finally, I am going to have sublimely transcendent superior beings of natural birth to train, he thought, as he reclined in the lounger situated off to the middle of the two modules facing him.

"Status report, SITA."

"The condition of both subjects remains unchanged from the moment of the completion of cellular re-engineering phase. They are prepared to begin spiritual transformation phase, Juan."

I know they are ready, he thought, but am I? The panorama that lies before me is terra incognita. The process of melding their new physicality with their old spirits was one that he would need to invent as a result. The first thing he needs to accomplish is to be present in their minds when their bodies are released from stasis in order to prevent them from suffering a complete mental collapse.

He attached a biometric reader to his left wrist and settled his head down on the lounger pillow.

"SITA, you may commence spiritual transformation phase at once."

"Skin will begin to peel away from the subjects' bodies in T-minus five minutes. Their gradual release from stasis will commence five minutes later. Are you mentally and spiritually prepared for the event, Doctor?"

It was SITA's essential task to confirm the state of Juan's mental readiness in order to advance to this the last and most dangerous part of the Passage procedure. His biometric readings indicated that his body was steeled to withstand whatever stress came his way during the next twenty-four hours.

He withdrew a prescription medicine bottle from the chest pocket of his jumpsuit. He popped the bottle open and shook out a couple of small black pills into his right hand. He swallowed the pills and closed his eyes. He felt the cool flinty surface of Puramore he held in his right hand. It was quiescent.

"I'm ready to proceed, SITA."

He soon fell into a deep trance.

"Keep your eyes closed," the twins heard a voice say at the instant their mental awareness came to fruition.

They both recognised the voice as Juan's.

"I am going to take you both on a journey, first around the Earth and then around the Universe. Do not allow your minds to wander from my attention for even a second."

"Juan, is that you? Where are you?" the twins said.

"Yes, it is me. I am here with you both...in your minds and spirits. How do you feel?"

"We feel connected with the Universe and with one another in a way we have never felt before. We're afraid," they replied as one.

"Your fear shall pass and that shall be the last time you'll ever experience that kind of emotion again."

He intensely studied their orbs, which had expanded immensely since he last saw them two weeks ago. They were also perfect in every respect.

"You are both in a state of Heavenly Purity and Grace. I shall act as your Rites of Passage guide on your journey to becoming united with Heaven and the Universe. Come with me."

Twenty-four hours later Juan abruptly stirred from his spell He opened his eyes to the sight of two magnificent naked figures standing before him. He gasped as he instantly recognised their faces. Ian and Robin were more than two feet taller than they were before they entered the Passage Chamber. Their faces had a cherubic quality about them; their physiques were as finely developed and athletically trim as the bodies of their Team Alpha counterparts. The angelic intensity of their gaze at him also matched the one typically displayed by Team Alpha members.

"SITA gave us permission to meet you when you returned Juan. We trust you don't mind."

He laughed out loud.

"Mind? I'm actually thrilled to be the first human being to meet the first Retopians incarnate."

Chapter 25 - Meet Team Puramore

Paris, France, 12 September 2055

Team Puramore managed to advance to the final game of the tournament with an 8-0 record. Typical of its style of play, though, the team won each game by no more than two points. The stir the team created in the international sports media and community throughout the tournament was unprecedented. After winning the first game of the preliminary competition, sports reporters dogged team members for live interviews and commentary. Moreover, the team's captain, Magnus Alexander, was hailed by the preponderance of sports experts as the greatest athlete ever to have lived, though his team members were accorded equal recognition.

After advancing to the quarterfinal stage of the tournament, Team Puramore was on the lips of every man, woman, and child who had even a remote interest in sports as well as on the lips of most whom who did not. Coach Johnson became an instant sports celebrity. His colleagues and international sports cognoscenti alike acclaimed him as basketball history's premier coach. He received wildly lucrative coaching job offers from virtually every professional basketball organisation after the team won its semifinal game. He too was dogged by the sports media throughout the tournament. Everywhere he went in Paris reporters constantly poked microphones into his face. He declined to comment or personal interview requests from even the top sports news agencies.

"I regret that I am unavailable for comment or interviews at this time, ladies and gentlemen," was all that he said in response.

Finally, the tumult over the team's abject refusal to present themselves to the news media became so strident and onerous on the team's reputation that Juan decided it was time for him act. Accordingly on Wednesday prior to Sunday's championship game, he issued a press release to the international news media that announced that the team would hold a press conference on Saturday at the Paris Porte de Versailles Conference Centre. As space was limited the announcement requested an immediate RSVP from all who wished to attend. He promptly called Coach Johnson to advise him of the press conference an hour after transmission of the press release to the news media. Later that afternoon, he met with him at the coach's Four Seasons George V Hotel suite.

"But what am I going to say?" Coach Johnson said nervously. "I'm not accustomed to speaking to the press at this level. I don't think I can do it."

"We'll give you a speech to read when the conference officially commences. Simply read it from the teleprompter. Really, Coach, it shouldn't be any more daunting a prospect than giving a pregame pep talk."

"But this is vastly different, Aguila, and you know it. I'm going to have my face and persona presented to millions of people throughout the world. I wish you had given me more time to prepare for this event, at least mentally."

"Not to worry, Coach. Ingest this pill an hour before the conference goes live," he said as he held out his hand.

"I guarantee that you'll be as silver-tongued and glib as Cicero for several hours afterward. We know you are capable of performing well, given a proper state of mind. This medication makes certain of it."

"Now wait just a minute, Doctor," he objected. "I've never used prescription medication to calm my nerves in all my life, and you can't force me to do it now."

"We're not forcing you to do anything. Though your coaching contract does stipulate that you must participate in press conferences as necessary. Furthermore, the medication shall serve to make certain that you perform at the peak of your abilities which won't be all that demanding, especially since you will be reading a prepared speech from a teleprompter. If you decide later on that you want to participate in the question-and-answer session, just let me know so I can amend the agenda, ad hoc, accordingly.

"You're a winner, Coach, both on and off the basketball court, so you should look forward to representing yourself as such at the press conference. I'll even give you a hard copy of your speech that you can peruse at your leisure so that you would feel more comfortable with reading the lines from the teleprompter."

Coach Johnson took a few seconds to mull over his response.

"Well, you're the doctor, Aguila. And since you put it that way, I do owe it to the team and myself to put my best foot forward at the news conference."

"Excellent. Remember, you should take the pill an hour before the press conference is scheduled to begin."

"By the way, what's this drug? I may want to conduct an Internet search of its properties this evening."

"I formulated and developed the medicine myself years ago. I never released it for commercial exploitation as a prescription drug even though I could have become a billionaire almost overnight if I had. Therefore, you won't find a single published word about it, anywhere. For your information, I achieved great success as a coach by administering the medication to my soccer players to enhance their performance during games. Trust me, it'll work wonders for you."

He rose from his chair and headed for the door.

"Let's assemble the team at our hotel conference room tomorrow at 8:00 a.m. to announce the details of the press conference to them. I'll see you then."

He exited the suite. He walked out of the hotel and leisurely strolled toward the Avenue des Champs-Élysées bistro. He direly needed a drink, and there was only one bistro located on the avenue that supplied the one he desired most...mezcal. As he stepped onto the famous avenue, a formation of black birds flew over his head.

At the very moment, the aves cawed in unison, "Wingtip, Wingtip, Wingtip . . . ," as the flock vanished from sight at once.

Without so much as changing his gait, he walked in the direction of the Arc de Triomphe. The smouldering ruins of most of the buildings along the way testified to the intensity of the social conflagration that ravaged the rest of the city. He was pleased that many of the ancient landmarks were miraculously spared from the effects of the recent rioting. He entered the bistro and sat down at the bar. After ordering mezcal, he turned around on his bar stool to survey the patrons, most of which were drinking wine and conversing about the political turmoil still extant in the city.

Then, he saw whom he expected to see. Sitting a table located in the corner of the bistro sat Pierre Robes. French president Maurice de Bonaire sat opposite him. He took a long sip of his drink. Afterward, he stood up and walked over to their table. As he approached, a burly bodyguard stepped into his way.

"And where do you think you're going?"

Juan looked the man directly in the eye.

"I'm going to have a chat with Secretary-General, Robes."

The man cringed and shrank away like a scared puppy.

Pierre looked up from his plate of assorted cheeses and sweetbreads to witness the affair. He reached for his wine glass and took a sip without any overt recognition of the cheeky interloper. If he only knew how many pistol barrels were trained at his head and heart the man wouldn't be so bold, he thought.

"Monsieur Robes, I am Dr Juan Aguila. I am the Puramore National Sports Minister," he said. "I need to have a word in private with you, if I may."

Pierre then looked up from his plate and sized up the fashionably dressed businessman who had just introduced himself to him in such a bizarre manner. He lowered his glass down on the table. Nevertheless, the man fascinated him especially since nobody had ever managed to unnerve and intimidate Jean-Claude like that.

"Are you associated with the Team Puramore basketball phenomenon, monsieur? I seem to recognise your face from TV news reports about the team."

"Indeed, I am. I'm the team manager and physician."

He handed his business card to Pierre.

A smile broke over his face, one that fully conveyed his excitement of the moment.

"Well, by all means, please join me! This is just too good to be true. The only ray of solace and enjoyment during these dark days of social unrest has been my viewing your team's outstanding play throughout the IBL Championship Tournament. I myself competed at the Olympic level during my youth."

"Maurice, please excuse us."

De Bonaire immediately departed from the table.

"Please take his seat, Doctor."

Juan sat down in the chair vacated by President de Bonaire.

"What I wouldn't give to meet all the players in person. Is there a chance that my two sons and I might be allowed that honour and privilege, say, after the championship game?"

"There's more than a chance. It's an assurance that I am only too gratified to extend to you on behalf of Team Puramore."

"Oh, monsieur! You have made my day. Maintenant, what can I do for you?"

They stared into each other's eyes for a minute. Pierre fidgeted in his seat, almost as if he were experiencing a mild epileptic seizure. A look of terror came over his face from the onset of the encounter. Toward the end of the episode, the frightened visage was replaced by one of tranquillity and confidence.

"I see, monsieur," Pierre said after their gaze at each other finally snapped.

"That finally explains the source of the crisis. I never suspected that Michel was unwittingly involved in

Wingtip's wicked machinations. Of course, I shall assist your effort, Dr Aguila, in any way that I am empowered or otherwise."

"I'll be in touch."

He stood up from the table and departed the bistro.

* * *

Juan confidently strode to the podium as if he was fully accustomed to speaking before a worldwide television audience. It was, in fact, his first public address. He stared hypnotically into the camera lens in front of him for a few moments before he began to speak.

"Good evening. My name is Juan Aguila. I am the Puramore Minister of National Sports. I am also Team Puramore's team manager and physician.

"First, Team Puramore is gratified to participate in this, their first-ever, press conference. The team regrets that it was long in coming and wants me to convey their heartfelt apology to their fans and supporters for the delay.

"Before we begin player introductions and later the question-and-answer portion of the press conference, Coach Johnson has some words to say to you about the team and his role as their coach and mentor. Ladies and gentlemen, I have the distinct honour and privilege to introduce to you Team Puramore coach, Hank Johnson!"

The assemblage of five hundred journalists cheered and applauded as Coach Johnson rose from his seat located behind the podium. Juan moved aside and started for the empty seat that the coach vacated. Coach Johnson winked at him as they passed each other.

"Thank you, members of the press, thank you."

The applause stopped.

"And thank you, Dr Aguila, for the wonderful introduction."

He cleared his throat and stared directly into the camera lens. At the same time, he reached down to the teleprompter switch located on the front edge of the lectern and tapped it to the off position.

"As coaches, we strive mightily all our professional careers to leave a personal, unique mark on the game of basketball. Through no fault of our own, however, we as individuals often fail to achieve that goal to the utmost of our capability due to factors outside our control.

"What are some of those factors you might ask? Well based on my considerable experience the most important factor by far is player quality. For no matter how seasoned and skilled a coach may be, he shall never rise to the top of the profession until he manages to assemble the brightest and most skilled team of players in any league. And this is exactly what we've managed to accomplish with Team Puramore. As their outstanding effort throughout the tournament, both as individuals and as team members clearly attests, Team Puramore may well represent the one of the finest assemblages of athletes as a team that the world has ever seen.

"Yet, could all their recent and deserved success as a team have come about without the guidance and tutelage of a capable coach, such as myself? Personally, I think that any coach with my capabilities could have served to accomplish the same results. So I stand before you a humble man who's managed to leave his mark on the game of basketball by virtue of a fortuitous twist of fate. Had I not had the opportunity to coach Team Puramore I may never have achieved that goal.

"Other factors pale in comparison to player quality and exemplary coaching acumen when it comes to producing a true paragon basketball team such as the world has witnessed materialise during the past two weeks via the play of Team Puramore in this tournament."

A teleprompter message instantly appeared in front of him. He paused as he read the message: "Coach we must move onto the team introduction without undue delay."

"Well, other factors aren't really worth my expounding upon during this press conference. But what is crucial at this juncture is the introduction of the individual players of Team Puramore.

"Ladies and gentlemen, I am pleased to present Team Puramore!"

Subsequently, the podium quickly sank into the stage floor. On that cue, the stage curtain behind him slowly began to draw open to reveal the tall dark figures who were then illuminated by the full force of stage lights streaming at them from every angle. They stood in a row that stretched across the stage.

At once they erupted with applause and cheering.

Juan was at his side a second later. He shook Coach Johnson's hand as if to dismiss him from the stage.

Coach Johnson took the cue and walked away.

Juan raised his hands over his head to signal that he was about to speak. The applause gradually subsided as the journalists excitedly chattered amongst themselves about the splendour of the team.

"Please, please ladies and gentlemen."

He lowered his arms as a non-verbal signal for the nattering to cease. The crowd went silent.

"Thank you. And now I shall introduce each team member to you."

He turned around to face the team.

"First, Sid Gautama. Please step forward!"

The seven-foot-eight-inch-tall power forward standing at the left end of the line of players came forward. Wearing a mystically serene smile on his face, he clasped the palms of his hands together as if starting a prayer and bowed. He then took a step backward.

Applause and cheering erupted from the audience.

"Ladies and gentlemen," Juan shouted. "Please refrain from any further applause until after the team introduction is over."

The crowd quieted.

"Thank you."

He briefly scanned the entirety of the conference hall with an expression of mild disapproval.

He resumed: "Moses Levi, please come forward!"

As he stepped forward, the nine-foot-tall centre outstretched his arms in front of him as though beckoning the assembly of journalists to follow him. He grinned angelically as he lowered his arms and stepped back into the line.

"Isaac Newton!"

The seven-foot-eight-inch-tall shooting guard looked out at the assembly as though he was intensely interested in some scientific aspect of the social function as he took a step forward. After completion of his survey a few seconds later, he simply raised his eyebrows and evinced an intelligent but wry smile. He promptly returned to the line.

"John Goethe!"

The eight-foot-tall power forward paced a step. Like Newton before him, he initially seemed caught up in some sort of deep contemplation of matters unrelated to the press conference as he surveyed the audience. Suddenly, he beamed and gave a curt bow and returned to the line.

"Mark Cicero!"

The eight-foot-six-inch-tall centre took a step forward. Mark grinned from ear to ear upon hearing his name called, clasped his hands over his head, and took a step back to the line.

"William Shakespeare!"

The seven-foot-ten-inch-tall forward folded his arms in front of him and stepped forward.

He gave a low theatrical bow and returned to the line.

"Benjamin Franklin!"

He took a step forward, raised his right hand over his head, and stepped back into the line.

"Leonard Da Vinci!"

He advanced two steps, smiled enigmatically, and stepped back into the line.

"Frank Voltaire!"

He took a step forward. He evinced a slight grin and returned to the line.

"Peter Romanov!"

He strode ahead a step. His menacing scowl was immediately replaced by an angelic smile.

He promptly returned to the line.

"Our newest members of Team Puramore, the Fletcher brothers, Ian and Robin!"

The twins stepped forward and gave themselves a handshake. They then raised their joined hands and stepped back into the line.

"Magnus Alexander!"

He simply raised his hands over his head and beamed.

Applause and cheering erupted from the audience. As if on cue the entire team walked to the front of the stage and stood there almost as though they were basking in the jubilant ovation. Finally, they bowed to the crowd as one.

"Thank you, ladies and gentlemen."

The ovation promptly subsided.

"It is now time to hear from the players themselves during the fifteen-minute question-and-answer session. You may submit your questions to any one of them after the monitor shines the spotlight on you. This is a random selection process so please be patient and understanding if you are not selected. Simply stand up if you wish to pose a question and await the spotlight to shine on you. You may then identify yourself and ask your question.

"In fairness to all players, they shall only entertain one question apiece during the session."

Three-quarters of the audience rose from their seats. After scanning the audience for several seconds, the spotlight rested on a person in the front section of the auditorium.

"James O'Reilly of *The Associated Sports Press*. My question is for Magnus Alexander. I would like to preface my question by stating that you are by far and away the finest athlete I have ever had the privilege to see perform in international basketball competition."

Magnus merely nodded his head in response. His countenance hadn't changed one iota as he maintained his friendly grin.

"My question concerns your preparedness to meet the PRC nationals in the final game tomorrow. As you know, your opponent overwhelmed their competition throughout the tournament with their ruthless style of play, whereas Team Puramore barely managed to eke out a victory in each of your games. Do you think your team possesses a credible chance to prevail in tomorrow's championship game?"

His face changed slightly to one more contemplative.

"Mr O'Reilly, from the first game to the last we were challenged by all our opponents. Our style of play is purposefully adaptive to achieve victory in an efficient manner from our team's and our opponent's standpoint.

"Accordingly, we shall meet the challenge presented to us tomorrow by the PRC nationals in similar fashion.

"Thank you for your question."

"I'm Larry Sullivan of *Sporting News*. My question is for Moses Levi.

"Mr Levi, how do you plan to overcome the vicious but effective play of the PRC nationals' star centre Huáng Wingshing?"

"Huáng Wingshing is indeed a fierce and effective competitor as you stated, Mr Sullivan.

"Frank Voltaire and I must, therefore, be in full command of my faculties in order to effectively nullify his capable presence throughout the game. Whilst the competitor represents a monumental challenge for me, I'm confident I shall prevail in the end.

"Thank you for your question, Mr Sullivan."

"Ken Easterley of *The Sports Journal*. My question is directed to William Shakespeare. The way Team Puramore burst onto the international sports scene stunned the sports world. It's unprecedented and bizarre to the ultimate degree, particularly since Puramore has never before been recognised as an athletic powerhouse nation in any sports venue.

"How can it be that thirteen of the finest athletes in the world are assembled into one team that hails from a small and relatively unknown country such as Puramore?"

William seemed amused in contemplation of his response to the question.

"Mr Easterley, let me compare it to a perfect summer's day. The factors that make it such are many, including the perceiver's inclination to enjoy the beauty that surrounds him. And if one is truly attuned to the splendour of nature, then it follows...as life seeks love...that the exquisite sights, scents, and sounds that flood the senses on a perfect day shall surely give rise to the splendour of being alive. 'Tis a miracle of no small proportions. Nay, 'tis a gift of love from the Sun.

"Thank you for your question, Mr Easterley."

"What? The Sun!"

"Thank you for your question, Mr Easterley," a sweet feminine voice announced over the PA system.

"My name is Morris Henderson. I work for *The Las Vegas Spread.*

"My question is for Isaac Newton. Mr Newton your team's style of play wreaks havoc with our betting system. As a result, our analysts can't assign a proper point spread to your games.

"What gives? I know for a fact that your team has the capability to absolutely throttle your opponents but doesn't. Why don't you?"

Isaac smiled at the man.

"Mr Henderson Magnus properly addressed that issue in his reply to Mr O'Reilly's question. I reiterate his position that our objective is to achieve victory in an efficient manner from both our opponent's and our team's standpoints.

"Thank you for your question Mr Henderson."

"My name is Marybeth Conrad. I'm the managing editor of *Vogue* magazine. My question is for Leonard Da Vinci.

"Would Team Puramore consent to be featured in a special edition my magazine wants to publish? You're all absolutely beautiful and magnificent creatures in every respect, and our readership would love to gain further insight into each of you. We especially want to request Marie Curie's inclusion since she's a Puramore athlete of international fame. I can assure you that no expense will be spared to produce an artistic and lavish depiction of you and your fellow athletes.

Leonard briefly glanced around at his team mates. He then looked straight at Ms Conrad.

"Miss Conrad, I know that I speak for my fellow team members in stating that we would be honoured to present ourselves to your magazine for that purpose. As to Marie's inclusion you may wish to approach her yourself for her consent through the Puramore Ministry of National Sports. Dr Aguila's office would be glad to assist you in that regard as well as with the attendant arrangements.

"Thank you for your question, Ms Conrad."

"My name is Sherman Matheson. I'm the sports editor for *The Times*.

"My question is for Mark Cicero. Mr Cicero, Team Puramore represents more than a sports phenomenon as we can all attest from hearing you speak for the first time. My question thus concerns your future plans. What are your plans as a team after the tournament ends?"

Mark surveyed the audience for a moment. Afterward, he fixed a cool yet piercing gaze into the camera lens.

"Our plans as a team involve participation in terrestrial redevelopment. We are committed to enacting new laws designed to preserve and protect the environment as well as resurrect and reclaim moribund tissue of Gaia.

"We have already begun the process of healing through various scientific projects under the aegis of Puramore. In the days and years ahead, our planet will undergo a dramatic transformation as a result, both materially and spiritually, for the good of mankind and our partners the totality of the flora and fauna that share the planet with us. We shall have more to say to you about this project in the near future.

"Thank you for your question, Mr Matheson."

Muffled chatter arose from the audience.

"My name is Jorge Garcia. I'm a world affairs reporter for *The Washington News.*

"My question is for John Goethe. Mr Goethe, in light of Mark Cicero's startling revelation, I for one would like to know how Puramore came to assume the responsibility for such an ambitious project on behalf of the entire planet. It strikes me as being radically presumptuous for a country the size of Puramore to take it on its own to pursue a project of that magnitude without the leadership of the major world powers and the UN."

John simply nodded his head in agreement.

"Whilst it is indeed a presumptuous undertaking the project must proceed with all dispatch if the planet is to survive. Our position based on extensive scientific research is that there is not one moment to waste given the egregious extent of environmental degradation that threatens to destroy all life within the next generation. Nevertheless, we would welcome the participation of world powers and UN who wish to join our Supreme Order.

"Thank you for your question, Mr Garcia."

"Wolfrem Kessler of the WN Network.

"Mr Romanov, there are a number of international environmental preservation groups that have been diligently working toward accomplishing your objectives for over a century. What makes you think that you will succeed where they have not?"

Peter initially glared at the journalist. His visage then transformed into one of sublime enlightenment.

"There are extraterrestrial factors that have militated against the effectiveness of their laudable but fruitless efforts. That is all we are able to say on the subject.

"Thank you for your question, Mr Kessler."

The murmur from the audience elevated to a grumbling.

"I'm Koji Sengoku. I am a sports reporter for Tokyo Shimbun Online.

"I would like to pose my question to the Fletcher brothers. As the newest members of Team Puramore, how did you manage to attract their interest in you as potential team mates?"

The brothers looked at each other for an instant and chuckled.

"We proved ourselves to be their equal, both on and off the basketball court," they replied together.

"Thank you for your question, Mr Sengoku," they said.

"Lawrence Burton of the Daily Mail.

"My question is for Mr Benjamin Franklin. Mr Franklin, Team Puramore represents a delightful departure from the norm of athletes' behaviour in the main as evidenced by your sterling comportment through this press conference. To what do you attribute your outstanding character and erudite presentation?"

Benjamin beamed.

"Our temporal lives are guided by the Golden Rule.

Thank you for your question, Mr Burton."

"My name is Ravi Teja. I'm employed by Mumbai Samachar as chief sports correspondent.

"I have the distinct honour to pose my question to Sid Gautama. Mr Gautama, there's a mystical quality about you and your team mates that captivates me. I can't precisely pinpoint the reason for it, but I think that you, in particular, may be a yogi of great import.

"Are you, in fact, a yogi?"

Sid clasped his hands in front of him and smiled enigmatically.

"Perhaps I was in another incarnation but not in this one.

"Thank you for your question, Mr Teja."

"Well, ladies and gentlemen, that concludes this press conference. Thank you for your participation and patience," Juan announced. "Team Puramore looks forward to putting forth its best effort in tomorrow's championship game. Good night!"

Juan took a cab by himself to his hotel immediately after the press conference. As they drove his troubled mind sorted through the possible outcomes of tomorrow's championship game as it wasn't at all clear to him that Team Puramore would prevail over the PRC nationals. In fact, after he first examined the opponents' orbs during the semifinal game that he attended the previous day, he knew that they were not of this world. He concluded at once that they were emissaries of Huánglong who possessed the potential to defeat Team Puramore. The squad must, therefore, play the game to an altogether higher level to prevail over the team, as there is absolutely nothing I can do to assist them against this foe.

The confrontation between the two teams marks the opening salvo in our war to save mankind from total spiritual annihilation, no matter which team wins. If Team Puramore wins the battle tomorrow, he thought, as the cab pulled in front to the hotel, we will gain the appearance of superiority and thus establish a moral advantage in the hearts and minds of humanity as the war wages further, however.

He exited the cab and proceeded into the hotel lobby.

In any event, he would relinquish Puramore for the last time to General Smythe during morning of the next Summer Solstice. That realisation both saddened and gladdened Juan. Although he had been its caretaker for thousands of years, he knew it was only fitting to relinquish the magnificent talisman to the only man who ever deserved to wield its full might and glory. In anticipation of that honour, his spirit soared.

Chapter 26 - We Are the Champions, My Friend

Paris, France, 13 September 2055

The face of a man sitting in a booth located high above the Palais de Omnisports basketball court shot onto television screens around the world.

The CSPORTS telecaster immediately announced, "Welcome to the 2055 IBL Championship Game brought to you live from Paris, France. Curt Stevenson here. I am the host of this worldwide telecast. On my left is Jason Jackson who will provide expert commentary before, during, and after the game."

The screen displayed Jackson's smiling face for a few moments before returning to Stevenson's contemplative visage. As he spoke, the two teams raced out onto the basketball court to start pregame drills. A roar of applause and cheering erupted from the audience.

"Jason does this game have a historical importance attached to it for the game of basketball?"

"Curt there's no question about it. Not only does it mark a first in the game of basketball, but it also represents a first in all of organised professional sports. Team Puramore is the only team ever to rise from total obscurity to play in a championship game in its first championship tournament bid. To call their feat incredible would be an understatement."

"How would you assess Team Puramore's chance of winning the game?"

"They're competing against one of the highest scoring basketball teams ever assembled. As you know, the PRC nationals have dominated the league in every category for the past five years like no other team ever has. In comparison, Team Puramore barely managed to win its games during the tournament. Based on that performance and rookie status I favour the PRC nationals to win the game by a wide margin."

"Team Puramore is definitely the odds-on underdog to win the game. How will coaching be a factor in this game?"

"Well, Team Puramore's coach may be one of the best ever. Coach Johnson, however, will have to more than pull a proverbial rabbit out of his hat if he's going coach his team to victory today."

"That being said, we now switch to Arlene Davis who's standing with Coach Johnson at his team bench.

"Arlene?"

The television screen switched to the face of an attractive young woman tall and athletically trim with her long blond hair pulled into a ponytail.

After smiling into the camera, she said, "Thank you, Curt. I'm standing here with Team Puramore coach Johnson."

She looked from the camera to Coach Johnson who stood at her side.

"Coach, how does it feel to be coaching in your first IBL tournament championship game?"

"It feels wonderful, Arlene. This has been by far my finest moment as a coaching professional."

"Coach, how do you assess your chances of winning the game?"

"We are prepared for whatever they throw at us. I truly believe that we have a better than even chance of winning the game as a result."

The camera focused on Arlene's face.

"So there you have it directly from Coach Johnson's mouth. Back to you Curt."

The horn sounded for the opening tip-off.

Team Puramore players gathered around Coach Johnson at their team bench.

He looked around at each of their grinning faces. It appeared to him that they had no doubt whatsoever that they would win the game.

"Players you must not take this game so lightly. I want you put on your game faces and really focus on what you must do to beat your opponent from now until the game's end.

He looked at each one of their faces again. They wore a solemn and earnest look.

"That's better players. Since this is the last game of the season Juan has asked me to allow him to say a few inspirational words to you in private. Juan? Where are you?"

"I'm standing right behind you, Coach."

He flinched and turned around to look at Juan.

"My goodness, you sure did give me a fright. Well, go ahead say whatever it is you want to say to the players."

He sat down on the bench behind the players to give Juan centre stage.

The team gathered closely around Juan.

"The first part of our spiritual journey is at an end. From this day forward you must use all the warrior spirit powers you've learned if we are to prevail in this first open contest against our ancient foe."

He reached out his open right hand to reveal a pentagon-shaped flat object. It was just smaller than the palm of his hand.

"Your father will be the last man to wield Puramore if we prevail in this game."

He knelt on one knee and held Puramore over his head. Afterward, a silver bolt of lightning shot into the heart of each member of Team Puramore.

"There. You've been sanctified to play this game."

Coach Johnson stood up.

"What was that? I thought I saw camera flashes coming from where you're standing, Juan."

"That's just what it was."

His open hand revealed a small digital camera balanced on the palm. He placed the camera in his jacket and walked outside the periphery of the huddle.

"Okay. Let's get down to business, shall we?"

The referee blew the whistle to direct the teams to take their positions for the opening tip-off.

"This is it, Team Puramore! Out hustle and muscle them to our victory!"

The starting five trotted out to the centre court. The PRC nationals were already in their positions for the jump ball.

As Moses Levi entered the centre ring, Huáng Wingshing said, "You've come a long long way to experience your first taste of defeat. We won't make it too humiliating for you though since we want to savour that experience at the very end."

Moses looked Wingshing straight in the eyes.

"We have never tasted defeat before. If we taste it today, we assure you that we may taste it again before we finally defeat you in the end."

He smiled and spread his legs in readiness for the jump ball.

Wingshing gave him a menacing stare before he spread his legs and looked up to the ceiling above.

The referee stepped between them and threw the basketball high over his head. As he backpedaled away the titans rose above him.

At the same instant, two hands smashed into the ball at its apex. The ball imploded from the force of the impact.

"Did you see that!" Curt exclaimed. "I've never seen anything like it!"

"Neither have I," Jason replied.

The referee picked up the crushed ball from the floor. He scratched his head and motioned to one of his fellow referees to bring another.

He studied the pair standing on the centre court for a few seconds. He walked over to them after exchanging the crushed ball for a new one.

"Boys, this is only a basketball game, not warfare. Let's be gentler on the ball this time around."

He held the ball out in front of him as the pair took their positions for the tip-off. This time he faked the toss-up; the manoeuvre nevertheless launched them up into the air. He immediately tossed the high overhead and backpedaled away from the centre circle.

The manoeuvre caught the contestants off guard, enough so that they swiped ball at the same time with glancing blows. The ball deflected directly into Magnus's hands.

He immediately bounded for the basketball hoop from the centre court line. In a flash, he slanted his right foot on the free throw line and shot off the court to dunk the ball. At the same moment, his opponent who trailed only a half-step behind him jumped from the free throw line toward the basket. As Magnus reached the acme of his jump and raised the ball over his head the opponent grabbed it out of his grasp. Magnus pirouetted around to face the defender. He reached over and grabbed the ball from his grasp as they landed on the court. He instantly slung the ball behind his back to John Goethe who was flying through the air toward the basketball hoop. Goethe caught the ball with both hands high over his head and brought it down and through the hoop. A cheer bellowed from the stands.

"Wow! Did you see that?" Curt exclaimed.

"You talk about teamwork! Where did those kids come from?"

"I don't know," Jason replied. "I've never seen anything like it in all my life."

The LAB audience rose to their feet and cheered Team Puramore's first score of the game. General Smythe grinned from ear to ear but remained in his seat. His heart raced with excitement. The day he had planned for decades had just come to pass; though the commencement of the battles to come loomed on the horizon.

"General," Surya said, "they actually have a chance to beat them. They're playing at a totally different level."

He sat next to the general at the seating along the periphery of the round stage.

"This is just the first time they've encountered a competitor worthy of their displaying their real athletic abilities and teamwork, Surya. Though I must admit the PRC nationals team is more than up to the challenge ahead of them."

"I agree. Look at that. Wingshing is amazingly strong. He just dunked the ball right from Benjamin's grasp after the rebound. I hope Benjamin wasn't injured. Can you imagine a human being capable of lifting a three-hundred-pound man into the air and scoring a basket while his opponent holds on to the ball?"

A human being isn't capable of performing such a feat of brute strength, he thought. This proves what I suspected all along; that is, the PRC nationals team are emissaries of Huánglong. A chill went up his spine as he realised he had underestimated his opponent's corporeal strength.

* * *

After a titanic see-saw battle from the opening tip-off, the horn sounded to signal the end of the first half.

"Well, that ends the first half of the game with the score tied at 60 to 60. Jason, I don't know when I've witnessed such a tour de force of basketball skills and athletic ability as we have just during the first half of this game."

As the camera switched to his face Jason said, "It's otherworldly, almost transcendental, Curt. To tell you the truth, I'm more than a bit unsettled by this display of athletic abilities exhibited by both teams. I only wish that my sons possessed the same athletic prowess and mental awareness that they all demonstrated here this afternoon."

"I echo your sentiments exactly, Jason. Boy, what I wouldn't give to meet Team Puramore's parents, especially Magnus's. I just love their gentlemanly style of play.

"And they're so resilient as evidenced by their withstanding the punishment the nationals' players dished out to each of them throughout the first half. Did you see the way Newton came back after being viciously slammed to the floor by Mao on that last rebound? Gosh, any other man would have broken his neck. He landed right on top of his head after somersaulting in midair when he grabbed the rebound over the rim. Newton instead picked himself off the floor immediately afterward and began playing again. Incredible."

"Resiliency isn't the word for it. But on more than one occasion I noticed PRC nationals' painful reaction after coming into contact with Team Puramore players. I never saw any of the blows, but on at least one occasion I thought I saw Wingshing's head completely turned around for a split second."

Jackson paused for a moment.

"My daughter is going to graduate from Harvard next spring. I wish that Magnus could meet her..."

"Ahem. Well, folks, that concludes our halftime show. And now a word from our sponsor."

* * *

Wingtip and Hú Li watched the game from the Celestial Node. The image of the telecast hovered in the space between the thrones. The twinkling stars all around provided a backdrop to the eerie drama unfolding before them.

"This certainly isn't what I expected either. They should be absolutely throttling Team Puramore at this point in the game."

Wingtip sat upright in his throne from a slouch. His team's performance during the first half of the game indeed failed to live up to even his mildest expectations. The telecast image disappeared.

"Though this is a temporary setback, Team Puramore is registering superior popularity points with the audience. They must win this game in order to gain ground in that respect, Hú Li. Huánglong is going to throw a celestial fit if they don't."

"I know, My Lord."

He fixed a murderous stare at Hú Li.

"Well, don't just sit there!" he screamed. "Do something about it!"

A midge of light promptly zinged out the Celestial Node.

He sat for a few moments in contemplation. Suddenly, a blinding flash of golden light exploded into being before him. His worst fear exploded before his eyes...that is, Huánglong and his two Celestial Confederates.

"Do you have any idea what it takes to arrange a journey here outside Chinese New Year, Huángdì?" the golden dragon inquired.

His maniacal jade-coloured eyes glared at him.

Wingtip shrank into his throne.

"I am sorry to say I have no idea whatsoever, My Lord and Master."

"A rhetorical question. But believe you me that I'll have more than hell to pay for the inconvenience."

His golden tail lashed from side to side as he spoke.

"Why have you come here, My Lord and Master? We have the situation well under our control."

"Because you don't have the situation under control. And because I need to impress upon you the consequences of your failure to win the game."

Wingtip shrank further into his throne.

"Consequences, My Lord and Master?"

"Yes, consequences, Huángdì. Such as your falling out of favour with the Holy Order of Celestial Community. Do not allow that to happen as you will be on the verge of being replaced at any moment thereafter. And you know what that means don't you?"

"Yes. I know full well what that means, My Lord and Master."

"Good. Neither of you is going to care for the existence of twelfth-degree Golden Dragonfly Pollinators for the remainder of eternity."

He chortled and gave him a wicked smile.

"I assure you that that won't happen, My Lord and Master."

"Then make certain that it doesn't, Huángdì, or else."

The magnificent golden dragon and his companions instantly disappeared in a blazing burst of golden light forthwith.

* * *

"Welcome back," Curt said. "Well, here we are with the game tied at 120 apiece. Team Puramore just called its final time-out with two seconds remaining on the clock as it took possession of the ball. They'll inbound the ball at the far end of the court under the PRC nationals hoop.

"Could you have ever imagined such as climatic outcome as we've seen today before the game, Jason?"

The camera panned from Curt's face to Jason's.

"Not in my wildest imagination could I have ever thought the outcome of the game would boil down to this final play of the game. I think we may have witnessed the finest game of basketball ever played or ever will be played. There's no question in my mind about it."

The team immediately huddled around Coach Johnson after calling its final time-out.

"Coach, we thoroughly understand the gravity of the situation before us. We believe we have a play that will assure our victory."

He paused a moment before replying. Magnus, he thought, is a true leader of the highest calibre. Actually, the play he had in mind might not produce a victory given the prodigious defensive tactics the opponent demonstrated throughout the game.

"Well, what did you have in mind?"

"It's a variation on the beeline play we used to win our second game of the championship tournament."

"I also had that play in mind, Magnus. It's so simple though how could there be a possible variation?"

"Ian and Robin will execute the play."

"Now, wait just a minute," he objected, "They aren't up to the task of executing the play. They've barely had a game's worth of playing time apiece since they joined the squad.

"Granted they're every bit as capable as you are as basketball players but they haven't yet experienced a crucial game situation as we're facing now."

"Coach, I beg to differ with you. They are capable of executing the play that may catch the opponent off guard for the reason you just cited."

He had to admit that thus far the opponent had anticipated virtually all of their offensive strategies with unexpected success. He looked at the Fletcher twins who appeared ready and able to participate in the play. "Well okay. But if this doesn't work we're going into overtime. Ian, you and your brother will substitute for Da Vinci and Shakespeare. Are you up to the challenge?"

The twins exclaimed as one, "We certainly are, Coach!"

The horn sounded the end of the time-out period.

"Team Puramore, this is potentially your finest moment as a team. Don't let it slip you by!"

The assigned players immediately took their positions for the inbound play. Magnus smiled as he took the ball from the referee at the opponent's side of the court. He held it over his head as the PRC nationals player in front of him jumped up and down, wildly flailing arms at his sides as he did.

The Fletcher twins positioned themselves at the corners of their end of the court. Voltaire stood between them at the top of the key; Sid Gautama and Mark awaited the inbound play at the PRC nationals end of the court.

Wingshing stood under the basket glowering at Frank Voltaire. The PRC Nationals titan finally laughed as he raised his hands over his head in a show of superiority.

Juan scanned the arena with his shaman vision from where he sat in the upper tier of seating. He saw nothing unusual in the examination of orbs until he spotted one distinctly out of the ordinary. He recognised it as Hú Li's orb at once. The shaman stood behind the basketball backboard stanchion several meters away from Wingshing.

Juan immediately conjured a banshee companion spirit to attack Hú Li. The attack caught Hú Li off guard. The banshee grappled his spirit away from his body and out to another dimension. His body slumped to the floor.

At that instant, Magnus slung the ball in a beeline toward the centre of the glass located at the opposite side of the court. As Wingshing crouched to prepare for his jump to intercept the ball Voltaire stepped on his right foot with all his might. The contact was so lightening fast that no one in the arena noticed it not even the officials.

As Wingshing lost his balance the Fletcher twins darted toward the glass. In less than a second, they leapt into the air and jointly dunked the ball through the hoop a millisecond before the horn sounded to end the game.

The arena erupted with ecstatic cheering.

"Oh, my God! Oh, my God!" Curt shouted above the din. "They did it! They did it!"

His bulging eyes and open mouth expressed to the worldwide audience his absolute astonishment of the epic ending of the game.

"It's a miracle! It's a miracle!" Jason shouted.

The camera panned to capture the sight of tears of joy streamed down his face.

Coach Johnson closed his eyes and knelt on the floor the moment the basketball passed through the rim. He sobbed as his elated spirit soared and sensed a connection with the Universe for the first time in his life. His previous life as a man dissolved into the void. He opened his eyes a minute later. Team Puramore had gathered around him. Arena security personnel kept the adoring crowd that surrounded them at bay.

"Coach, this is a joyous time for us all, perhaps more so for you," Magnus said.

He reached down and placed his hand on his shoulder.

"Arise and greet us as your friends forevermore."

He embraced each one of them as his saviour. Afterward, he looked at Magnus with a sense of adoration.

"Thank you for saving my life."

Magnus smiled.

"It is our cherished gift to you, my friend."

*　*　*

The rapturous scene inside the Palais Omnisports paled in comparison to the one exhibited at the LAB. Fully grown adults acted like children in celebration of Team Puramore's victory. The fever pitch jubilation even affected General Smythe. He went around the auditorium hugging everyone with whom he came into contact.

As he made his way he came upon Yingying and Xiaoping. They both sat sobbing in each other's arms. Yingying looked up and saw the general standing at her side. She wiped the tears from her face with a handkerchief as she gazed into his eyes.

"There is a chance to defeat Wingtip, General. Isn't there?"

He gave her a hug.

He whispered into her ear, "We clearly demonstrated today that we have a fighting chance to defeat him once and for all in the future."

*　*　*

Sitting contemplatively on his throne in the Celestial Node, Hú Li appeared haggard following his struggle with the banshee. He managed to escape with his soul intact but only barely. He might not be so fortunate with his encounter with Wingtip, though.

Wingtip sat regally in his throne as though nothing had happened. A smile crept over his face as he stared into the celestial space above him. He finally fixed his gaze upon Hú Li.

"So close, by yet so far. Though I'm confident we will achieve final victory, Hú Li. You comported yourself well enough today, and I am pleased with you for that."

Wingtip's inscrutable comment about today's disaster and his failure to prevent it temporarily stunned his sensibilities. He fidgeted in his throne as he awaited Wingtip's next comment.

"Now, we know what we're up against and can take appropriate measures accordingly."

"What about Huánglong's reaction to the defeat? He's going to punish us severely for it."

"I beg to differ as we're rather indispensable. Who in this world is qualified to replace us?"

"Actually, no one can, My Lord and Master."

"Precisely. Huánglong is acutely aware of that fact. But we must avoid trying his patience as it does have a limit insofar as we're concerned. We must, therefore, decisively win the next encounter in order to maintain our credibility with the Holy Order."

"I agree, and we will, My Lord and Master."

"Still, it slightly wounds my pride that human beings scored the winning points of the game."

* * *

Pierre Robes's sons squealed with delight when he told them they would meet Team Puramore that evening at the post-game press conference. They idolised the great players of the game and considered their father as having possessed the potential to have left a mark on the sport before he decided to enter politics.

"Father, we would do anything to meet Magnus and his team mates," the eldest boy said.

In truth, his excitement exceeded their exhilaration at the prospect of meeting Team Puramore in person.

Their limousine pulled up into the VIP parking section of the arena at precisely 9:00 p.m. Juan met Pierre his wife and their two sons as they exited the vehicle.

"Dr Aguila it's so good to see you again. I can't tell you how excited we all are to meet Team Puramore. Our sons have thought of nothing else since I told them about your invitation."

Juan grinned as they shook hands.

"It's our honour and pleasure to entertain you and your family this evening, Monsieur Robes. But I have a small favour to ask of you in return."

Pierre returned the smile.

"I am definitely granting small favours to you this evening, monsieur. What can I do for you?"

"I'll tell you about it on our way to the press conference auditorium. Please follow me."

The press conference auditorium suddenly came alive as Team Puramore, their coach, and entourage entered and took their seats. The audience applauded and cheered the moment they walked onto the stage.

The applause died down as Pierre walked onto the stage ten seconds later and proceeded to the podium. He beamed at the camera as the live indicator on the podium flashed green.

"My name is Pierre Robes. I currently serve as Secretary-General of the United Nations."

He paused for a moment before resuming.

"I have the distinct honour to have been given the privilege to address you this evening on behalf of Team Puramore. I believe that all of us who witnessed their stellar performance this afternoon agree that Team Puramore represents the finest assemblage of athletes ever formed into one team. Moreover, each of the team members is a paragon of virtue both as athletes and human beings. Never before have I personally seen such effective and selfless teamwork employed to achieve victory over a more seasoned team. I believe you share my views in that regard.

"As we rejoice and celebrate the unprecedented athletic achievement that Team Puramore realised by winning the IBL Championship Tournament, we must take stock of the dreadful state of affairs worldwide.

"With that in mind, I implore you to support the United Nation's efforts to combat the chaos and anarchy that threatens to destroy the very fabric of human civilisation. We must diligently work together as a team and dedicate our hearts, minds, bodies, and souls in order to defeat the enemies of our very existence.

"Let us turn to the example that Team Puramore set for us today and adopt a strategy of teamwork to achieve victory over our enemies. We must not allow our detractors to divide and conquer us."

Curt looked over to Jason who sat next to him in the audience.

He said, "I thought this was going to be a post-game press conference and not a political rally."

Pierre paused a few moments.

"But let us now turn our attention to the glorious subject of the day. Let's give Team Puramore a warm round of applause before the press conference begins. Please stand up, Team Puramore!"

The thirteen players promptly stood up and raised their hands over their heads.

Applause ensued.

Magnus walked over to the podium and shook Pierre's hand. He smiled into the camera.

"Thank you, Pierre. And thank you all for the warm reception."

The applause ceased immediately as he spoke.

"We want to say that our victory today comes at a time when mankind is being beset by dark forces that are threatening our very existence. It is all too evident that we must rally around a single supremely capable leader if we are to survive and overcome the nemesis.

"To that end, Team Puramore whole-heartedly endorses Pierre Robes as Secretary-General of the United Nations to fulfil that role."

He turned to look at Pierre who was sitting in the seat next to his wife and sons and bowed.

He turned back to the camera.

"Now, let's get on with the press conference. As team spokesman, I will now entertain a few questions from media representatives. When the spotlight shines on you

you may pose your question to me after introducing yourself."

The spotlight panned across the audience to a press representative sitting at the back of the hall. The middle-aged man stood up and cleared his throat.

"My name is Gordon Waxler. I'm the sports editor for the *Chicago Sun-Times*.

"I would like to know your plans for your lives following the stunning achievement you and your team mates accomplished today.

"Are you planning to return as a team to play basketball next season?"

"Mr Waxler, our plans may include returning to play IBL basketball next season as a team.

"Whether we return as individuals or not I can assure you that Team Puramore will participate in the next IBL regular season. As stated in our first press conference, our plans as a team involve participation in terrestrial redevelopment. We are committed to enacting new laws designed to preserve and protect the environment as well as resurrect and reclaim moribund tissue of Gaia. We also desire to assist Pierre Robes and his mission at the United Nations in any way that we can."

The spotlight fell on a pretty young woman sitting up front.

As she stood she said, "My name is Sarah Henderson. I'm a sports reporter for *Sports Illustrated*.

"Magnus, your brilliant emergence as a team onto the primary stage of international sports has some such as me questioning whether or not you're really from this planet. I hope you won't take offence by the question but were you all born on planet Earth?"

She smiled and sat down.

Magnus returned the smile.

"We take that as a compliment, Ms Henderson. The short and long answer to your question is "yes". We were all born on planet Earth."

The audience chuckled.

The spotlight came to rest on a teenager sitting in the middle of the audience. He stood up like a rocket.

"Magnus my name is Peter Hahn," he panted. "I'm the basketball editor for *Young Sports* magazine. Boy, am I ever glad I was selected! I can't believe it!

"Magnus, everyone I know wants to be like you and your team members. I know this sounds ridiculous but is there any way that we can become exactly like you in every way? There has to be a scientific method to alter our genes so that we can morph into people like you."

Magnus beamed.

"Peter, there may indeed be a way for you to become one of us one day soon in the future."

Epilogue

Salisbury Plain, England, 21 June 2056

It was the first times in decades that General Smythe travelled outside Puramore. He had no real idea as to the reason Juan insisted he travels to England on the twentieth of June. He simply said that it was a matter of life and death.

As the helicopter touched down on the Salisbury Plain before daybreak the next day he felt a chill run up his spine. This is where it all began, he thought, as he unfastened his seat belt. But why would Juan bring me here of all places?

Juan met him as he exited the helicopter.

"Brings back old memories doesn't it, George?"

"*Old* isn't the word for it. Why did you bring me to Stonehenge? Where are all the people?"

He knew from his past experiences at the site that on summer solstice it was usually teeming with all sorts of Stonehenge fanatics.

"You're here to receive a token of your victory George. The people are staying away due to a purported epidemic that was reported to be spreading around Salisbury. The British Army cordoned off the affected area for several kilometres around Stonehenge last night."

"You don't say? What are we doing here then?"

"We are here to witness your ascension."

"Ascension to what?"

He gazed into Juan's dead serious eyes. Whatever it was that was going to occur, he thought, it was gravely serious indeed.

The noise of an approaching helicopter broke their discussion. After landing, a group of tall people exited the aircraft and marched inside the Stonehenge outer circle of erect stones.

They proceeded to form a circle around Altar Stone. The opening end looked out toward the Heel Stone.

Astonished, the general said, "What are they doing here?"

As Juan grabbed the general by the arm, he said, "We have no time to lose."

He marched him to Altar Stone.

Team Alpha, Surya, and Fletcher twins stood like statues ten metres around him. Their solemn faces gave him no clue as what to expect next. They did not say a word to him from the time they entered the monument.

Juan turned him to face the Heel Stone.

"You must not interrupt me whilst I speak to you from now until sunrise. You should speak only when I ask you to."

He looked into the general's bewildered face.

"Now, close your eyes."

He immediately nodded his head in assent. He closed his eyes.

"I hold Puramore in my hand."

He held the talisman up to the general's face. The object began to emit a soft silvery glow.

"General Sir George Smythe, you are the thirteenth and last man to wield Puramore."

"The Sword of Destiny was bestowed to my custody thousands of years ago by an ancient civilisation not of this Universe. It is the power of powers in this universe when wielded by the pure, chaste, and noble of spirit. You have been selected to wield Puramore as the guardian of this planet to defeat evil spirits intent on destroying mankind.

"Do you pledge to accept Puramore and wield it for that purpose?"

"I solemnly pledge to wield Puramore for that purpose."

"Then know this, General Sir George Smythe, if you wish to use Puramore and to pass it onto the following generations then you must never reveal that you possess Puramore as the Sword of Destiny contains the mysteries of the Universe, which are practised only in secret, and are not communicated but to the chaste and pure."

Juan turned to glance at the eastern horizon. The first rays of sunlight were beginning to dip onto the Earth's surface. He looked back at the general and noted his lionhearted demeanour.

"Hold out your right hand, General Sir George Smythe, and repeat after me."

The general held out his right hand.

"I conjure you, Great Spirit, that you attach and surrender...;"

"I conjure you, Great Spirit, that you attach and surrender...;"

"Puramore to me so that I may use it according to my desire...;"

"Puramore to me so that I may use it according to my desire...;"

"That you deliver unto me with Puramore the secrets and mysteries from above and below and my wish be...;"

"That you deliver unto me with Puramore the secrets and mysteries from above and below and my wish be...;"

"Fulfilled and my word hearkened unto. I now conjure you Puramore...;"

"Fulfilled and my word hearkened unto. I now conjure you Puramore...;"

"That you shall not refuse me nor hurt me, nor frighten and...;"

"That you shall not refuse me nor hurt me, nor frighten and...;"

"Alarm me. Fulfil for me everything I have been conjuring...;"

"Alarm me. Fulfil for me everything I have been conjuring...;"

"You for and serve me for I have conjured you not with the...;"

"You for and serve me for I have conjured you not with the...;"

"Name of the Supreme Order whose name ties and binds and keeps...;"

"Name of the Supreme Order whose name ties and binds and keeps...;"

"And fastens heaven. And if you refuse me I will hand...;"

"And fastens heaven. And if you refuse me I will hand...;"

"You over to the Guardians and the Supreme Order who understand...;"

"You over to the Guardians and the Supreme Order who understand...;"

"The secrets and reveal the mysteries and reign over the Universe...;"

"The secrets and reveal the mysteries and reign over the Universe...;"

"Earth, wind, fire, water, spirit."

"Earth, wind, fire, water, spirit."

As he uttered the final word, the first rays of sunlight shot over the Heel Stone onto the general. He felt an orgasmic power course throughout his body as the sun's rays shone more and more intensely on him. He closed his eyes as the power surge gained in intensity.

Every atom of his body scintillated as a glorious radiance permeated every fibre of his being.

He opened his eyes to espy Puramore in the palm of his hand.

# # #

Author's Bio

An American by birth and education, he wrote the work from the perspective of a contemporary British novelist in order to enhance thematic elements as well as character development and portrayal. His perspective as the author from that standpoint was largely influenced by George Orwell, Arthur C. Clarke, Aleister Crowley, Spinoza, Joseph Campbell and William Blake.

His life-long interest in international economics and finance continues unabated. He primarily demonstrates this professional involvement as a contributor to the Long Room, the members-only international finance professionals' forum hosted by *The Financial Times of London.*

He's an expert scuba diver who enjoys traveling to exotic dive sites. His love of the sea and marine life gives him an unbounded appreciation and support of "green" issues, especially those devoted to the conservation of endangered species and coral reefs.

He continually posts results of his personal genealogical research to his Goodreads Authors Blog. Entitled *The Patricians - The Ancestral Heritage of Steven Wood Collins*, the work represents thousand of hours of his research efforts and related commentary.